FAR FROM PERFECT

A LOVE FROM THE HEARTLAND NOVEL

FAR FROM PERFECT

Barbara Longley

Montlake
Romance

Published by Montlake Romance
P.O. Box 400818
Las Vegas, NV 89140

ISBN-13: 9781612185897
ISBN-10: 1612185894

This book is dedicated to Laurel Otis & Thomas Menton,
Jeffrey Otis & Austin Wiebe. I'm proud to call you family.

CHAPTER ONE

ONE FOR THE BASKET OF colors, one for the basket of whites. Ceejay sat in the middle of the living room floor and sorted through a mound of dirty laundry. While most people abhorred this kind of chore, she found a soothing cadence in all things mundane. If only navigating her way through life were this simple—one for the basket of colors, one for the basket of whites.

"Babe." Matt sauntered into their tiny living room. "Toss me your keys. I'll pull your car around and meet you out front."

Her heart tap-danced against her rib cage. Maybe it would be best to wait a few more days before telling him about the baby. She glanced up at him. "Why don't *you* carry the laundry, and *I'll* pull the car around?"

"You're not done sorting yet, and I'm itchin' to go." Reaching out a hand for her keys, he flashed his dimples, a sure bet for getting his way. Faded jeans and a tight black T-shirt emphasized his lean, muscular frame, while his chestnut waves and sexy brown eyes made him look like he'd just rolled out of bed. Matthew Wyatt looked like her downfall.

"You know where my latest issue of *Motor Sport* is? I wanna bring it along."

"It's on the bedside table, right where you left it." Ceejay snatched up the rest of the whites and shoved them into one of the baskets. Rising from the floor, she pulled her keys out of her back pocket. "Here." She nudged the basket toward him with her foot and dropped the keys on top. "Take this one with you so I don't have to carry both. I'll get the magazine on my way out."

"Thanks." He leaned in and gave her a peck on the cheek, and a moment later the apartment door shut.

She hefted the remaining basket to her hip and retrieved the racing magazine from the table next to his side of the bed. Grabbing her purse from the couch, Ceejay slung the strap over her shoulder and made her way downstairs to the exit. They rarely locked their second-floor apartment. Crime was mostly nonexistent in their small town. Besides, who in Perfect, Indiana, would want their secondhand crap anyway?

Maneuvering through the heavy doors to the street, she noticed the basket of laundry Matt had taken sitting in the middle of the sidewalk. She scanned the street for her old Honda Civic and frowned. Her boyfriend and her car were nowhere to be seen. Ceejay placed her load next to the other basket and sat down on the concrete steps in the hot July sun to wait.

Matt had probably run into one of his buddies in the parking lot. Most likely he'd forgotten all about her in his rapture over a discussion about motors and racing. What a relief it would be once he gave it up. Her insides always knotted up when he raced, and she couldn't relax until he emerged unharmed from whatever souped-up late-model stock car he raced around the oval track.

Sweat trickled down her left temple. Lifting the damp curls off the back of her neck, she got up and moved closer to the street to sit in the shade of the large boulevard oak. The *tick-tick-tick-tick-whirr* of a sprinkler across the street marked the passage of time, and the electric hum of a cicada in the still afternoon heat made her edgy.

What could be taking him so long? Ceejay glanced at her watch. Nearly twenty minutes had passed. Fuming, she left the laundry and walked around the building to the parking lot in back. Matt wasn't there. Neither was her car.

Ceejay walked all the way around the block, peering down every street for a glimpse of him, until she'd come full circle. The two baskets of laundry caught her attention, and dread lodged itself in the pit of her stomach. She stopped in the middle of the sidewalk while her mind ran through all the possibilities, coming at last to an unhappy conclusion.

No, Matt wouldn't do such a thing. He wouldn't. Ceejay dug through the baskets until clothing, towels, and sheets were strewn all over the lawn. Other than a pair of raggedy jeans, some briefs, and a worn T-shirt, none of it belonged to him. Why hadn't she paid more attention? Oh, yeah. Because she had other things on her mind, like an unplanned pregnancy.

She tore back into the building, raced up the stairs and through their apartment to the cramped bedroom they'd shared for the past six months. There were two small closets in opposite corners of the room. One was his, the other hers.

Ceejay approached his closet as if it harbored all the dreaded monsters from her childhood nightmares. Her hand froze on the doorknob. It took a supreme effort to open the door, and once she did, she regretted the act. All that remained of their love story were a few empty hangers and a pile of old racing magazines on the dusty floor. Well, not quite all. She took a few steps back and placed her hand over her abdomen. He had left her with something to remember him by. Only he didn't know it.

Replaying the past few weeks in her mind, she searched for clues. Why would he leave? It had been his idea to move in together, not hers. She'd never put any pressure on him other than to suggest he quit racing and find a real job.

Another sinking feeling hit her, and she dashed back to the living room. Falling to her knees in front of their ratty old couch, Ceejay slid her arm underneath to where the lining hung loose from the wooden frame. Frantic, she reached around in all directions. He'd taken it. All the money she'd saved for nursing school, her way out of Perfect, gone.

Crap. He was halfway to somewhere else by now—with her car.

Nausea hit her hard. She pushed herself up from the floor and dashed to the bathroom. Once nothing was left inside to come up, she rinsed her mouth and grabbed some tissue to blow her nose. Turning to toss it into the trash, she spotted Matt's reason for leaving.

There it was. Mystery solved.

The early pregnancy test she'd taken the day before lay on the bottom of the empty can, dead center with the +*yes* facing up. No mistaking that message. He must've found it when he took out the trash. While she'd been waiting on tables at her aunt's diner, he'd freaked out and packed up.

Sinking down to the cool tile floor, she stared at the plastic wand for a long time—long enough for all of her dreams to sputter out like a wet match. How could such a tiny piece of plastic have such an enormous impact on her life?

She got up and dragged herself to the phone. Once her car and money were reported stolen, all the sad, sordid details of her bad judgment would be a matter of public record. Might as well rent a billboard, because the news would be all over town by tomorrow noon.

"Warrick County Sheriff's Office. How may I direct your call?"

"Hello, Inez. This is Ceejay Lovejoy. Is Sheriff Maurer around?"

"Hold on a minute, Ceejay. I'll put you right through."

A bad Muzak rendition of "Free Bird" filled her ear. And here she thought her day couldn't get any worse.

"Hey, Ceejay. How's your aunt?"

"Oh, she's fine, Sheriff. I'm calling to report a theft."

"A theft? Hold on a tick." The sound of a drawer opening and paper shuffling came over the line. "All right, tell me what's missing."

"My boyfriend, five thousand dollars in cash, and my car." The other end of the line went quiet. "Sheriff Maurer?"

"Where'd you get that kind of money, Little Bit?"

"I've been saving all my tips from the diner and everything I earn selling beadwork at the craft fairs." She fought hard not to cry. "It was for nursing school. I've been accepted at the University of Evansville. Classes start at the end of August."

"Why on earth didn't you keep your money in the bank?"

"That's a very good question, Sheriff, and if I had it all to do over…" Her voice went wobbly, and the sheriff cleared his throat as if he were the one choking up.

"Did you and Matt have some kind of fight? Maybe you'd like to wait awhile. Could be he'll cool down and come on home tomorrow."

"No. We didn't have a fight, and he's not coming back." The image of the pregnancy test flashed through her mind. Ceejay bit her bottom lip to keep from blurting out the real reason her boyfriend had hared off.

"You're certain this isn't just a misunderstanding?"

"I'm certain."

"I'll need the year, model, and make of your car and your license plate. Do you have the VIN number?"

"I do. Hold on, and I'll go get it." She set the phone on the kitchen counter and ran back to the closet, where she kept the cardboard box full of important documents. Ceejay returned with her car registration, gave him all the pertinent information, and then hung up. Her mortification complete, she made for the one piece of furniture worth squat in their entire apartment—the rocking chair that had once belonged to her mother. The mother she barely remembered.

Setting the chair in motion, Ceejay started counting the cracks in the living room ceiling. As long as she focused all of her attention on the numbers, she could ignore her breaking heart and pretend she wasn't pregnant, alone, and scared shit-less. When the light began to fade, she counted the forward and backward movements of the rocker.

Footsteps in the hall brought her to a halt. Sucking in her breath, she went still. He'd come back. Matt had come back for her. She listened and watched. The knob turned, and the door opened a crack.

"Ceejay, come on now. Let's go home."

"Aunt Jenny?" Disappointment pressed her hard against the wooden spindles of the chair. "How did you know?"

"I had a feeling."

"Huh." Ceejay blew out shaky breath. "Sheriff Maurer called you, didn't he?"

Jenny switched on the lights and came toward her. The pity in her aunt's eyes forced her to turn away and start the chair rocking. Where had she stopped? Oh, yeah, 299, 300, 301.

"Gather some of your beadwork and whatever else you need. We'll send your cousins over tomorrow for the rest. I picked your laundry up off the lawn and loaded it into my car. Did you know you left your purse right there in the middle of the sidewalk?"

Her aunt stopped the chair's motion with a hand on the frame. "Come home, Little Bit. I never did understand what you saw in that boy. He rolled into town from God knows where, and after a year, you still don't know much about him. I swear you were just wearing that boy for his looks."

"He *was* good-looking." Hysteria rose like a bubble, bursting out in a laugh that took a turn for the worse. "He stole my money. He…he took the money I saved for school."

"I know." Jenny nodded. "I've been thinking—"

"When did you have time to *think* about this?" Ceejay's eyes flew to her aunt. "It just happened."

Jenny patted her shoulder. "You have your job at the diner, and once you get too far along in your pregnancy to wait on tables, you can take over the register."

Ceejay's eyebrows shot up. "You…you *know* about…?"

"You think I didn't notice those quick trips to the restroom with your face all pasty green? I've decided to turn the carriage house over to you. If you clean it out and fix it up, maybe you can find a renter. Along with the craft fairs, it'll give you a little extra income."

Not enough for college. Not nearly enough to make her dreams of leaving Perfect come true. Ceejay started counting her heartbeats. The plans she'd made for the future slipped through her fingers like water through a rusted bucket. "You've…you've already done so much for me. I can't accept it."

"Nonsense. You're family." Her aunt circled the room, picking up her basket of beadwork and other small items, tucking them into the basket as she went. "You and the baby will live with me in the big house, of course. It's way too much for one person, and I don't like rattling around in that big old monster by myself."

"Oh…Jenny…" Pushing her hand against her mouth, she tried to hold herself together. No use. Grief spilled out in great, gasping sobs.

Ceejay sprayed Windex on the windowpane and rubbed at the stubborn dust and grime hardened by years of neglect. Boxes full of Levolor blinds awaited installation, and the wood plank floors smelled like lemon cleaner and wax. Next, she planned to give the walls a fresh coat of paint.

The toilet in the tiny bathroom didn't work properly, and the faucet in the kitchen leaked, but her uncle had promised to look at both when he returned with the truck full of her belongings. Once she had everything in working order, she'd place an ad in a few of the local papers and stick a "for rent" sign out alongside the highway next to their mailbox.

She'd always loved the old brick carriage house. She and her cousins had played there on rainy days when they were children. Sometimes she'd hidden there with a good book when she'd needed to get away. Now it was hers, and she meant to take good care of the place.

"Ceejay," her aunt called from the back door of the big house. "Sheriff Maurer is here to see you."

Her heart took a nosedive. She walked slowly across the yard and into the kitchen, stopping by the sink to splash cold water on her overheated face before entering the foyer. "Sheriff Maurer," Ceejay greeted the burly man she'd known all her life. "How are you?"

Perspiration beaded on his upper lip and forehead. He fidgeted with the uniform hat in his hand, turning it around and around by the rim. "Hey, Little Bit. I'm fine." He used his hat to gesture toward the living room. "Why don't we all go have a seat while we talk?"

Ceejay followed his stocky frame into the living room. His short-cropped hair had turned mostly gray now, and his middle hung over his belt. He took a seat on the couch, and Ceejay sat in her rocker. She'd insisted they load it into her aunt's car before agreeing to return home.

"Would you like some iced tea, Harlen?" Jenny swept into the room with a plastic tray holding a pitcher and three glasses filled with ice. She wore a denim skirt that made a whooshing sound with each step and a blue cotton blouse that matched the color of her eyes. Her silver-streaked blonde curls made a bid for freedom from the clip at the top of her head.

"Thank you, Jennifer." Sheriff Maurer smiled. "I could do with something cold to drink."

Jenny set the tray on the coffee table and poured a glass for the sheriff. Ceejay shook her head when her aunt turned her way in question. Her stomach was kinked with tension, and she couldn't take anything right now.

The sheriff took a long drink. His Adam's apple bobbed away, and the sound of his swallows filled the room. With a satisfied sigh, he put the glass on the coaster set before him and turned to Ceejay, all business now that his thirst had been slaked. "We found your Honda just this side of the Kentucky border. Matt left it parked at a truck stop."

"What do I have to do to get it back?" She studied her folded hands.

"I'll have Deputy Taylor drive it here for you. You don't have to do anything but hand over a spare key." He cleared his throat and patted her knee. "I'm afraid the money's long gone."

What did she want to count, the knotholes in the floor or the planks? "Can I charge him with anything? Auto theft, or...or... what about stealing my money?"

"I'm afraid not. It doesn't work like that. Since the two of you were living together, it's a civil matter, more a breach of trust than auto theft. That goes for the money too. You kept the cash in the apartment. There's no way to prove who it belonged to."

How many times can a heart break before it stops beating altogether? She probably would've learned the answer to that question in nursing school. One glimpse at the sympathy in the sheriff's eyes set the refrain she'd heard all her life buzzing around her head like a big fat horsefly. *Poor Ceejay, abandoned by her own mother. Poor Little Bit, doesn't even know who her father is.* At least now the refrain would change. *Poor Ceejay, pregnant, unmarried, and abandoned...again.*

What is it about me that makes leaving so easy?

The desire to get away from Perfect sucked all the breath out of her lungs. She needed a new start someplace where no one looked at her like she was some kind of rescue puppy in a kill shelter. The floorboards drew her attention, and her lips moved without sound. Numbers never left, never took anything from you, and they didn't judge.

"What's she counting now, Jen?"

Poor little oddball.

"Hmm?" Jenny looked toward her. "The knotholes?"

Ceejay shook her head.

"Oh, it's the planks then." Jenny leaned toward the tray. "More tea, Harlen?"

"Naw. I've got to be going." The couch creaked as he rose to leave. "The deputies will be here shortly with her car."

Jenny rose with him. "Thank you so much for coming by personally. Will we see you at the diner for lunch tomorrow?"

"Of course. What's Monday's special?"

Her aunt accompanied him to the front door. "Meat loaf and mashed potatoes."

"Any chance you'll make one of your strawberry-rhubarb pies?"

"If we have any rhubarb left, I'll make one just for you."

The next best thing to counting was cleaning. She didn't wait for her aunt to return to the living room. Ceejay slipped out the back door quiet as a shadow, heading for the grime on the windows of the carriage house.

Attached to the living quarters, the large bays that once housed the carriages and tack of her ancestors now held cobwebs, dust, and the accumulated junk from several generations of Lovejoys, stretching all the way back to the Civil War. Here was a project offering an almost endless escape. If she played it right, paced herself, she'd have to emerge only for her shifts at the diner. She wouldn't have to face the curious stares, the pity, or the smugness any more than necessary.

Jenny stood in the doorway. "You're not alone, honey."

Ceejay nodded.

"You're young, not even twenty yet. You'll bounce back from this."

"Just how does one *bounce back* from an unplanned pregnancy? Once this baby is born, is everything suddenly going to fall into place?" She rubbed harder at the windowpane. "How am I going to manage raising a child on my own? I have no education and no future."

"You've got to make a plan."

"I *had* a plan. I *planned* to go to nursing school, find a great job, move away, and maybe even get married and start a family of my own someday." She swiped at the sweat on her forehead with the back of her wrist. "I wasn't stupid like some girls. We used birth control."

"What's meant to be—"

"The condom tore." She pressed her forehead against the cool glass and closed her eyes tight. "That's not fate, Jenny. *That's* an unfortunate accident resulting from an inferior product."

"You can still start nursing school."

"How?" She rolled her forehead against the glass. "The baby is due in the middle of the second semester, and I'm fresh out of options."

"You'll find a way. At any rate, you need to track Matt down."

"I have no intention of tracking that rat-bastard down." The thought of any contact with the source of all this pain turned her stomach. "He stole from me. How likely do you think it is that he's going to pony up any kind of child support? Besides, as far as I know, he's never held down a regular job. All he ever wanted was to get picked up as a driver by a big name on the NASCAR circuit, race cars, and drink beer with other motor heads."

Jenny wrinkled her nose and waved her hand in front of her face. "Oh, Lord. The wind is shifting."

The stench of hog farms to the west of Perfect permeated the carriage house. A wave of nausea roiled through Ceejay, and she made a beeline for one of the cleaning buckets.

The wind had shifted, all right, and it wasn't going to shift back anytime soon. Maybe never.

CHAPTER TWO
FIVE YEARS LATER

IRONIC. HE'D SURVIVED A SUICIDE bombing in Iraq, but his stepbrother hadn't survived the same Pennsylvania turnpike they'd been driving on for most of their lives. Noah shifted his balance as the remaining mourners trickled away from the Langford mausoleum. His prosthetic chafed, and exhaustion tugged at his already ragged edges. Leaning more weight on his cane, he tried to relieve some of the pressure.

His stepmother came to stand beside him. "The limo is waiting, and so is your father." Allison's eyes were red rimmed and swollen. "You know how impatient he is."

"He can wait." They stood side by side in the quiet, sharing their grief. Noah's mind drifted back in time to when his father had brought Allison and her young son home to meet him for the first time. Despite the vast differences in their natures, they'd hit it off immediately. He'd always been the reflective and responsible older brother, while Matt had been wild, hot-tempered, and impetuous. Memories of the many times he'd extricated Matt from his own acts of stupidity ran through Noah's mind. He chuffed out a breath of air and stifled a curse. He was going to miss his kid brother. No matter what, Matt always managed to make him laugh, and it had been far too long since he'd had anything to laugh about.

The damp March chill had him reaching to rub an aching leg that no longer existed. The healing skin grafts running up his left side itched like the devil. Panic and pain had become his constant companions.

Allison placed her hand on his coat sleeve. "I have a favor to ask."

"What is it?" Noah swallowed the lump in his throat.

"I can't bear to sort through Matt's things, and—"

"Let's get going." Edward Langford strode up to them. "Our guests will be arriving for the funeral luncheon before we do. I sent Paige on ahead with the relatives."

Noah glared at his father. "You were saying, Allison?"

She tugged him away from the mausoleum and turned them toward the waiting limo. "Would you mind clearing out Matt's condo? Everything can go to charity, of course, but there might be personal things we want to keep."

"Have some of the staff take care of it." Ed came up beside her. "Noah doesn't want to rummage through Matt's things."

"I'll do it," Noah said. "It should be taken care of by family."

His father jangled the contents of his pockets, a sure sign he'd worked himself up for something. "Have you given any thought to your future, son?"

"I've only been home from the VA hospital for two days, Dad. *Right now* is about all I can handle." He'd been avoiding this conversation, and his dad knew it. No slipping away or pretending to be asleep now.

"Give it a week or so, and then come work for Langford Plumbing Supplies. It would do you good and help you pull your life back together."

Noah tensed. For as long as he could remember, he'd been pressured into joining the family business, like all the Langford males since his great-grandfather had founded the company. Nothing about plumbing supplies appealed to Noah. He'd always wanted a career in the military. Even now the army would find a place for him in some office, or commanding a training unit, but he'd lost his heart for the job. Yep. That ship had sailed, and he no longer had any sense of direction. Almost thirty, no career, a wrecked body and a shattered mind. Now what? "I'm not interested in working for LPS."

"A Langford has always stood at the helm. You're next in line."

"What about Paige? She's the Langford getting the Harvard MBA. Why not let her take over?"

"Paige doesn't know thing one about plumbing supplies, and it's always been the men who've run the business."

"Are you hearing this?" He glanced at his stepmother. "Your husband's a sexist."

Allison nodded and turned her gaze toward the Philadelphia skyline and the benevolent Billy Penn statue keeping watch over their city.

"Paige is brilliant, Dad. You'd be a fool not to put her to work for LPS."

"Right. I'll put your sister in charge. She'll fall in love with some guy, get married, and have babies. Next thing you know she'll want to stay home, give teas, and support a whole host of charities like every other high-society woman in this city. We need you, Noah."

Allison slid into the limo after her husband. "Hush, Ed."

"I'm only thinking what's best for my son."

"No, you're not. You're thinking what's best for you and LPS." She reached into her purse for a tissue and dabbed at her eyes. "I just buried my son. Do you hear me? My *son*. Noah has just come home. I will not have you drive him away with your harping."

Warmth spread through Noah. Allison had rescued him from a desolate childhood filled with nannies and boarding school hell. She'd been the only mother he'd ever known and one of the few people who could stand up to his father. Noah leaned his cane against the seat and tried to make himself comfortable. "One thing at a time, and first on the list is Matt's condo. When I know what I want to do, I'll let you both know."

"Take your time." Allison patted his arm. "Maybe now you'll tap into the trust fund your grandfather set up for you. It'll give you some breathing room while you figure everything out."

"I still think—"

"Edward." Allison quelled him with a look.

Noah turned his attention to the scenery passing by the limo's tinted windows. As a Langford, he'd been born into the family wealth, while Matt had not. Painfully aware of the disparity, Noah had refused to touch the money in his trust fund. The family fortune meant nothing to him, or maybe being born a Langford meant he had more to prove—to himself and to the rest of the world.

After three days of visiting with relatives in town for the funeral, Noah was relieved to have a job to do. He turned the key and opened Matt's condo door, half expecting to see his stepbrother's ghost. The stillness inside sent a chill down his spine. He dropped the keys on the chrome-and-glass dining room table and wandered into the living room.

No one would mistake the place for anything but a bachelor pad. A single black leather couch faced a large entertainment center holding racing trophies, an enormous LCD TV, and video game equipment. Matt's coffee table bore the hardened, sticky outlines of take-out cartons from countless solitary meals, and racing magazines littered the floor.

A familiar, well-worn denim jacket slung over the back of the couch slammed Noah hard against the finality of Matt's death. His hair-trigger hold on reality snapped, and the blast-furnace heat of an Iraqi desert engulfed him in sweltering waves. Sweat beaded his forehead and made the back of his neck itch. Every excruciating detail from the worst day of his life came back in a rush—even the pain. Especially the pain.

"Lieutenant, civilian vehicle approaching from the east. Check it out, sir."

Noah dropped the map he'd been studying and snapped his attention to the battered old truck cruising their way. "We're still ten kilometers from Mosul. Intel reports this road has been secured." Mosul was a hotbed of insurgents, which was why his platoon's mission was so critical.

"Yes, sir, but that truck's heading straight for us like it means business. Could be carrying IEDs."

Noah grabbed the field glasses off the floor and peered into the oncoming vehicle. "It's a couple of kids, maybe sixteen or seventeen years old. Probably locals trying to catch a glimpse of the Iraqi officials we're escorting." He lowered the glasses and nodded toward the line of vehicles in front of them. "Radio ahead and have Staff Sergeant Reilly pick up the pace. If the civilians get too close, we'll fire a few rounds into the ground to warn them off. You hear that, Gunny?" Noah called over his shoulder.

"Yes, sir," he called down from the artillery hatch.

Private Jackson picked up the radio to call ahead, and they were soon clipping along at a faster rate. The civilian truck responded by adjusting its speed, going off road, and angling toward them. Frowning, Noah lifted the field glasses again. The driver and passenger were talking and laughing, not the fanatical look of men intent on martyrdom. Not likely jihad. Still, it wouldn't be the first time insurgents had used children to do their dirty work. "A couple of curious kids is all," he muttered to himself. "Gunny, fire a round into the dirt in front of them."

"I got a bad feeling about this, Lieutenant," Jackson shouted over the sound of the machine gun discharging above them.

What could he do? Order a couple of teenagers killed because they were in the same desert? Noah kept his eye on the vehicle.

The truck turned sharply and accelerated, setting a collision course straight for them. "Shit! Blow the suckers out of the sand! Shoot to kill, shoot to kill," he shouted his order, knowing it was too late. The truck increased its speed, plowing into their midst.

Detonating explosives lit up the road like the Fourth of July. The world became a kaleidoscope as Noah's vehicle flipped. Metal fragments and body parts flew through the air, littering the sand, while the screams of the dying echoed all around him. Noah was pinned under his Humvee. Burning pain seared the entire length of his left side up to his armpit. He tried to catch a breath through the grit and the smoke and searched the perimeter for his driver. He found him—parts of him, anyway, and then everything went black.

Trembling, Noah gasped for air. He leaned against the wall for support and waited for the panic to recede. Guilt tunneled through him like a ravenous worm, leaving his psyche full of holes. Five men died because of his hesitation. In his nightmares, the dead paraded in front of him, their hollow eyes a condemnation of his survival.

The worst part was, he couldn't predict what would set him off. Sometimes it made no sense at all. The tiniest incident with no discernible connection to Iraq would plunge him back into the middle of hell. He was trapped in some kind of time warp for the damned. Even after six months in the VA hospital with all that therapy, there were still days when the dead were more real than the living.

Wiping the sweat from his clammy forehead, Noah looked around at the artifacts of his stepbrother's short life. How like Matt to die at a time when he needed him the most. No matter how irrational the anger, his stepbrother's death left teeth marks in his soul. Taking a deep breath, he pushed himself off the wall. He had a job to do, and the sooner he got started the better.

Cleaning and packing could wait. He'd take care of the financial stuff first and look for a will. "One thing at a time. One thing at a time." Chanting his mantra, Noah headed down the hall toward the second bedroom, where Matt kept his computer. He glanced into the bathroom. Clothing overflowed from the hamper, as usual. Towels, dirty socks, and jeans lay in a heap on the floor.

Matt had always been full of glory dreams. He'd been determined to burn up the racetrack and make millions in endorsements. Gorgeous women were going to throw themselves at his feet. He'd be written up in racing magazines all over the world. Noah's dreams had been much simpler, or so he'd thought. See the world, fight terrorism and tyranny, take a stand on the side of freedom and justice.

None of their dreams had turned out the way they'd planned. He entered the second bedroom and turned on the iPod dock sitting on the shelf above the desk. He thumbed through Matt's music and selected U2, cranking up the volume until he couldn't hear his own thoughts. Taking a seat at the desk, he opened one drawer after another in search of the cheap address book where Matt listed his account information alphabetically. The passwords were right there for anybody to steal. How many times had he told his stepbrother his system sucked? Everything a thief needed in one place, so like Matt.

A bulky Tyvek envelope lay on top of the pile of folders and loose papers in the bottom drawer. Noah started to lift it out of the way when he noticed it was addressed. Curious, he pulled the envelope out and read: Ceejay Lovejoy, RR1 Box 65, Perfect, Indiana. Giving the bundle a squeeze, he wondered about the bulk. Who was Ceejay Lovejoy? Noah upended the unsealed envelope. Stunned, he watched several stacks of hundred-dollar bills hit the desk.

"What the hell?" He thumbed through the bundles, counting. Almost ten thousand goddamned dollars! He reached inside and pulled out a handwritten letter. Matt's familiar scrawl riveted his attention. Glancing at the date, his eyebrows rose. It had been written three years ago. Written and never sent.

Ceejay,

It's been two years since I left, and not a single day goes by that I don't regret stealing from you the way I did. I'm sorry I took your money and your car. When I found out you were pregnant, I panicked. I know that's no excuse, but you knew I never had any interest in getting married or having kids. If I'd stayed, I would've put pressure on you to end the pregnancy, and you would've put pressure on me to settle down. We would've ended up hating each other.

It's going to take me a while to scrape it together, but once you receive this letter, you will find a cashier's check for two times the $5,000 I took from you and a life insurance policy naming you as the sole beneficiary. It's the best I can do. I hope you can forgive me. I'm sorry, Ceejay. I never meant to hurt you the way I did, but it never would've worked out between us. This way, I saved us both years of misery.

Matt

It took reading the letter through three times before Noah could absorb it all. "What the hell, Matt?"

Noah leaned back in the chair, rubbed his face with both hands, and tried to pull his thoughts together. He'd always known Matt was irresponsible and more than a little self-centered, but never in his wildest imagination had he believed his stepbrother capable of such coldhearted, selfish cowardice.

He stared at the pile of cash covering the laptop keyboard. Why keep the cash here, and not in a bank? Stupid question. Matt liked to stay under the radar, and he'd probably been doing something slightly illegal to earn the money in the first place. Like side bets on the races maybe, or some other under-the-table dealings he really didn't want to know about.

Pulling his cell phone out of his pocket, he hit speed dial and waited for his father to pick up. "Dad, do you have a minute?"

"Sure. What's up?"

"Have you ever heard of Ceejay Lovejoy?"

"No. Why do you ask?"

"We need to talk." Noah ran a hand over his buzz cut. "Is that coffee shop down the street from your office still there?"

"What's this about, Noah?"

"Matthew left a letter and ten thousand dollars to a woman in Indiana." Or close to it. He'd throw in the last remaining bills himself. It was the least he could do. "She was pregnant with his baby five years ago. You and Allison might be grandparents." The other end of the line went quiet for several long seconds.

"Give me a couple of hours," his dad rasped out. "I'll meet you at the Gathering Grounds at three thirty p.m. Will that work?"

"Yeah. That'll give me some time to finish going through his desk. I'll see you then." Noah hung up and turned back to his task, his mind still reeling.

A couple of hours later, Noah headed out to meet with his dad. He gripped the steering wheel of his Ford pickup while the beginnings of a plan fomented. He'd seen more of Afghanistan and Iraq than he'd ever seen of the U.S. and knew very little of the country he'd fought to protect. Worse, he'd forgotten why he'd gone to war in the first place. Matt's letter had given him an idea, and the more he mulled it over, the more sense it made.

He'd buy a camper, hitch it to his truck, and travel to Perfect, Indiana. He needed to find out if Ceejay Lovejoy had kept his stepbrother's baby. If so, having a grandchild would go a long way toward healing his stepmother's broken heart—if the Lovejoys allowed them into their lives, that is. Maybe Ceejay and the child needed help and would welcome them with open arms. Or maybe she'd married by now and had a blended family. No matter what, he needed to know. They all needed to know.

If she hadn't kept the baby, he'd take off and travel around the U.S. until he got his head straight. Besides, if he didn't leave soon, he and his father were going to start some serious head butting. Not a good idea in his present state.

Noah pulled up to the curb next to the coffee shop, cut the engine, and snatched the letter from the seat next to him. Talking to his father would take patience, and he no longer had any to give. For Allison's sake, he had to keep it together. He did a visual check of the area and rooftops before entering. Habit.

Being in the coffee shop put him on hyperalert status. He scanned the room for...what? The enemy? He shook his head and let the scent of strong, freshly ground coffee penetrate the fog of apprehension gripping him. Noah located his father toward the rear of the room. Good. He'd be able to sit with his back against the wall and his eyes on the door.

"Hey, Dad." Noah slid into the wooden booth.

"I got you coffee." His dad pushed the cup toward him. "Let's see this letter."

Noah handed it to him and took a sip of the strong brew. His father ran a hand over his chin, and Noah noticed the old man had more lines on his face. He looked older, and right now, regret clouded his eyes.

"Don't mention this to Allison," his dad said. "It'll break her heart all over again if she gets her hopes up, only to learn..."

"I agree. That's why I came to you first." When it came to Allison, Noah had never doubted his father's complete and utter devotion. Noah had once believed he'd share that kind of love with someone someday. Dreams of a wife and family of his own had always been there in the back of his mind. Not anymore. He'd buried that hope in the desert sand along with his sanity.

"What was going on with Matt five years ago? What was he doing in Indiana?"

"You know what a temper he had." His dad took a deep breath and let it out. "Matt came to me asking for money to fund his pipe dreams. He wanted to become a big-time stock car racer, and LPS was supposed to be his biggest sponsor. I told him I'd give him a free ride to any college or trade school he chose. I even offered him a job at LPS again. He turned it all down and threw a fit. He said he'd find a way to make it without us and left. Your stepmother and I didn't hear from him for two years. By the time he returned, he had a gig with an outfit that paid him to drive for them."

"Why didn't I know about any of this?" He frowned.

"You were deployed. We didn't want you stressed about anything going on at home. Besides, what could you have done?"

Noah nodded, and his jaw clenched. "I also found a life insurance policy naming Ceejay Lovejoy as the sole beneficiary."

His father leveled a somber look his way. "If this Ceejay didn't keep the baby, I don't want Allison to know anything about this. It'd kill her to learn Matt walked away from his own flesh and blood. Her ex-husband did the same when Matt was only a couple of weeks old."

"I didn't know."

"Allison doesn't talk about it. She tried so hard to raise her son to be different." He sighed. "I guess I'll hire a private investigator, and—"

"I have a better idea." Noah straightened. "I'll head to Indiana myself. If Ceejay Lovejoy kept the baby, I'll take some time to get to know them before springing the Langfords on them."

"You're in no shape to go anywhere. Stay home. Work for LPS, and—"

"Dad, we've been through this more times than I care to count. LPS is not for me."

"I know. You wanted a military career, but that's over with now." He started fiddling with his empty coffee cup. "It would help if you had a job to go to every day. At least give it some thought, son." Staring at the artwork on the brick wall next to him, his dad swore under his breath. "What was Matt thinking?" He shot Noah a questioning look as if he had the answers.

He didn't. Noah shook his head and swallowed the rising bitterness. Committing such an act of selfishness was beyond his comprehension.

"At least we can give Matt's child every advantage we have to offer," Ed continued. "We'll set them up in his condo and give the mother a job."

"Wait," Noah said. "Think about it. If she'd kept the baby, wouldn't she have come looking for Matt? At the very least he owed her child support. That's the law, and if she knew about his connection to LPS, she'd have demanded a lot more than support after the way he treated her."

His father leaned back. "As angry as he was at the time, I doubt he mentioned the Langford name. Matthew was a Wyatt. How would she make the connection?" His brow furrowed. "She might have searched and found nothing. Where is this town anyway?"

"Perfect is on the Ohio River." Noah reached into his pocket for the Google map he'd printed and laid it on the table. "Evansville is the closest city. I know you mean well, but we can't just charge down there expecting her to welcome us with open arms. If she did keep the child, she's not going to uproot her life simply because we want her to." Noah shifted again. The hardness of the seat was beginning to wear on him. "I've been giving

my future some thought. I plan to buy a fifth-wheel camper
trailer—"

"What's that got to do with Matthew's child?"

"Hear me out." He fought against the urge to snap at his dad
and took a deep breath before continuing. "I'll head to Indiana
first. If there is no child, I'll hand off the letter, money, and insurance policy and be on my way. I want to see this country—"

"Noah—"

"Just listen." He glared. "I want to travel for a year. I need to
get my head together and figure out what to do with the rest of
my life." His gut knotted. "If I haven't found any answers by the
end of the year, I'll give LPS a shot." Man, he hoped it didn't come
to that. "If there is a child, like I said before, I'll stay nearby if I
can and try to get to know them before telling them about our
connection to Matt."

His dad scrutinized him for a long moment. "A Langford in
a camper trailer," he muttered and shook his head. "Langfords do
not live in trailers."

Noah grunted. "This Langford will." He had a mission, and
the forward momentum felt good.

❦　❦　❦

Perfect, Indiana—an idyllic post–Civil War town nestled on
the banks of the Ohio River. That's what the welcome sign said,
so it must be true. Main Street looked like something out of a
Norman Rockwell painting, with redbrick storefronts, colonial
blue and white trim, and potted geraniums blooming out of window boxes everywhere.

Even with a stop sign at every corner, it took only three minutes to pass through town. Noah pulled into a gas station on

the outskirts and filled his tank. He went inside, grabbed a soda from the refrigerated case, and handed his credit card to a gum-chewing teenager behind the counter. Her blonde hair was pulled into a ponytail, and she wore too much makeup, as if doing so might make her look older.

"You don't happen to know where Rural Route One, box sixty-five is, do you?"

The blonde popped her gum and shrugged. "I know everybody in Perfect, but I couldn't tell you any of their addresses. You got a name to go by?"

"Ceejay Lovejoy."

"She's my cousin." Her eyebrows rose, and she appraised him with frank curiosity. "How do you know the Lovejoys? I've never seen you around here before. You have an accent."

One side of Noah's mouth quirked up. She spoke with a southern Indiana twang, and *he* had the accent? "I don't know them."

"Oh?"

He could see her working up to more questions he had no intention of answering. "Can you give me directions or a landmark?"

"Sure. Just head on down the road about three miles. You'll see a rusty old 'carriage house for rent' sign right next to a black mailbox. That's their driveway." She placed his receipt on the counter. "You here to rent the carriage house?"

He signed the receipt without answering. Once he was back on his way, Noah lowered the window and inhaled the fresh spring air. Late May, and already the temps in southern Indiana reached the midseventies. It had still been chilly and damp when he'd left his parents' home in Pennsylvania. He scanned the side of the two-lane highway until he found the landmark the cashier had told him about, a tin sign rusted around the edges of the white paint and black lettering.

He turned onto the gravel driveway, and his palms grew damp. What would he say if he found out she hadn't kept the baby? *Um, hi. Here's ten thousand dollars and a life insurance policy worth ten times that amount. Sorry my stepbrother knocked you up, stole your money, and ran for the hills. Have a nice day.*

What if she owned a gun? Worse yet, what if she knew how to use it?

The right side of the drive boasted an orchard in full bloom with three different kinds of fruit trees arranged in neat rows, all perfectly pruned with wire frames around the trunks. Mature black walnuts lined the other side, leading the way to a large limestone manor house with a screened porch on the second floor and a columned veranda on the first. A variety of flowering shrubs grew in a well-tended row in front.

The house gave every appearance of being as carefully maintained as the yard and landscaping, until he got closer. He noticed the peeling paint on the columns and window frames, the rusted-out screening, and the sagging gutters with plant life sprouting over the edges. The roof needed replacing, and he suspected the windows did too. The elegant old home had seen better days.

Beyond the house at the bottom of a long, sloping lawn flowed the Ohio River. Another copse of walnuts separated the property from yet more farm fields sprouting green. Situated as it was, the waterfront property must be worth a tidy fortune, yet the maintenance of the home had been neglected. It bothered him. Was it due to a lack of interest or a lack of funds?

Noah pulled his truck and trailer around the circular drive and parked between a neon-green Volkswagen Beetle and an old

Honda Civic. He took a deep breath to shore up his nerve. Should he bring the envelope with him, or wait to see whether Ceejay still lived here?

His Google search had come up a blank, and he knew nothing about her. Once she found out about Matt's ties to the Langford empire, she might start seeing dollar signs. Things could turn ugly. On the flip side, if Ceejay still lived here, and he told her who he was from the start, she might slam the door in his face and refuse to have anything to do with the Langfords. It was what he would do if their roles were reversed. If Matt's child existed, he didn't want to risk losing his chance to get to know him or her.

Wait and see won out, and he left the envelope locked in the glove compartment, eased his way out of the truck, and took the stairs leading to the front door. The moment the brass knocker connected with the wood, loud barking erupted from the back-yard. The door opened to reveal a petite young woman wearing hospital scrubs with a name tag clipped on in front.

Ceejay Lovejoy regarded him with large, wide-set blue eyes. Red-gold curls framed her oval face, and a sprinkle of freckles dusted her nose and cheeks. All-American cute, in a girl-next-door kind of way. Noah's mouth went dry.

"Oh. Hello." She smiled up at him. "Can I help you?"

"Um, yes. My name is Noah Langford, and I..."

"Are *you* the guy who called about the carriage house a few days ago?" Her eyes slid over him, coming back to meet his gaze with obvious curiosity.

Was that appreciation he saw in her expression? "Uh..." Just then a small, dark-haired child inserted herself between the doorframe and the woman's legs. She had Matt's coloring, his brown eyes and dimples.

"I can say my ABCs," she announced.

He blinked hard and tried to catch his breath.

"Lucinda Mae, what makes you think this man is here to listen to you recite the alphabet?" Ceejay placed her hand on the little girl's head, smoothing her curls down in a maternal gesture. The child looked up at him, then swung her gaze back to her mother.

"What makes you think he idn't?" She stared up at him. "I'm gonna be six."

If she was already five, then she couldn't be Matt's daughter. Disappointment twisted his gut. "You are?"

"Now, Luce. Don't you remember when your cousins, uncles, and aunties all came over to celebrate your birthday?"

"I remember. I got presents." Lucinda's expression turned solemn.

"How many candles were on the cake?" Ceejay smiled as the little girl held up four fingers. "That's right. You *just* turned four. You have to turn five before you can be six, baby."

"But I'm *gonna* be six."

Ceejay shook her head. "There's no arguing with the logic of a four-year-old. Do you want to see the carriage house?"

"I—"

"Who's at the door, Ceejay?" a feminine voice called from somewhere inside the house.

"It's the folks from Publishers Clearing House Sweepstakes here to deliver your check."

Ceejay smiled and winked at him.

He lost his breath.

"I don't know why I bother." A woman he guessed to be in her fifties opened the door wider. She bore a strong familial resemblance to Ceejay.

"I'm going to be late for work. This is Noah Langford. He's here about the carriage house. Can you take care of it?" Ceejay pushed her daughter toward the older woman and slipped past him as she headed down the stairs with a wave.

He caught the faint scent of something floral and soft as she swept by. She smelled good, looked good, and judging by the interaction he'd witnessed between her and Lucinda, she was a caring and competent mother. Noah watched her walk to the ancient Honda and slide in behind the wheel. She had a sweet little figure too. His stepbrother must've been out of his mind. How could he walk away from her knowing she carried his child?

His insides were shaky, and he leaned on his cane. Matt had never laid eyes on his precious little girl, never saw how much she resembled him. It had taken Noah all of a minute to become completely captivated. He could only imagine how his stepmother would react. He swallowed hard.

"I'm Jenny." The older woman held Lucinda's hand. "Hold on a sec while I get the key."

Noah nodded. He had no place he had to be. Besides, the tour would give him time to pull himself together. Jenny returned with the key in hand and Lucinda in tow. Noah followed them around back, where the carriage house was situated. The dog, now inside the house, whined and barked as Jenny opened the gate to a small portion of the grounds that had been fenced into a small yard.

"Lucinda, why don't you go play in your sandbox while I show Mr. Langford around."

Nodding, Lucinda smiled up at him and trot-skipped away. Jenny unlocked the door to the living quarters adjoining the carriage bays.

Noah stepped inside. The faint smell of lemon cleaner wafted up around him. He was surprised to find a black walnut floor buffed to a high shine. The walls were painted a neutral cream color like so many rentals, contrasting nicely with the rich walnut. A few pieces of cheap, tattered furniture were at odds with the nineteenth-century architecture's coved ceilings and alcoved window seats.

"The furniture can go into storage if you don't need it," Jenny said.

He nodded, thinking the city dump would be more appropriate. She led him into a small kitchenette. Bright color on the wall drew his eye, a framed picture of a cardinal perched on the stem of a pink flower. He was amazed to discover the piece had been done in precise, intricate beadwork. A craftsman himself, he couldn't help admiring the piece.

"Ceejay did that." Jenny beamed. "She sells most of what she creates, but I wanted her to keep this one. It really brightens the place up, don't you think? The cardinal is our state bird, and the peony the state flower."

"She's very talented." Noah stepped back to admire how realistic the bird looked.

"There's a full-size bed in the bedroom and a bathroom with a shower through here." She nodded toward a short hallway. "We have a window air-conditioner in storage for the place. Rent is five hundred per month plus utilities. We require first and last month's rent up front." Jenny stood by the door. "Take a look around. When you're done, come on back to the big house."

Noah nodded, and she disappeared. He wandered around the apartment, poking through each room. Everything was in perfect order and squeaky clean. It reminded him of the carefully tended trees and shrubs. Ceejay's doing? He wanted to get to know her better, find out what made the mother of Matt's daughter tick before revealing who he was. Maybe he'd get a better sense of how she might react. His mind full of questions, he headed back to the front door and knocked.

"What do you think?" Jenny asked as she indicated the way into the living room.

"It's nice." Noah noticed the floors here were black walnut as well, along with the doors and trim. Rare. Walnut was costly and usually reserved for fine furniture. He should know. He'd spent all his afternoons after school working at his uncle Gabe's furniture restoration and replication shop. Remembering the peaceful hours spent in his uncle's steady, quiet presence brought a smile to his face.

Lucinda was coloring a picture laid out next to a stack of puzzles on the coffee table. Noah leaned his cane against the armrest and sat on the couch.

"If you don't mind my asking, what brings you to Perfect?" Jenny settled into the chair across from him.

"I had planned to travel for a year." He couldn't very well blurt out who he was and why he'd come. "But it's so quiet and peaceful here, I've decided to stay for a while." Quiet except for the stupid dog scratching and snuffling on the other side of the double doors behind him. The sound set his teeth on edge, and he started to sweat. *Not now.* He sucked in a deep breath and forced himself to concentrate. He couldn't afford to fall into a flashback in the middle of the Lovejoys' living room.

"That explains the truck and trailer parked out front." She nodded. "Where are you from?"

"Pennsylvania." The door behind them burst open, and the biggest, ugliest dog he'd ever seen came bounding through.

Instinct took over. Noah shot off the couch and snatched Lucinda out of the beast's reach. It hit him full force then—he held Matt's little girl in his arms. His niece. Allison and his dad were grandparents, and *he* was an uncle.

She giggled and squirmed in his arms. The dog reacted in a frenzy of barking, leaping in circles around him. "What is that thing?"

Lucinda patted Noah's face. "That's Sweet Pea."

Noah glanced at Jenny. Her intense scrutiny made him aware of how odd his reaction must seem. "What kind of dog is that?" The mutt was the color of mud-streaked ash, part of its coat smooth, part long and wiry. Its head was massive and draped in extra folds of skin. The mutt must have weighed at least a hundred and fifty pounds, maybe more, and drool hung from its jowls in slimy strands.

"Far as the vet can tell, he's part mastiff and part wolfhound. Sweet Pea is just one rung up from a floor rug, Mr. Langford. You can put Lucinda down. Other than accidentally knocking people over with his enthusiasm, he wouldn't hurt a flea."

Shaken, he set Lucinda in front of the picture she'd been working on. His stump throbbed from the sudden exertion. He limped back to the couch, grateful to take the weight off his prosthesis. "Call me Noah."

"This place has a history." Jenny leaned forward in her chair. "My great-great-grandfather fought in the Civil War. Southern Indiana wasn't his destination either." She smiled. "He left Georgia intending to buy land in Texas and start a ranch. I think the quiet got to him too. He settled here, married, and founded the town of Perfect. Something about this place appeals to the war-weary."

Noah shifted his weight.

"Am I wrong in assuming you're recently out of the military?"

"No, ma'am. Seven years in the army, followed by six months in the VA hospital. I got out in March."

"I lost my husband in Vietnam, along with a brother. Lovejoys have fought in every war this country has ever been in, including the American Revolution."

War was the last thing Noah wanted to talk about. Glancing at Lucinda, he focused on the picture she was drawing, a large red barn with happy stick people in front and a big yellow sun in the corner. Sweet Pea lay on the floor next to her, his tongue hanging out, content to drool on the rug while keeping an eye on Noah. "I noticed your daughter wore scrubs. Does she work in a hospital?"

"I raised Ceejay, but she isn't my daughter. She's my niece." She canted her head and studied him. "Does she have anything to do with your being here?"

Heat crept up his neck. His gut told him now was not the time for revelations. "What makes you think that?"

"Just a feeling." Jenny shrugged. "I get them sometimes, about people mostly, and sometimes about things to come."

"Aunt Jenny is speckle-ating." Lucinda looked up from her task. "Mommy told me she speckle-ates all the time."

"Who asked you, little Miss Buttinski?"

"Nobody." Lucinda started to squirm. "Uh-oh, Aunt Jenny. The wind is gonna shift."

"Well, don't let us stop you. Get going."

Noah frowned as he watched Lucinda hold the railing and take the steps one at a time. He turned toward Jenny. "What does shifting wind have to do with going upstairs?"

Jenny laughed. "It's what Lucinda says when she has serious business to attend to in the bathroom. Stick around. You'll make the connection soon enough."

"Hey." Lucinda called from the second-floor landing. She pressed her tiny face up against the railing and peered down at him. "Will you still be here when I come back?"

"Do you want me to stay?" Noah held his breath.

Lucinda nodded solemnly.

"Then I will."

CHAPTER THREE

CEEJAY ROSE UP ON TIPTOE in front of the sink and looked out the kitchen window at the mystery man sitting in her backyard. She hadn't been able to get him off her mind since he showed up at their front door three days ago. Noah wasn't movie-star good-looking, but he had an interesting face—the kind of face a girl could spend hours getting to know better. She liked how his eyes were mostly green with brown flecks, and he had a great smile. Still, it wasn't his looks that piqued her interest. She knew a bird with a broken wing when she saw one, and that drew her like nothing else could.

"What are you doing?" Jenny swung into the room and set two canvas grocery bags on the table.

"I'm watching our new tenant." Ceejay glanced over her shoulder. "It's only two o'clock. How come you're home so early?"

"My new assistant manager is working out well, which means I can finally cut back on my hours." Jenny pulled cartons of diner leftovers out of one of the bags and placed them in the refrigerator. "What's Noah doing that's so interesting you have to stare at him out that window?"

Ceejay turned her attention back to the mystery man and smiled. "Far as I can tell, he's in a stare-down contest with Sweet Pea. My money's on the dog."

Jenny laughed. "That stupid mutt broke through another hook-and-eye on the kitchen doors after Noah's tour of the carriage house. The moment the dog burst into the room Noah shot off the couch like a rocket and lifted Lucinda into the air."

"Really?" Ceejay frowned. "Why would he do that? Sweet Pea would never hurt Lucinda."

"He didn't know that. I think he's one of those people who can't help themselves. The instinct to protect is in his blood."

"I don't know." Ceejay wiped her hands on a dish towel and helped her aunt put away the groceries from the second bag. "What do we know about him?"

"We know he's recently out of the military and trying to figure out the rest of his life. It's clear he's hurting. Something brought him here to heal."

"There you go speculating again." Ceejay shook her head. "According to his rental application, he's unemployed and doesn't seem real motivated to change that status."

"He just got out of the VA hospital two months ago. Give him some time." Jenny folded the canvas bags and shoved them into the broom closet. "Where's Lucinda?"

"Still napping. I'm going to go talk to Noah."

"Invite him to dinner while you're at it. I have enough ham and mashed potatoes to feed an army, and he looks like he could use a few good meals."

Nodding, she headed out back, letting the screen door close with a loud thwack behind her. Noah didn't stir as she approached, and Sweet Pea kept vigil at his feet. It wasn't until she stood right next to him that she noticed the trembling. He stared at nothing, his face tight and pale as if he suffered great pain. He had the look Lucinda got sometimes when she had night terrors. What kind of hell was he seeing?

Sweet Pea nudged Noah's clenched fist and sidled closer to lick his face. Noah came to with a gasp, shoving Sweet Pea away. "Get off me, you slobbering sack of—"

Ceejay cleared her throat.

"I didn't see you standing there." Noah swiped at his face with the sleeve of his T-shirt.

"I don't think you saw anything here. Are you all right?" Her nursing instincts kicked in, and she had to fight the urge to soothe him with a touch.

He nodded. "I have…flashbacks. From the military."

How stable was he? She'd heard of vets with PTSD becoming violent during flashbacks, and she had a daughter to protect. She sat down in the lawn chair next to his, determined to find out more about him. "Are you all settled in?"

"Yes, thanks."

"I went over your application and the lease. I've been watching you for a few days now, and—"

"You've been watching me?"

His lopsided grin and hopeful expression did funny things to her insides, and heat flooded her cheeks. "Let's just say every time I pass a window I have a tendency to look outside, and there *you* are sitting in *that* chair. Your application didn't list any employment. I'd be happy to introduce you to some of our local businesses, and if you want I could—"

"I'm paid up."

"My aunt handled your application and the lease. I didn't have a chance to talk to you first, or to ask questions. I know you're paid up for the month, but I'm a little concerned that without a job—"

"I have money."

"I'm sure you do. It's hard to miss that shiny new truck and camper parked out front, but don't you want to work?" She couldn't imagine sitting around every day with nothing to do. It would drive her crazy. He opened his mouth to reply, and she held up a hand to stop him. "I'm sorry. It's small-town nosiness on my part." She shrugged. "I just want to make sure you're going to be a steady tenant."

He raised an eyebrow. "Do you have a better prospect waiting to move in?"

She narrowed her eyes at him. "Maybe I do."

"You don't."

"You don't know that."

"Yes, I do." He smirked. "Your aunt told me no one's lived here for eighteen months."

Dang. Even his smirk was sexy. "Only because I haven't advertised. I've been too busy finishing school and starting my career to bother. This is a very desirable location. The carriage house is a registered historical landmark, not to mention charming. There are plenty of folks who'd love to live here by the river." She lifted her chin, smug in the soundness of her argument. A breeze kicked up out of the northwest, nullifying her position on a single inhalation.

"What is that *stench*?" Noah glared at Sweet Pea.

"It's not the dog." Ceejay sank back into the chair. "Occasionally the wind shifts in the wrong direction. What you smell is hog farm."

"Ah, the wind shifted." Noah laughed. "I get it."

"Get what?"

"Never mind. What do people around here do for fun?"

Ceejay's brow rose. Their conversation had taken an unexpected turn, and she wasn't in any hurry to turn it back. Hmm.

Something to think about. "There's a movie theater and a mall halfway between Perfect and Evansville, a racetrack outside of Boonville, and a few bars with dance floors and live music nearby."

She didn't mention the monthly Polka Fests or the pancake breakfasts and spaghetti dinners held in the local churches. And a man from Philadelphia probably would *not* be interested in joining the local farm families when they gathered to help one another butcher a few hogs for personal use. How many fall days had she spent making pork sausage and pickling pigs' feet with the women while the men took care of curing the hams? Nope. She shuddered with embarrassment. That she did not want to share.

"I'm not interested in racing"—Noah turned his face away— "or dancing. What about places to eat? Are there any restaurants nearby?"

"My aunt owns a diner in town. It's open for breakfast and lunch six days a week."

"When's your next night off? Maybe we could head into Evansville, go see a movie and get a bite somewhere."

Her heart started to riot in her chest. He wanted to spend time with *her*. Was it possible she'd been on his mind the way he'd been on hers? "You're asking your landlady out on a date?"

"You don't have to think of it as a date if you don't want to. Pick out a children's movie. We can bring Lucinda." Noah's face turned red. "I don't know anybody else here. It would be great to have some company while I familiarize myself with the area."

"So now you're saying you wouldn't want to date me?" Was she flirting with him? Huh. If so, her flirting skills certainly were rusty. No, make that nonexistent. They'd gone extinct sometime during the years she'd struggled to get through school while taking care of her daughter and working at the diner.

His face turned a deeper shade of crimson. "I'm not saying that either."

"My shift doesn't start until four p.m. tomorrow. Why don't I show you around Perfect? I'm sure you'll want to know where to buy groceries and do your laundry."

"Is there a furniture store?"

"You don't like shabby chic?"

Noah shook his head. "If you'd like, we could stop by your aunt's diner for lunch after the tour."

"Mommy?" Lucinda called out the back door.

"I'm here." Ceejay turned to watch Lucinda cross the yard, clutching her favorite stuffed animal. Lifting her daughter onto her lap, she snuggled her close and kissed the top of her warm head. Lucinda yawned and stuck two fingers into her mouth. "Fingers, Luce."

Lucinda took the fingers out of her mouth and smiled at Noah.

"Hey, there, princess." Noah touched the end of her nose, and pointed to the stuffed bear clutched in her arms. "Who's your friend?"

"Boo-Bear." Lucinda handed the bear over for Noah's inspection.

Ceejay smiled at the exchange. Most of the guys she'd tried to date in college had ignored Lucinda or bolted when they'd found out she had a daughter. Not Noah. He'd protected her from a dog he didn't know, and for some reason, Lucinda trusted him. She didn't ordinarily warm to strangers so quickly.

Birds with broken wings needed a safe place to mend. Maybe Jenny was right, and Noah came here to heal. Still, there was the PTSD to consider. "Do you mind if I ask you a personal question?"

Noah handed the bear back to her daughter. "Not if you don't mind my asking questions back."

"Fair enough." She hesitated, unsure how to begin such a touchy subject. Maybe directness was best, like ripping off a Band-Aid in one swipe. "What happened to your leg?"

"I lost it in a suicide bombing near Mosul, Iraq, along with five of my men."

"*Your* men. You were an officer?"

"First lieutenant." Noah leaned his head back and studied the sky. "I commanded a platoon. I had planned to have a career in the military."

"I know what it's like to have the rug yanked out from under you." Ceejay ran her fingers through her daughter's sleep-tangled curls. "When you have flashbacks, is that the day you relive?"

Noah turned to face her. His brow creased, and a haunted look filled his eyes. "It is."

"That was way too personal." She averted her gaze. "I'm sorry."

"It's all right." One corner of his mouth turned up. "Now it's my turn. You wore scrubs the other day. Do you work in a hospital?"

She nodded. It still filled her with pride to say the words. "I'm a pediatric nurse at Deaconess Hospital."

"You like what you do?"

"Very much. I plan to go back to school in a few years. Maybe I'll become a nurse-midwife, or a nurse-practitioner."

"Your aunt mentioned she raised you. What happened to your parents?"

Ceejay shifted Lucinda's weight in her lap. "Did I mention Jenny's invitation to dinner? She always brings home some of the daily special leftovers from her diner. Today it's ham and mashed potatoes. Come to think of it, it's always something and mashed potatoes. Her meat loaf is amazing, and her peach cobbler is to die for. The recipe's a secret handed down from generation to generation stretching all the way back to the Civil War."

He stared at her and didn't say anything.

"I can't see how my sad little history could possibly interest you."

"It does."

"Here's the thing." He'd been so open with her, answering the personal questions she'd asked without hesitation. She'd agreed to answer his questions in return, and she meant to keep her word. Still, it wasn't easy. She stared at the sandstone bricks of the carriage house, one, two, three…"My mother had chemical dependency issues." Four, five, six…"She dropped me off here one day, and that's the last we saw of her." Seven, eight, nine…

"What's kemcal deep ends issues?" Lucinda asked.

"Nothing you need to worry about, Luce."

"What happened to her?" Noah persisted.

"Mommy, you're squeezing me too tight."

"Sorry, baby. Why don't you go on in and help Aunt Jenny with supper? Take Sweet Pea with you."

"OK." Lucinda slid off her lap and headed for the back door. Sweet Pea trotted beside her, his tail a whirligig in the air.

"I was only three at the time. I don't know what happened to her." Noah had thrown a stone into the hornet's nest, stirring up the sting.

"Sure, but you're an adult now. Doesn't your aunt know?"

"I don't think so. I asked a lot when I was younger, and Jenny always told me 'she's gone.' That's all. Just, 'she's gone.'" Memories of her aunt cuddling her on her lap, reassuring her that she'd always be there for her filled her with warmth, followed by the anxiety that always chased through her at the mention of her mother.

"Doesn't not knowing bother you? It would bother me."

"I never think about it." *Liar.* "Jenny has been a mother to me for as long as I can remember."

"You've *never* looked for her?"

She launched herself from the lawn chair. "We always eat at six. I'd better go see what kind of trouble Lucinda's getting into." She counted her footsteps all the way to the back door, and just for spite, she pushed Sweet Pea back outside as she went in.

Ceejay finished rubbing her daughter dry and wrapped her up in the towel. Taking a seat on the edge of the claw-foot tub, she reached for the wide-toothed comb to work through Lucinda's curls.

"Do we get to ride in Noah's truck, Mommy?"

"I don't know. Your car seat is in our car."

"I wanna wear a dress."

"Of course you do." She sighed. "If you wear a dress, though, you won't be able to use the slide if we stop at the park." Such a familiar battle, and one she knew she wouldn't win. At least Lucinda had finally given up wearing her plastic rain boots every day. They stank so bad by the time she lost interest, Ceejay had been forced to throw them out.

Lucinda was quiet while she mulled things over. "I can still play on the swings and the go-round."

Ceejay glanced at her watch. They were already running late. "A dress it is, then. Hop up on that stool, and brush your teeth."

Three wardrobe changes later, and they were on their way out the back door to the carriage house. The windows were open, and she could hear Noah talking to someone. She couldn't help but listen.

"No, Dad, don't tell Allison yet...I *do* understand. I just...No. Give me a little more time...Yes...Of course I will." Noah walked out of the carriage house with his cell phone pressed to his ear. "Have it sent here. I'm sure there's a VA hospital in Evansville. I can arrange for PT."

Their eyes met and held. She turned away and fussed with the collar on her daughter's dress.

"I've got to go. I'll call you later." Noah snapped the phone shut and slid it into his back pocket. He raised his eyebrows at her. "Eavesdropping?"

"Of course not. We came to pick you up for our trip into town." She shrugged. "So, who's Allison?" And what secret did he want to keep from her?

"Jealous?" His tone was teasing.

"Don't be ridiculous." Her face grew hot. She had been a tiny bit jealous, but mostly nosy, and that was just as bad. "We don't even know each other."

"Can we ride in your truck, Noah?" Lucinda tugged at his jeans.

"If it's OK with your mother." Noah smiled at her. "You look very pretty in that dress, Lucinda. Where's Boo-Bear?"

"He can't come with." Lucinda's fingers edged up toward her mouth.

Ceejay reached for her daughter's hand before the fingers found their target. "We can go in your truck if you don't mind transferring Lucinda's car seat."

"I don't mind at all." He held his hand out to Lucinda, and she put her free hand in his.

They walked with Lucinda between them to the back gate, and a pang of longing shot through Ceejay. What would it feel like to be part of a nuclear family, with a husband and maybe a few siblings for Lucinda? For a full year after Matt left, she'd been swamped with self-pity for the things she'd never had, and for the things her daughter would lack.

"Can Sweet Pea come too?" Lucinda asked as the big dog trotted up to the gate, eager for a walk.

"That'll be the day," Ceejay muttered.

Lucinda nodded. "Yeah, that'll be the day."

"I don't mind if he rides in the flatbed."

"Sweet Pea won't get anywhere near your truck, my car, or anything else on wheels."

Noah shut the gate behind them with Sweet Pea looking like his hopes had just come to a tragic end. "What did you see in that monster? Why on earth choose a dog like that?"

"We didn't choose Sweet Pea. He chose us. Folks like to take their unwanted pets for rides in the country. They drop them off by the side of the road and drive off. Generations of Lovejoys have had dogs, and none of them came from pet stores or breeders."

Noah stopped and turned back to look at Sweet Pea. The dog's tail beat out an optimistic rhythm. "That's a dirty trick to play on a dog."

"I agree. Sweet Pea sat by the side of the road for two days waiting for his people to come back for him. We brought him food and water and tried to coax him home with us." She placed a hand on her daughter's shoulder. "It was Lucinda who finally convinced him he had a new home. Sweet Pea loves kids."

"He's my dog." Lucinda nodded.

"How long ago was this?"

"Two years. He was already as big as a pony, but the vet figured he was only about six months old."

"Can I have a pony, Mommy?"

Another familiar battle. "Not today, Luce."

Noah handed Ceejay his cane. "How do you get him to the vet's?"

"We don't." She watched him wrestle the car seat out of her Honda. He had a great butt, and as he worked, his jeans tightened over his thighs in a very nice way. He backed out of the car and straightened, his brow rising slightly as she brought her gaze back up to his face.

Crap. He'd caught her checking him out. Flustered, she rushed on, "Our veterinarian makes house calls. He's also a large-animal vet for the surrounding farms, so he's on the road anyway."

As they drove toward the highway, Ceejay pointed to the orchard. "See those fruit trees? My great-grandfather planted a new tree for each of his children when they were born. My grandfather continued the tradition, and now we supply the diner with seasonal fruit ourselves. We have peaches, pears, and apples."

"I have a tree," Lucinda piped up from the backseat. "Mine's peach. Can we plant a tree for Noah?"

Noah glanced in the rearview mirror at her daughter, and a smile softened his features. Every change in his expression kicked up a butterfly stampede in her chest. She swallowed hard and forced herself back under control. She shouldn't be this affected by a man she hardly knew, especially given her track record. "Maybe we can give him one of the walnut trees along the drive. They were planted by Lovejoys too." They turned onto the highway. "When you get to the edge of town, take a left on

First Street. There's an IGA grocery store two blocks down, but don't buy your meat there."

"Is there something wrong with it?"

"Not that I know of. It's just that we have Offermeyer's butcher shop too. All the meat is locally produced. Offermeyer's makes great sausage and smoked hams." She shrugged a shoulder. "We like to support the local economy."

Noah pulled into a parking spot near the butcher shop. Ceejay hopped out and freed Lucinda from her car seat. "On the next street over at the far corner is where you'll find the Laundromat and dry cleaner's. Let's start with Offermeyer's." She led the way through the butcher shop door, accompanied by the chime of an old-fashioned bell hanging from the top of the frame. The delicious aromas of smoked meats and spices permeated the shop. Noah inhaled audibly beside her. "Smells good in here, huh?"

Noah sniffed again and nodded.

"Hey, Ceejay." Dennis Offermeyer came out of the back to stand behind the refrigerated display case. "How're all the Lovejoys?"

"We're all fine, Denny. How are Gail and the kids?"

"Great. Thanks for the teething tip you gave my wife. We're all sleeping better now. Hey, Lucinda Mae, when are you coming over for another playdate?"

"I don't know." Lucinda looked up at Ceejay in question.

"Soon." She glanced down at her daughter. "I'll give Gail a call."

"You do that. What can I get for you today?"

"Nothing right now. I'm giving Perfect's newest resident a guided tour." She turned to Noah, who stood behind her. "This is Noah Langford."

"Welcome, Noah. What brings you to Perfect?" Dennis stared openly with small-town curiosity.

Ceejay noticed the color creeping up Noah's neck. "He's recently out of the military," she blurted.

"Wow. Welcome home. My youngest brother's unit is about to be deployed." Dennis reached over the case to shake Noah's hand. "Where are you staying?"

Noah shook his hand briefly. "I'm renting the Lovejoys' carriage house."

"You don't say." Dennis's brow rose slightly, and his glance went from Noah to her and back again. "Did Ceejay tell you how far back our families go? All the way—"

"Back to the Civil War?" Noah shifted restlessly.

"That's right." Denny's appraising stare remained fixed on him, and Noah's anxiety was palpable.

"Time to go." She ushered Noah toward the door. "I'll arrange that playdate with Gail."

"Do that," Dennis called as they left.

Out on the sidewalk, Noah stopped and ran his hand over the back of his head a few times. "Maybe we could just look around and skip the introductions for today."

"Sure. We'll give that a try." Ceejay lifted an eyebrow. "Welcome to small-town America. Most of the families here have roots stretching way back. Try keeping a secret in a place like this." She shook her head. "There's no such thing as privacy here. Denny will be talking about you for the rest of the week. I'll bet he's on the phone to Gail right now."

"I can't see why. There's nothing special about me."

"Other than you're new to town and fodder for speculation, do you mean?" She laughed.

After the rest of the tour, several unavoidable introductions, and a stop at the park, she directed him to her aunt's diner. "This diner originally belonged to my aunt's in-laws. Jenny started working here as a teenager. That's how she met her husband. When her in-laws passed, they left it to her."

Lucinda reached for Noah's hand again, and another annoying twinge of longing tugged at Ceejay's heart. *Stop it!* She had a daughter to think about. Maybe Lucinda's growing attachment to him wasn't such a good thing. Her own attraction to him was disturbing enough. Who knew how long he'd stick around, and she didn't plan to stay either. Once her debt was paid off and she had some savings, her new life would begin. Ceejay opened the door to the smells of good country cooking and strong coffee.

"Hey, Little Bit, been a while since we've seen you around here," Bill called from behind the window to the kitchen. This set off a chorus of heys and hellos from the staff and locals, making her cringe. How she longed to enter places where everyone *didn't* know her name—or her entire life history.

"Little Bit?" Noah nudged her.

"It's what people *used* to call me when I was little." She glared at him.

"I've got news for you." He leaned down to whisper. "You're still little."

She huffed and turned away from him to return the greetings. Sheriff Maurer stood up beside his table in the corner and waved them over. Ceejay wove her way around the Formica tables with Noah and Lucinda trailing behind her.

Sheriff Maurer hitched his pants up by the belt and eyed Noah with professional intensity. "Is this the new tenant your aunt told me about?"

She nodded. "Sheriff, this is Noah Langford. Noah, this is the Warrick County sheriff, Harlen Maurer."

"Jenny tells me you're recently out of the military." The sheriff held his hand out while sizing Noah up. He wore his cop-on-duty look, as if Noah might be potential trouble.

Noah shook his hand. "Yes, sir. First Lieutenant Noah James Langford, First Armored Division, Fourth Brigade, Task Force Iron."

"You don't say." Harlen nodded. "Why don't you join me? There aren't any other empty tables right now."

"I got to ride in Noah's truck," Lucinda told the sheriff.

"Did you now? Was it as good as my patrol car? Does his truck have a siren?" Sheriff Maurer took his seat and lifted Lucinda onto his lap.

"Nope, but it gots really big tires and a flatbed." She shook her curls. "But I didn't see a bed."

"Well, now, that's something." Sheriff Maurer patted her head.

Jenny bustled over with a plastic booster chair. "I was hoping you'd find your way to the diner, Noah." She placed the booster on an empty chair. "Come on now, Luce. Let's get you settled." The sheriff gave her up to Jenny, who put her into the booster and pushed the chair close to the table. "Do you want coffee? We also have sweet tea, lemonade, and soft drinks."

"Can I have a soft drink, Mommy?"

"Sure, a 7UP." Ceejay watched Noah take the seat with his back against the wall. A fine sheen of sweat had broken out across his forehead, and he'd gone pale. He glanced at her, and she caught the panic in his eyes before he turned away.

Here she was a health professional, and she hadn't even considered his PTSD. Strangers introducing themselves all morning and asking personal questions must've been hard to handle. Being enclosed in a room full of people he didn't know would be even worse. Sheriff Maurer's scrutiny had probably pushed him over the edge. Ceejay wanted to throw her arms around Noah. She wanted to shield him from the speculation running rampant through the diner—through Perfect. She had firsthand experience with that kind of scrutiny, and even without PTSD it wasn't pleasant.

With her back to the rest of the diners, Ceejay gave her aunt an imploring look with a slight nod in Noah's direction. As usual, Jenny sized up the situation in a heartbeat.

"Mostly we get our lunch customers from the local businesses and surrounding farms." Jenny inserted herself between their table and the curious stares aimed their way. "The rush will be over soon. We know everyone here."

Noah nodded.

"Can I sit with you, Noah?" Lucinda squirmed in her booster.

"Sure." His tightness eased. "If your mother doesn't mind."

"I don't mind." Bless her daughter's little Lovejoy heart. Lucinda was passed to Noah. He held her on his lap as if she were some kind of precious hothouse orchid. A pleased smile erased the panic she'd glimpsed a few seconds ago.

"Today's meat loaf day. You don't want to miss Jen's meat loaf." Sheriff Maurer beamed at her aunt. "She's the finest cook in the county."

"Sounds great," Noah said. "I'll have coffee, too."

"Can I have ice cream?" Lucinda asked.

"Maybe later." Ceejay relaxed. The diner gradually emptied, and Noah seemed more at ease for the rest of their meal.

After lunch, she strapped Lucinda into her car seat for the ride home. Her daughter yawned and fell asleep almost at the same moment Noah started the engine. He pulled out of the parking spot and headed the wrong direction out of town. "Home is that way." She pointed with her thumb.

"I know. I thought we'd take a drive through the country before heading back." He tapped the clock on his dashboard. "It's only one thirty. We have plenty of time." He shifted in his seat and glanced at her.

"Don't even think about it," she muttered.

His eyebrows shot up. "Think about what?"

"I'm not going to have another discussion with you about my mother."

"I wouldn't dream of bringing her up again."

"Good."

"Today I thought we'd talk about your father. Where is he?"

She rolled her eyes. "I don't know who my father is, and neither does Jenny. No one knows." She crossed her arms in front of her. "Why are you doing this anyway? Does it make you feel better about your own life to pry into mine?"

"Maybe. I don't know." He shook his head. "I've been in the army for seven and a half years. When you live in a militarized zone, you get to know people really fast or not at all, because there might not be a tomorrow. I haven't had a normal conversation with anyone outside of family in a long time. My social skills are rusty." His eyes met hers for an instant. "I'm just trying to get to know you."

"All right. I can understand that." She stared out the windshield.

"I said I wouldn't bring your mother up, but I wanted to tell you that my mother abandoned me, too."

"Huh?"

"She died a few days after I was born of a rare condition, an intrauterine embolism."

"Oh, Noah, she didn't abandon you. Your mother didn't have any choice in the matter."

"Maybe yours didn't either."

She watched the passing farm fields and started counting corn rows.

He glanced at her. "My father's a tyrant and a tough son of a bitch."

"At least you know who he is."

"You could find yours."

"You never did say who Allison is." She glanced at him. "It sounded like you don't want her to know you're here. I'm sure reentering civilian life takes its toll after what you've been through. Is she someone you left behind, because things got too tough to handle after you returned from Iraq?"

Noah pulled the truck over to the shoulder of the road and shoved the gearshift into park. He twisted around to face her, his eyes boring into hers. "That's not who I am, Ceejay. I don't leave people behind."

CHAPTER FOUR

CEEJAY SCOWLED AT HIM ACROSS the cab of his truck. "I don't know you well enough to judge what kind of man you are, and it makes no difference to me whether you stay or go, if that's what you're thinking."

Her words hung in the air between them like a neon lie. Oh, she cared all right, in much the same way she cared about Sweet Pea and all the other strays the Lovejoys had taken in over the years. Come to think of it, Matt had been a stray himself when he'd rolled into their town.

Noah's grip on the steering wheel tightened. "I might've lost my direction, but I'm no stray."

She blinked at him with a confused expression. "I never called you a stray."

"You didn't have to." Red flashing lights behind the truck drew his attention, and Noah looked into the outside mirror to see Sheriff Maurer getting out of his patrol car. *Great.* He lowered his window.

The sheriff peered past him into the truck. "Everything all right, Ceejay?"

"Everything is fine, Sheriff." She leaned forward in her seat and pointed with her thumb. "Noah here just had a point to make, and he can't seem to manage talking and driving at the same time."

Noah let his breath out in an exasperated sigh.

"I might as well make it clear, son." Sheriff Maurer turned to face him. "I'm mighty protective when it comes to the Lovejoys, especially Ceejay and Lucinda."

"Yes, sir. I got that." *You and everyone else in Perfect.* He'd endured all the once-overs and *you'd better not hurt our girl* looks he could stomach for one day. "If you don't mind, I'll make a U-turn here and take them home."

"U-turns are illegal. I'd be forced to issue a citation." He jutted his chin toward the highway. "There's a dirt road up ahead. I suggest you turn around there." The sheriff touched the brim of his hat and nodded to Ceejay before walking back to his car. He drove off in a burst of acceleration and a cloud of dust meant to remind Noah who wore the badge in Warrick County.

Noah pulled his truck back onto the two-lane highway and tried to get a handle on the woman sitting tight-lipped beside him. She hadn't made any effort to track her parents down and probably never tried to find Matt. Did she fear what she might find, or she was happier not knowing? Either way, it made no sense to him. Ceejay was a complex puzzle he couldn't resist trying to solve. Complex and adorable. Glancing at her out of the corner of his eye, he noticed her lips moving while she stared at the farm fields. "What are you doing?"

"Counting corn rows."

"Why?"

Ceejay lifted a shoulder and let it drop. "Habit."

No use commenting further. He'd already upset her enough for one day, and this probably wasn't the best time to open the can of worms labeled *Lucinda's daddy.*

Medevac helicopters hovered in the air above him, the sound of their engines bringing him back to pain-filled consciousness. Noah tried to will himself back into oblivion, but the desert grit blasting into his open wounds like tiny shards of glass kept him front and center. Medics worked over him. One of them pushed a needle into his right arm and held a bag of clear liquid above his head.

His entire left side burned, and excruciating pain throbbed through his left leg like he was still trapped under his Humvee. Glancing around at the chaos, he watched body bags being zipped closed over soldiers he'd known—soldiers he'd lived and served with for the past thirteen months.

How had the medics managed to match body parts to soldier? Maybe they hadn't. Maybe it didn't matter to them. His men deserved to have their own arms and legs. It was up to him to see that they got them. Noah struggled to rise.

"Easy, Lieutenant." The medic at his head pushed him back down by the shoulders. "We're going to get you out of here."

Noah fought to throw him off. "My men. I need to get to my men."

"We're taking care of them. Easy now. You're going home."

Noah thrashed and twisted, tangling in something that wouldn't let him go. He shouted and woke covered in a cold sweat. It took a few seconds for him to register where he was, and what was making the noise outside his apartment. *A damned lawn mower?* He reached for his watch on the nightstand and squinted at the dial. "Who the hell mows their lawn at 0600 hours on a Sunday morning?"

Disentangling himself from the sheets, he swung his good leg over the edge of the bed and sat up to rub his face. His mind still reverberated with the images of his nightmare, a terror triggered by the sound of the lawn mower. His landlady was about to get a piece of his mind. Noah scanned the tiny bedroom for clothes. He fastened the prosthesis to his stump, pulled on yesterday's jeans and T-shirt, and headed for the door, grabbing his cane on the way out.

Early morning dew covered the lawn where the sun hadn't yet hit the grass, dampening the bottoms of his jeans and chilling his bare foot. Noah followed the sound of the lawn mower to the front of the house and nearly got mowed over.

"Watch it!" Noah glared as the stranger sitting on the riding mower came to a stop millimeters from his prosthesis.

The kid cut the engine and stared back, his surprised expression shifting to suspicion. "Who are you?"

"I'm the angry tenant you woke up, that's who. It's a little early to be cutting the grass, don't you think?" His hands balled into fists. "Who are you?"

"Noah." Jenny leaned over the porch railing. "I'm sorry Teddy woke you. We should have warned you he might show up at any time. Come on up to the veranda for coffee. Go on now, Ted. Finish up, and then come join us."

The fight-or-flight adrenaline rush still pumped through Noah's veins. He needed to take a few breaths before he'd be ready to join anyone for anything. Why hadn't Jenny and Ceejay asked him to cut the grass? He would've been glad to help out. Shifting his balance, he glanced up at Jenny. "I can mow the lawn for you."

"I'm sure you can." The lines around Jenny's eyes creased with warmth and humor. "Come on up. Coffee's waiting."

She disappeared from the railing, and Noah was left feeling ridiculous. Why had he said that? It wasn't his grass to cut, and this wasn't his territory to protect. Teddy might be a stranger to him, but he certainly wasn't to the Lovejoys. He shook his head. Out of habit, he kept the young man in his field of vision as he made his way up the veranda stairs.

Jenny sat at a wrought-iron patio table painted white and surrounded by wicker chairs with flowery cushions. "It's fresh." She gestured toward some kind of thermal container placed among a few mismatched mugs, a container of cream, and another of sugar.

Noah pulled one of the frilly chairs out and sank down. He reached for a mug and filled it with steaming coffee. "Thanks." Noah inhaled the rich aroma, relaxing in increments as he leaned back and sipped the strong brew.

"I'm sorry my nephew woke you so early. He comes by when he can, and we never know when to expect him. He farms with his father, so it all depends on his priorities for the day."

"I can do the mowing if you'd like," he repeated his offer. "I don't handle surprises well."

"We don't expect our tenants to do chores for us."

"I know you don't, but you've been feeding me, and you've made me feel welcome. I'd like to return the favor."

"I appreciate the offer, but Ted is working off a debt. I'm sure we can find another way you can help out if you want." She smiled. "I've been meaning to tell you, if you want to store your camper in the bay area of the carriage house, feel free. Maybe while Ted is here he can help you move it."

"Thanks, I'll do that." Noah leaned back in the chair and drank his coffee. Birdsong filled the early morning air, and the sound of the lawn mower had an altogether different ring to it now. It had transformed into the nonthreatening, ordinary sound of everyday life. He breathed in the scent of freshly mowed grass, and the last of his tension slipped away.

Watching Ted mow the lawn while he sat on his ass drinking coffee made him aware of how soft he'd grown. Idleness had never been easy for him. Now it worked on his nerves. Doing chores around the place would help, and the Lovejoy women could certainly use a hand. Maybe if he started taking care of things around here, Ceejay's drive to see him employed would be satisfied. "Ceejay's been pushing me to get a job."

"Has she?"

Noah nodded, remembering how she'd brought it up again on their way back from his tour of Perfect.

"How do you feel about that?"

"You saw how it was at the diner. Put me in an enclosed space with strangers, and I start to sweat and get the shakes."

"Give it time. You won't always feel that way." Jenny twisted in her seat to face him. "If you want, why don't you make a habit of stopping by the diner? Get used to people where you know you're safe. I'm always there, and I'll introduce you to everyone. Before you know it, they won't be strangers anymore."

"Is Sheriff Maurer there often?"

"Almost every day."

Noah shook his head. "He's going to run a background check on me." Jenny's laughter brought a smile to his face.

"I suspect he already has. Harlen and I grew up together. Both of us were born and raised here." She straightened the cream and sugar containers in the middle of the table. "We even dated some in high school."

"Is he married?"

"No, he never did marry."

"You probably broke his heart in high school and ruined him for any other woman," he teased. "You remind me of my stepmother."

"Do I?" Jenny peered at him over the rim of her coffee mug. "Are the two of you close?"

He nodded. "My mother died a few days after I was born, and my stepmother raised me."

"Growing up without your mother is something you have in common with my niece."

"I guess." Noah reached over to refill his mug. "Ceejay mentioned she doesn't know what happened to her mom, only that she dropped her off here when she was three, and that's the last either of you saw of her."

"How long have you been here now, three weeks?" Jenny's eyes widened. "She told you all that?"

"It'll be a month on Tuesday." Noah nodded.

"Well, well." Jenny expression grew pensive, and she gazed out toward the orchard.

"Do you know what became of her?"

"Of course I do, but I won't bore you with that old tale." Jenny swatted at a fly that had settled on the table. "Whenever any of us brought her mother up, Ceejay would get so upset it broke our hearts. So we stopped bringing her up. I guess it never occurred to me that she didn't know."

Know what? Maybe if he pushed a little, Jenny would tell him. Noah leaned forward in his chair. Or maybe she could shed some light on why Ceejay never looked for Matt. "What about…"

The front door opened and Ceejay came out looking like a disgruntled angel wrapped in a blue cotton bathrobe. Even though the robe had seen better days, she still looked sexy as hell. Morning sun caught in her tangled curls, turning them into a halo of spun copper and gold. Noah's breath caught in his throat. Embarrassed by the way his body was reacting to her, he forced himself to focus on Ted mowing the lawn, on the coffee in his mug now strategically held in his lap, on anything that would help him get a grip.

"I'm gonna kill Teddy." She plopped down in a chair, grabbed one of the mugs, and filled it with coffee and cream.

"Good morning to you too." Jenny patted her arm. "Is Lucinda still sleeping?"

"You know Luce." She stirred sugar into the mix in her mug. "She could sleep through Armageddon."

Just like Matt. Noah smiled as he remembered some of the things Matt had slept through. Once he'd found him standing next to a dresser with his elbow propped on the top, sound asleep.

"You find being rudely awakened this early in the morning amusing, Noah?" Ceejay asked.

"Uh...no." How was it Ceejay could look so fresh and lovely first thing in the morning, while he always woke up a sweaty mess? Lord, he hoped he didn't reek. What about morning breath? "Thanks for the coffee, Jenny." He rose to leave.

"Aren't you going to stick around and talk to my nephew about moving your camper?"

"Another time." Heat crept up his neck, and he beat a hasty retreat to the privacy of the carriage house. *Damn.* Being around Ceejay tied him into knots and brought home with excruciating clarity all the ways he didn't measure up.

❧ ❧ ❧

Three days later Noah still couldn't get the sleep-rumpled image of Ceejay in her bathrobe out of his thoughts. When he spoke to her at dinner, or as their paths crossed coming or going, he couldn't help picturing her as she'd been that morning. Adorable. He rose from the dinette table, stretched, and checked his watch. It was almost 1000 hours. She was probably awake by now. Moving into the living room, he looked out the window toward the big house just as the back door opened.

Sweet Pea lumbered down the steps, followed by Lucinda. Noah watched his little niece make her way toward the sandbox. He couldn't fathom trading in a daughter for an asphalt race-track. Matt had been a fool. Noah grabbed his cane and headed for the door.

Lucinda had settled herself next to the sandbox with a shovel and a variety of plastic cups and pails. She smiled up at him.

"Hey, what are you doing there, Luce?"

"Making stuff, see?" She pointed to several little hills.

"Can I help?"

Her eyes lit up. He looked around for something to sit on and dragged one of the lawn chairs over. "How about we make a castle?"

"I don't want a castle. I want a pony."

He lowered himself into the chair. Lucinda needed a swing set and a playhouse back here. Maybe he'd look into one of those put-together kits for her. Sweet Pea ambled over to investigate and nudged Noah's hand with his wet nose. He scratched the big mutt behind the ears and studied the sandbox. His last experience with sand had been the day he'd lost his leg—one of the worst days of his life, trumped only by his stepbrother's death. "A pony, huh?"

Lucinda nodded and looked up at him with wide-eyed trust in his ability to produce a pony out of dry sand. Noah searched for a spigot at the back of the house. "Do you know where your mommy hooks up the hose to water the garden?"

"There." Lucinda pointed to the side of the house where a vegetable garden flourished in tidy rows.

"Great. Let's see if there's a hose or a bucket nearby." Leaving his cane on the ground, Noah hoisted himself from the chair and limped awkwardly toward the gate. He hated the unyielding stiffness of his prosthetic and hoped his dad had shipped the new one he'd custom-ordered before leaving Pennsylvania. The flexible carbon-fiber blade type was used by athletes, and he looked forward to getting around without the damned old-man cane.

Noah found an aluminum bucket next to the spigot, filled it, and limped back. "I'm going to pour, and I want you to use your shovel to stir. Can you do that?"

Lucinda nodded and picked up her plastic shovel.

He let the water trickle out of the bucket while she stirred. He saved some for the finishing touches and settled himself back into the chair. The two of them bent over the project and began to work. He concentrated on forming a pony's long head using one of the smaller buckets, while Lucinda made a pile that would become the body.

"It gots to be a mommy pony," Lucinda informed him.

"All right." He molded the wet sand for the head.

"No, Noah. Use *this* one." Lucinda handed him a disposable cup like the ones used at keggers.

"You're a bossy little thing, aren't you?"

"That's what Mommy says." Her face puckered. "What's *bossy* mean?"

"It means you know what you want, and you know how to get it." He touched the end of her nose, leaving a few particles of wet sand clinging to her skin. "It's a good thing, sweetheart, and you do it well."

"Oh." She accepted her due and went back to work.

Noah lost all track of time and found himself smiling as the image of a pony lying on its side emerged. He shoved his chair out of the way and sat on the damp lawn with his prosthetic stretched out straight to the side. "Take your shovel and start smoothing out the sides there, Luce, and I'll work on the tail."

"Are you gonna stay wif us for a long time?"

"Maybe. I don't know yet. Would you mind if I stayed?"

"No." Lucinda stopped working to gaze earnestly at him. "I like playing wif you."

Noah had to swallow a few times before he could trust his voice. "I like playing with you too, kiddo."

"Hey, what're you two up to out here?"

Noah startled, and a surge of adrenaline hit his bloodstream. He struggled to stand. What would Ceejay think of a grown man playing in a sandbox?

"We made a pony, see?" Lucinda pointed to their sculpture, and Ceejay stepped closer to look.

"Wow, you did make a pony." She smiled at Noah. "That's really something. I've been watching you two work out here for a while. Now I see what kept you both so occupied."

Her smile held only warm appreciation, and he relaxed. It was natural for Ceejay to keep an eye on her daughter, but he couldn't help wondering whether she still occasionally peeked out her windows to look at him. God, he hoped so. "It's been a long time since I've played like this. Lucinda is a great little teacher." He winked at his niece. She beamed back.

"Lucinda and I are heading into town. Do you need anything?"

"Groceries." Noah wiped his hands on his pants. "Why don't we make a day of it and do something fun?"

"Like what?"

"Is there a zoo or an amusement park somewhere near?"

Lucinda jumped up and down. "The zoo! I want to go to the zoo."

"There's Mesker's Park Zoo in Evansville," Ceejay said, her expression open and friendly. "It's about an hour's drive from here."

"What time does your shift start today?"

"This is my day off, and I'd love to go to the zoo."

"Great. We can stop at IGA and run errands on the way home."

"All right." She smirked. "But you might want to change your pants first."

Noah looked down at himself. His khakis were grass stained and covered with wet sand and dirt. "Right. Give me a few minutes. We'll take my truck." He had to force himself not to rush back to his apartment, and hoped she hadn't noticed the stupid grin he couldn't seem to keep off his face.

❧ ❧ ❧

"Can we go in there, Mommy?" Lucinda pointed to the zoo's gift shop set conveniently close to the exit doors.

"I don't think so, Luce."

Noah held his niece's hand, and had for most of the day. He'd savored every moment her tiny hand held his with so much trust. That Ceejay had allowed it and had been so relaxed and open all day hadn't escaped his notice either. "Come on, Ceejay. I'd like to buy her a souvenir."

"You don't have to do that." Her brow creased. "You've already done so much. You drove, paid our admission, bought us lunch, and you don't even have a—"

"I told you. I have money."

Concern filled her eyes. "Yeah, I know, but—"

"I want to get her a gift." Lucinda had already tugged him through the entrance. "How about something small, like a plastic animal."

"Oh, all right. As long as it's something small," she capitulated. "A plastic animal, Lucinda Mae. That's it."

"OK, Mommy."

Noah let his niece pull him through the aisles. He'd been aware of Ceejay's eyes on him the entire day, and it was no different now. She stood back and watched as he and Lucinda located the wire bins filled with the toy models of the animals they'd seen together.

"What should I get?" Lucinda asked him.

He pulled a black jaguar from the pile and turned it over in his hands. "It's up to you, sweetheart."

"I liked the giraffes and the camels we saw." Lucinda dropped his hand and knelt on the floor to sort out her favorites from the heap. "Can I have more than one?" She turned a hopeful expression toward her mother.

"Nope. Just one." Ceejay shook her head.

Lucinda's face puckered with disappointment, but it looked so practiced that Noah had to bite his tongue to keep from laughing. If Ceejay hadn't been there, he'd be such a pushover for that tactic. "Just one, kiddo. Your mom has the final say."

"OK." She turned back and pulled out a plastic hippopotamus. "This one, please."

"The hippo it is." He tousled her curls and took the toy from her, heading for the cashier with Ceejay and Lucinda trailing behind. He paid for the toy and handed the bag to Lucinda.

"What do you say?" Ceejay raised an eyebrow at her daughter.

"Thank you, Noah."

"You're welcome. I had a great time with you and your mom today."

"Me too." She yawned and clutched her prize to her chest. "Will you carry me to your truck?"

"Lucinda…" Ceejay shook her head.

"It's OK. I'd love to carry her. How about piggyback style. Would you like that?" Her head bobbed away in happy agreement. "All right." He handed his cane to Ceejay. "Here we go." He swung her high in the air over his head to his back as she shrieked and giggled. Lucinda's arms and legs wrapped around him. She laid her head on his shoulder, and his heart melted. Ceejay moved to his side, handed him his cane, and slid him a shy smile that scrambled his insides.

"You've been great today. With Lucinda's constant chatter and nonstop questions, most guys would've run for the hills by now."

"Is that why you stayed in the background?" he teased. "Were you waiting to see if I'd run, or taking advantage of the break?"

"Both." Her smile blossomed, and she reached out to rub her daughter's back. "Thank you for today. Lucinda and I don't do things like this often enough."

"It's been a struggle for you, hasn't it?" Anger at his stepbrother's selfishness knotted his stomach.

Ceejay nodded and averted her gaze. "It's better now that I'm done with my degree and working as a nurse. But, yeah. While I was going to school, I didn't have the time or the money to take her anywhere." She sighed. "There's no guilt like mother's guilt."

"What do have to feel guilty about? You are an amazing role model for her."

"Do you really think so?" Her eyes widened, and she peered up at him as if to gauge his sincerity.

"I do. You faced challenges, overcame them, and got your nursing degree in order to provide a better life for the two of you." Lucinda had fallen asleep, and he tightened his hold. "That's something to be proud of."

Ceejay's posture straightened, and her chin came up a notch. "Thank you."

"You're welcome." They'd reached his truck, and he turned. "She's out. Take her, and I'll get the door." They managed to get Lucinda strapped in without waking her. They climbed into his truck to set out for Perfect and the grocery store. "It sure is quiet when she's asleep." Noah shook his head and sighed. "I don't know how you do it."

She laughed. "I'm used to her."

They drove to town in companionable silence, and he replayed the day in his mind, turning the new memories over one by one. Everything had been new and exciting for Lucinda, and her reactions had kindled a new appreciation in him. He'd even enjoyed her barrage of questions.

He'd managed to convince his dad to give him more time before he revealed their connection to Matt. By then, Ceejay would know him well enough to realize he and his stepbrother were nothing alike. She'd already begun to trust him, and he sensed she didn't give her trust easily. "Is there a children's museum in Evansville, or a water park or something?"

"Sure. Why?" She shot him a questioning look.

"Maybe we could take Lucinda on another outing on your next day off."

"I'd like that." She glanced his way with another shy smile lighting her face, and then turned to watch the passing landscape.

His chest swelled, and heat crept up his neck. He checked Lucinda in his rearview mirror. "She's going to wake up once we get to the grocery store, isn't she?"

"Yep. Enjoy the quiet while you can. I do."

As he predicted, Lucinda woke from her nap ready to race down the aisles of the grocery store. Between the two of them, they managed to pick up what they needed and herd the little girl back to his truck. Noah piled their groceries into the back while Ceejay loaded Lucinda into her car seat. He climbed into the driver's seat, eager to get home and take a nap. He'd have to start running or working out soon. He was sadly out of shape and still tired far too easily.

"Noah, what animal did you like best at the zoo?" Lucinda asked from the backseat where she played with her plastic hippopotamus.

"I'd have to say the jaguars. How about you?"

"The hippopotmus."

"It's *hippopotamus*, Luce," Ceejay corrected.

"*That's* what I said."

Noah exchanged an amused look with Ceejay as he pulled out of the parking lot and turned the truck toward home. The sun hung in an orange haze above the western horizon, and the air had grown heavy with humidity. Maybe they'd get rain tomorrow.

"Noah, my aunt and I were talking." Ceejay fidgeted with a thread hanging from the hem of her blouse. "She says if you want, you could help out at the diner a few days a week. It's not much, but it would be a great way to get to know everyone in town."

"Not interested." Did she really see him as busboy material? His pride took the hit, and a bruise formed under his skin. "I didn't ask for your help."

"I know, but we could all use a hand now and then. I just thought you might enjoy getting out a few days a week." She reached out and touched his arm, and the simple gesture sent an electrical current sizzling through him.

"At least give it some thought."

"No thanks." Wasn't it bad enough he was only half a man? Did she have to remind him?

"OK. The diner is out. Couldn't you go to college for free on the GI Bill?"

"I already have a degree."

"You do?" Her eyes widened. "What in?"

"I have a political science degree from Penn State. I wanted an education before enlisting."

"Why?"

"Because a degree helped me move up the chain of command faster." He glanced at her. "You have to have a degree if you want to be a commissioned officer."

"Oh." She nodded. "What can a person do with a political science degree?"

"Besides a career in the military, you mean?" Bitterness laced his tone.

"Yeah, besides that."

"I could go into government, or get a law degree. I'm not interested in either." He raised an eyebrow at her. "I suppose you have your life all figured out?"

"I do." She lifted her chin. "Once I'm done paying off my student loans and what I owe my aunt, I plan to look for a job in a large city. I figure it'll take me about two more years before I can relocate."

"Bull. If you were going to move, you would've done it already." He turned to her. "The post office still delivers checks through the mail, last time I checked."

"You don't know what you're talking about," she huffed. "I *am* going to leave. I just need some time to save enough money to set it all up."

"Why do you want to move? What's wrong with Perfect?"

"Everyone knows my entire life history. That's what."

"Sure, but they also care. Have you considered how relocating might affect Lucinda?"

"We were talking about you, not me. Don't you want something in your life to keep you busy?"

"I'm not fit for employment." Noah glanced in the rearview mirror. Lucinda had stopped playing with her new toy. Her face was a picture of concentration as she listened to every word they said. He fought to keep his tone even. "Don't you get it? When I'm around too many people it makes me feel like I'm backed into a corner, and the only way out means a fight." He forced himself to relax his grip on the steering wheel. Ceejay meant well. "What kind of job doesn't involve contact with people?"

"You seem all right with me and Jenny."

"That's different."

"How so?"

"Your aunt is like a carton of sunshine to go." He sent her a pointed look. "*She* understands what I'm going through."

Ceejay's forehead creased as she considered his words. "If Jenny's like sunshine to go, what am I?"

"You're a scab I can't stop picking."

She glared at him. "Lovely."

"Would you prefer a mosquito bite I can't stop scratching?" He shot her a quick look. The disgruntled expression on her face went a long way toward restoring his good mood. "Believe me, I've been giving the job thing some thought. I know it's not good for me to sit around with nothing to do. I have a few ideas."

"Oh, yeah?" Her expression turned skeptical. "Let's hear one."

"I noticed your house could use some work. The trim needs to be scraped and painted. The gutters are a wreck, and the windows should be replaced. How about if I do the work in exchange for rent?" In some small way, maybe he could make up for the years of struggle she'd suffered because of his stepbrother. Plus, he'd have something to occupy his time, and he'd be helping the family in a way that Matt should have done from the start.

"Do you know how to do all that stuff?"

"I grew up in the construction business. Plumbing on my dad's side, and my uncles taught me all there is to know about carpentry and cabinetmaking. I can do everything except the electrical."

"Hmmm, and I suppose all that will take a year. So, you'd live rent free for the duration of your lease."

He laughed. "I hadn't thought of that, but it will take some time. If you hired a contractor to do everything, it would cost a fortune, and that doesn't include the roof. Your house is huge, old, and in need of updates and repairs. What I'm offering is a great deal for you and your aunt, and it will give me something to do. That's what you want, right?"

"Since the house belongs to Jenny, I'd have to discuss it with her."

"Let me know once the two of you have decided." Noah turned into the driveway and passed the orchard. A silver BMW SUV was parked in front of the porch. The Pennsylvania license plates read LPS2. *Shit.* So much for more time to get to know the

Lovejoys. What happened to change his dad's mind? He wanted to pound his head against the steering wheel.

"We got company," Lucinda trilled from the backseat.

"Looks that way, Luce. Pennsylvania license plates." She glanced at him. "Now, who do we know from Pennsylvania?"

"Listen, you remember when you kept asking me about Allison?" Noah parked and cut the engine.

"Sure I remember. You never did say."

"She's my stepmother, and that's her SUV."

Ceejay opened her door and hopped out. "Great. Can't wait to meet her." She freed Lucinda from her car seat and lifted her to the ground.

"Is she Noah's mommy?"

"Kind of." Ceejay grabbed her groceries from the back.

Lucinda squirmed. "I need to go to the bathroom bad."

"OK, sweetie. Let's go."

"Wait, she's not just my stepmother, she's—"

"Later," Ceejay called over her shoulder as she scooted up the front steps with Lucinda. "We'll meet you inside."

"Great." Noah reached over to unlock the glove compartment and snatched the envelope containing Matt's letter, the insurance policy, and the cashier's check. His groceries could wait. The shit about to hit the fan couldn't.

CHAPTER FIVE

CEEJAY SET HER BAGS ON the floor inside the front door and hurried her daughter up the stairs to the bathroom. She could hear voices from the living room as they went, and curiosity about Noah's family consumed her. Once Lucinda had finished and washed her hands, Ceejay picked her up and carried her back downstairs to the spot where she'd left her bags. "Why don't you go join Aunt Jenny and our guest while I put these away? I'll be there in a minute."

"I wanna stay wif you." Lucinda clutched her plastic hippo to her chest and stared up at her with big round owl eyes.

"Ceejay, honey," Jenny called from the living room, "there's someone here who'd like to meet you and Lucinda."

"We're coming," she called back. The groceries could wait a few minutes. "Come on. Let's go meet Noah's stepmom." Lucinda's fingers crept up toward her mouth. Ceejay took her by the hand and led her toward the living room. "It's OK. You can sit on my lap."

An attractive middle-aged woman sat on one of the chairs across from Jenny. She wore an expensive pantsuit and designer shoes. A matching handbag rested on the floor by her feet.

Chestnut-colored waves framed her large brown eyes. Not a single strand of gray—Mrs. Langford was no stranger to upscale salons—perfect makeup, a great smile, and dimples. Something about her seemed vaguely familiar.

"I'm Allison Langford." She smiled warmly. "You must be Ceejay. Noah has told my husband so much about you."

"He has?" Though Allison had spoken to her, Ceejay noticed her eyes never left Lucinda. "I don't know what Noah had to say about me, but it's a pleasure to meet you, Mrs. Langford."

"Please, call me Allison. This is Lucinda?"

Ceejay nodded and glanced down at her daughter, who had two fingers firmly planted in her mouth.

"Oh, she's lovely." Allison's eyes filled with tears, and she held her arms out toward Lucinda. "Come here and let me look at you. I'm your grandmother."

"What?" Confusion and disbelief reverberated through her. Ceejay heard Noah enter the room behind her. Was he so desperate for normal that he'd spun some kind of wild tale for his family? "I'm afraid there's been some kind of misunderstanding. I've only known Noah for about a month. He's not Lucinda's daddy."

"Allison." Noah's strained tone filled the awkward pause that followed. "I asked Dad for more time, and he agreed. What happened?"

"Your new prosthetic arrived at our house. I found the box on the porch for the UPS guy. It had been redirected to Perfect, Indiana, and I knew something was up. You said you were going to travel and camp, and suddenly there's an address in a small town in Indiana." The corners of her mouth turned down.

"You know your father can't keep a secret from me once I get wind of it. I couldn't wait to meet Lucinda. I...I thought you would've told Ceejay the truth by now." Allison's eyes were filled with hurt. "Obviously you haven't."

"Told me the truth about what?" Ceejay spun around to face Noah, searching his face for clues. What had he told his father? How could Allison believe she and Lucinda were in any way related to her?

"Let's all take a deep breath." Jenny patted the place next to her on the couch. "Ceejay, come sit down."

Tugging Lucinda along with her, Ceejay crossed the room and perched on the edge of the cushion. Lucinda climbed onto her lap.

Noah placed a large envelope beside her. "Matthew Wyatt was Allison's son and my stepbrother."

"Matthew Wyatt?" For a blessed second her mind went completely blank. Then understanding dawned in a rush that sent heat to her face. Allison's dimples, chestnut hair, and brown eyes...no wonder she looked familiar. "All this time..." She couldn't tear her gaze from Noah. "Why didn't you tell me?"

He ran a hand over the back of his skull. "I was working up to it."

"Working *up* to it?" Mortification burned a hole right through her all the way to the floorboards. "So that's what all the prying and time spent together has been about. You weren't interested in getting to know *me*, you were working up to *this*?"

Noah shoved his hands in his pockets. "I thought if we had some time to get to know each other first, breaking the news would be easier."

All the pain and rejection she'd suffered when Matt left reared up, along with red-hot anger at Noah's deception. He hadn't wanted to know her at all, and that stung way more than she wanted to acknowledge. "I want you gone. Consider yourself evicted."

"You can't evict me." He widened his stance. "I have a lease."

"Regardless, I want no part of you, the Wyatts, or the Langfords."

Allison's muffled cry penetrated the fog of shock and confusion wrapped around Ceejay's brain. Noah's words echoed inside her head. "*Was* Allison's son? *Was?*" She managed to tear her gaze away from Noah long enough to look at Allison. Matt's mother wept into a handkerchief held to her face. The breath left Ceejay's lungs in a rush. "Matt is…"

Allison nodded. Ceejay turned toward the bricks in the fireplace and started a desperate tally of the bricks. *One, two, three…* Her chest had grown so tight it was a wonder she could breathe.

"Why don't I take Lucinda upstairs for her bath?" Jenny patted Ceejay's knee. "You all stay here and talk this through."

The fingers flew out of Lucinda's mouth. "I don't wanna take a bath. I wanna stay here."

"I'm sure you do, but we're going upstairs anyway. Your mommy needs to talk with this nice lady and Noah."

Lucinda started to cry. "I wanna talk to the nice lady too."

"Go on, Luce. I'll be up to kiss you good night in a little while." Ceejay handed her to Jenny.

Noah moved to sit next to her. "Matt left you a letter along with the money he owed you."

"The money he *owed* me?" Her eyes widened and her throat tightened. "You make it sound like he *borrowed* my entire life savings. That's not how it happened. He *stole* that money from me—along with my car."

"I know." Noah reached around her to retrieve the envelope and placed it on her lap. When she made no move to open it, he did it for her, pulling out the contents. "He also made you the beneficiary of a life insurance policy."

"H-how did he…what happened to him?" She stared blindly at the pile of papers in her lap.

Noah spoke in a low tone. "He died in a car accident."

"Racing?" She closed her eyes.

"No," he answered. "He was hit head-on by a drunk driver."

"Oh."

"I'm so sorry," Allison whispered. "I'm so sorry about the way my son treated you."

Ceejay opened her eyes and focused on the documents Noah had placed in her lap. A cashier's check made out to her for ten thousand dollars rested on top of a handwritten letter and the thick insurance policy. Somehow she managed to slide the check aside to read the words Matt had written. Big mistake. The pain grew worse.

"I need air." She stood, letting the pile in her lap fall to the floor. "If you'll excuse me…" She placed one foot in front of the other and made it out the front door. *Not far enough.* She kept on walking until she reached the middle of the orchard.

Lying down on the soft, cool grass, she stared up into the canopy of leaves and the small peaches, pears, and apples growing on the branches above. Her mind should've been spinning. Instead it remained blank and still like the eye of a hurricane. Any minute now the storm would tear her apart.

The tiny orbs of fruit weren't easy to count in the twilight. Good. A challenge was exactly what she needed, because she didn't want to think about Matt, Noah, or anything at all. Maybe tomorrow she could do that, but right now, it was all too big, and too much to handle. Taking refuge in numbers felt far safer than examining how Matt's death and Noah's betrayal affected her.

"Ceejay!" Noah called.

"Go away," she shouted back. No good. He came to loom over her, forming a dark silhouette against the gathering dusk. She began her inventory of the peaches.

"Talk to me." He set his cane on the grass, lay down beside her, and reached for her hand.

She snatched it away, but not before the warmth of his skin registered against hers, making her heart ache even more. "I have nothing to say to you."

"What are you doing out here?"

She pointed to the trees. "Three, four, five…"

"Is that how you deal with everything? You count corn rows and fruit?"

"No. Sometimes I count bricks or cracks in the ceiling, even stars. Maybe you should give it try the next time being around people sends you into a panic." She glared at him. "Do you think that awful letter and a check make everything hunky-dory in my world?" Her breath hitched, and she clamped her mouth shut.

"No." He turned on his side to face her. "Why didn't you ever try to find Matt after he left?"

"Why would I look for someone who'd made it abundantly clear he didn't want me or his baby?"

"Child support."

"The guy stole everything I had! Why the hell would I expect financial help from him?"

"It's the law."

"He didn't have anything I wanted." She shook her head. "Matt used me, and I was the naive little fool who let him." The sympathy in his eyes had her focusing on the trees above. "I didn't want the contact. A check each month would've been a reminder of how disposable I was to him. Why put myself through that?"

"Matt's actions had everything to do with him and nothing to do with you. You aren't disposable. How old were you when all this happened?"

"Nineteen."

"I'm sorry. I—"

"I don't want your pity." She sat up and wrapped her arms around her knees.

Noah propped himself up beside her. "You think *I* pity *you*?"

She glanced at him. "Don't you?"

"Damn, Ceejay, do you really think you're the only one who gets wet when it rains?" He rapped his knuckles against his fake limb and then his skull. "Take a good look, sweetheart. I'm more likely to be on the receiving end when it comes to the pity dole."

"I don't pity you either."

"Don't you? Who would want a guy like me? I'm damaged goods. I don't even have a job."

"You can always find a job, and a missing limb doesn't make you undesirable." Her head started to throb.

"No?" His scrutiny became intense. "Could you ever want a man like me?"

Not a question she wanted to answer or even admit to herself—not while tonight's revelations still burned. He'd lied about who he was, about why he wanted to get to know her and Lucinda, and that betrayal, right when she was beginning to trust him, scorched her from the inside out. "I'm not going to stick around Perfect much longer." Ceejay pulled at the grass around her feet. "The money Matt left will make relocating a whole lot easier."

"I didn't ask if you planned to stay. I asked if you could want a man like me."

"You do realize your timing sucks, right?" She scowled at him. "You should've asked that question before I found out you lied to me."

"I didn't lie."

"Yes, you did. You said you came for the carriage house."

"No, *you* said that. *I* couldn't get a word in edgewise. Once I met you and Lucinda, I decided to take advantage of your assumption, that's all."

"Right. Matt took advantage of my assumptions too." She rested her cheek on her knees. "I assumed he was an honest man. I assumed he meant it when he told me he loved me. Instead of telling me who you were, and why you showed up at my front door, you decided to *take advantage*. You're no different."

"It's not the same at all. I'm not—"

"Do you think my money and car are the only things Matt stole?" She blinked back the angry tears. "While my college friends were out dating and partying, I was juggling school, work, and caring for a newborn—always exhausted and always broke." *Always alone and heartbroken.*

"Wait." She raised her head to glare at him. "Why the sudden interest? Why are you people showing up now? Lucinda is four years old." He didn't respond. Could she sink any lower, feel any more like dog poo on the bottom of somebody's shoe? "Matt didn't tell anyone about me, did he?"

Noah shook his head. "None of us knew you existed until I went through his things and found the envelope."

"It's time you left." Ceejay shot up. "Last time I checked, the post office still delivers large envelopes. You should've put it in the mail, because coming here was a waste of your time."

Noah struggled to his feet. "Don't blame Allison for any of this. Lucinda is her granddaughter. She only wants the chance to be a part of her life."

She kept walking. Allison's SUV was still parked in front of the house. She walked around to the back. Taking the stairs off the kitchen, she headed for her daughter's room. Lucinda must be wound up tight about now. It'd be a miracle if she could get her settled down enough to sleep.

The sound of happy voices stopped her outside Lucinda's door. No, Jenny wouldn't…reaching for the doorknob, she braced herself and walked in.

Jenny and Allison sat on opposite sides of Lucinda on her bed. Her daughter had been bathed and dressed in a summer nightgown. Her favorite book lay open on her lap, and Boo-Bear was nestled against her chest. Even Sweet Pea had insinuated himself into the happy tableau. He lay stretched out on the rug by Lucinda's bed, barely lifting his head to acknowledge her. It was all too much, too sweet, and too happy.

The moment Lucinda saw her, she got up and started jumping on the mattress. "Mommy, Mommy, Allison is my grandma, and you know what?"

Her stomach lurched. "What?"

"She's gonna spoil me rotten. That's what she said."

"Yay."

"You know what else?" Lucinda cried. "Noah is my uncle."

"You don't say." She sent her aunt a silent plea. "I think you've had enough excitement for one night. It's way past your bedtime. Say good night, and I'll tuck you in."

"It is getting late." Allison rose from her place on the bed. "I should be going. Is there a motel or a bed-and-breakfast nearby?"

"Nonsense," Jenny waved a hand in the air, "you'll stay right here. We have plenty of room if you don't mind helping me put fresh linens on one of the spare beds."

"Are you sure I'm not imposing?"

"I'm sure. We'd love to have you."

Ceejay sent her aunt an angry scowl, but Jenny ignored her. *Wonderful.* Betrayed by her own aunt.

Jenny kissed Lucinda on the cheek and headed for the door. Allison followed, stopping beside Ceejay before she left. "I know this has all been a shock. I hope we'll have the chance to get to know one another…"

Guilt stabbed at her as she looked into the older woman's warm brown eyes. None of this was Allison's fault. Still, she had no words to offer. Hurt flashed through Allison's eyes as she hurried off after Jenny.

She was being petty, but she couldn't seem to help herself. Having the past thrown into her face with no warning had stirred up the cauldron of emotion always simmering just below the surface. She wanted to scream. She wanted to fling things against the wall to watch them shatter like she'd shattered the day Matt walked away with her ability to trust.

Instead, Ceejay tucked her little girl into bed, sitting with her while Lucinda talked herself out and fell asleep. Leaning close, she inhaled her sweet little girl scent, kissed her forehead, and left the room to head for the sanctuary of hers. Once she was behind the closed door, the tears started. Matt. Dead. She'd always harbored the tiny hope that he'd show up one day, begging to be a part of their amazing little girl's life.

Her thoughts turned to Noah. She'd risked opening up and had begun to trust him, even sharing mortifying details about her life. What a fool to believe he wanted to get to know her. All this time he'd been working up to dropping this bomb in her lap. She didn't want to acknowledge the hollow ache of disappointment eating at her, but it was there. Something about Noah drew her, and she'd wanted to get to know him better. She'd allowed herself to believe he felt the same.

A knock on her door sent her heart racing. She swiped at her eyes. "Who is it?"

"Just me." Jenny opened the door a crack. "Can I come in?"

"Sure."

"I found your groceries by the front door and put them away."

"Thanks." Ceejay opened her dresser drawer and pulled out her pajamas.

"Ceejay, you can't blame Allison and Noah for Matt's actions."

"I don't. I blame them for barging into my life uninvited, and I blame Noah for being dishonest about his reasons for being here." She gritted her teeth to keep from crying again.

"Fair enough." Jenny leaned against the door. "For Lucinda's sake, you might consider forgiving them. Maybe the right thing to do would be to give the Langfords a chance. Allison is her grandmother, and Noah is her uncle. Family is a good thing."

"Jenny, they didn't ask first. Maybe if they had, maybe if they'd written a letter, or called on the phone…It's the deception and the intrusion without any consideration that I can't forgive. Not today, anyway."

"Maybe tomorrow, then." Jenny pushed off the wall and opened the door. "Sleep on it."

All she could manage was a mute nod. The lump in her throat made speech impossible.

Ceejay awoke in a sullen mood despite the sunlight pouring through her bedroom window. Glancing at her digital clock, she sat up. It was already nine o'clock. Why hadn't Lucinda come to her demanding breakfast? Maybe all the excitement from the night before had tired her out so much she'd slept in.

She got up, grabbed her robe, and headed for her daughter's room. Empty. Ceejay looked out the window into the backyard. Maybe she'd conned Noah into another sand sculpture. No sign of either of them.

The happy sound of Lucinda's giggles floated up the back stairs as Ceejay headed for the kitchen.

"Grandma, make another one, only this time, make it Minnie instead of Mickey."

"All right, sweetie, but you be careful on that chair."

She walked into the kitchen. Lucinda stood on a chair beside Allison in front of the stove. They both turned. Two faces haloed in chestnut waves with identical dimples and large brown eyes. The same chin. Ceejay's heart twisted every which way.

"Grandma is making pancakes. Mickey and Minnie Mouse." In her excitement, Lucinda lost her balance and almost tumbled from the chair. Allison steadied her with an arm around her shoulders.

Ceejay walked over and lifted her daughter down. "Let's go sit at the table so you can eat them."

Allison turned back to the skillet and busied herself with flipping pancakes. "Would you like some?"

"No." She settled her daughter into her chair.

"I understand how you feel, and I have a fair idea what you're going through." Allison placed a plate of cartoon-shaped pancakes drenched in syrup in front of Lucinda.

"I doubt that." Ceejay made a point of looking at the huge diamond glittering on Allison's left ring finger.

"Noah's father is my second husband. I haven't always had it so easy."

"Then I'm sure you know what it's like being pregnant and unmarried in a small town like Perfect," she muttered. "I'm certain you know what it feels like to have your boyfriend steal everything you own. Not a good time, is it?"

"No. It isn't, and there's nothing I can do to change what happened. Lucinda is my granddaughter." Allison's voice shook, and her chin quivered. "All I want is the chance to know her."

"It takes more than genetics to make a family. Matt gave up any right he had to fatherhood the minute he walked out on us. In my book that nullifies your claim."

"We didn't know about you and Lucinda." Allison's eyes filled. "If we had, steps would've been taken to—"

"Look, there are reasons why I never came looking for Matt or any of his family. I didn't invite you into our lives. How can you expect me to make you feel welcome?"

"We can't change the past, but please," Allison pleaded, "let us make it up to you and Lucinda."

"You have. Noah delivered the check and the insurance policy. We're all set. Thanks."

Allison gasped and rushed out of the kitchen. Ceejay leaned down to cut Lucinda's pancakes for her, and the sour taste of her own bitterness turned her stomach.

"Why were you so mean to my grandma?" Lucinda sniffled.

Lucinda's tears bit at her conscience. "You're too young to understand."

"Is she going to go away?"

"I don't know." *I hope so.*

Lucinda squirmed out of her chair. "Is my uncle Noah gonna go away, too?" she cried. "I don't want them to go away. You go make it better right now, Mommy." Lucinda stomped her foot and crossed her arms in front of her.

She sighed. "If you aren't going to eat these pancakes, let's go upstairs and get you dressed."

"Are you going to 'pologize to my grandma?" Lucinda's voice wobbled.

"Not today, Luce." How long would it take for news to get around town that Matt's mother had barged into her life, and that her new tenant was her ex's stepbrother? She wouldn't be able to show her face in town. The pity, the disapproval, and the smug *I'm so glad it's you and not me* looks would be far too much to bear. Shame and humiliation swamped her. Had she truly believed she'd left all that in the past?

One more worry insinuated itself into her psyche. What must Noah think of her? Did he pity her as well? He said he didn't, but how could he not? At any rate, he couldn't think very highly of her. She didn't think much of herself right now. Allison didn't deserve the anger being thrown her way. Intellectually she knew that, but emotionally? Not so much, and she was helpless to rein it in.

The rage always simmering just below the surface had taken on a life of its own, turning her into a monster even she didn't recognize. She just wanted to run away and start over. As long as she remained in Perfect, she had no chance to escape her past. The idea of leaving never looked so good, and now she had the means to make it happen.

CHAPTER SIX

LAST NIGHT HAD BEEN A disaster, and Noah had only himself to blame. Still, one part of his conversation with Ceejay kept looping through his mind.

"Could you ever want a man like me?"

"You should've asked that question before I found out you lied to me."

He examined her words from every possible angle, replaying every moment they'd spent together. Did she mean if he'd asked her the day *before* Allison arrived, she would've answered *yes*? A picture formed in his mind—Ceejay in his arms, smiling up at him, her eyes filled with trust. He wanted that—and more. The sudden, visceral need nearly staggered him.

Fall back, soldier. Regroup.

He had a target in his scope; now came the hard part. What did he possess in his arsenal that could get through the Kevlar Ceejay had wrapped around her heart? How could he earn her forgiveness and gain back her trust now that she'd placed him in the "not to be trusted" category—like Matt? Like her mother.

"Noah?" His front door opened, and Allison peeked around the edge.

"Come in." Noah set the book on his lap aside and rose from the ratty old couch. He hadn't read a single word anyway. "Do you want coffee? It's fresh."

"No, thanks." She entered, clutching a long cardboard box with a UPS packing slip taped to the side. "Coming here unannounced was a mistake. I should've listened to Ed and waited."

"Don't blame yourself. This is my fault." He took the package and gestured to the couch.

Allison perched on the edge. "Ceejay made it clear I'm not welcome." She pointed to the box as he leaned it against the wall. "I wanted to deliver your new prosthetic and say good-bye before I leave."

"You're welcome to stay as far as I'm concerned." He sat beside her. "I'll bunk in the camper, and you can have my room." He rubbed his face. "I should've told Ceejay who I was from the start. I don't know how, but I'll fix this. I swear."

"You always were the one to shoulder every burden, whether it had your name on it or not." Allison patted his knee. "All of this is Matt's doing. It wouldn't have made any difference if you'd told Ceejay who you were."

Allison smoothed out the creases in her slacks. "Despite what Ceejay thinks, I do understand what she's going through. I've never told you about Matt's father. I tried to tell her, but she wouldn't listen."

"You don't have to."

"I want to." She lifted her chin. "Maybe it'll give you some insight."

Noah squirmed. Personal stuff from the only mother he'd ever known was uncharted territory. He nodded, trying to look more interested than alarmed.

"I married Matt's father when I was nineteen. I was pregnant. My family didn't approve of Mark." She shook her head. "That's putting it mildly. They couldn't stand the loser, but I married him anyway, and it caused quite a rift."

Allison picked at nonexistent lint on her sleeve. "Matt was a colicky baby. He cried nonstop, starting up like clockwork at five in the afternoon and conking out around midnight. Mark couldn't stand it. He'd pace and shout, slam things around, tell me to shut the baby up or else."

"Or else what?" Noah frowned. "Matt was an infant. It's not like he had any control."

"His threats were nonspecific." She stared off into space. "Just *or else.* The afternoon he left, we'd been fighting. Mark had quit his job because he didn't feel he was being treated with enough respect." She shot him an incredulous look. "He did unskilled manual labor, for crying out loud. That measly income was all we had, and he gave it up because of his stupid, immature, male ego!"

"Sounds like you're still angry."

"Of course I'm still angry. Even after all these years what he did still floors me, and that's what you have to understand about Ceejay. She hasn't gotten over what Matt did to her. When someone abandons you like that, there's never any closure."

Noah shook his head. "You and Mark were too young to be parents."

"Would you have done such a thing?"

"No."

"Exactly. Anyway, that afternoon, Matthew started wailing, and Mark pitched a fit. I sent him to the store for diapers, thinking it would give him time to cool down. He never came back." Allison turned to face him. "That kind of trauma leaves a permanent scar. His betrayal hollowed out a place inside me the size of the Grand Canyon, and anger was the most natural thing to fill it with." Allison rose from the couch. "Maybe I will have a cup of coffee."

Noah started to rise.

"Stay put. I'll get it."

She returned with two mugs and handed one to Noah before sitting down and setting her cup on the floor. "It's been a long time since I've talked about all of this." She gave him a small smile. "I had no job, no education, and a newborn who depended upon me alone. It was the lowest, most frightening point in my life."

"You had your family."

"I didn't think so at the time. We were estranged, and if Mark's family had shown up after I'd managed to claw my way out of that black hole, I would've slammed the door in their faces. Ceejay is reacting exactly like I would have."

Noah thought about his step-uncles and grandparents. Allison was the youngest and the only girl in a family of five children in an Irish Catholic family. They all adored her, but he knew how stubborn and proud they could be. "They came through for you in the end."

"They gave me a job in the family business with the expectation that I'd come through for myself, which I did. Ceejay's aunt did the same for her. She provided her with the support she needed to make her own way. We're both very lucky to have had that kind of help. It's been worse for Ceejay, though. Perfect is a small town, and she and Matt weren't married."

Allison slapped her knees. "That's enough of the maudlin. Lucinda is adorable, isn't she? She has Matt's eyes and his coloring. She's precocious as all get out."

"Yeah, she is." Noah reached for his stepmother's hand and gave it a squeeze. It couldn't have been easy to reveal so much about her past. "Give Ceejay some time, Mom. She'll come around."

Allison sucked in her breath. "You haven't called me Mom since you were little. I wish you'd never stopped."

Noah nodded, unable to speak.

Allison cleared her throat. "I suppose you'll be heading out now as well?"

"I'm staying. The cycle you described has to stop somewhere." The only good to come out of yesterday's fiasco was that he now understood why Ceejay never looked for her mother or for Matt. The people in her life who should've cared the most left the quickest. She did her own kind of leaving in return, the only way she could—by shutting them out of her life and mind completely. He didn't want to be shut out.

Allison's eyes widened. "Do you have feelings for Ceejay?"

"I hardly know her." Heat filled his face. *Could she want a man like me? Half a man with a shattered mind and a busted rudder?* "Lucinda needs to know she has a place in the Langford family, and that we care about her. If I leave now, it would be another abandonment of the next-generation kind."

Allison's eyes held a knowing look. "It took a patient and persistent man like your father to tunnel through all the walls I put up."

"Patient? Edward Langford, right? We're talking about my father?"

Allison laughed. "You'd be surprised by what lies beneath that crusty shell of his. I love your father. He taught me how to trust again."

Noah straightened. "How?"

"He didn't give up on me. He held on like a barnacle and wouldn't let go. I couldn't shake him loose no matter how hard

I tried." Her expression turned wistful. "Believe me, I tried. All the times I pushed him away, what I really needed was proof that he'd stick around, and he knew it. Your father is very intuitive."

He shot her an incredulous look.

"It's true. He understands me like no one else ever has." Allison grinned. "He can be a jerk, but there's no doubt in my mind that he's *my* jerk, and he always will be."

Noah smiled. Fondness for his hard-assed father warmed his insides. Yep, Edward Langford could be an ass, but Noah had never doubted that he cared. That was what made it especially difficult when they butted heads. No matter how far off the mark his actions, his father's motives sprang from a fierce love for his family.

Allison scanned his tiny living room. "If you're going to stay, you might think about making this place more comfortable. It's a darling apartment, but it looks like no one lives here."

"I've been meaning to buy furniture and a few other things I need." Noah ran his hand over his scalp. "I'm not good at that sort of thing."

Allison rose from the couch. "I'm sorry I didn't get a chance to thank Jenny or say good-bye." She rifled through her handbag and pulled out her car keys. "Keep me updated. Maybe given some time, Ceejay will soften."

"Wait." He pushed himself up from his place on the couch. "Help me pick out some stuff for the apartment today, and I also need a child's car seat for my truck. Then I'll take you to Jenny's diner. You can thank her yourself." Noah squared his shoulders. "I'm not giving up, and neither should you."

"I won't." Allison threw her arms around him for a quick hug. "I have a granddaughter, and she's already stolen my heart.

If anyone can chip away at Ceejay's anger, it's you." Her voice quavered, and she sniffed. "Let's go shopping."

Noah finished giving directions for the furniture delivery company. He shoved the receipt into his back pocket and headed for the children's section of the department store, where Allison had promised to stay until he came for her. As he wended his way through the crowded mall, his insides coiled up like steel ready to spring. Too many people. Too many whining children being pushed in their strollers at a snail's pace. All morning he'd listened to people complain about the dumbest shit, bickering with one another about nothing.

Time to go.

His stepmother stood by the register. A happy-to-be-shopping expression lit her face as the clerk rang up the little girl dresses piled high on the counter. She caught a glimpse of him, and her smile disappeared. "What's wrong?"

He wiped the sweat from his forehead. "I've got to get out of here."

"All right. We're almost finished." She handed the clerk her credit card.

Shoving his hands into the front pockets of his jeans, Noah nodded and tried to hold on to the unraveling end of his sanity. *Maybe you should try counting the next time being around people sends you into a panic.* Ceejay's words came back to him. He took a deep breath and started counting the racks of children's clothing. Pacing through the maze of garments, he came to the women's lingerie section, stopping amid the mannequins dressed in bits of satin and lace.

The image of Ceejay in her bathrobe with the morning sun gilding her hair flashed through his mind. The coil inside him eased. To hell with counting clothes. He'd rather count the freckles sprinkled across Ceejay's cheeks, or gaze into the pure blue depths of her eyes. Now that calmed him.

Noah pictured her face, tender with love as she ran her fingers through Lucinda's hair. What would it be like to have that look turned his way, or to feel her touch on his skin? One side of his mouth quirked up.

"All right." Allison thrust the bag full of little girl outfits at him. "Let's go."

"Lucinda is going to love these," he said. "She wears nothing but dresses."

Allison looped her arm through his. "I remember when Paige went through that phase."

"Yeah, me too. She used to tell everybody she was going to be a princess when she grew up."

"She kind of is," Allison whispered.

Noah laughed, and she glanced at him.

"Feeling better?"

"A little." He held the door open, and a blast of Indiana heat and humidity enveloped them. They crossed the parking lot to his truck. Noah placed the shopping bag next to the new car seat he'd already installed in the backseat. Helping Allison into the cab, he wondered if Ceejay would allow Lucinda to have the dresses. It would break his stepmother's heart if she didn't. He settled himself into the driver's seat. "Are you hungry?"

"Famished. Shopping does that to me."

"You're in for a treat. Jenny's diner is like something straight out of the fifties. Black-and-white tiled floor, red Formica, and vinyl booths, and it's all original. The food is country comfort all the way." Would Jenny be as angry with him as Ceejay was? He hoped not. He'd grown fond of her, and he valued their friendship. "How did Jenny react to all this mess? Did you two talk about it last night?"

"I showed up at their door believing you'd already told them who I was. I introduced myself as Matt's mother and your step, and Jenny welcomed me with open arms." Allison's brow furrowed. "She didn't seem at all surprised."

"That's Jenny." He remembered when she'd asked if his being there had anything to do with Ceejay. Maybe she did have some kind of special radar when it came to people.

"What happened in the mall, Noah? When you joined me in the children's department, you were so pale."

"It's hard to explain." His grip tightened on the steering wheel.

"Try. I want to understand."

He eased out of the parking lot into the traffic. "In a militarized zone, you're hypervigilant and pumping adrenaline twenty-four seven. Any minute could be your last, and you never know how the end might come. IEDs turn up everywhere."

"What's an IED?"

"Improvised explosive device. Insurgents don't fight fair. You lose people close to you far too often and never lose sight of the fact that they aren't just soldiers. Somebody has lost a son or a daughter, a wife or a husband. Lots of soldiers are parents themselves. That leaves a kid somewhere without their mom or dad. Living under that kind of constant stress puts things into perspective." He glanced at his stepmother. "Everything petty is stripped away."

"What does all that have to do with the mall?"

He blew out a breath. "I have no patience. Getting trapped behind a couple arguing over whether the toilet seat gets left up or down makes me want to knock heads together. Being stuck behind a family pushing a stroller, or getting trapped in a crowd of strangers sends me into a panic. I have post-traumatic stress disorder, Mom. Paranoia, irritability, rage, panic, anxiety, and flashbacks. This is my life."

"I know your diagnosis." She rested her hand on his forearm. "Until today, I didn't understand what it meant. This is the first time I've seen what it does to you. If I could make it better, I would."

"I know." Warmth flooded through him. "It's something I have to learn how to cope with. Perfect is a good place for me to be right now. It's quiet, peaceful, and I'm having fewer meltdowns."

"I wish you could've found that closer to home." She propped her chin on her fist and stared out the window.

The past few months must have been brutal for her. She'd spent every spare minute she could at his side while he'd been in the VA hospital, and then, just when he'd been ready to be discharged, she'd lost Matt. "Isn't Paige home for the summer?"

"No. She and some of her friends are sharing a house near campus. She has an internship for the summer that she's really excited about." She sighed. "You all grew up too fast."

Noah made a mental note to call his little sister. Maybe he could talk her into going home on the weekends. He checked the dashboard clock as he pulled into Perfect, hoping the lunch rush had ended. The thought of facing Jenny made his palms sweat.

"Damn." He pulled into a parking space near the diner.

"What is it?"

"Sheriff Maurer is here."

"You don't like the sheriff?"

"He doesn't like me." Noah took the key out of the ignition and breathed deep. His heart was pounding. "Let's do this thing."

"You make having lunch here sound like one of your military missions. Are you sure you want to eat here?"

He ran his hand over the back of his skull. "It sounded like a good idea when I suggested it, but…"

"We don't have to go in."

"Yes, we do." He opened the door of his truck and climbed out.

He helped Allison down and guided her inside the diner. It was nearly empty. Jenny and the sheriff shared a table toward the back. Jenny spotted them and rose from her chair, her expression welcoming.

She gestured toward the table she shared with the sheriff. "Join us. I was just telling Harlen about your visit, Allison."

Great. "Sheriff Maurer, this is my stepmother, Allison Langford. Mom, this is Sheriff Maurer."

"Call me Harlen, ma'am." Sheriff Maurer stood up and eased a chair back for Allison. "Jenny told me about your recent loss. I'm sorry to hear it."

Noah blinked. This was *not* what he'd expected. The sheriff turned a baleful glare his way. Oh, good. Back in familiar territory.

"Thank you, Harlen, and please call me Allison." She sat down. "Jenny, I stopped by to thank you for last night and to say good-bye."

"You just got here," Jenny cried. "Can't you stay for a few days?"

A young woman with menus tucked under her arm came by with a cloth and swiped the table clean while Jenny and the sheriff lifted their coffee mugs. "Today's special is spaghetti and meatballs with garlic bread," she said, handing them the menus.

"That sounds good. I'll have the special and an iced tea." Noah took the seat with his back to the wall.

"Same here." Allison handed the menus back. The server went to place their order, and Allison turned to face Jenny. "I can't stay. Ceejay doesn't want me here, and I respect her wishes."

"As far as I'm concerned, you're always welcome. I hope you realize she's not really angry at you," Jenny said. "She's angry at Matt. You and Noah just happen to be in her line of fire."

Sheriff Maurer turned a glare his way. "You did lie to Ceejay and her aunt, though. Isn't that right, son?"

Noah swallowed. Why did they have to have this conversation in front of the sheriff? He turned to face Jenny. "I should've told you both who I was, but I wasn't sure how the news would be received. I couldn't risk losing the chance to get to know Lucinda."

"I figured you were here for a reason." Jenny leaned back and studied him. "I had a feeling it had something to do with my niece. I know your heart is in the right place, even if you went about things all wrong."

"Thank you." He blew out a breath.

"I suppose you'll be taking off with that fancy camper now," Jenny remarked.

"No, ma'am. I'm staying." Noah caught a glimpse of something pass through her eyes. Satisfaction?

Sheriff Maurer grunted and leaned back in his chair, crossing his arms over his chest.

Noah shifted. "I talked to Ceejay about an idea I had. Your house needs work, and I need something useful to do. I'd appreciate it if you'd let me make some of the repairs."

"Noah comes highly recommended," Allison added. "There's nothing my stepson can't do, and you won't find a more skilled craftsman anywhere."

"The deal I proposed to Ceejay was that I do the work in exchange for rent."

Jenny shook her head. "We don't expect you to—"

"I know you don't. I want to do this."

"The carriage house belongs to Ceejay, and so does the rental income. In her present state of mind, it's not likely she'll agree."

"I'll keep paying rent, then. I have money. What I don't have is an occupation, something to keep me busy. Look at this like it's part of my PTSD therapy. You'd be helping me out, and we'd all benefit."

The laugh lines around Jenny's eyes creased. "Since you put it like that, I don't see how I can refuse."

Their server arrived with steaming plates of spaghetti each topped with three gigantic meatballs. Noah's mouth watered at the delicious, garlicky scent, and his stomach growled.

"I've got to be going." Sheriff Maurer pushed himself away from the table. "It's been a pleasure meeting you, Allison."

"Thank you, Harlen. I hope we'll see each other again soon."

Sheriff Maurer nodded, and turned his cop-on-duty look toward Noah. "I'll be keeping an eye on you."

"Yes, sir. I figured you would." Not even Sheriff Maurer could destroy his new sense of purpose. "How did that background check on me turn out?"

The sheriff made a chuffing sound, put his hat on, and sauntered out of the diner without answering.

"He did a background check on you? Whatever for?" Allison twirled her fork into the spaghetti.

"For Ceejay and Lucinda's sake, of course." Jenny nodded. "Harlen and I have been friends almost our entire lives. He's very protective."

Noah could respect that. He'd be the same way in the sheriff's shoes. Jenny and Allison kept a stream of happy chatter going. Noah paid no attention. He had more important things to attend to, like forming a strategy for winning Ceejay's forgiveness.

Now, that really did present a challenge.

CHAPTER SEVEN

CEEJAY SNAPPED HER CELL PHONE shut and groaned. According to the life insurance company, she needed a certified copy of Matthew's death certificate to file her claim. Noah hadn't included one in the envelope he'd dropped on her lap, which meant she'd have to track one down or talk to him. Her insides pitched a fit, part righteous anger, part guilt. *Nope. Not ready for that.* Besides, now that he'd delivered the goods and come clean about who he was, he'd probably break his lease and take off.

Why did that churn up all kinds of regret? What she ought to feel was relief.

The image of Noah sitting on the damp grass by Lucinda's sandbox flashed through her mind. He'd taken the time to sculpt a pony out of sand for her little girl. How many men would do that? Not any she'd met. The rare look of joy on his face when Lucinda asked to sit on his lap, his patience with her daughter's endless chatter at the zoo, the way he held her hand and watched over her…Ceejay's eyes misted up.

She blinked the sentiment back. Yeah, all those things were great, but none of it erased the fact that he'd lied, and none of it erased Noah's connection to Matt. She didn't need that constant reminder in her life.

"Mommy, more milk, please."

"Coming right up." Ceejay set her cell phone on the counter and crossed the kitchen to the fridge. "Almost finished with that sandwich?"

Lucinda nodded as Ceejay filled her cup. "What would you like to do this afternoon, Luce?" The phone on the kitchen wall rang, and she crossed the room to answer. "Hello?"

"This is Edward Langford."

Her heart rate surged. "Noah's not here. Maybe you should try his cell."

"I'm not calling for Noah. Is this Ceejay?"

She took the handset from her ear and stared at it for a second before bringing it back. "Yes?"

"My wife came home in quite a state. She says you're unwilling to let her get to know our granddaughter."

"That's right. I don't appreciate the way you Langfords have barged into my life uninvited."

"I'm hoping I can change your mind. We're in a position to make your lives easier."

She frowned. "I don't know what you mean."

"We have money, and—"

"You're trying to bribe me?" She wanted to laugh. *What arrogance.*

"Lucinda can go to the best private college available. She'll always have whatever she needs. Call it bribery if you want. I see it as providing for my family."

"Look, we're doing just fine, Mr. Langford. I've already started a college fund for *my* daughter, and just because Matt was her father doesn't make us *family.*"

"Think about it. We—"

"Lucinda is not for sale. Thank you just the same." She hung up and tried to get her anger under control. "Who does he think he is?"

"Who, Mommy?"

"Um, nobody important, baby. Finish your lunch."

There it was again, that twinge of guilt. Intellectually she knew the Langfords had nothing to do with Matt's actions, but emotionally? She was still too raw with shock to think rationally. Maybe once she had a new job and her new life had begun, she'd feel strong enough to deal with Lucinda's grandparents. Not now, though.

Sweet Pea kicked up a ruckus from the backyard, and the rumble of a large truck pulling up in front of the house had Lucinda scrambling out of her booster. Ceejay followed her to the front door already open to let in the breeze.

"Uncle Noah," Lucinda cried with delight as she slipped out to the veranda.

"Hey, sweetheart," Noah greeted her from his place on the gravel driveway. A white truck with "Johnston's Rental Equipment" written on the side maneuvered around and backed up onto the grass as close to the house as possible.

Ceejay leaned over the railing. "What's all this?"

"It's the scaffolding equipment I need to start working on the house."

"I never agreed to the deal."

"I know." Noah glanced her way. "Jenny gave the OK for the work to be done, and I'm doing it whether you agree or not. I'll keep paying rent."

"You're not taking off with that fancy camper?" Should she tell him about his father's attempt to bribe her? No. For all she knew, Noah had put him up to it.

Noah moved to stand beneath her. He didn't have his cane, and his limp was barely noticeable. His eyes met and held hers. "I'm not leaving."

Her heart and her stomach fluttered in tandem. Confusion swirled through her until she couldn't think straight, let alone breathe. "Doesn't matter to me one way or the other. I'll be the one leaving once I find a job."

"When you do, you let me know. I'll be there to help you get settled into your new place."

Noah's gaze never wavered from hers, and his intensity sent her back a few steps.

"I don't wanna move." Lucinda hopped down the stairs and ran to put her hand into Noah's.

"Don't worry about that now, Luce. Let's go finish your lunch, and then we'll call the Offermeyers to invite Celeste and Brandon over to play. You'd like that, wouldn't you?" The sound of another vehicle coming down the gravel drive drew her attention. Her cousin Teddy pulled his old beat-up Chevy pickup next to Noah's newer, shinier Ford.

He swung out with a broad smile. "Hey, Ceejay."

"Hey, Teddy. What brings you here?"

He sent Noah a pointed look. "Jenny ordered me to help Noah with the work on the house."

Noah frowned. "I don't need your help."

"Maybe not." Teddy sauntered over to the men unloading the steel pipes for the scaffold's framework. "But you might as well take advantage, because I'm not getting on Auntie's wrong side on your account. Me and her have a deal."

Noah grunted, and one of the truckers approached him with a clipboard and a pen.

"She and I have a deal." Ceejay corrected Ted's grammar for her daughter's sake.

"You have a deal with her too?" Teddy's eyes widened in mock surprise.

Ceejay scowled at him. "Lucinda, come up on the porch, and stay out of the way. I'll go make that call."

"I'll keep an eye on her." Teddy lifted Lucinda and spun her around in a wide arc.

Her daughter's gleeful shrieks filled the air. "She just ate lunch. You might want to put her down before she throws it up all over you." She smirked at her cousin before retreating to the house.

I'm not leaving. Noah's words sent ripples of emotion through her, touching off all kinds of internal chaos—hope and despair being uppermost in the maelstrom. Nope. She couldn't afford to get sucked into the hopeful part. No matter how wonderful he seemed, or how her insides turned to mush under his green-eyed scrutiny, the potential for pain Noah Langford represented made him a risk she couldn't afford to take.

He'd said some words that had touched upon her vulnerabilities, that was all, and words didn't mean shit. Picking her cell phone up from the kitchen counter, she swallowed the lump in her throat and punched in the numbers.

❧ ❧ ❧

"Mommy, Mommy! Can we have some jars? We wanna catch fireflies." Lucinda hopped up and down on the wooden floor of the veranda while her playmates nodded away in happy agreement to the scheme.

Ceejay's hands were full with the plates and cups she'd cleared from their outdoor picnic of hot dogs, potato salad, and fresh strawberries. "Sure, open the door for me, honey. I'll be right back with some jars, and we'll poke holes in the lids." Brandon beat Lucinda to the task, opening the door in an exaggerated show of male gallantry. "Why, thank you, kind sir." She tipped her head, carried her load into the kitchen, and deposited the dirty dishes into the sink. She gathered three mason jars with lids, a hammer, and a nail and returned to the waiting children.

"It's going to be a while yet before you can spot fireflies."

"That's OK. We'll catch grasshoppers until it gets dark," Brandon said.

Nine-year-old Brandon was the oldest of the three, and Celeste was a few months older than Lucinda. "I'm counting on you to watch the girls. All of you need to promise you'll stay away from the river." She looked from one child to the next until certain they understood she meant business. "I'll join you when the dishes are done, and I'll be watching from the window." She took a seat on the top step of the veranda and set the jars down. "Stay on this side of the walnut trees. Fireflies and grasshoppers love the tall grass along the edge."

"I know." Lucinda flopped down on the step beside her.

Ceejay punched holes in the lids under the watchful eyes of the three children. "Remember what I said. Stay clear of the river." She handed them each a jar, and they ran off in a flurry of excited giggles. Sweet Pea followed behind with his tail in perpetual motion.

How many times had she played the same game with her cousins and friends? Her aunt had issued the same warning about the river, had punched holes in countless jar lids with the same hammer and possibly even the same nail. Both were kept in a kitchen drawer and had been for as long as she could remember. Come to think of it, the nail was squared like the ones used in the nineteenth century. Ceejay studied the nail, imagining all the generations of Lovejoy children who had chased fireflies in the tall grass by the walnut grove.

How would moving affect Lucinda? She surveyed the orchard and the sloping lawn leading to the Ohio's banks. Rising from the step, she turned back to study the limestone home built by her ancestors at the turn of the century. The huge old house had replaced the original log cabin the family had lived in for decades. Lovejoys had occupied this land since 1868, and all her life she'd wanted to leave. Soon her dreams would be realized.

Why did the prospect suddenly feel daunting? She shook her head. *I've never gone anywhere or done anything, that's why, and it's about time that changed.* It was nerves, that was all. Maybe she'd take Lucinda to Disney World before the move. That would be a great start to her new life, and she could afford it. Once they were settled, the rest of the insurance money would go into Lucinda's college fund.

Gazing back toward the orchard, she sought the peach tree her uncles had planted when she and her family had celebrated Lucinda's birth. Her baby girl had been christened in that orchard, and the tree had been planted right after the ceremony, like all the trees preceding hers. The porch door hinges creaked behind her.

"I'm off to play bridge," Jenny told her. "What are you doing out here, Little Bit? I can hear the children in the backyard."

"Thinking."

Jenny came to a stop beside her. "You know, when Tobias Lovejoy returned to Atlanta after the Civil War, he found his mercantile burned to the ground."

Ceejay nodded. She'd heard the story a thousand times.

"The surviving Lovejoys wanted to rebuild and start over. Not Tobias. He wanted to head west and start over somewhere fresh. Even so, he helped them rebuild their business before he left."

"Has Noah ever asked what side the Lovejoys were on in the Civil War?"

Jenny chuckled. "No, he never has, and I haven't mentioned it either."

She sighed and turned to face her aunt. "I want to leave Perfect. You know that, don't you?"

"I've always known. I imagine what you're feeling right now is similar to what Tobias felt, and I'm sure it's a mixed bag."

"It is. I'm excited and scared to death all at the same time. I'm suffering from an attack of nostalgia right now."

Jenny laid her hand on her shoulder. "You won't be satisfied until you've seen for yourself what it's like to live somewhere else. I understand. Just don't forget your roots are here. You have a place to come home to when the world feels too big for you to handle."

"I'd better get those dishes done." She blinked back the sting of tears. "Go play bridge, and say hello to Sheriff Maurer, Uncle Jim, Aunt Mary, and everybody else for me."

"I'll do that." Jenny gave her a quick hug and headed to her car.

She returned to the kitchen and filled the sink with sudsy water. The children's excited shrieks floated in through the window. Smiling, she watched them running through the tall grass in the gathering twilight, their faces alight with joyful innocence. She wanted to chase fireflies. She wanted to run through the tall grass and feel the tickle against her legs like she had as a child.

Leaving the dishes to dry in the rack, Ceejay slipped out the back door, coming to a stop when she saw Noah watching the children from inside the small fenced yard. His hands hung by his sides. All his attention was riveted on the scene before him. Something about his posture, the way his shoulders were hunched forward, wrenched her heart. She approached, trying to see things the way he saw them. His breathing came in shallow starts and stops, and he trembled.

Childish laughter and Sweet Pea's frenzied barking filled the night air. The purity of their play held a glow all its own. Lucinda, Brandon, and Celeste hadn't a care in the world. In a flash of insight she glimpsed what being a soldier had cost Noah. Compassion overrode her own petty grudges. She walked over to him, slipped her hand into his, and laced their fingers together. "Noah."

He tugged her into his arms, crushing her against his chest so tightly she feared he'd break a rib. His tremors reverberated through her. She stiffened for a fraction of a second, easing once she realized there was nothing sexual about his need to hold her. She put her arms around him and ran her hands up and down his back, offering comfort and acceptance.

"I..." His voice broke. He cleared his throat. "I wanted to travel. I thought maybe it would help me remember...why I... why I went to war."

"I know," she murmured in a soothing tone. The warmth of his shuddering breaths against the bare skin of her neck sent a delicious tickle down her spine.

He straightened and rested his chin on the top of her head. "I don't want Lucinda to see anything but good in this world." He gave a shaky laugh. "Not very realistic, is it?"

"Maybe not." Ceejay pulled back so she could look into his eyes. "But I think I get it, or I might if you'd explain."

He shook his head. "I don't know if I can. It's about how safe and secure they feel. They've never been touched by anything remotely evil. I've seen…things. Things done…children who were used to fight dirty."

"That can't be easy to deal with."

"I've lost the capacity for the simple kind of joy they're feeling tonight. I'm afraid I'll never get it back. I don't know what it's like to feel secure anymore. I don't want that for Lucinda. I don't want that for any child." He drew in a shaky breath. "Watching them play brought it all back."

Ceejay held his face between her palms. "If I could take the pain away from you, I would. In a heartbeat." Some of his tension eased, and his hold on her shifted from desperate to something softer, more tender.

"Allison said the same thing." He swallowed hard a few times. "I have nightmares."

"They'll fade with time. You won't always feel this raw. Things will get better."

"I wish…"

She waited for him to continue. He didn't. "What do you wish? Tell me." She laid her cheek against his chest and listened to his heart pounding too fast. He smelled so good, masculine, with traces of the soap he used mixed with his own unique scent. She wanted to plant her nose against his bare skin just to breathe him in. It felt way too good to be in his arms—way too good to press so close to his warmth.

"I wish I'd met you before…"

"Before you lost your leg?" she whispered against his shirt.

"No."

She felt him shake his head. "Before Matt?"

He made a disgruntled sound in his throat. "No, not that either."

"What then?" Ceejay sucked in a breath laced with his scent and held it.

"Before my mind fragmented, before I broke. I wish we'd met back when I was whole and not damaged goods." His hands ran up and down her back at a frantic pace. "I know I screwed up. I should've told you who I was from the start. Can't you forgive me?"

Conflicting emotions churned through her. How could she explain that her attraction to him scared her to death? She didn't trust him, didn't trust her own judgment when it came to men. Noah wasn't to blame for the baggage she carried, but he sure hadn't helped her leave it behind by lying.

"You have to forgive me."

She lifted her head to reply, and his lips covered hers in the most bone-achingly tender kiss she'd ever been a party to. Her arms slipped around his neck like they had their own agenda, and she kissed him back.

"Mommy, why are you kissing my uncle Noah?"

CHAPTER EIGHT

CEEJAY SHOVED HIM AWAY WITH so much force he almost toppled. Noah managed to remain upright, but the transition from warm, willing woman in his arms to empty air left him off-balance in an altogether different way.

"Noah needed a hug, Luce. That's all." Ceejay ran a shaky hand through her curls and put more distance between them. "Run along and play. Mrs. Offermeyer is going to be here any minute now."

All three children stared wide-eyed for a few seconds before running off to huddle under one of the walnut trees. They placed the mason jars in the center of their circle and bent their heads to whisper over the captive flicker of firefly light. "News of that kiss will be all over Perfect by lunchtime tomorrow." She scowled and crossed her arms in front of her.

The movement drew his attention to her breasts. In the dim glow of the back-door light he could just make out the outlines of her hardened nipples against the thin blue cotton of her tank top. He ached to touch her and couldn't tear his eyes away.

"Brandon will tell his mom. She'll tell Denny, and he'll tell anyone who happens into the butcher shop."

He'd just bared his soul and begged for her forgiveness. Now she wanted him to apologize for kissing her? For a moment he'd been in heaven. There wasn't anything sorry about it. "Ceejay—"

"I need a death certificate to file a claim with the insurance company."

"Huh?" He ran his palm over the back of his skull.

"A certified death certificate for Matt." Her tone was all business now, like their tongues had never touched. "There wasn't one in the envelope you gave me, and I need it to file the life insurance claim."

"Oh. Right. I'll call Allison and have her send one." All sweetness and passion one minute, and shoving him away the next. He'd stepped into a field full of land mines and had no idea how to navigate his way through it to safe ground.

She studied the ground and rubbed her hands up and down her arms as if she were cold, though the temperature was still in the eighties. "The Fourth of July is next week. I wanted to warn you. My extended family and half the town will be here for our annual pig roast. My ancestor is Perfect's founder, and it's a tradition for us to host the event."

What the hell was she talking about now? *Focus.* "Right."

She pointed across the river with her thumb. "The pyrotechnics set the fireworks off directly across the river from our place."

"Loud explosives and a crowd of unfamiliars. Got it. Thanks for the warning."

"Plus alcohol. Beer mostly."

"Great. Food, fireworks, and drunks." Noah slid his hands into the front pockets of his jeans to keep himself from dragging her back into his arms. "Will Sheriff Maurer be here on the Fourth?" He watched the corners of her mouth turn up. She bit her bottom lip to nip her smile in the bud.

"He'll be here, but he won't be on duty." Headlight beams swept over the lawn. "That'll be Gail. Gotta go."

He watched her walk away. Had he imagined her response? No. She'd melted into him like chocolate on a s'more. Now her defenses were firmly back in place. No matter how often his stepmother had pushed his father away, what she'd really wanted was proof that he'd stick around.

"Damn." He hoped the same was true for Ceejay, because he didn't think he'd survive the alternative.

Erotic images of Ceejay naked and in his arms woke him. He forced his breathing to slow down and kicked the tangled covers off his overheated body. Lord, what he'd give to feel her beneath him, on top of him. Hell. He'd settle for anywhere in his proximity so long as she was naked. Noah blew out a frustrated breath. The physical discomfort he could deal with, but the ache of wanting her tied him into knots beyond his capacity to untangle.

The clock on his nightstand glowed a green 0500 hours. No use trying to fall back asleep. At least he hadn't been visited by the dead. Maybe horniness would prove to be his talisman against ghosts. He had Ceejay to thank for a full night without the usual specters. Facing a cold shower seemed a small price to pay. He got up and headed for the bathroom.

After his shower, he read the news on his laptop while he ate breakfast to the background sound of birdsong outside. The dark, rich scent of his morning coffee made the carriage house feel like home. It was home. When had that happened?

Once he was certain it wasn't too early to start work, he carried his cereal bowl and mug to the sink, gathered his tool belt and the bucket of supplies, and headed for the house. The scaffold had been positioned to the left side of the front of the house. First order of business would be the gutters. Maybe a good cleaning, paint job, and caulking would suffice. If not, he'd see about getting new gutters at wholesale through his uncles.

A classic Mustang convertible outclassed his truck in the driveway. Noah couldn't resist a closer look. The aqua-blue coupe had to be from the sixties. "Sweet." Running his hand over the original finish, he looked inside at the cream-colored leather bucket seats. His jaw clenched. Who did it belong to? Noah straightened and glanced toward the house. Maybe another man was sitting at the kitchen table with Ceejay right now, laughing and drinking coffee. His entire being rebelled at the idea.

She had the right to spend time with anyone she wanted to, and there wasn't a thing he could do about it. Besides, she deserved better than all the *dysfunctional* he had to offer. He might as well get his ass up on that scaffold, start working, and stop thinking he had a snowball's chance in hell with her.

Once he was secure on his perch, Noah pulled a plastic scoop from the bucket. A quick examination proved the gutters had some life left in them. He scooped out a handful of sprouting seedlings and decomposing leaves just as the front door opened beneath him. He strained to hear the sound of another man's voice.

Ceejay emerged from under the frame, wearing short cut-off jeans and a skimpy bathing suit top. She wore her hair up in a ponytail, and garden tools dangled from her hands. Noah watched her walk to the tidy patch of vegetables next to the house. She knelt on a foam pad and started to pull weeds from between the tomato plants. As she reached deeper between the vines, her bottom stuck up in the air, wiggling with each tug.

All the blood from his head rushed south of his waistband. He leaned out over the end of the platform for a better look.

"You better not be ogling my cousin."

Noah jerked and twisted around, grabbing for the metal frame to keep from falling. His right leg sent the plastic bucket of supplies sailing over the edge. It landed with a clatter a few inches to the left of Ted. Shoot. If only he'd had time to aim it better. "You idiot."

Teddy laughed and leaned over to pick up the packages of sandpaper and tubes of caulk from the ground. "I'm here to help," he called as he straightened.

"You can help by disappearing." Noah glanced Ceejay's way. She stood watching him with her hand shielding her eyes from the sun. Had she seen the whole thing? Noah muttered a stream of expletives under his breath.

Ted scrambled up the scaffold to stand beside him. "Auntie wouldn't like it if I disappeared."

He glared.

Ted grinned back. "What are we doing today?"

"Cleaning out the gutters. Then we'll sand, paint, and caulk. I'll scoop. You sand. No talking."

"Did you notice my wheels?"

Noah's brow rose. "The Mustang is yours?"

"Yep, it's a four twenty-eight Cobra Jet Deluxe. She's got a V-eight engine with two hundred thirty ponies under the hood. There are only three thousand, three hundred thirty-nine of them in the world, and *that* one belongs to me."

He couldn't ignore the note of pride in the kid's voice. He glanced over his shoulder at the Mustang. "Impressive."

"If you start being nicer to me, I might let you take her for a ride."

Noah grunted and turned back to the gutters. "Get to work."

"The Mustang belonged to Jenny's husband." Teddy gave him a sidelong look. "He died in Vietnam. The car sat in the carriage house under a tarp for as long as I can remember. Once I was old enough to have a job, I asked Jenny to sell it to me. She refused, and then she gave it to me when I graduated from high school. She said I could have the car in exchange for my help with odd jobs around here for the next five years. Stuff like mowing the lawn and fixing things."

"That explains why these gutters are in such sad shape."

Ted's brow rose. "I'm working on them now, aren't I?"

"How's she run?" Noah glanced at the Mustang again.

"Like a dream." Teddy puffed out his chest. "I took the entire engine apart, cleaned it up, and replaced all the gaskets and rings. She has all her original parts and only fifty thousand miles on the odometer."

"Your aunt doesn't have any idea how much that car is worth, does she?"

"Jenny's no fool." Teddy raised an eyebrow and faced him. "She did the research and let me know exactly what it was worth the day she handed over the keys and the title. Money isn't important to her. Family is."

Noah's gaze strayed back to Ceejay. Her shapely bottom was back in the air bobbing away with each pull. Maybe one night while she was at work, he'd plant some weeds in the vegetable garden by the tomatoes.

"So, what was it like? Being in the military, I mean. I'm thinking about enlisting."

His attention turned back to the kid. "For lack of anything better to do?"

"Partly. My folks want me to go to college. I'm not interested."

"But you *are* interested in becoming a human target for zealots and martyrs." Noah pointed to his prosthetic. "Do you have a burning desire to try out the latest and greatest in prosthetic technology, or are you just determined to become an adrenaline junkie?"

"Lighten up." Teddy scooted around him to sand the cleared part of the gutter. He blew out a long breath. "I don't know what I want to do. That's why I'm asking."

"How old are you?" Damn. Ted blocked his view of Ceejay.

"I'll be nineteen in August."

"You have time to figure your life out. Don't rush into anything. Why not take a few classes at a junior college while you're waiting for inspiration?"

"I've never been any good at school."

"Learn a trade, then." He stopped scooping to frown at Ted. "I thought Jenny said you farm with your father."

"Yep. We raise hogs, grow soybeans and corn. My parents want me to go to school to learn the latest and greatest in pig technology." Teddy shook his head. "Man, I really don't want to take over the family farm. Do you have any idea what hogs smell like?"

"I've caught a few whiffs."

"Being a hog farmer doesn't exactly make me a chick magnet."

Noah laughed. "And you think fake limbs and being messed up in the head will improve your odds?"

"The uniform might."

"Damn, you're young." He shook his head.

"So everyone keeps telling me." Ted picked a piece of flaking paint from the gutter. "Do you plan to go into business for yourself? Is that why you're doing all this work on the house? Jenny says you know everything there is to know about carpentry and painting and stuff. Maybe I could work for you. We could be partners or something."

"I'm not getting paid for this job. Neither are you."

"I know, but you could teach me things. I've lived in Perfect my whole life. I could get us more jobs. Paying jobs."

Even annoyed as he was, Noah couldn't help feeling pleased. It had been a long time since anyone looked up to him. "Why me?"

"You're not a Lovejoy." Ted rolled his eyes. "Do you have any idea what it's like to be one of us? I have two uncles, their wives and children, Aunt Jenny, two great-uncles, three great-aunts, and about a hundred first and second cousins, and that's only on the Lovejoy side. I can't go anywhere or do anything without running into family."

He swallowed. "Are they all going to be here for the Fourth?"

"Pretty much. Why?"

"Just wondered."

"So, what do you think? Can I be your apprentice?"

"Nine-tenths of this kind of work is pure tedium." Hell, who was he kidding. He didn't have any idea what to do with the rest of his life either, and he was going to be thirty. This job was time-fill, nothing more. Something to keep him busy until...*until what*? "Are you sure you want to learn how to clean and paint gutters? Do you really want to scrape and sand peeling paint for eight hours at a stretch in the hot sun for the rest of your life?"

"Not when you put it like that."

Noah grunted. He used to know what he wanted to do. He'd commanded a platoon of soldiers, and now he couldn't even command his own life. Once, he'd been certain and confident. His soldiers had looked to him for leadership, and he'd given it without doubt, without hesitation.

The one time he did hesitate, everything went to hell.

His heart pounded against his rib cage, and his mouth went dry. He tried to catch a glimpse of Ceejay to calm himself and couldn't. What the hell was he thinking? His chances of winning her over, of sharing anything even remotely normal were next to nonexistent.

A cold sweat and the shakes broke over him. The dead paraded through his fractured mind—accusing. Damning.

"A couple of curious kids is all," Noah muttered to himself. *"Gunny, fire a round into the dirt in front of them."*

"I got a bad feeling about this, Lieutenant," Jackson shouted over the sound of the gun discharging above them.

"You all right, Noah? You look kind of pale."

❦ ❦ ❦

It had only been a handful of days, but already his muscle tone was coming back. He'd traded in his PTSD pallor for a working-man's tan. Having a reason to get out of bed each morning and the satisfaction of a job well done lifted his mood.

He ticked off a mental to-do list for the day. With Ted's help, the job was going faster than he'd anticipated. The kid's company was even growing on him. When Ted stopped flapping his tongue, he'd turned out to be dependable and hardworking. He learned quickly and did a great job.

The gutters in front were done and they'd moved on to the porch on the second story. The brand-new circular saw he'd bought sat on the veranda, ready to go. Today he planned to tear out the rusting screen and frame in some new windows, turning the space into a three-season porch. He had Ted stripping the paint from the floor and trim on the inside so they could restore the space to its original glory. He walked around the side of the house with a smile on his face, eager to start the day.

The sight of Ceejay wrapped in her blue bathrobe and sitting at the table knocked the breath out of him and sent his heart pounding. Her hair was a riot of curls around her face, and he caught a glimpse of one bare leg tucked under the other. She had her laptop open, and she concentrated on the screen.

Noah climbed the steps and took the chair across from her. "What are you up to this early in the morning?"

"I'm working on my résumé." She spared him a glance. "Did you ask Allison for that death certificate yet?"

All his well-being dissipated. "Uh, no…I—"

"Are you procrastinating on purpose, or did you just forget?" She sat back and fixed him with a look that had him feeling like a dung beetle under a magnifying glass.

"It slipped my mind. I'll give you Allison's number, and you can call her yourself." Maybe if he could get the two talking, Ceejay's attitude toward his stepmother would soften.

Her mouth tightened into a straight line. "I'd prefer it if *you* made the call."

"I'm not the one who needs the certificate."

"Yes, but you *are* the one who said you'd do it." She lifted her chin.

The front door opened, and Jenny came out, keys dangling from her hand and her purse draped over an arm. "Noah, I'm glad you're here." She gave him a sunny smile. "Did Ceejay already invite you to our Fourth of July celebration?"

"No, ma'am, but she did warn me about it." He watched the color flood Ceejay's cheeks.

Jenny frowned at her niece. "We'd love to have you join us. The festivities start around seven p.m."

"Thanks. I will." He sent Ceejay a triumphant smirk. "Is there anything I can to do help?"

Jenny was already moving down the steps. "My brothers are coming over tomorrow. Why don't you and Teddy take a break from the house? You can help them set everything up."

"We'll do that." He waited until Jenny was in her car before turning back to Ceejay. "You don't want me there, do you?"

"I didn't think you'd *want* to come." Ceejay stared at her computer screen. "Drunks, strangers, and fireworks don't seem like something you'd enjoy."

"If you don't want me there, just say so."

"OK. I don't want you there."

"That's tough." Ted's Mustang came into view. He got up and grabbed his supplies. "I'll be there anyway. You may as well forgive me, honey, because I'm not going anywhere, and it's going to get damned awkward if you don't."

"Don't call me *honey*, and it won't get awkward because I won't be around much longer."

"You're not leaving the planet. Lucinda is my niece. She's a part of my life, and I'm a part of hers. I'm not giving that up." *And I'm not giving up on you.*

"Call Allison." Ceejay snapped her laptop closed and stomped back into the house.

He raked his fingers through his crew cut. How could one tiny female who looked so sweet be so damned stubborn? He wasn't the one who had wronged her. Why did she refuse to make that distinction?

Noah scoped out the grounds from his position next to the carriage house. Families had laid blankets down on the grass at the top of the slope. They played board games or cards. Some were eating. Lawn chairs in circles filled the more level spaces by the riverbank. Lovejoys manned the long line of food-laden tables under the canvas pavilions he and Ted had helped set up the day before.

The smell of pork, baked beans, and roasted corn on the cob made his mouth water, but not even the promise of great food was enough to entice him away from the safety of the wall against his back.

Too many strangers milling around. Too many firecrackers going off at random, sounding like gunfire and threatening flashback hell. It took a supreme effort for him to remain in the present. He swiped at the sweat on his brow. Everywhere he looked, children darted through the crowd, playing games of tag and keep-away. Their shrieks set him on edge.

He swallowed hard. He had to face this, or he'd become the town freak, always hiding in the shadows with his back against a wall. Hell, he already was the town freak. His eyes settled on Ceejay. She ladled baked beans onto plastic plates while talking and laughing with the families making their way through the line. Watching her calmed him. Maybe he could make it to the space behind her and hang out in the periphery.

Hell. No.

There were fewer people down by the river. An old willow tree grew near the water's edge. If he could make it there without incident, he swore he'd find a spot near the hanging foliage and sit on the lawn like everyone else. He sucked in a breath and pushed away from the wall. One step, two.

"Hey, Noah. Good to see you." Denny Offermeyer approached. He held his daughter with one arm. She wore a bright blue sundress, and her tear-streaked face was pressed close against his shoulder. Denny offered his hand.

Noah reached out and shook it. "Hey, Denny. What's wrong with Celeste?" Good. He sounded kind of normal.

"She tripped on something and went down hard." Denny gave the little girl a squeeze. "She'll be OK in a minute. Say, I hear you've been helping the Lovejoys out with their house. That's real nice of you."

"It gives me something to do, and I'm happy to help." He forced a smile.

Denny winked. "I also heard the kids caught you and Ceejay in a kiss."

"Uh…"

"Daddy, I want to get down now."

"All right, sweetheart." Denny leaned over and set her on the ground. "You go find your brother and stick close." He watched his daughter scamper off before turning back to Noah. "Why don't you and Ceejay come join us when she's done serving up those baked beans? Our blanket is right over there." He pointed in the general direction behind him.

"Thanks, maybe we'll do that." *Fat chance.* "I'm heading over to get something to eat now." Noah nodded and started moving toward the pavilions. "I'll pass the invitation along to her." Once Denny had turned away, he changed direction and headed for the willow. Maybe after there wasn't such a long line, he really would get himself something to eat. His stomach growled in protest as he moved farther away from the enticing smells.

He made it. Savoring his small victory, Noah pushed his hands into the front pockets of his cargo shorts and watched the river wind its way around the bend. What would it be like to walk up behind Ceejay, put his arms around her, and tell her that

Denny and Gail were expecting them to join their family for the fireworks display?

He imagined her glancing back at him over her shoulder, her eyes alight with love. Maybe she'd call him honey or sweetheart. She'd turn in his arms and plant a kiss on his cheek. He lost himself in those images of normalcy—ordinary moments spent with Ceejay as part of a couple. Maybe she was one of those women who liked to hold hands when they walked together. He hoped so. She'd—

"Noah Langford, you son of a bitch!" Teddy shoved him around by the shoulder and poked a finger into his chest. He held a plastic cup of beer in his free hand. Not his first by a long shot. "I just found out who you are." Ted poked him again.

"What the hell are you talking about?" Noah took a step back out of Ted's reach and tensed, battle ready. Adrenaline surged through his bloodstream.

"You're that asshole's brother. The one who broke my cousin's heart, stole her money, and left her knocked up." Ted tossed the plastic cup to the ground and lurched toward him with his fists in the air.

Noah stepped aside.

"I oughtta kick your ass. I'm *gonna* kick your ass." He lunged again, and again Noah dodged him.

Ted pivoted and took a swing just as a series of *pop-pop-pops* rent the air. Noah snapped, and his fist connected with Ted's chin. Out of the corner of his eye, he saw a flash of bright blue, a sundress. *Celeste.* Ted reeled backward, knocking into her. There was a splash, a shriek, and a child bobbed down the river. Sweet Pea ran back and forth along the riverbank, barking like crazy. Another splash and the dog was in the water too. *Great.*

Ted scrambled up from the ground. "Jesus! Celeste's in the river." He dove toward the riverbank.

Their battle forgotten, Noah snatched him back by his belt and tossed him to the ground. "You've been drinking. Stay put."

Noah ran along the riverbank, keeping Celeste in his sights. She was being carried away at an alarming rate. With the current as strong as it was, he feared he wouldn't be able to catch her. He had to get ahead of her. Celeste screamed for her daddy, and he caught a glimpse of the terror in her eyes just as Sweet Pea collided into her. She went under, and all thought left him.

He dove in headfirst and searched for a flash of blue or the paleness of her skin underwater. Sweet Pea paddled between him and his target, stirring the water into a froth and making it more difficult to see. Noah came up for air just as Celeste popped up to the surface, coughing and gasping.

"Sweet Pea, come. That's a good boy. Celeste, grab his tail." Noah swam toward the dog. She was crying now, but she managed to get a death grip on the dog's tail. Screams and shouts reached him from the shore, but he kept his attention focused on the dog and the child. Sweet Pea swam close enough to reach. Noah grabbed his collar. He took hold of Celeste's dress and pulled her toward him.

"I've got you now. It's all right. I won't let you go." She sobbed and threw her arms around his neck. The current had taken them around the bend. Now that he had the dog and the child, he could think straight. He'd run out of energy long before they reached shore if he fought the current. Instead, he let the river carry them, and steered at an angle toward land.

With only one foot to kick with, and his arms full, they weren't getting close to shore fast enough. He needed his arms. His heart raced, and he had trouble catching his breath. He was tiring fast. What if he couldn't get them to safety? "You're on your own, buddy. Go home." He let the dog loose and hoped for the best. "Celeste, honey, I want you to ride piggyback. Can you do that?"

She nodded. Her eyes were as big as saucers, and her chin trembled.

"That's good." Noah maneuvered her around to his back. "Hold on tight, now." Her tiny arms squeezed around his neck. The pressure on his Adam's apple made it even harder to breathe, but at least he had his arms free. He aimed toward shore, aware of the crowd gathered there in the tall grass. Sweet Pea swam in circles around him. "Go on, you stupid mutt."

The dog seemed to sense what Noah needed him to do, and straightened his course toward land, paddling along beside them. Finally, he felt the sandy bottom beneath his foot. He threw himself toward the bank. Someone pulled Celeste from his back. Denny and Ceejay's uncle Jim took his arms and dragged him out of the water. He collapsed onto his stomach and sucked in huge gulps of air.

This was all his fault. Shame tore him apart. He couldn't tolerate the backslapping gratitude coming at him from all sides. Sweet Pea chose that moment to shake the water from his coat, and the crowd started talking and laughing at once, diverting attention away from him.

When everyone started making a fuss over Celeste, Noah slipped away. He didn't belong here. If he wasn't screwed in the head, he wouldn't have reacted to the firecrackers going off. If the popping sound hadn't flipped his trigger, he wouldn't have taken the swing at Ted, and if he hadn't taken the swing, Ted wouldn't have knocked Celeste into the river. No matter how he looked at it, Noah couldn't deny that his PTSD had put a child's life in peril. Maybe it was time to leave Perfect before he caused any more casualties.

Celeste had come far too close to becoming another ghost haunting his dreams.

CHAPTER NINE

Horrified, Ceejay watched Ted shove Noah around and poke him in the chest. She raced to get to them before things got out of hand, but couldn't. The whole scene played out before her in slow motion as Celeste fell into the Ohio. She ran behind Noah down the path winding alongside the riverbank. Her heart leaped up her throat when he dove in after the little girl.

Once Denny and her uncle dragged the two to dry land, the breath she'd been holding came out in a rush. Ceejay put her hand over her racing heart and turned away from the crowd. She needed to gain control over her emotions. God, if Noah hadn't gone in after Celeste...what if Ted had fallen in, inebriated as he was? She blinked at the sting of tears and searched for Noah. Everybody from the party had come down the path after her. With so many bodies pressing close, she could only imagine what he must be going through. While everyone fussed over the soaking, distraught child, she watched him slip away. Her fear morphed into anger. She located Ted standing a few yards away and made her way toward him. "You moron!" She smacked the back of his thick skull.

"Ow." Ted frowned at her.

"What were you thinking? Don't you know any better than to poke a veteran suffering post-traumatic stress?"

"He hit me." Ted rubbed his swollen chin.

"You took the first swing." Ceejay put her hands on her hips and glared at her idiot cousin. "You're lucky he didn't snap your head off."

"Why didn't you tell me he's Matt's brother?"

"He isn't. They were stepbrothers, as in no shared genetic material whatsoever. The Langfords didn't know I existed until after Matt died. You can't blame Noah for what Matt did to me." She had, though, and the hypocrisy of her own words came back to hit her hard. Other than the fact that he'd kept his connection to Matt to himself, Noah had been nothing but good and kind. She'd repaid that kindness with her own displaced wrath.

Jenny joined them with Lucinda in tow. "I told you Noah was one of those people who can't help themselves. Being a hero is in his blood." She turned a baleful eye toward her nephew. "And you...I'd better hear a sincere apology coming out of that mouth once you've sobered up."

"I'm sorry, Aunt Jenny."

Jenny sighed. "Not to me. You need to apologize to Noah, and why are you drinking? As far as I know, you aren't legal yet."

"Dad said I could have a beer."

"*A* beer." Ceejay cocked an eyebrow. "How many does *a beer* add up to in Teddy world?"

Ted's shoulders raised a notch. "A few."

Ceejay shook her head. "You'd better ride home with your folks tonight, or plan to stay here, 'cause I'm not letting you drive."

"I'm not twelve."

"You sure?"

Jenny placed her hand on Ceejay's shoulder. "Go fix Noah a plate. He never ate, and after all that exertion, he must be starving about now."

Her daughter had two fingers firmly planted in her mouth, and her eyes were as big as saucers as she took everything in. "Lucinda, stay with Aunt Jenny." Shooting another glare Ted's way, she headed back to the food. Denny caught her before she reached the pavilion.

"Where'd Noah go? Gail and I want to thank him."

"I'm sure he went to get cleaned up and change into dry clothes. If you want, you can take Celeste inside and give her a quick bath. Borrow something of Lucinda's for her to wear. She'll be more comfortable."

"Thanks. I'll tell Gail. We were hoping you, Noah, and Lucinda would join us for the fireworks. Gail will be heartbroken if she doesn't get the chance to thank him personally."

"I don't know if—"

"Didn't Noah tell you? We talked about it before Celeste went into the river."

"He didn't get the chance. I'm going to bring him something to eat. I'll see if he wants to watch the fireworks, but I wouldn't count on it. I think the explosions are hard on him."

Denny frowned. "Oh. Right. I didn't even think about that."

"I'll talk to him, and if he's up to it, we'll find you."

"Good enough. I'd better get back to Gail and the kids."

She continued on her way to the food. Did they see Noah and her as a couple now? One kiss and the whole town was probably planning their wedding. She hated the lack of privacy, hated the way everyone stuck their noses into everyone else's business. That kiss didn't mean anything. Noah had been suffering, and she'd reacted, that's all. Even so, she had to admit, his kiss was the best she'd ever had...and she wouldn't mind a second helping.

She heaped two plates with generous piles of everything. With practiced ease, she balanced the load and headed for the carriage house. Ted wasn't the only one who owed Noah an apology.

She knocked on the door and waited. When Noah didn't answer, she maneuvered the plates so she had a free hand to twist the doorknob. "Noah?" she called out as she let herself in. The shades had been drawn, and Noah sat in the gloom on an unfamiliar couch. Come to think of it, the room was filled with unfamiliar furniture. Ceejay flipped the light switch and took a look around. "Wow. When did you get all this?"

New period pieces had turned the space into a cozy home while still managing to appear entirely masculine. A flat-screen TV had been mounted on one wall, and an overstuffed leather chair and ottoman took up the opposite corner. A thick floor rug with geometric designs in muted tones of sage, tan, and cream complemented the wood floor and trim perfectly, and mission-style end tables flanked a matching couch where Noah sat. He'd changed into dry shorts and a T-shirt. His prosthetic was off, and he was massaging the stump with both hands.

"It must hurt after running like you did." She nodded toward his stump. "Do you want something for the pain?"

He didn't look at her, but reached for his prosthetic and put it back on. "What do you want?"

"I brought you something to eat."

"I'm not hungry."

"Sure you are. I'll just warm some of this in the microwave." Ceejay walked to the kitchenette and deposited the plates on the counter. She opened one of the cupboards, took note of the brand-new set of ceramic dishes, and pulled out a dinner plate. "What do you want? I brought a little of everything."

"I *said* I'm not hungry."

"I heard what you said, but you never fixed yourself a plate tonight, and then you took that long swim in the Ohio. How could you not be starving?" He'd come up behind her, and she glanced at him over her shoulder. The despair in his eyes had her turning to face him. "You're Perfect's newest hero. Why are you looking like that?"

Noah's jaw tightened, and his gaze slid away from hers. "Like what?"

"I don't know." She started opening drawers, looking for silverware. "Kind of like you've lost all hope. Where do you keep your forks and spoons?"

Noah moved around her and jerked a drawer open with enough force to cause the stainless steel inside to clatter. "Why are you here?"

"I brought you something to eat."

"Thank you." His tone was flat and cold. "Now, please leave."

"I'm trying to be nice here, and you're making it difficult." She crossed her arms in front of her and stared at him.

"For how long?"

"What?"

"How long are you going to be nice *this* time?"

Ouch. Even though she had it coming, apologizing to him lost its appeal. "I don't get it. What's eating you? Everybody in town is waiting to shake your hand, and you're holed up in the dark like—"

"Shake my hand?" A strangled, choking sound broke free from deep in his throat. "For what?"

"For saving Celeste's life."

"If it hadn't been for me, she wouldn't have needed saving." Noah crossed the room and sat on the edge of the couch. He propped his elbows on his knees and buried his face in his hands. "Please leave."

"Don't tell me you're blaming yourself for what happened. You're not the one who started it, and how could you know the child would pick that moment to walk behind my idiot cousin? You're not—"

Noah's cell phone started to ring. He grabbed it off the end table without sparing her a glance. "Hello," he snapped. "Sorry... now is not a good time, Mom. Can I call you back? OK...thanks." He set the phone back on the table. "The death certificate is in the mail. Stay. Go. I don't care either way." He shot up from the couch and headed for the bedroom, slamming the door shut behind him.

She stood frozen in the middle of the living room. Should she force her way into his bedroom and insist he talk to her? Leaving him like this didn't feel right. She glanced at the piles of food she'd brought. Dammit, she had come to see that he ate and to apologize. She meant to do the apologizing part before she lost her nerve.

"Noah." She rapped her knuckles against the bedroom door. Muffled curses came from the other side. Taking her life in her hands, she opened it anyway and walked inside. He was lying on his bed with one arm pressed over his eyes. A lamp on the bedside table filled the room with soft light, casting him in shadow and sharp angles.

"I've changed my mind," he grumbled. "You aren't a mosquito bite I can't stop scratching. You *are* the mosquito, buzzing around my head in the dark and driving me crazy."

"I came to apologize."

He lifted his arm to stare at her in surprise. "For what?"

"For taking my anger at Matt out on you." She watched the play of emotion cross his face before he dropped his head to the pillow and covered his eyes with his arm again. She waited for some kind of response, anything. The seconds stretched out end-on-end between them. "That's it? You aren't going to say anything?"

"Your timing sucks."

"Seems like something we have in common." She moved to the edge of the bed. "Are you going to accept my apology or not?"

"Did you accept mine?" He pushed himself up to sit and leveled her with a look hard enough to dent her heart.

Heat crept up her neck and into her face. Stubborn, stupid man. "Fine. You'd better put that food away before it spoils." She fisted her hands by her sides and took a step back.

Before she could escape, he caught her wrist and drew her close. "Oh, no, you don't. You're not leaving until we get this straightened out between us. Why can't you meet me halfway, Ceejay?"

His eyes were filled with hurt, and his vulnerability tugged away at her resistance. If she let herself fall for him, she didn't know if she'd ever recover once he left. "I'm not mad at you anymore, but it doesn't change anything. I'm still leaving Perfect, and I—"

"And you don't trust me."

"It's not you, it's—"

"Damn straight it's not me. Why do you want to leave Perfect so badly?"

Ceejay's voice rose. "You don't know what it's like to have everyone in town know everything there is to know about you.

Otherwise, you wouldn't have to ask." She tried to free herself from his grasp. His hold tightened.

"All right, then tell me what it's like."

Blinking hard, she clamped her mouth shut. She didn't want him to see her as the pitiful, abandoned toddler, the fatherless girl, or the abandoned pregnant teen. A lump the size of Mount Rushmore lodged itself in her throat. More than anything, she wanted Noah to see her the way she wanted to be—strong, independent...desirable.

She wanted him to see her as a woman worth fighting for.

Where had that come from? Frantic, she searched for something to count. The slats on the blinds would do. Turning to face the window, she started a silent countdown. Noah took both of her hands in his and drew her down until she sat on the bed.

"Don't. Don't shut me out. Tell me what's going in that head of yours, honey, or we'll be here all night." His gaze slid over her face, coming to rest on her mouth. He leaned in and brushed his lips across hers. "Come to think of it, that's not such a bad idea."

A pleasurable shiver ran down her spine and warmth flooded her. "A few great kisses don't make me your *honey*. We haven't even gone on a date, and I've already told you more than once why I want to leave."

"Explain it again. Only this time, say it real slow so I'll understand." He tucked a strand of hair behind her ear. "You think my kisses are great?"

She couldn't help smiling at the hopeful tone in his voice. Somehow he managed to make her believe he really did want to know what was going on with her, like he really cared. Had Matt ever made her feel that way? She searched her memory for a time Matt showed genuine interest in what was on her mind, her fears, or even her hopes. Her search came up empty, and it was probably her imagination in overdrive when it came to Noah. Wishful thinking, nothing more. "Everybody knows…"

"What do they know?"

"My sad story. My mom, no dad, then Matt…"

"You still haven't tried to find out what happened to your mother?"

"No, I haven't, and I don't plan to either. You're missing the point here. I want to start over someplace where no one knows I *have* a history. I want to live in a city with more to offer than this small town. What if Lucinda wants to learn how to play the violin or take ballet? Do you have any idea how far I'd have to drive to get her to lessons if I stay here?"

"You and Lucinda have deep roots in Perfect. You have family here."

"Lord, don't I know it." She sighed. "You can't swing a dead cat by the tail around here without hitting a Lovejoy. That's reason enough to make a break for it." Noah chuckled, and the sound sent a thrill reverberating through her. "I've been thinking about your situation, too."

"*My* situation?"

"You can't spend the rest of your life taking care of Aunt Jenny's house."

He let go of her, scooted down so he lay on his back, and placed his arm over his eyes again.

"Now who's shutting who out?"

"I'm doing the best I can," he gritted out.

His anguish went right through her. Ceejay snuggled up to his side and wrapped her arms around him. This time, she was the one to initiate a kiss. She'd do anything to wipe the despair from his soul. He didn't respond at first, but lay stiff and tense beside her.

She teased and coaxed with her tongue against his sealed lips until his tension eased. He opened for her, and took over. His hands explored her rib cage, and his palms brushed the sides of her breasts. Noah Langford was bliss and heartache wrapped up in one sexy wounded warrior. Ceejay melted into him, savoring each stroke, every electrifying brush of his fingers.

"I forgive you," he whispered against her lips, ending the sentence with another bone-melting kiss.

Oh, God. The way he held her against him, the feel of his tongue sweeping into her mouth, she could become addicted to his touch, to the way he smelled. She was in real danger when it came to Noah.

He flipped her onto her back and covered her with his delicious male hardness and warmth. "Can you meet me halfway here? Forgive me, Ceejay."

"I have. I'm not mad anymore. I—"

"Noah?" Ted called from the living room.

Ceejay shoved herself out from under him and scrambled off the bed. Curse her idiot cousin.

"Why do you do that?"

"Do what?" She ran her fingers through her hair.

"Pull away from me like you're ashamed." He sounded hurt and more than a little angry.

"Noah, you here?" Ted called again.

"I'm not ashamed, it's—"

"Never mind." Noah rose and headed for the door. "I'm here. Hold on," he called back.

Ceejay followed. It was embarrassment, not shame. How could he not know the difference? Here she'd come to make amends, and somehow she'd managed to hurt him again.

"I haven't been in here for years." Ted stood in the middle of the living room, surveying his surroundings. "The place looks good."

The minute her cousin spied her exiting the bedroom, his eyebrows shot up, and his eyes flicked from her to Noah and back again.

Wonderful. "I brought Noah some food."

"He's eating it in bed?" Ted smirked. "Let me guess. You're—"

"Now do you get it, Noah? He'll be torturing me for the next decade. If this doesn't make my reasons for leaving clear, I don't know what will."

"She's right, you know. I will tease her. I'm really good at it."

"You have something to say to me, kid?" Noah crossed his arms in front of him, widened his stance, and straightened to military posture. He stared at Ted with a steely expression, and Ceejay caught a glimpse of the commander he'd been. His shoulders were broad, his waist trim, leading to narrow hips—heat sluiced through her in a rush. She had to look away, and turned her gaze to Ted.

"Yeah." Ted raked his fingers through his hair. "I'm sorry I came at you like I did. It won't happen again, and I hope we can continue to work together without any hard feelings."

"Apology accepted." Noah nodded once. "Maybe I'm hungry after all." He ran his hand over his belly and studied the food on the counter.

Noah hadn't looked at her since she'd jumped away from him. Were the two of them too screwed up to work their way toward common ground? Maybe two birds with broken wings could never fly, and no matter how much she wanted him, they'd always remain grounded. She had to get out of there. Without a word, she slipped out the door, giving Ted a knuckle to the shoulder as she passed.

"Ow. Why do you keep hitting me?"

Ceejay held Matt's death certificate in front of her. It had taken her an entire day to work up the courage to take a look. Paper and ink with an official-looking embossed stamp, that's all it was. It didn't seem real, this declaration that the boy she'd given her heart to, the boy who had fathered her child, no longer existed. Lucinda would never meet her father. Like she'd never met hers. The piece of paper in her hands represented another kind of abandonment—the permanent kind.

Lord, she needed time. Time to come to grips with Matt's death, Noah's connection to him, the Langfords...Why didn't anybody get it? This had all come at her too fast. Sighing, she folded the certificate up and tucked it into the envelope with her insurance claim. On her way to work, she'd stop at the post office, make copies of everything, and send it off.

At least she'd had a fantastic phone interview this morning, and for a great job too. And despite the awkward way she and Noah had ended the Fourth of July, they were talking again. She had a lot to be thankful for. Everything was falling into place. Her dreams were finally coming true, and she wanted to share her news with someone. Not just anyone—she wanted to tell Noah.

Ceejay fixed herself an iced coffee and another for Noah. The day was overcast and humid, and the chilled glasses beaded with condensation immediately. She placed them on the veranda table and walked down the stairs to peer up at the scaffold. He wore a tool belt low on his hips. His muscle shirt emphasized his well-defined biceps and the width of his shoulders. She took a moment to appreciate the view before calling out. "Hey, do you want to take a break? I brought iced coffee."

"Sure." Noah climbed down and settled himself at the table. He accepted the glass she handed him. "Thanks. You're looking happy this morning."

"I am. I had a really good phone interview with Riley Hospital for Children in Indianapolis." She sighed and leaned back in the wicker chair. "I think I might get the job."

"How long a drive is it from here to Indianapolis?"

"It's a little over three hours from Evansville, so about four hours from here, which would be perfect. We wouldn't be so far from family that we couldn't head home for visits when we want, and it's a big city with lots going on all the time."

"That's great. When will you hear?"

"The HR rep said she'd call Deaconess for references and get back to me by the end of the week. I might take some time off before the move. Maybe Lucinda and I will go to Disney World or something. We've never been on a real vacation." Noah nodded, but she couldn't read his expression.

He swiped a streak through the condensation on his glass. "I've been thinking about what you said a couple of nights ago."

"A couple of nights ago?"

"The night of the Fourth of July party."

She blinked in confusion, trying to recall everything she'd said that night. "Which part?"

"The part about not calling you honey because we've never gone on a date. Do you remember?"

Her heart skip-hopped, and her mouth went dry. She nodded.

"When's your next night off? I'd like to take you out for dinner and a show."

She should say no, but on top of everything else that had gone right today, the thought of a real date with Noah tempted her beyond good sense. One date, and in a month she'd put about four hours' distance between them. After a while he'd lose interest, and so would she. Heartache safely averted.

"Ceejay?"

"Sure. I'd like that. I'm off this Saturday."

"Great. Indianapolis isn't that far away. I'm sure I can find an RV camp outside of town. I'll look for a place that rents spots by the season, so I can spend plenty of time with you and Lucinda."

She swallowed hard. *Damn.*

CHAPTER TEN

"I PLAN TO TAKE YOU somewhere fancy Saturday night, Ceejay. Dress up." Noah took a sip of the coffee she'd brought him and watched for her reaction.

"Great." Color flooded her cheeks. She looked everywhere but at him. "I should go get Lucinda up from her nap." Her chair scraped against the wood as she rose. "Then I have to get ready for work."

Noah bit the inside of his cheek to keep from laughing as she fled. He'd figured out right away where her thoughts had taken her. Hell, he'd practically seen the wheels turning inside her head. She expected him to fade from her life once she moved, so a date or two seemed safe. Wrong.

He was beginning to understand how her mind worked. The pleasant thrill of triumph bounced around his insides. She'd agreed to go out with him, and he couldn't keep the smile off his face. Now all he had to do was figure out where to take her.

He leaned back into the frilly cushion. Stretching his leg out in front of him, he surveyed the sawdust and scattered tools on the Lovejoys' front lawn. After he finished his coffee, he'd clean up and go for a run along the riverbank with Sweet Pea. Time to get back in shape, and the new prosthetic made jogging possible. Maybe he'd buy some weights and a bench.

Jenny's neon-green Beetle bounced along the ruts in the gravel driveway and pulled up next to his truck. Noah got up and went down the stairs to help her with the bag she always carried home from the diner. "You're just the woman I wanted to see."

"I am?" Jenny handed him the canvas sack and turned to retrieve her purse from the front seat.

"Yep. I need your help." He followed her to the kitchen and placed the bag on the counter.

Jenny unpacked the leftovers and put them in the fridge. "I'm all ears."

"I have a date with Ceejay Saturday night, and I want to take her somewhere special. Any suggestions?"

Her brow rose, and she stopped fussing with the food to stare at him. "Ceejay agreed to a date?"

Noah nodded, and his smile disappeared. Maybe she didn't want her niece involved with a head case like him, not to mention his connection to Matt.

"Good for you." Jenny folded the canvas bag and shoved it into the broom closet. "She hasn't said yes to a date since the end of her sophomore year in college. It's about time."

A surge of relief made him shaky enough to pull out a chair and take a seat. "You don't mind?" He ran his hand over the back of his skull. "I know I have...issues, but—"

"Stop it, Noah. I couldn't be more pleased." Jenny took the seat across from him. "Now, let me think. You'll want to take her somewhere romantic."

"I was hoping you might know of someplace near a theater. Do you think she'd enjoy seeing a play?"

"I do, and I know just the place." She reached over and patted his arm. "The Red Geranium in New Harmony is close to a theater. The restaurant is lovely, romantic, and the food is wonderful. The theater in town used to perform Shakespeare every summer." Her tone grew wistful. "I wonder if they still do."

"You've been there?"

"My husband proposed to me at the Red Geranium." She sighed. "So long ago. New Harmony is far enough away that you're not likely to run into anyone Ceejay knows. She'll like that."

"Uncle Noah!"

Lucinda ran straight for him, and he hoisted her to his lap. "Hey, sweetheart, all done with your nap?" She nodded and leaned against him. Strong emotion welled up. He couldn't love her any more than he did if she were his daughter. God, he wished she were his daughter. He never would have walked away from the two of them. What the hell had been wrong with Matt?

"What're you all up to in here?" Ceejay walked in wearing her scrubs. Sweet Pea ambled by her side.

"Just visiting." Jenny winked at him.

Ceejay picked her car keys up from the counter and slung her purse over her shoulder. "Are you free to watch Lucinda Saturday evening?"

"It's Harlen's turn to host bridge night, but I'm sure he won't mind trading."

"I'll have Lucinda fed and ready for bed before I leave."

"Where are you going on Saturday, Mommy?"

"I'm going out on a date." Ceejay tousled Lucinda's hair.

"Who with?" Lucinda's fingers edged up toward her mouth.

Noah caught her hand in his. "With me, if that's all right with you."

Lucinda twisted around to look up at him. "Why can't I come?"

"Who would stay home with me if you go with Noah and your mom?" Jenny feigned a look of sadness.

"Harlen can stay with you, Aunt Jenny. I want to go with Uncle Noah and Mommy."

"Maybe next time." Ceejay leaned over and kissed her daughter's forehead. "I'm off to work."

He watched her leave. Sitting in the Lovejoys' kitchen with Jenny across from him and Lucinda on his lap filled him with a sense of rightness and belonging he hadn't experienced in a long, long time. Normal. He had to blink back the sudden sting behind his eyelids. Lucinda reached around and patted his cheek as if she knew what he was feeling.

The phone mounted on the wall rang, and Jenny pushed herself up from her chair to answer it. Noah savored the new feelings as he held his niece close. He let his mind wander to Saturday and his first date with Ceejay. Would she like it if he bought her flowers? He needed to get on the Internet, make reservations, and see what was playing at the theater.

"That was Gail Offermeyer." Jenny took her place at the table again. "Their mare foaled early this morning with twins. Gail invited Lucinda over to see the new babies and to stay for supper."

Lucinda slid off his lap. "Can I go?"

"I told them your mom can bring you tomorrow. I'm not feeling up to par this afternoon. All I want is a good sit down on the porch with my feet up and a glass of sweet tea."

"I can take her." The words were out of his mouth before he had time to think.

"You sure?" Jenny's eyes went wide. "I know how hard it is for you to be around strangers, and you've never met Gail." She gave him a pointed look. "She hasn't had the opportunity to thank you for saving their baby girl from certain death."

Was he up to Gail's gratitude? *No.* A fine mist of sweat broke out on his forehead. "I'm sure. You'll have to give me directions."

"The Offermeyers have the farm about two miles down the highway. You can't miss it. Take a left on the dirt road where you see a small school bus shelter that looks like a miniature barn. Denny's folks built it when he and his brother and sisters were growing up."

"Let's go." Lucinda tugged at his hand.

"I have to clean up first. I'll come get you in a little while."

"I'll call the Offermeyers and let them know you're bringing her," Jenny said as she rose from the table.

Thirty minutes later Lucinda was buckled into the car seat in his truck, and they were inching their way down the Lovejoys' driveway. "Ted needs to get a grader over here to fix this road," he muttered.

"Uncle Noah?"

He glanced at her in his rearview mirror. "What is it, sweetheart?"

"How come I can't go out with you and Mommy?"

"Sometimes grown-ups like to do things that wouldn't be much fun for little kids, but I promise we'll all do something together again soon."

"Like the zoo?"

"Sure, or maybe we can see a movie and go out for pizza afterward. Would you like that?"

"I love pizza."

"You and I are out together right now, aren't we? And this time your mom didn't get to come with us. That's just how it is sometimes." He watched her in the rearview mirror as she processed that bit of information.

"Uncle Noah?"

"Hmmm?"

"I wish you were my daddy."

Noah's throat closed. "I wish I was too, but we might have to settle for my being your uncle. It's the next best thing." He stopped the truck and turned to face her. "You know I love you, right?"

She nodded, her eyes solemn. "I love you, too. *That's* why I wish you were my daddy."

He reached out and smoothed a curl out of her face. "Nothing would make me more proud." Could he make it happen? Even if nothing came of his relationship with Ceejay, maybe he could adopt Lucinda. Little girls needed fathers to love and protect them. Lucinda deserved that, and if she were his, he'd see to it that Allison got to be the doting grandmother she longed to be. He put his truck back in gear and turned onto the highway. Ceejay would never agree.

Resolve coursed through his veins. A new challenge.

Noah splashed aftershave on his palms and rubbed his face and neck. He took the new shirt and tie off the hanger and put them on with military precision. Scrutinizing himself in the small bathroom mirror, he went over his mission.

Directions to the Red Geranium and the New Harmony Theater were tucked into the glove compartment of his truck. *Check.* Tickets to see *A Midsummer Night's Dream* would be waiting for them at the will call window of the theater. *Check.* Showered, shaved, and dressed. *Check.* He glanced down to make sure he wore matching shoes. *Check.* He'd brushed his teeth and gargled with mouthwash. *Check.*

Ten minutes till go time.

His stomach flipped. His first date with Ceejay. Hell, his first date with anybody since…crap. He couldn't even remember his last date. What would they talk about during the hour-long drive to New Harmony?

When did I turn into such an idiot? We talk every day. He grabbed his sport coat off the bed and moved to the living room to sit on the couch. He had nothing to do and eight minutes to kill before he could knock on her door without appearing too eager.

He should've bought her flowers. Maybe a single rose. Next time he would. He glanced at his watch again. Sitting here was driving him nuts. *Maybe if I walk real slow…*He shot off the couch and headed for the door.

Noah took note of the SUV parked in the driveway. *Damn.* He'd hoped to leave before Sheriff Maurer arrived. He sucked in a breath and knocked. The door opened. Sheriff Maurer stood between him and the Lovejoys. "Sheriff." Noah greeted him with a nod.

"I hear I missed all the excitement on the Fourth. You did a good thing, son."

"I was nearby." Noah shrank away from the words of praise. "Someone else would've gone in after Celeste if I hadn't, and Sweet Pea got to her before I did. I noticed you weren't there."

"I was held up at the station. Holidays are always busy days for us. Made it for the fireworks, though." He stepped back and held the door open. "I understand you're taking Ceejay out this evening."

"Yes, sir."

"You remember what I told you. I'm protective when it comes to the Lovejoys."

"How could I forget?" Noah gritted his teeth and slid through the door past the sheriff.

"Uncle Noah," Lucinda called from the second-floor landing. She wore a summer nightgown, and her curls were still damp from a bath. "You're dressed up."

"I am, and I see you're all ready for bed."

Lucinda nodded, and Ceejay appeared behind her dressed in a short, floral print sundress with thin straps where the sleeves ought to be. The dress emphasized her sweet little figure, and the high-heeled sandals she wore drew his eyes to her shapely legs as she walked down the stairs.

"She reminds me so much of Jennifer at that age," Sheriff Maurer muttered.

Noah raised an eyebrow and glanced at the older man.

"Harlen, will you help me move the food into the dining room?" Jenny came out of the kitchen with a ceramic bowl full of coleslaw in her hands.

Sheriff Maurer's posture straightened. "Be glad to."

"My, don't you look handsome." Jenny smiled at Noah.

"Thanks." Noah moved to the door and opened it for Ceejay. "We should be going." He got a whiff of her perfume as she passed by. She always smelled good. Their date was just starting, and all he could think about was holding her in his arms and kissing her good night—all night. Once the door shut behind them, he leaned close to whisper in her ear, "You look fantastic." Her head tilted toward her shoulder like maybe his breath sent a shiver down her spine. He hoped so.

"So do you."

Noah opened the door to his truck and helped her in, then took his place at the wheel. "I hope you like Shakespeare. I've got tickets for *A Midsummer Night's Dream*. We're having dinner first."

"I've never seen a Shakespeare play, but I've read a few."

"Never seen Shakespeare? Where'd you go to college?"

"The University of Evansville, and yes, they have a theater. I just never had the chance to go." She smoothed out the skirt of her dress. "Being a single parent is a full-time job, and so is taking a full load of college credits, plus I worked at the diner."

Great. They'd been in his truck, what, all of ten minutes, and already he'd stuck his one good foot in a cow pie. "How are your plans for the big move coming along?"

Her expression brightened, and Noah settled back to listen as she chattered on about her move and taking Lucinda on their first real vacation. He loved the sound of her voice and the way it washed over him like soft summer rain. He nodded and made the appropriate responses, encouraging her to continue.

Ceejay lit up from the inside out as she launched into her plans to find a little house for her and Lucinda to rent. "I'm going to try to find a place that will let us have Sweet Pea."

"You'll have to get some horse-sized tranquilizers to move him." Noah shot her a wry look. "Make sure the landlord doesn't see him before you sign the lease."

"I hadn't thought of that. Good idea." Her brow creased. "It would break Lucinda's heart if we couldn't have him with us."

"I can always bring him with me for visits."

"You'd do that?"

"Which, visit or bring Sweet Pea?"

"Both." She turned to look out the window at the passing countryside. "Of course, it's all contingent on my getting the job."

"Haven't heard yet?"

"Nope."

"Don't worry. You have skills and experience. If you don't get this job, you'll get the next." The pleased expression she turned his way made his head spin. He'd best focus on getting them to New Harmony in one piece.

By the time he pulled into the Red Geranium parking lot, he'd regained his equilibrium enough to shut the engine off and scramble out of his truck so he could help Ceejay out. He ushered her along the redbrick sidewalk leading to the crimson-colored doors.

"Oh, it's so charming." She stopped to look around at the garden surrounding the rustic country inn. "I've never been here before."

"Your aunt recommended it. Did you know her husband proposed to her here?"

"I've heard the story." Her eyes sparkled as she glanced at him. "Several times, and it's very romantic."

The happy smile on her face sent his heart soaring. "I reserved a table inside in case it was really hot out. I hope that's OK. If you prefer, we can ask for a patio table."

"No, inside is fine."

He opened the door and followed her to the hostess stand. Noah couldn't take his eyes off Ceejay. She'd lit up with excitement the moment they'd parked the truck, and he loved watching her take it all in. They were led to a table by a window overlooking the garden. Potted red geraniums filled the windowsill, and the table was covered in a red-checkered cloth topped with white linen. A large candle burned in the center.

Noah pulled her chair out for her before taking the seat in the corner, the seat facing out with his back to the wall. A busboy immediately brought water, and their server greeted them and set menus and the extensive wine list on the table. "Shall we get a bottle of wine?"

"That would be nice." Ceejay opened her menu, started reading, and frowned.

"What is it?"

"It's so expensive," she whispered.

"I don't want you to worry about it. I'm not." Noah reached across the table and lowered her menu until she looked at him. "Tonight is for us, Ceejay. Order whatever you want, and don't give the cost a second thought." He watched her bite her lower lip, her brow still creased while she thought it over. Adorable. Sexy as hell, and so damn charming. "I mean it, Ceejay."

She glanced at him, all shy and sweet, and his heart nearly stopped.

"Are you sure?"

"I'm sure." His chest swelled. He could do this for her, make her feel like a princess for the evening.

She sighed, and all the tension left her body. The smile was back, and she looked like a kid in a candy store. "All right, if you aren't going to worry about it, neither am I. I'm thinking seafood, the jumbo sea scallops with the ginger cream sauce. What are you going to have?"

"The rib eye steak."

"Hmm." She touched her chin. "You'd want red wine with that, and I'd want white with the seafood. Shall we compromise and have a blush?"

"Perfect. How about the Maryland-style crab cakes for an appetizer?"

"You sure know what to say to get to a girl's heart," she teased.

What would the establishment think if he lifted Ceejay out of her chair and held her in his lap for the entire meal? What would they think if he fed her one bite of her meal at a time from his hand to her luscious mouth? Noah spread the linen napkin over his lap, trying to hide the evidence of where his thoughts were taking him. "Save room for dessert."

The meal was a blur to him. Maybe the rib eye was good, but he hardly tasted it. All his attention had been riveted on the morsels going into Ceejay's mouth, and the warmth lighting her eyes as he attempted to keep a coherent conversation going. She leaned back and put her hand on her stomach. He followed the movement, wishing it were his hand there.

"I'm so full I'm afraid I might fall asleep during the play."

"If you feel the need to nap, you can lean against me." The server refilled their coffee cups and laid the leather case holding their bill on the table. Noah didn't even look at the total. He would've paid three times whatever it was just to watch Ceejay enjoy herself. He reached for his wallet and slipped his credit card into the leather. "We have time to walk around the grounds before the play if you'd like."

"I'd love it. It'll give me some time to digest the amazing meal I just had. Thank you, Noah. This was wonderful."

"The evening's not over yet."

He should be watching the play. Instead, Noah's concentration was riveted on the woman next to him. His eyes snagged on the rise and fall of Ceejay's chest while she breathed. He wanted to hold her hand. What if she pulled away when he reached for her? Unpredictable. That's what she was. Willing one minute, shoving him away the next. She'd been all warm honey during dinner, though. That had to count for something.

Ceejay shifted in her seat and leaned closer. He caught a whiff of her perfume, and his pulse surged. Should he go for it, risk the rejection? He wanted her fingers twined in his. Hell, he wanted her naked and in his lap with his arms around her. Were they too old to make out in his truck? He inched his hand closer to where hers rested on her purse. She glanced at him with a half smile, looped her arm through the crook of his elbow, and slipped her hand into his.

All the air left his lungs. He leaned back and held himself perfectly still, waiting for her to change her mind and pull away. She didn't. His entire world narrowed down to one thing—her hand in his. Hers was soft, warm, and small, while his was large and callused. He twined their fingers. Even in the dim light the differences in their skin tones fascinated him.

"Shouldn't you be watching the play?" Ceejay leaned close to whisper.

"I am." The way she smelled made him weak in the knees. He tightened his hold on her fingers. Now that he had her skin next to his, he didn't intend to let go.

She shook her head, gave him another heart-stopping smile, and went back to watching the stage. He sank back into his fantasies about the good night kisses to come and tried to shift in his seat to relieve some of the pressure in his lap.

After the curtain closed, they followed the crowd out of the theater and down the concrete stairs to the sidewalk. The night air had that velvety, still quality it sometimes took on during the summer. They moved along the sidewalk with the rest of the throng leaving the theater. Other than her brief visit to the restroom during intermission, Noah had managed to keep his hold on Ceejay's hand for the entire production. Their bodies touched occasionally as they walked. He'd be heading for a cold shower once he put her safely behind the door to her house. He didn't want to rush things with her. She'd bolt. "Did you enjoy the play?"

"I did. Dinner was wonderful too. Thank you for a lovely evening." Her free hand came to rest on his forearm. "You did really well in the theater."

Noah frowned. "Huh?"

"You sat with your back to the wall at the restaurant like you always do, but you couldn't do that at the theater. It didn't seem to bother you, even though we were surrounded by strangers."

"Oh." He relaxed. "That's because…"

"You were too occupied with other…*things* to pay attention?" She laughed. "So, tell me, Noah, did you enjoy the play?"

"Sure." Heat crept up his neck.

"I don't see how you could've. I don't think your eyes were on the stage for more than sixty seconds for the entire performance."

"Shakespeare is all about the prose. I listened."

She laughed again. "Liar."

She had him. What was he supposed to say? *I watched your breasts through most of the performance. I'd like to see them bare now, please.* That would go over well. Wait. She didn't sound annoyed or angry. Maybe…no. Not going to risk making a move on the first date. But they'd known each other for a few months, and that counted. Didn't it?

They'd reached his truck, and he opened the passenger door for her. He had to let go of her hand once she climbed in. Would she give it back? Knots. Ceejay Lovejoy had turned him into the human equivalent of a giant pretzel. A pretzel with aching, blue balls. He let his breath out slowly, slid into his seat, and started the engine.

"You're awfully quiet. Are you OK?" Ceejay slid her hand over his forearm.

"Sure." He concentrated on the traffic leaving the theater and tried to ignore the bolt of electric heat the contact caused.

"So, what *were* you doing while I watched the play?"

"I was concentrating."

"On?"

"I had to make sure you didn't stop breathing during your first Shakespeare play."

She glanced at him, her eyes sparkling with amusement. "How thoughtful."

"Yep." He tried to swallow, but his mouth had gone dry. "I'm a thoughtful kind of guy."

"What would you have done if I'd...stopped breathing?"

"Hmmm. Mouth-to-mouth, of course. Maybe a little massage." Were they really having this conversation? All the signals she was sending flashed *go*. He gave the accelerator a nudge. He couldn't get them parked in that dark driveway fast enough. Too bad he couldn't drive right up to his front door.

"It's good to know my life is in such good hands this evening." Her lips pursed like she was trying hard not to laugh.

"Definitely." He stared out the windshield. "Does this mean there might be a second date?"

"Maybe."

"Maybe?"

She shrugged.

Damn. And there it was, the push back after he'd gotten a little too close. *Don't back down, soldier.* "How about something more casual next time? A movie might be nice."

"I hear you drove Lucinda over to the Offermeyers' to see the new foals." She changed the subject. "How'd that go?"

"It went fine. Lucinda put her arms around one of them, and she wasn't going to let go." He chuckled at the memory. "Wanted to bring him home."

Ceejay sighed. "That doesn't surprise me."

"Couldn't she have a pony? I mean, with so many of your relatives living on farms, isn't there a place for one small horse?"

"Horses are expensive." She held up her hands and started ticking off the costs on her fingers. "Shoes, shots, worming, tack, feed, boarding fees, riding lessons. I can't afford all that."

"I could help."

"One, it's not your responsibility, and two, you don't have a job."

"That again?" He glanced at her. "I have money."

"When you say that, do you mean your *family* has money? 'Cause I get that."

He tightened his grip on the steering wheel and bit down hard on the reply he knew better than to make. Where had he taken a wrong turn? Ah, yes. Asking for a second date. Noah racked his brain for a way to turn things around while his truck ate up the distance to her front door. Silence reigned in the cab for far too long. "Ted is doing a great job on your aunt's house. He learns fast."

Ceejay glanced at him. "Good. It's keeping him out of trouble."

"Does he get into trouble a lot?"

"More than most of my cousins. He's the wild one of the bunch." She shook her head. "He's always been more like my pesky little brother than a cousin. He loves to torture me."

"You have lots of cousins?"

"Tons. What about you?"

"I have a bunch too. Nowhere near your clan, though." His grip on the steering wheel eased, and the Lovejoys' driveway came into view. Had he salvaged things enough to get her into his arms? He turned onto the gravel and inched his truck along, parking as far from the front door as he could without being too obvious. He unbuckled his seat belt and turned to face Ceejay— with no clue what to say.

"I had a nice time tonight, Noah. Thank you." She started to make moves to get out.

Who the hell invented bucket seats? "Me too. Hold on to that thought." He swung his door open and raced around the truck to get to her door. Helping her down put them in proximity. Noah drew her close, and shoved the door shut. Then he kissed her before she had time to object.

He didn't dare pull her too close, but, oh, man—her soft lips opened beneath his—he couldn't get enough of her. She closed the gap between them, pressing her delectable body close, and encircled his neck with her arms.

Take it slow. He broke the kiss and looked deep into her eyes, wanting to say…something, but what? All the blood in his brain had rushed to his groin hours ago. Speech was beyond him. Her gaze roamed over his face. Their eyes met and held, and he saw a need in her as great as his own. *The hell with slow.* He backed her up against the truck and took her mouth the way he wanted to take the rest of her.

She ran her hands up his torso and across his chest. He groaned and slid his hands up her sides and around to cup her breasts. She didn't push him away. God, they were a perfect fit in his hands. Her nipples hardened, and he ran his thumbs over the fabric covering them, catching her gasp with his mouth.

Slow down. She's not a one-night stand. She's…

The effort to rein himself in sent a shudder through him. He broke the kiss, drew her into his arms, and rested his chin on top of her head. The sound of their heavy breathing filled the air. Ceejay leaned against him and sighed.

He had to say something, redirect his lustful thoughts. Now that she was all friendly, maybe this would be a good time..."I've been thinking."

Another sigh escaped her. "About what?"

"Lucinda."

"What about her?"

"She needs a father." Ceejay went still in his arms. He pulled back slightly to look at her face. "I'd like to adopt her."

He almost went down on his ass from the force of her shove.

"Where did that insanity come from?" Ceejay fisted her hands on her hips.

"Think about it." Desperation clawed at him. His heart hammered away in his chest, and his palms started to sweat. It had all sounded perfectly reasonable in his head. Why wasn't she reacting the way he'd expected? "You'd have someone to share in the responsibilities. I'd help with child support and with the cost of college. Little girls need fathers. I want to be hers."

"Let me get this straight." She paced the length of his truck and came back to face him with her arms crossed in front of her. "You show up on my doorstep without telling me who you are, rent my carriage house, spring the Langfords on me without warning, and now you want to adopt *my* daughter."

He nodded.

"So, taking *me* out was all about wanting to be Lucinda's daddy?"

"No! It's not like that. I—"

"I don't need your help." She glared at him. "Did it ever occur to you that one day I might get married? When that happens, she'll have a father."

His chest tightened, and he had to lean against the truck. "No. That never occurred to me."

"Huh." She snorted. "Well, thanks a lot."

"I didn't mean it like that." Noah ran his hand over the back of his skull. "What difference would it make, anyway? He'd be her step. I'd be her dad. I wouldn't have a problem with that." *Like hell I wouldn't.*

"You and Ted have a lot in common." She sent another glare his way and headed for the house.

"What's that supposed to mean?"

"Think about it," she called over her shoulder. "It'll come to you."

Ted's an idiot. "Damn."

He'd slowed things down, all right. Brought them to a screeching halt. He sucked in a breath and pushed off the truck to head for his apartment and a cold shower. There ought to be more female soldiers. They'd confound the insurgents until they didn't know up from down. Then the enemy would be easy pickin's.

CHAPTER ELEVEN

CEEJAY DIDN'T KNOW WHAT UPSET her more, the fact that Noah thought he should adopt her daughter, or that he'd taken her out on a date solely to further that harebrained scheme. He made her crazy. Once she was safely inside, she slipped the sandals off her feet and dropped them by the front door. Swiping at the tears dampening her cheeks, she headed upstairs to check on Lucinda.

Disappointment ate at her. And embarrassment. The man could turn her into a quivering mass of sex-starved Jell-O with nothing more than a freaking *look*. The one that smoldered and said he wanted more than kisses. Had she imagined the heat? Was it *all* one-sided?

Of course it was.

He'd been softening her up for the *big announcement*. How'd he put it before? Oh, yeah. He'd been *working up to it*.

*Poor Little Bit, abandoned by her own mother...*She closed her mind to the painful refrain echoing inside her heart and balled her hands into fists. *I'm not that little girl anymore.* She was a grown woman with a great career and a bright future. This time, she'd be the one to walk away.

Sweet Pea waited for her at the top of the stairs. "Hey big guy, you love me, don't you?" She gave him a scratch behind one ear. His tail started to whip back and forth, and he followed her to Lucinda's door. Ceejay opened it slowly and tiptoed in to stand next to the bed. She gazed at her little girl through the sheen of tears blurring her eyesight. Lucinda had Boo-Bear clutched to her chest. She slept on her side with her covers thrown off. Two fingers were firmly planted in her mouth, and her dark curls clung to her damp forehead. She looked like an angel. *My angel.*

Getting through college had been an uphill struggle all the way. Being responsible for an infant, working at the diner, and taking a full load of credits—she'd had no time for herself. She'd never been able to go out and party or blow off steam like her friends. Her circumstances had set her apart and kept her isolated, but not once had she ever regretted her decision to keep Lucinda. Not once. A fierce love and the certainty that she'd walk through fire for her little girl filled her until she ached from the force of it.

Ceejay disentangled the sheet twisted around Lucinda's legs and pulled it up to her chin. She smoothed the ringlets from her forehead. Leaning down, she kissed her good night. The scent of baby shampoo and soap wafted up from her sleeping form. Lucinda never doubted being loved or wanted. Ceejay had made sure of that. She'd worked hard to be the kind of mother Lucinda deserved. She straightened and tiptoed toward the hall.

Did Noah find her so lacking as a parent that he felt he had to step up to the daddy plate? What gave him the right to judge her, anyway? *Damn him.* Hot tears traced down her cheeks again. She slid out of the room, closed Lucinda's bedroom door behind her, and leaned against it.

She didn't need the Langfords looking down their noses at her. The sooner she moved away the better.

❦ ❦ ❦

Ceejay finished drying their breakfast and lunch dishes just as her cell phone started ringing. She hurried to snatch it up off the kitchen table. "Riley Hospital" showed on the caller ID. Her heart raced. "Hello?"

"Is this Ceejay Lovejoy?"

"Yes, it is." She ran a shaking hand through her curls.

"This is Emily Larkins with the human resources department at Riley Children's Hospital, Ms. Lovejoy. I'm calling to let you know that all of your references checked out, and we'd love to have you join our nursing staff."

Ceejay wanted to jump up and down and make a lot of noise. She didn't. "I accept. I need to give Deaconess notice, find a place to live, and arrange the move. When do you need me to start?"

"Would the first of September give you sufficient time?"

"That would be perfect. Thank you."

"I'll be putting some paperwork in the mail today, and we'll let you know when we schedule the next staff orientation."

"Great. Thank you so much. I'm really excited about joining Riley Children's." Ceejay barely heard the rest of what Emily Larkins said after that. Her ears rang, and excitement thrummed through her. She closed her cell phone and danced her way from the kitchen into the living room.

"What are you doing, Mommy?" Lucinda looked up at her from her place on the rug. She had her plastic horses set up inside their plastic paddock and stable.

"I'm dancing a happy dance." She'd give her notice at Deaconess tonight. That would give her the entire month of August off, and that sent her into another twirl. She had the money from the cashier's check Noah had given her. Ten thousand would be enough for the move and a vacation, and she'd pay her aunt back the eight grand she owed her once the insurance check arrived. Maybe she'd even buy herself a new car. "I'm taking you to Disney World."

"We're gonna live in Disney World?"

"No, silly. We're going to Disney World for a vacation."

"What's a vacation?"

"Something we've never had. We'll invite Aunt Jenny too."

"And Sweet Pea?"

Ceejay laughed. "Nope. Sweet Pea is going to have to stay here." Maybe Ted could come stay at the house and watch the dog for them. Lucinda had caught the spirit of the moment and rose to dance with her. Ceejay grabbed her hands and twirled them both in a circle.

"What's going on in here?" Jenny beamed at them from the foyer. She had her canvas bag full of diner leftovers in her arms.

"I got the job in Indianapolis. I just got off the phone with HR, and the best part is I don't have to start until September."

"That's wonderful, Ceejay. Congratulations."

Lucinda bounced in place. "We're going to vacation!"

"Will you come with us, Jenny? I want to take you and Lucinda to Disney World. We can stay in their most luxurious resort and have all our meals served to us for a change."

"That sounds lovely." Jenny plopped down on the couch. "I don't remember the last time I went on a vacation."

"Mommy, can we bring Uncle Noah too?"

"No." Ceejay stopped dancing. She pushed back the hurt and disappointment Lucinda's question stirred up and glanced at her aunt.

Jenny set her canvas grocery bag on the floor. "Lucinda, do you think you can drag this bag to the kitchen for me?"

Lucinda grabbed the handles and lifted the sack. "I can carry it."

"You sure can. Thank you, sweetheart." Jenny waited until she'd left the room before turning to Ceejay. "I noticed you've been avoiding Noah for the past two days. Date didn't go so well?"

"Oh, the date went fine."

"Then what's the problem?"

"I want this to be a family vacation. That's all. He's not family." Ceejay stared at the porcelain figurines decorating the fireplace mantel. One, two, three...

"I wasn't referring to Disneyland."

"We're going to Disney *World*. It's in Florida. Disneyland is in California."

"Ceejay..."

"He wants to adopt Lucinda, OK? Right after the good night kiss he sprang it on me." Ceejay moved closer to the figurines and turned her back to Jenny. "I don't want the Langfords to be a part of our lives."

"They already are whether you want it or not. Allison Langford is Lucinda's grandmother. Noah is her uncle."

"Matt walked away. I never looked for him or his family, and I've never asked for a thing from the Langfords. They didn't even know Lucinda existed." She swallowed the rising bitterness. "I want things to go back to the way they were."

"You don't mean that. Think about Lucinda. I would think you, more than most, would understand how important family is to a little girl. Would you have wanted me to turn your father away if he had suddenly appeared at our door when you were little?"

Jenny's words stung. Ceejay closed her eyes and gritted her teeth while anger and shame circled each other inside her like boxers looking to throw the first punch.

"Noah cares a great deal about you and Lucinda. He might go about it all wrong, but his heart is in the right place. He wants to help."

She shook her head. Not what she wanted to hear when her pride had been so badly bruised.

"You have feelings for him, don't you?"

"I do not!" She let out the breath she'd been holding and turned back toward her aunt. "He mostly just pisses me off."

"Like I said." Jenny chuckled. "He couldn't get under your skin the way he does if you didn't feel something for him."

"Aunt Jenny, I put all the leftovers away." Lucinda skipped into the room.

"Oh, boy." Jenny rose from the couch. "Let's go see where you put everything. Can you show me?" She took Lucinda's hand.

"I have to get ready for work." Ceejay watched the two people she loved most in the world head to the kitchen before she walked upstairs. Ted would be working on the second-floor porch—with Noah.

The old, derelict space with its rusted-out screens, peeling paint, and rotting wood had been turned into an inviting three-season porch. The smell of new paint and varnish filled the entire second floor. Ceejay placed her fingers on the edge of one of the French double doors where it was taped and opened it enough to poke her head through. "Hey, Teddy." She ignored Noah, even though her heart raced at the sight of him. "I have good news."

"Yeah?" Ted didn't stop painting, but he glanced at her over his shoulder.

"I got the job in Indianapolis."

He stopped working and turned to face her. "Good for you, Ceejay."

She edged her way onto the drop cloth covering the newly refinished floor. "I was wondering if you'd be interested in house-sitting and taking care of Sweet Pea for a week. I'm taking Jenny and Lucinda on a vacation."

"I can do it." Noah stared at her from beneath his lowered brow.

"I'd be happy to pay you, Ted. How's a hundred fifty sound?"

Ted looked from her to Noah and back again. "That sounds great. Let me know when you have your plans firmed up."

"I will." She gave him a big *I'm happy* grin. "I'm giving my notice tonight, and I'm taking the whole month of August off. Will you help me move?"

"Sure."

Noah put his drill down and started toward her. "Ceejay…"

"Gotta go." She backed out and pulled the doors closed.

"What'd you do to piss her off this time?" Ted asked Noah behind the door.

Curiosity burned through her at the sound of Noah's low murmured reply.

Ted laughed. "Yep, that'd do it."

What had Noah said? *Let it go.* His reply didn't matter. She'd managed to avoid him since their date. She intended to avoid him from now on.

Ceejay parked her car in the driveway and glanced at the dash-board clock before shutting the engine off. Almost two a.m. She smiled, remembering how excited everyone at work had been when she'd told them her big news. They'd insisted on taking her out after work to celebrate.

Exhausted, she wanted nothing more than to fall into bed. She yawned as she got out of her car and headed for the front door. Fumbling with her purse, she put her cell phone and keys away as she climbed the veranda steps.

"Ceejay."

"Crap!" Her purse slipped from her hands and hit the floor. She bent over to pick everything up that had spilled out. "You just took a good five years off my life, Noah. What are doing out here, anyway? It's late, or early. Whatever."

"Feeding the mosquitoes, mostly—and waiting for you." He rose from the shadows to loom over her as she stuffed her things back into her purse. "We need to talk."

"It couldn't have waited until tomorrow?"

"No."

"I really don't have anything to say, other than no. You can't adopt my daughter." She rose, slung the strap of her purse over her shoulder, and tried to edge her way around him to the door.

He caught her around the waist with one arm and hauled her close. "That's fine. In fact it's better. You don't need to say anything. Just listen." He led her to the steps and drew her down to sit next to him.

"Noah…"

"All you have to do is listen." He glanced at her. "Matt stole your car and your money. He abandoned you at a time when you should've been able to depend on him for support."

"Not only me. Lucinda too." She started to rise, and he grabbed her hand and tugged her back down. She clamped her lips shut and fought the urge to pull away and run for the door.

"I know. My stepbrother lied, cheated, and used you, and I can't even imagine how awful that must've been. I'm sorrier than you'll ever know." He swallowed hard. "But I didn't do that to you. My family didn't do that to you, and it's time you got over being angry at us for something we had no control over."

"I know it wasn't you!"

"That's not what I'm getting here. Did it ever occur to you that I want to adopt Lucinda because it'll make your life easier?"

"No, it didn't. I'm thinking it's more because you think I'm a lousy mother."

He jerked around to face her. "How can you say such a thing, much less think it? You're a great mom, and Lucinda is one lucky little girl to have you. Did it ever occur to you that my adopting Lucinda is the only way I can make amends for what my asshole of a brother did, or that it's another way I can get closer to you?"

He ran his hand over the back of his skull, a gesture so familiar to her now that her heart turned over. "It's not up to you to make amends for Matt. You can't fix what he did." She stared out into the dark orchard. "I don't want you to get any closer."

"Why not?"

Why couldn't he just let it go and leave her be? She shook her head.

"Come on, Ceejay. Spill it. I'm not letting you leave this porch until you do, and let me tell you, the mosquitoes are fierce tonight." He slapped the side of his neck as if to prove his point.

They sat in silence for several minutes with her hand firmly grasped in his. She couldn't take it anymore. Stupid, stubborn man. "The reason I don't want you to get any closer is because it'll make it all the more difficult when you leave. I don't want Lucinda to go through that. Satisfied?" She turned away and struggled to keep her tears from falling.

"What makes you so certain I'll leave?"

"You will." Everyone else had. Why would he be any different?

"You don't know that." His voice was tinged with hurt. "And you don't even think I'm worth the risk to find out, do you?"

He thought she saw *him* as not being worth the risk? Stunned, Ceejay couldn't think of anything to say. He had it all backward.

"I'm Lucinda's uncle. That makes me family."

"Yeah, Matt was family too. He was her *father.*"

"Damn, you're hardheaded." He blew out an exasperated breath and stood on the step. Stuffing his hands into his front pockets, he stared straight ahead into the darkness. "Give me that second date, Ceejay, and a third. I want you, and I think you want me too. Constantly pushing me away is taking a toll. I'm not Matt, and I shouldn't have to bear the brunt of your anger toward him." He glanced down at her. "Take a chance on me. That's all I'm asking. Give us a shot."

"What if it doesn't work out?" Her voice sounded small, even to her own ears.

He scowled. "At least we'll know we tried. Isn't that better than always running away because you're afraid you *might* get hurt?"

She sucked in her breath. He was right. She was the one who'd been doing the running, and all because of her own fears and insecurities. All those dreams of a family of her own, a man to love her—she'd stuffed those hopes deep down because she feared they'd never happen for her.

What would it be like to let herself go and to fall in love with Noah? Hell, she was already more than halfway there. He was everything she could want in a man—smart, considerate, openly affectionate, and great with Lucinda. Almost perfect.

She frowned as she watched him turn the corner of the house and disappear. He thought she didn't see him as worthy? He wanted *her*? "Shit," she muttered. "It's gonna be another sleepless night."

🐏 🐏 🐏

"What're you still doing here, Jenny?" Ceejay ushered her daughter into the kitchen for breakfast. Her aunt was usually gone by the crack of dawn. "Why aren't you at work?"

"I took the day off." Jenny sat at the kitchen table with a craft magazine laid out before her on the table. "I have my yearly checkup scheduled for later this morning. I can't even have coffee. That's the hardest part." She winked at Lucinda and turned the page in front of her.

"What time do you need to be at the clinic?"

"Not till eleven. You got home awfully late last night." Jenny turned another page of the magazine. "I heard you come in."

"My friends took me out after work."

"I heard voices on the porch."

Heat flooded Ceejay's cheeks. She caught her aunt's eye and nodded toward Lucinda.

Her aunt chuckled. "What was Noah doing out on the porch at that hour?"

"I don't know. Maybe he couldn't sleep and wanted some fresh air."

"Oh, he wants something all right, but I don't think it's *air*."

"I'm going to go get my laptop." Ceejay fled the kitchen, and Noah's words came back to her full force. *I want you, and I think you want me too.* She wanted him all right, and it was driving her crazy. She was halfway up the stairs when someone knocked on the front door. Turning around, she called out to her aunt. "I'll get it."

She opened the door and came face-to-face with Noah. His green eyes bored into hers like he was mining her soul for answers. He opened his mouth to say something, then shut it again.

"Where's Ted?" She opened the door wider for him to enter.

"He's on his way." He gestured toward the stairs. "I need to get to the porch. I have to come in through the house."

"Sure. The porch looks great, by the way. It's probably better now than when it was first built." *Lame, so lame.* For the second time in the past thirty minutes, her face flamed. "I was heading upstairs for my laptop. We're going to make our vacation plans this morning."

"I can watch the house and the dog for you while you're gone."

"I know. Thanks." She started up the stairs with him right behind her. Hyperawareness of his nearness kicked her pulse up a few notches. "Ted could use the cash, though, and he's here almost every day anyway."

"What about that second date, Ceejay?"

"Still thinking." They reached the second-floor landing. Facing him was almost too intense, and her heart had lodged itself in her throat.

Noah took her by the shoulders and turned her to face him. Placing a finger under her chin, he raised her face and brushed his mouth over hers in a barely there kiss. Flutters and tingles zinged through her. Who knew such a tiny touch could cause so much chaos?

"Let me know once you've decided." He kissed her again and let her go.

She swallowed. "I will."

He nodded and walked down the hall. Man, he had a great butt, and he'd certainly filled out nicely in the few months he'd lived with them. His muscle tone had improved now that he was more physically active. If she were to be honest with herself, she'd have to say he was drool-worthy.

"You're checking me out, aren't you, honey?" he called without looking back.

"You wish."

His laughter made her heart sing a brand-new tune, and she floated all the way down the hall to her room. She grabbed her laptop and headed back to the kitchen. *So this is what happiness feels like.* How could everything suddenly be so good in her life? A new job, the prospect of living in a big city, her first-ever vacation, and a man who wanted her.

Ceejay walked back from the mailbox and flipped through the pile in her hands. She came across an envelope addressed to her from Langford Plumbing Supplies. Frowning, she tucked the rest of the mail under one arm, tore the envelope open, pulled out the letter, and began to read.

Dear Ms. Lovejoy;

I hope you've had a chance to reconsider your position regarding visitation with our granddaughter, Lucinda. As I mentioned during our previous conversation, we have much to offer. It is foolish on your part to reject the advantages to you and Lucinda based solely on the grudge you bear for my recently deceased stepson...

She tore the letter into little bits. She didn't like Edward Langford's pushiness, or the implication that she could be bought, that having them in Lucinda's life was all about *advantages*. Calling her foolish hadn't done much to make her more receptive to the idea, either. Maybe if he'd presented his case differently, if it was about getting to know Lucinda, loving her, then she could forget his arrogance. Was Allison like him? She'd seemed warm enough, but had she put her husband up to the phone call and this letter?

Confusion and guilt buzzed around in her head. She didn't want their relationship with Lucinda to be predicated by the advantages they could offer. Maybe she'd discuss it with Noah, explain her position, and have him talk to his folks. Why couldn't they give her some time, let her be the one to make the first move?

She walked back to the kitchen, put the mail on the table, and threw the scraps of paper into the trash. Her list of rental units and telephone numbers lay on the counter. She glanced at the "Award-Winning Hogs" calendar on the kitchen wall and started to calculate. Five more shifts spread out over the next nine days, and then she'd be free. If she called and set up appointments to look at her list of possible homes, she could head up to Indianapolis next week on her days off. Lucinda would love staying in a motel with a pool.

The kitchen phone rang, interrupting her thoughts. She rose from her place at the table and picked up the receiver. "Hello."

"Is this Jennifer Hoffman?"

"No, this is her niece. She's at work. Can I take a message?"

"Yes, I'm calling on behalf of Dr. Jacobs, from the radiology department at United Health Clinic. Could you have Mrs. Hoffman return my call as soon as possible?"

"Sure. Hold on a second." She set the receiver on the counter and grabbed a piece of paper and her pen from the kitchen table. She hurried back to the phone. "I'm ready." After she wrote all the necessary information down, she hung up with a frown. Probably nothing.

"Mommy, me and Sweet Pea are hungry." Lucinda came in through the kitchen door with the dog behind her.

"Huh. Had a conversation with him about it, did you?"

She nodded.

"Gotta make a few more playdates for you, Lucinda. With children, not dogs or ponies."

"Can I have—"

"Don't even say it. You already know the answer."

"But—"

"No ponies, Luce. We're going to be living in a city. How about taking violin lessons?"

Lucinda's brow scrunched. "What's a violin?"

"It's a musical instrument." She opened the refrigerator door. The shelves were full to overflowing with diner leftovers. Time to send a bucket home with Ted for her uncle's hogs to dine on. Speaking of Ted—maybe the two guys working upstairs could help reduce the volume. "Run upstairs to the porch and see if Ted and Noah want to eat lunch with us."

Her daughter's expression went from disappointment to glee in a nanosecond. "OK."

Soon she heard male voices and work boots coming down the stairs. A good sound. Long ago, the old place had been filled with the deep voices of the Lovejoy men, and she was certain the house missed all the noise a large family generated. Noah and Ted walked into the kitchen and headed to the sink to wash their hands. Ceejay's heart did a somersault when Noah's eyes caught hers.

"We have a fridge full of leftovers. What do you two want?" She turned back to the food to hide her blush. "I could make meat loaf sandwiches, meatball sandwiches, or I can heat up some roasted chicken, and all of the above come with...?" She turned expectantly to Ted and Lucinda.

"Mashed potatoes!" Lucinda cried.

Noah laughed. "I could go for a meat loaf sandwich."

"Throw me some chicken and mashed potatoes, and I'll heat them in the microwave." Ted shook his head. "You know it's illegal for Aunt Jenny to bring these leftovers home, don't you? We could set up a barrel for her, and I could pick it up every day for the hogs. Lots of farmers are doing that now."

"I know. You tell me at least once a month. You need to have this conversation with Jenny."

"Nope. I've tried. You'd have better luck." Ted grabbed four plates from the cabinet. "Say, Noah, I have this friend who's in a band. They've got a gig at a club in Evansville this weekend. He gave me a couple of free tickets. You wanna go check them out Saturday night?"

"A huge hall full of strangers and loud music?" Ceejay whipped around and glared at her cousin. "I don't think so."

Noah's eyebrows shot up, and she bit her lip.

"First of all, I was asking him, not you, Nurse Nosy." Ted glared right back. "What do you think, Noah? I hear this club is a huge draw for hot chicks." He raised an eyebrow. "I can be your wingman, or you can be mine, depending on who we meet."

Noah opened his mouth to reply, and Ceejay cut him off. "Bad plan."

"I'm in. Let's do it." Noah grabbed silverware from the drawer and set it out on the table. "A night out might be fun."

"Great." Ted smirked at her. "If any of the ladies ask what I do for a living, I'm telling them I'm a contractor in the home remodeling industry. I'd appreciate it if you'd back me up on that."

"Don't bring up the hogs?" Noah laughed. "All right, so long as you introduce me as your boss."

Ceejay fumed. The thought of Noah flirting with other women made her edgy. What was Ted thinking? No way would Noah be able to handle a crowd of rowdies like that. She slapped a piece of meat loaf between two slices of bread, cut it in half with a vengeance, and dropped it on the plate in front of Noah.

"Thanks." Noah smiled sweetly. "Pass me the ketchup, please."

"Get it yourself." She stomped back to the counter. "Lucinda, what do you want?"

"A pony."

Ted and Noah laughed, and it was all she could do to keep from lobbing cold mashed potatoes at the three of them. "What would you like to *eat*?"

The microwave dinged, and Ted removed the plate. "You want a chicken drumstick and potatoes, Luce?"

"Yes, please. Mommy, we gotta have a vegetable or a fruit, right?"

"That's right. How about grapes?"

"While you're up, could you *please* get the ketchup?" Noah glanced in her direction.

"Didn't hear me the first time?" she grumbled.

Ted laughed. "I think you've pissed her off again."

"I don't know how." Noah rose from the table and came to stand behind her at the fridge. He reached around her and plucked the bottle of ketchup from the door compartment. "Didn't do anything."

He brushed against her back, igniting a heat wave. She huffed out a frustrated breath and grabbed the grapes. "Come get the rest of these leftovers before you head home, Ted. I'll put the bucket on the counter."

Ceejay grabbed the bowl of grapes and took them to the sink to wash, and placed a handful on a paper towel for her daughter. While she made her own sandwich, she let the chatter between her daughter and the men buzz around her. Noah and Ted discussed work they had to do, what they'd move onto next, and Lucinda piped in with excited comments about vacations and Disney World.

The two men gulped down their meals, brought their dirty dishes to the sink, and left. The room went back to being way too quiet.

After she'd cleaned up from lunch, read Lucinda a story, and tucked her in for a nap, Ceejay went back to the kitchen and made some calls. She surveyed her list of possible rental houses. She'd managed to set up three appointments for next week. Hopefully, one of the units would work out. She stood up and stretched. Better get that bucket for Ted. He'd be heading home soon. Then she'd go wake Lucinda. The front door opened. She glanced at the kitchen clock and grabbed the message she'd taken for her aunt.

Jenny swept into the kitchen, smiled her way, and set her things on the table.

"You've got a message here from the radiology department at United." Ceejay handed her the slip of paper. "You're supposed to call them back right away."

Jenny's brow furrowed as she took the paper. Ceejay started unloading the bag. Once the food had been crammed into the fridge, she turned to face her aunt. "Make that call, and don't worry. Most callbacks are because they want to take another look at something that ends up being nothing."

"I will."

"I'm going to get Lucinda up from her nap."

Twenty minutes later, Ceejay walked into the kitchen to find her aunt sitting at the table and staring into space. Jenny's mouth was set in a straight line, and she looked pale. "Jenny?"

"Where's Lucinda?"

"She'll be down in a minute. What's wrong?"

"I...they want me to come in tomorrow...for a biopsy."

"Oh, Jenny." She leaned down and gave her aunt a hug. As a nurse, she knew how these things went. "Nine times out of ten it's nothing but fibrous tissue or a cyst."

Her aunt nodded.

"I'll take you."

"I'd appreciate that."

She hugged her aunt's shoulders again and straightened. "Probably nothing." Statistics were in their favor, and most likely Jenny's biopsy would turn out fine. Still, Ceejay needed someone to tell *her* that everything would be all right. A rush of longing swept through her. She wanted Noah.

CHAPTER TWELVE

Noah peeled blue tape from the freshly painted walls and thought about the lunch he'd had with Ceejay earlier. She cared enough to be concerned about him, and a thread of pleasure still tugged through him because of it, but hell. Didn't she see him as a man capable of making his own decisions? That part pissed him off. "You *do* know I'm not going to any club with you Saturday night, right?"

"Yep." Ted snorted. "I know."

Wadding up the sticky mess in his hands, Noah moved to the next window frame. Maybe laying it all on the line with her had been a mistake. The last thing he wanted or needed was to be coddled, and he sure as hell didn't need her protection.

"You *do* know I don't have any musician friends, right?"

"Figured as much." Noah glanced at Ted. "Why'd you say it?"

Ted shrugged. "Because I know my cousin."

"Meaning?"

"Haven't you noticed the way she looks at you?"

"Sure." Noah sighed. "I'm *real* familiar with her look of annoyance."

"Man, I may be young, but you're blind."

Noah stopped pulling tape and turned to him. "What am I missing?"

"Ceejay has it bad for you." Ted raised an eyebrow at him. "She looks at you like you're the last hot fudge sundae on earth, and she can't find a spoon."

"I don't think so."

"You saw her face when I brought up other women, right?"

Noah summoned her image. When they were talking about the club, her mouth had been turned down, her expression definitely displeased. "She looked…"

"Like she just ate a bug?" Ted laughed. "Jealousy is a powerful motivator."

Was it possible he'd misinterpreted her reaction? It would explain why she'd gotten so cranky. "What did you hope to accomplish?"

"First off, I like to push her buttons. She's easy to rattle, and it's fun. Second, she needs a shove in the right direction."

Ted saw *him* as a partner material for Ceejay? A gratifying ping bounced through Noah. "What makes you think pushing her my way is a good idea?"

"Everyone can see the way you two look at each other." Ted shot him an incredulous look. "You could both use a shove."

"How do I look at her?" Noah frowned. Had he been that obvious?

"Like she's a thick T-bone steak grilled to perfection and served with all the fixings, and you can't find—"

"A knife and fork?" Noah laughed. "Hell, I'd use my hands."

"Exactly. Why'd you agree to go to the nonexistent club?"

"I didn't like the way she answered for me." Noah surveyed the porch. His stump ached as it always did when he'd spent too much time upright. "I'll put the new hardware on the doors, and we're done here. Tomorrow we'll start on the outside window frames."

"Why are you doing all this?"

"All of what?"

"Putting in all these hours on a house that doesn't belong to you, spending your own money on materials."

"It's complicated."

"Break it down."

"Matt."

"OK, I get that part, but it's not your deal. Never was. Plus, the house belongs to Jenny, not Ceejay."

"PTSD."

"Come again?"

"I need something to do, but…" Noah glanced away.

"Can't face working for somebody else?"

Noah nodded.

"You ought to start your own business. You can do all this." Ted gestured to the finished three-season porch. "You definitely have skills, and this kind of work doesn't require lots of talking or interacting with the customers."

"It does. You don't know what it's like to face an unhappy customer or some asshole who's trying to get something for nothing. I do. I grew up in this type of business." Noah shook his head. "I couldn't handle some irate homeowner in my face because the color of the paint didn't turn out exactly the way they thought it would. I'd snap."

"That's what you have me for." Ted pointed to himself with his thumb. "I'm great with people."

"You sure this is what you want to do with your life?" *Is this how I want to spend my life?* He surveyed the three-season porch, with its refinished hardwood floor and trim, new windows and fresh paint. Returning the old home to its former glory satisfied him. The job gave him a reason to get up in the morning, but he suspected the good feelings had more to do with the people living in the house than the work itself.

"For now." Ted's expression grew serious. "At least give it some thought."

"I will." Noah threw the wadded-up ball of painter's tape into the cardboard box full of debris. "You think Ceejay has it bad for me, huh?"

"I know she does, and it scares her shitless." Ted scowled at him. "If you hurt her, there will be consequences."

Noah widened his stance and crossed his arms in front of him. He gave Ted his best military glare. "You threatening me, kid?"

"Hell, yeah. I'll sic Sheriff Maurer on your ass."

Noah threw his head back and laughed, and Ted joined in. He was the right direction for Ceejay.

Now all he had to do was convince her.

"Noah, check out that civilian truck heading our way."

He dropped the map he'd been studying and stared in horror. Ceejay was driving the Humvee, and he knew what was coming. "Stop the vehicle."

"That truck—"

Where was that hammering noise coming from? Bile rose in his throat as he searched for the new threat. "It's an order. Stop the Humvee and get out. Now."

"Noah, I don't like the looks of that vehicle. Could be insurgents..."

Panic clawed at him. Not Ceejay! "Stop this goddamned vehicle. Run!"

"...might be carrying improvised explosives."

"Why won't you look at me? LOOK AT ME, *Ceejay.*"

"Noah, I don't have a good feeling about this."

Why the hell didn't she respond to his order, dammit? His gaze flew to the truck full of explosives heading straight for them. No, no, no...can't let this happen. Not Ceejay. Not her!

"STOP!"

"NOAH!"

He woke with a start, drenched in sweat, with the pounding on his door synced to the pounding in his chest.

"Noah, I know you're in there."

"Dammit." He drew in a breath and glanced at his clock. Almost 0100 hours. What the hell? "I'm coming," he shouted. "Give me a minute." The pounding on the door stopped. His heart was another matter. He threw his blanket off, swung his good leg over the edge, and reached for his prosthetic. Clearing the cobwebs from his brain, he took off for the door. Ceejay needed him.

He made it in seconds, turned the dead bolt, and almost tore the door from the hinges getting it open. She stood in the dim glow of the backyard light, still wearing her scrubs from work. He ran his eyes over her. She looked all right. "Who's hurt?"

"Nobody."

"Fire?"

She shook her head, and some of the tension leached out of him. "What is it? What's wrong?"

"I...I need to talk to you."

"Now?" He stepped out of the way to let her in and shoved the door shut behind them.

She nodded, and her eyes pooled with tears. What else could he do but draw her into his arms. "What's wrong, sweetheart?"

"This isn't going to make any sense," she mumbled into his chest.

Probably not. "I'm listening."

"It's...complicated."

When wasn't it complicated between the two of them? Her warm tears dampened the front of his T-shirt, and his insides melted. "All right. It's complicated. Maybe between the two of us we can work it out." He pulled back to look into her face. "You've come this far, right? I'm here, and you have my undivided attention."

Having her in his arms and in his apartment wreaked havoc on him. Already he was hard and wanting her, and they hadn't even kissed. *Not cool. She's in tears, dammit.* His jaw tightened, and he tried to focus on her distress rather than his need to get deep inside her. "Let's sit down."

She nodded against him, and he inhaled the clean, flowery scent of the shampoo she used. His groin tightened even more. *Shit.* He led her over to the couch and waited until she sat down. There was no hiding the way his boxers tented in front. She noticed. Eyes wide, her gaze slid over him and his dick jerked in response—*boy, howdy, here I am.*

"I'm going to go throw some pants on. Be right back." *Pull it together, soldier. Straighten up.* Hell, he couldn't get much straighter, or much more *up.* He slipped into a pair of jeans, grabbed a few pieces of tissue, and headed back to the living room. Taking a seat beside her, he handed the wad of tissues over. "What's going on?"

Ceejay wiped her eyes and blew her nose. "It's Jenny."

"What about her?"

"She…she has to have a biopsy later this morning, and…" She bit her lower lip.

The gesture was too much to bear. Noah leaned close and brushed a kiss across her forehead. She sent him a look so full of vulnerability that he snatched her up and held her on his lap. He loved how tiny she was and how good she felt in his arms. "Go on."

"It…it got me thinking." She put her head down on his shoulder and sighed. "I wanted to talk to you before we know the results."

Noah frowned. Where the hell was she going with this?

"You're worth the risk, Noah," she whispered against his neck.

"That's good." He went on full alert. Had he heard her right? "I'm glad you think so."

"I want to be with you."

"*With* me?"

"Tonight."

He gulped. "I want to be…uh…*with* you, too, but don't we want to take things slow? We've only had the one date."

"Technically we've had three." She looked up at him through her lashes and pressed her palm against his chest. "The tour of Perfect and our lunch date."

Could she feel how hard his heart was beating? "That wasn't really a—"

"And our trip to the zoo."

"We can wait. There's no rush." Even if it meant his balls fell off. He didn't want to get it wrong with her. For reasons he didn't care to examine, getting it right with Ceejay was an all-encompassing imperative. *Everything* depended on it. "You're upset about Jenny right now."

"That's just it." She straightened and twisted in his lap to face him. "I don't want to wait until we know the results. If it's good news, you'll think I'm with you to celebrate. If it's bad news, then you'll think it's because I need to be comforted."

He blinked. "I'm not that deep. Once I have you in my bed, I won't be thinking at all." The way she smiled at his words undid him. "But, um...obviously you've...given this a great deal of thought." Not that he followed her logic. What the hell was he doing, trying to talk her out of his bed?

She nodded and shifted in his lap. "I've *been* thinking about it since you showed up on our front porch."

Say what? Her movements sent searing heat pulsing through him, robbing him of reason. He leaned in for a kiss. She wrapped her arms around his neck and pressed her sweet little breasts against his chest. He deepened the kiss, losing himself in her softness and curves, her feminine scent. His heart took flight. *Ceejay.*

No way around it. This mission would involve getting naked.

He broke the kiss and nuzzled the tender spot where her neck met her shoulder. "I...have scars."

"Shoot, this is me you're talking to. You think I don't?"

He grinned against her skin. "I'm not talking about emotional scars, honey. My left side was badly burned. It's not pretty."

"Oh." Ceejay cradled his jaw and planted little kisses all over his face. "And here all I've been worrying about is whether or not you have a condom."

He struggled to focus. *Condom.* "Yeah, I do." He always kept one in his wallet. No reason it wouldn't still be there, and his wallet was on the end table—next to his bed. He rose from the couch with her still in his arms. "Damn, you smell good."

"So do you."

She nibbled his neck, sending shivers cascading down his spine. He took her to his bed and laid her down. Retrieving the condom from his wallet, he thanked his lucky stars it was still there. "Are you sure about this?" One last chance to pull away, and then he'd be all over her like green on grass.

She nodded.

He worked his way out of his clothes and lowered himself beside her. "Um, what about…does the prosthetic bother you?" God, he'd never been so exposed, or so vulnerable. He held his breath.

"Nothing about you bothers me." She ran her hands over his shoulders and drew him to her. "I think you're gorgeous. Let me see those scars."

"Wait, if you're going to do a physical, Nurse Lovejoy, I get to play the doctor."

Her giggle was all the encouragement he needed. He removed her clothing one piece at a time, tasting and kissing every inch of her body with all its intriguing dips, swells, and curves. He reveled in each new discovery. Every adorable freckle was cause for celebration. Perfection.

She flipped their positions so that she straddled him. Gently, she ran her hands over the tightness of the scarring along his side. "It looks like you were sandblasted."

He swallowed hard. "Essentially, that's what happened. Superheated bits of sand blasted into my skin after I was already burned from the explosion."

"Oh, Noah, these scars are a part of you, part of what you've lived through. I don't see anything here that isn't a turn-on to me." She leaned over and kissed the puckered skin all along his side. Straightening, she twisted around and unfastened his prosthetic and slipped it off, placing it on the floor beside the bed. Her touch on his stump was gentle but sure.

Her acceptance brought tears to his eyes. She ran her hands over him like he wasn't scarred and broken. No part of him went untouched, unkissed. He couldn't move, the pleasure was so great, so healing to his battered soul.

The urge to touch her back, to be in command, soon over-rode everything. He slipped the condom on and rasped out, "My turn. Dr. Langford is on the job." Her throaty giggle nearly had him plunging into her. Too soon. He sat up, bringing her with him, and put his arms around her until every inch of her torso was tight against his. He kissed her hard, his tongue delving deep inside the softness she offered up without hesitation. Moving her beneath him, he started a deeper exploration.

He flicked his tongue over one pebbled nipple, watching the way it tightened even more to his touch. Her skin, so warm and soft under his hands, nearly unhinged him. He forced himself to slow down, but she was ready, slick with heat for him. The sounds of pleasure she made when he touched her, the way she moved beneath him, urgent and hot—in her arms he was whole. Whole and all male—confident, decisive, in charge. Until he entered her—then he surrendered control for sensation. He felt her come around him and soon followed, coming apart in her arms.

This is heaven. This is home.

He didn't want to leave her body, but his weight had to be too much for her. Noah rolled to his back and tucked her up beside him, too sated and spent to say anything. He stared at the ceiling while trying to figure out how he'd gotten so lucky.

Her breathing soon took on a steady, slow cadence. She'd fallen asleep, and he didn't want to disturb her by getting up. Did she always fall asleep after sex? He couldn't wait to find out. Grinning at the thought, he ran his hand up and down her arm. Her hair, a riot of soft, gold and copper curls, tickled his skin. He could get used to going to bed each night with her beside him and waking every morning to see her sleepy blue eyes gazing at him, filled with…

She stretched and sighed. He ran his fingers through her silky hair. "Didn't mean to wake you."

She kissed his chin and smiled. "I gotta go soon anyway."

"Not yet." Noah swung himself up and put on his prosthetic. "Stay for a while longer," he said on his way to clean up and dispose of the condom. Why wasn't he one of those optimistic bastards who kept several condoms in their wallets, or a boxful in the drawer of his bedside table? Once was not enough with her. He stood in front of the toilet, and then he noticed the tear. "Aw, hell." He blew out a breath and shored up his nerve. "Ceejay, honey?" he called.

"Hmmm?"

He had to smile at the satisfied purr in her voice, even though the shit was about to hit the fan. "The condom tore."

"Not funny. Don't even joke about something like that."

Noah flushed and called back, "I'm not joking."

"No. You *have* to be. Do you have any idea what happened the *last* time a condom broke?" she cried. "*Lucinda* happened. That's what."

A thumping noise came from the bedroom. He finished washing and returned to find her jumping up and down in place. "What are you doing?" He couldn't take his eyes off her bouncing breasts.

"I'm a health care professional." She glared at him. "I know full well this doesn't work, but I'm doing it anyway."

He frowned. "Doing what anyway?"

"I'm trying to make it harder for any of your escaped swimmers to reach their destination. Why are you smiling? This is serious."

He shook his head.

Her eyebrows rose. "And why are you doing *that*?" She pointed to his growing erection.

"I'm a guy. You're naked." He shrugged. "What guy wouldn't do *this*"—he gestured to his groin—"with a beautiful naked woman jumping in his bedroom?"

She stopped and turned her wide-eyed gaze on him. "You think I'm...really?"

"Absolutely." He swept her with a look. "The damage is already done, right?" His hands itched to touch her again, and he stepped closer. "No reason why we can't go back to bed and do it again."

"You did *not* just say that!" She raked both hands through her curls. "How long has that condom been in your wallet, anyway?"

"Um..." No way in hell was he going to admit how long it had been since he'd needed a condom. "A while."

"They do expire, you know."

"Didn't think about that before we—"

"I can't believe you're being so calm about this. What if—"

"If you're pregnant, I'll marry you."

She sent him a mutinous look.

Hell. Wrong answer?

"Well, isn't that the romantic proposal every girl longs to hear." She put her hands on her bare hips. "What makes you think I'd marry you, anyway? You don't even have a job."

"I'm worth millions, Ceejay. I have a trust fund my grandparents set up for me the day I was born. I can't touch the principal until I'm fifty-five, but the interest provides a very nice living. I don't have to work, and neither would you."

"I like working, and besides, the job thing isn't about the money." She threw her hands up in the air and paced around in a circle. "It's never been about the money."

Confusion clouded his brain. "What is it about, then?"

"It's about finding your passion in life. It's about doing something that takes you out of yourself and out of your PTSD."

No doubt about it. He'd forgotten all about PTSD, the scars, and his missing leg while he was inside her. Best therapy ever. He wanted more. "I'm passionate about you."

"It's not the same thing. Sexual passion isn't enough." Her eyes held a pleading look. "I don't want that kind of dependence. I want a partner who has something to share at the end of the day. It's about having your own life. I want that for you. Don't you see?"

He did see. Noah swallowed hard. He had to get a life before he had a life to share. Ceejay watched him. What did she expect him to say? "You said you were willing to give me a chance."

She nodded.

He blew out a breath. "Ted wants to go into the home repair business together."

"Is that what you want to do? Are you excited by the prospect?"

"I don't know." He rubbed the back of his skull. "Maybe."

"You've never once talked to me about the work you're doing on my aunt's house."

"I'll figure something out."

"I hope so. I really, really hope so."

"Promise me one thing."

"What's that?"

"Don't get one of those morning-after pills or…" He watched her eyes narrow. *Oh, shit. Wrong thing to say. Again.*

She made a growling noise and stomped out of the bedroom. He followed. "Wait."

Her hand was on the doorknob.

"Ceejay, wait!"

"What now?" She glared at him over her bare shoulder.

"You might want to put on some clothes before you leave."

"What difference does it make?" She shoved past him on her way back to the bedroom and snatched her things from the floor. "We live in the middle of nowhere right next to nothing."

She slammed the door behind her as she went, and Noah was left standing in his living room—naked and grinning like a fool.

New mission. Find his passion in life.

He hadn't had nearly enough sleep last night, but considering the reason, he couldn't complain. Noah yawned while his coffee machine spit dark liquid into the glass pot. Before he found his passion, he had to get his laundry done. Hauling it into town was not his idea of fun. He looked at his kitchen sink for a moment, mentally tracing the path of the plumbing. The kitchen wall butted up against the carriage bays. Was there running water in that part of the building? He'd never looked.

If the carriage bays were already wired for electricity, and if there was water, maybe the Lovejoys would let him install a washer and dryer. Noah filled a mug with coffee and headed out of his apartment to investigate.

Each of the two bays had its own set of double barn doors opening out, and a single entry door stood off to the left. Noah tried the handle of the regular door to see if it was locked. It wasn't. He'd noticed long ago that he was the only one on the place who locked anything. Habit. Paranoia. He flipped a light switch he found inside the door, and a low-watt bulb overhead came to life. Great, there was electricity. Once his eyes adjusted to the dim interior, he started to explore.

On the wall meeting his kitchen, he found a huge steel and concrete utility sink. An antique wringer washing machine gathered dust beside it. Ceejay's voice rang through his head. *Generations of Lovejoys stretching all the way back to the Civil War have washed their clothes in this very spot.* He grinned, and his mind drifted to the possibility of being a father. Odd. The thought didn't freak him out nearly as much as he thought it would.

The outlets weren't grounded, but it wouldn't take much to update the wiring. He turned to survey the rest of the area. Large timber beams supported the structure, including the ceiling joists. The Lovejoys didn't mess around. The carriage house had been built to last. South-facing windows would provide good light if they were cleaned, and if the bay doors were open, there would be ample ventilation.

A pile of lumber partially covered with a tarp caught his eye, and he went to investigate. Pulling the tarp back, he sucked in a breath. Black walnut two-by-fours, six-by-eights, and wider planks had been stacked for who knew how long. He ran his hand over one of the pieces. Man, what he could do with such a treasure made his hands twitch.

He glanced around and found an old, scarred workbench with a few vises of varying sizes fastened to the edges on either side. A dusty miter box sat next to a mason jar full of rusty nails. He lifted one of them and found it had a squared head like the handmade nails used in the nineteenth century.

Excitement thrummed through him. He already had a table saw. He'd need a jigsaw, a lathe, mallets, and chisels. He longed to shape the wood into something useful and lasting. He wanted to turn the pile of black walnut into furniture.

His mind spun. He'd have to ask Jenny about the lumber. Maybe she'd let him buy it. Would Ceejay be willing to rent the space to him? The partition between the bays had been torn out years ago. He'd get an electrician in here to update the wiring and add more overhead lighting. He'd build shelving to hold his tools and equipment.

If he *was* going to be a dad, he wanted to make something for his child with his own two hands. It had to be heirloom quality and built to last for the generations of Langfords to come. An image formed in his mind. He knew what he wanted to make.

A cradle.

What if Ceejay isn't pregnant? Hell, it didn't matter. She would be one day, and he *would* be the father.

Noah froze. A fine sheen of sweat broke out on his brow, and his heartbeat surged in retaliation to the flip his stomach did. "Damn." He'd fallen hopelessly, irrevocably in love with his tiny, freckled, adorable little mess of a woman.

He glanced at his watch. Only 0700 hours. Too early to beat on the Lovejoys' door. What had Ceejay said last night? The biopsy was scheduled for midmorning, so her aunt wasn't going in to work. Jenny was an early riser like him. Maybe she'd be on the porch with her air pot full of coffee. Did he want to bother her with this while she had so much on her mind? If nothing else, he could offer support. He flipped the light off and headed for the big house.

"Morning, Noah," Jenny greeted him from her place at the wrought-iron table. She had a cross-stitch project on her lap, and the table had several twists of thread strewn across the surface. "Come on up for coffee."

Noah tossed the cooled contents of his mug in the grass before he joined her. "Thanks. I don't know why, but your coffee always tastes better than mine." He filled his cup from the air pot and took a seat. "I was hoping I'd find you here." What could he say to the woman who'd come to mean so much to him? "Ceejay told me about…"

"The biopsy?"

He nodded. "Anything you want me to do, or if you need anything, you let me know."

"Help Ceejay. That would go a long way toward easing my mind."

"That goes without saying."

She studied him for several seconds. "If you don't mind my asking…"

"I'm crazy about her," Noah blurted. "I mean…" He scrubbed his hands over his face. The revelation still buzzed through him like a live wire, and the energy wanted an outlet. "Maybe that's not what you were going to ask. Sorry."

"Oh, that's quite all right." Jenny chuckled. "It is what I was going to ask, and I'm glad to hear it. You're a good man, Noah."

He fought the urge to squirm in his chair. How did being messed up in the head and clueless about what to do with his life add up to being a good man? "Thanks."

"I love this old place." Jenny sighed and stared out toward the orchard. "I've been meaning to thank you for all the work you've done. The porch is gorgeous. Can't wait to put some wicker furniture up there."

"You're welcome. Working has been good for me." His gaze went to his camper, still parked in their driveway. "I was snooping around in the carriage bays this morning."

"Oh?"

"I found a pile of black walnut under a canvas tarp. I was wondering if you might be willing to sell it to me."

"What do you want with that old pile of wood?" Her brow furrowed.

"I plan to make furniture with it."

"You can do that?"

Noah nodded. "One of my uncles does antique furniture restoration and replication during the months when the construction business is slow. I started working with him when I was fourteen."

"In that case, help yourself. You can have it."

"I'd feel better if you'd let me buy it."

"Consider it barter for some of the work you've done on the house."

"All right. I will. Do you think Ceejay would let me rent the bays?"

"I don't believe she'll have any objection. Your lease is for the carriage house, and you could always argue that the bay area is part of the carriage house."

"Great. I want to get the electrical updated, so I can install a washer and dryer."

The door opened and Ceejay walked out. She wore her blue bathrobe. God, he loved that ratty old robe. She sent him a shy smile that lit up his insides. He couldn't take his eyes off her. It was all he could do to keep from leaping up, grabbing her around the waist, and kissing her breathless. "Good morning, honey."

Her cheeks turned a delightful shade of pink, and her eyes darted to her aunt and back to him. "Morning." She filled a cup with coffee and doused it with cream and sugar before she sat down.

Noah cleared his throat. "Would you mind if I turn the bay of the carriage house into a workspace?"

"Nope. It's a registered historical landmark, though, so you can't make structural changes."

"I won't. Anything you want me to help you with today?"

A thoughtful expression crossed her face. "I was going to bring Lucinda with us to the hospital. Would you mind watching her for a couple of hours?"

"I'd love to. Maybe the two of us could visit the Offermeyers' foals again."

Jenny smiled at him. "She'd enjoy that. Their phone number is on the list tacked up by the kitchen phone."

"I know you wanted me to store my camper in one of the bays, but is it OK if I leave it where it is? If not, I can rent storage space somewhere else."

"It's fine for now." Jenny rose. "I'm going to go make myself some breakfast. You two want anything?"

"I'll fix myself something when Lucinda gets up," Ceejay said.

"I already had breakfast." Noah watched her leave, and then turned to Ceejay. "Am I forgiven?"

"Not entirely." She fussed with arranging the edges of her robe so that they overlapped. "Sometime today one of us has to make a drugstore run for condoms that *aren't* expired."

"Today?" *As in I might get lucky again tonight?* He grinned so hard his cheek muscles hurt. "I'll take care of it." He loved watching her squirm. Admitting they were *with* each other was really hard for her, and he now realized it had nothing to do with being ashamed and everything to do with long-held defense mechanisms. Intimacy frightened her, and she was shy. He loved that, too.

Her eyebrows shot up. "In town?"

Noah nodded.

She twisted a curl around one of her fingers. "People are going to talk."

"True, and when they do, I'll be standing right beside you." He rose from his place and came to stand behind her. Placing his hands on her shoulders, he gave her a squeeze, leaned close, and whispered, "No matter what."

"Oh, I'm not worried." She tilted her head back to look at him. "I mean, really, what are the odds that I'd get pregnant twice the same way?"

He frowned. What *were* the odds? "Regardless—"

"Thanks for taking Lucinda this morning. She can be a handful, and all my attention needs to be on Jenny."

"Not a problem." He moved to lean against the veranda railing. "When are you free for that movie?"

"Thursday night would be good. Do you know what you want to see?"

"Doesn't matter. You choose." He winked. "My job will be making sure you don't stop breathing."

A sudden burst of laughter caused her to choke on the coffee she'd just gulped. She covered her mouth, but coffee dribbled down her chin anyway. "Always looking out for me. I like that about you." She wiped her face with the sleeve of her robe.

"That's the kind of guy I am." Noah grinned and leaned in to kiss her forehead. "Gotta go. I have stuff to do." He started down the stairs.

"Wait. I need your cell phone number, and you need mine. Call me if you have any trouble with Lucinda, and I'll call you from the clinic when we're on our way home."

Noah pulled his phone from his rear pocket. "Give me yours, and I'll call you in a little while so you have mine."

Her expression changed, and her eyes grew bright with unshed tears. She recited her number for him. "What if Jenny's biopsy turns out to be..."

Noah came back up the steps, pulled a chair around to face her, and sat down. "It's going to be fine." He took her hands in his.

She bit her lip and nodded.

"What do you need? Tell me."

"Just this. Let me talk about it." She sighed. "Chances are everything will be all right, but even the thought of anything happening to Jenny..."

"I know." Noah tucked a curl behind her ear. "I'm here if you need anything."

"Thank you, Noah. Go on now. I'll be fine." She squeezed his hands before letting him go. "Come get Luce at ten."

He brushed a kiss across her lips and tore himself away.

CHAPTER THIRTEEN

THIS RANKED UP THERE AS one of the worst mornings of her life. Everything had happened in such a big hurry. Jenny's biopsy, followed by the call the next day, and their appointment today. Ceejay gripped the steering wheel so tightly her knuckles stood out in stark relief. At least it kept them from shaking like they had when they'd met with the surgeon and the oncologist. "They caught it early, Jenny. That's good."

Her aunt nodded, but her mouth formed a straight, tight line against her abnormally pale skin. The past two days had been a surreal blur. Reality hadn't completely sunk in until they'd sat across from the surgeon forcing her aunt to make a decision. Radical mastectomy or a lumpectomy, and might she consider a double mastectomy as a cautionary measure against developing a tumor in the other breast? God, what a question!

Everything had been so clinical, so professional. Cold.

Nothing about Jenny was cold, dammit.

Ceejay couldn't get enough breath into her lungs, and she bit her lip hard to force herself to concentrate on driving home safely. She was almost grateful that she had to work later. Having something to do would keep her sane. "Do you want me to ask Noah to watch Lucinda tonight?"

"No, of course not. I want to do it. I need to…to…"

Her aunt's voice faltered, and Ceejay's heart faltered with it. "OK. I just didn't want to add to your stress."

"Nothing about being with Lucinda is stressful. You know how much I love her." Tears trickled down her aunt's cheeks. "I…I've always loved you like you were my own daughter, and… and Lucinda is the closest to a grandchild I'll ever have!"

"I know." Ceejay blinked hard and reached a hand out to her aunt. Jenny grabbed for it and held on tight. "We love you too, Jenny. We're going to get through this. The doctors said your prognosis is good."

"They also said they won't know anything for certain until they have a chance to check my lymph nodes."

"They're optimistic, so we're going to be optimistic too." The ever-present bug bodies on the windshield of her ancient car drew her attention. One, two three…no. She had to be strong for Jenny. "It's not the most aggressive type of cancer. We do know that for sure."

"Cancer. I hate that word."

"Me too." Ceejay turned into their driveway, pulled up next to her aunt's car, and parked. Noah and Lucinda were on the veranda. It looked like they were playing cards. Her throat closed. He'd been so great these past few days. She climbed out of her car and headed for the porch. Sweet Pea lolled over the edge of the top step and stretched out across the floorboards. She gave him a scratch behind his ears on the way up the steps, eliciting a round of tail thumping.

"Mommy, Uncle Noah taught me how to play Go Fish." Lucinda held her hand of cards up for her. "See?"

She sent him a look of gratitude. "Wow, Luce. Looks like you're winning too."

"I am," Lucinda crowed. "Aunt Jenny, do you wanna play wif us?"

"I'd love to, honey. Just let me get a glass of sweet tea first. Anybody else want some?"

"I can get it," Ceejay headed for the door.

"No, I want to. You sit."

Noah held up his coffee mug. "I'm good, and Lucinda has juice."

"I'd love a glass." Ceejay waited until her aunt was gone, let out a loud breath, and slumped into a chair. She felt as if she hadn't breathed deeply for days.

"You all right?" Noah reached across the table for her hand.

She nodded and twined her fingers with his. "Her surgery is scheduled for Thursday morning. I have to cancel our date."

"Not a problem. There will be plenty of movies for us to see in the future."

"Thank you." She swallowed hard. "You've been so...I don't know what I would've done without your help these past few days."

"What's surgery, Mommy?"

What did you tell a four-year-old when it came to cancer? "Aunt Jenny has some bad cells growing inside her, and surgery is what the doctors do to take those bad cells away."

"Am I gonna get bad cells growing inside me too?" Lucinda's expression turned fearful.

Ceejay ran a hand through her daughter's curls. "No, of course not."

"Come here, sweetheart." Noah held his arms open, and Lucinda scrambled out of her booster seat and into his lap. He wrapped his arms around her. "You don't need to worry. You're a very healthy little girl, and everything is going to be fine."

Lucinda snuggled against him and slipped two fingers into her mouth. Ceejay didn't have the heart to call her on it. If sucking her fingers gave her comfort, so be it. For today, anyway.

"Will you play Go Fish too?" Lucinda peered at her from her place on Noah's lap.

"Sure. Sounds like fun." She gathered up the deck of brightly colored children's cards and started to shuffle them. "Where'd you get these?"

"At the drugstore in Perfect."

"Oh." Her insides fluttered. He'd made the drugstore run for condoms. She imagined how quickly that little tidbit would be spread all over town. *Wonderful.*

Jenny pushed the screen door open with her hip and placed a glass of tea in front of Ceejay before taking her seat. "I'm ready to kick your butts. Let's play Go Fish."

It almost felt normal, sitting at the wrought-iron table and playing cards like the possibility of her aunt's cancer being terminal didn't loom large over everything.

❦   ❦   ❦

"So, I hear you're seeing this Noah fellow now." Her uncle Joe leaned forward in the uncomfortable hospital waiting room chair. "Is that true, Little Bit?"

Ceejay sent a glare Ted's way. He raised his brow and pushed off the wall he'd been holding up to move closer. What would it be like to have a private life that was…private?

"I've been on one date with him."

"Has he asked you out for another one, honey?" Aunt Kathy asked.

Ceejay's face grew hot, and she surveyed the hospital waiting room filled with Lovejoys. Jenny's brothers, their wives, a third of her cousins, and her great-aunt Edna. She cringed. "Yes, he asked me out for another date," she replied loudly enough to satisfy everyone's curiosity at once. They all relaxed. After all, she hadn't blown her first date with Noah. Ceejay let out a huff of air and shook her head. What would they think if they knew she'd thrown herself at him the other night? Another wave of heat scorched her cheeks.

Great-aunt Edna gave her walker a shake. "Ought to bring him to church with you this Sunday."

This set off a round of murmuring assent, and Ted laughed. Her other cousins looked up from their texting or magazines to smirk her way. They'd all been in this hot seat a time or two, and she was sure they were relishing the moment.

"Bring him to Sunday dinner after the service." Aunt Mary came to sit beside her and gave Ceejay's knee a pat.

Ceejay pushed herself back against the fake leather chair. "I don't even know if he goes to church."

"Can't hurt to ask." Uncle Jim raised an eyebrow at her, like it was her moral obligation to bring Noah into the flock.

Floor, open up and swallow me now! She started to reply and stopped when Jenny's surgeon appeared at the entrance of the waiting room. Everyone went silent, turning as one to study the doctor's facial expression for clues.

His brow rose slightly. "All of you are Lovejoys?"

Rising from her place, Ceejay replied, "Yes, sir. We're all related. How did the surgery go?"

"Mrs. Hoffman is being moved to ICU as we speak. The surgery went very well. I believe we got all of it…"

A collective sigh filled the room.

"I want to caution you here. Though the surgery went well, we still have to wait for the pathologist's report." He reached up and took the surgical cap off his head. "Visitation is strictly controlled in the ICU. No more than two or three people at a time, and the hours are limited due to the intensity of the care provided." His gaze traveled around the room. "It will be several hours before she's awake and ready for company. You might want to take advantage of this time. Go home, and get some rest, do whatever you need to do. She'll be moved to her regular room tomorrow morning. What she needs now is quiet and rest."

"I'd like to see her before I leave." Ceejay stepped forward. "Can you have a nurse come tell me when my aunt is settled?"

"Will do." The surgeon nodded and left.

Her knees went weak, and a round of shoulder patting and hugging started up all around her. No way was she going home before seeing Jenny. Aunt Mary caught her up in a hug, and Ceejay hugged back, tears of relief springing to her eyes.

"We'll be back tomorrow, honey. Maybe you should go home and get some rest like the doc said. Come back tomorrow when she's awake."

"I will." She watched as everyone gathered their things and started their mass exodus. "I'm just going to the cafeteria for coffee, and then I'll check on her before I go home."

"You do that." Her uncle Jim pulled her in for a bear hug. "Call us if you need anything."

"OK." She followed her family to the elevators. The uncles and aunts took the first, and her cousins piled into the next one with her.

"Noah is kind of hot." Her cousin Carrie nudged her with an elbow.

"He is." She nodded. And now everyone would be speculating, watching. Her insides knotted. What if she and Noah didn't last? The thought of all that pity coming at her sent her heart into overdrive. Why couldn't she have been born into a small, nonintrusive family in a large city? The elevator doors opened. "I'll see you all soon." She hurried off to the cafeteria.

Ceejay returned to the hospital waiting room with a Styrofoam cup of really bad coffee in her hand. She frowned and came to a stop. "Sheriff Maurer?"

He sat slumped in one of the chairs and stared at the floor with a grim expression. "Hey, Little Bit." He straightened and started to turn his uniform hat in his hands. "How'd the surgery go?"

"It went well." She took the chair beside him and set her coffee on the end table. "We have to wait for the pathologist's report on her lymph nodes, but her surgeon believes they got it all."

An audible sigh shuddered through him. "Thank God." He rubbed at his eyes, and his lips tightened. "I've been in love with your aunt since she was in the third grade."

Ceejay blinked, and she didn't know what to say. He'd been a part of their lives forever, a fixture in the landscape of her childhood, and she'd never suspected. "I...does Jenny know?"

"No. I couldn't do that to her."

"I don't understand." She glanced at him. "Do *what* to her?"

He leaned his head back against the wall. "She and I dated some in high school, even though she was a couple of years behind me. Then she started working at the diner, and it was all over." He let out a strangled laugh. "Mike worked for his parents back then. I didn't stand a chance against him. Captain of the football team, good-looking, even worse—he was the genuine article, a good guy."

"But what about—"

"After he died?" He regarded her with his brow lowered. "After my own tour of duty in Nam, I went into law enforcement."

"What does going into law enforcement have to do with anything?"

"Do you have any idea how high the divorce rate is for law enforcement officers? I couldn't risk it. I didn't want to put her through any more pain than she'd already been through after losing Mike."

Ceejay fought the urge to snort. "I'm sure the divorce rate is high because of the stress involved with the job, but surely it's much less stressful in rural areas, right? I mean, how much crime is there in Warrick County?"

"You'd be surprised." He started turning his hat again. "Used to be a lot simpler than it is today. Now we have meth labs, drug rings, gangs, sex offenders, you name it, we have it."

"Sheriff—"

"You can call me Harlen. I'm not here as the sheriff right now, and I've known you since you were this high." He held his hand out to indicate how tiny she'd been. "You're like family to me."

She swallowed the lump in her throat and rested her hand on his forearm. "Harlen, I'm not the one who needs to hear all this. Tell Jenny how you feel."

He slumped forward and rested his elbows on his knees. "I don't know. What if...what if she doesn't—"

"Don't you think she deserves the right to make up her own mind? Give her the choice."

"Maybe it's too late. I should've told her decades ago. Each year I didn't made it easier just to keep things the way they are." He shook his head. "Now, I don't know if—"

A nurse walked into the waiting room and called Ceejay's name.

"I'm here." She rose from the chair.

"If you'd like, you can sit with your aunt for a little while." The nurse smiled. "Her doctor told me you're a nurse."

She nodded. "In pediatrics." Ceejay turned to the sheriff. "Do you want to come with me?"

He nodded. They followed the nurse down the white concrete and linoleum hallway to the ICU. Jenny was hooked up to monitors, a catheter, and two IV drips. Ceejay had known what to expect, but seeing her like that, her skin so pale and drawn— she had to cover her mouth to keep from crying out. Harlen placed his hands on her shoulders and gave her a squeeze. She froze, surprised by the comforting gesture.

"Jenny's going to be fine." He guided her to the chair beside the hospital bed, made her sit, and then he dragged another one over for himself. He put his elbows on the bed and held Jenny's hand in both of his with so much reverence, Ceejay almost fell apart.

"Harlen, promise me you'll tell her how you feel. If anyone deserves to be happy, it's the two of you."

She heard the ragged intake of his breath as he brought Jenny's hand to his mouth and kissed it. He didn't answer, but kept a tight grip, as if he feared letting go.

She knew the feeling.

Thirty minutes later, Sheriff Maurer walked out of the hospital with her into the heat and humidity. A fine sheen of perspiration formed on her brow, and Ceejay picked up her pace. The inside of her old car would be an oven until she got moving. "Will I see you here tomorrow, Sheriff?"

"Count on it. Do you know when you'll hear from the pathologist?"

"No." The thought of that last hurdle sent a rush of adrenaline through her.

He stopped. "If I'm not there when you get that report, you call me."

"I will."

He nodded and veered off toward his patrol car. After all this morning's tension, she needed to get home and give her daughter a hug. The minute she opened her car door, a wave of sauna-like heat engulfed her. She really needed to buy a new one, a compact with air-conditioning that worked. Any day now that big insurance check would be direct-deposited into her checking account. First order of business would be a new car.

Once Jenny was home and on the mend, Ceejay would start her search for a house in Indianapolis again. Plus, with her aunt's surgery behind them, they would all appreciate their upcoming vacation even more.

Everything would be back on track once they got the all clear from the pathologist.

The scent of freshly mowed hay poured into the car. She rode the rises and dips on the rural two-lane, taking comfort in the familiar rhythm of the gently rolling hills. The world had that almost ripe late-summer feel to it. It had been this time of year when Matt had walked out of her life. She took a deep breath, inhaling the sweet alfalfa and clover-spiced air.

She wouldn't think about Matt. Just because her life had gone to shit one late July day years ago didn't mean it would turn to shit again this July.

Turning onto their gravel driveway, she came head-to-head with a pickup truck heading out. She pulled over into the grass to let the truck by and pasted a smile on her face as she leaned out her window.

"Hey, Ceejay." Aunt Jenny's best friend leaned forward to talk around her husband. "We just stopped by to see if there's anything you need." Her warm brown eyes were filled with concern.

"Thanks, Mrs. Weber. We're fine for now." Her throat tightened, and warmth filled her. She'd known the Webers for as long as she could remember. She knew practically everyone who lived in Perfect, and they had all reached out to her and Jenny with calls, offers to babysit, cooking, cleaning—whatever they needed.

"How's your aunt?" Floyd rested his elbow on the window frame and poked his head out of the cab of his truck. "How'd the surgery go?"

"The surgery went really well. Jenny's resting in the ICU now. They're going to move her to a regular room tomorrow, so she can have visitors."

"Oh, that's good. We'll stop by to see her." Mrs. Weber smiled. "You take care, now, and give that little girl of yours a big hug for us."

"I will. Thanks for stopping by." Ceejay waited for their truck to pass and pulled up alongside Ted's Mustang. Noah's truck was there too, but neither of them was working on the house. Maybe they were taking a break, or maybe it was too hot to work outside today. She got out of her car, walked up the veranda steps, and went inside.

The quiet sent a chill down her spine. Empty. Jenny should be here about this time in the afternoon, unloading her canvas bag of diner leftovers. "Hello," she shouted. No one answered. Ceejay walked to the kitchen and dropped her keys and purse on the table. Several plastic containers and plates filled the space. Breads, pies, cakes, and cards. A lump formed in her throat again. So many people had come forward to show they cared. Ceejay had never given this part of small-town life much thought. Maybe because she and Jenny were usually among the group bringing meals to neighbors in need, and this was the first time they had been on the receiving end.

Sweet Pea barked from somewhere behind the carriage house, and Ceejay slipped out through the kitchen door and made her way to the back. The deep cadence of Ted and Noah's conversation drew her. She needed this, the sounds of normalcy. Life. Swallowing hard, she opened the back gate and rounded the corner. "What're you all up to?"

"Mommy!" Lucinda ran into Ceejay's knees and threw her arms around her legs.

Ceejay hugged her and surveyed the bay through the open doors. Noah and Ted were installing a washer and dryer on either side of the old washtub. A pile of new tools stacked in the middle of the concrete floor caught her eye. "Wow. What's all this?"

"Stuff for my workshop." Noah sent her a smile. "We went shopping this morning."

Lucinda beamed up at her. "I'm helping."

"Oh, yeah? What's your job?" She ran her hands through Lucinda's silky curls, grounding herself in the feel of her daughter's warmth.

"I'm sweeping." She let go and ran to pick up the child-size broom lying on the floor. "This is my broom. Uncle Noah said so."

Ceejay blinked back the sudden sting of tears as all the worry and stress she'd been under came surging to the forefront. Noah dropped what he was doing and came to her side. Wrapping his arms around her, he rocked her back and forth. She relaxed against him. "You're all sweaty," she mumbled into his shoulder.

"I've been working in this heat most of the morning. Do you mind?"

She wrapped her arms around his waist. "Nope." Resting her cheek against his chest, she let all the fear and tension slip away. Peace stole over her, and she sighed. "Can I just stay here like this for the rest of the day?" Noah chuckled, and she loved the way the sound and vibration filled her.

"Did Aunt Jenny wake up before you left?" Ted asked from behind the dryer vent he was taping.

"No." She moved out of Noah's arms. "I sat with her for a while, though. Sheriff Maurer stopped by to see her too."

"That was nice of him." Ted straightened up and wiped the sweat from his face with the hem of his T-shirt. "I came straight here after I left the hospital. There's been a steady stream of neighbors stopping by to see if you need anything."

"I know." She nodded. "I ran into the Webers on the way in, and I saw all the food in the kitchen." The bane and blessing of small-town life—everyone knew everyone else's business, but they also reached out a helping hand when trouble struck. "I have to get ready for work." Two more shifts at Deaconess and she'd be free. She dearly needed the time off before her new job started. Jenny would need a lot of help while she recovered from her surgery. "Lucinda, you're going to go to Uncle Jim and Aunt Mary's with Ted tonight. I'll pick you up tomorrow morning."

"I want to stay here wif Uncle Noah."

"I know you do, but—"

"Let her stay in her own room." Noah twined his fingers through hers. "I'll sleep on a couch."

"We talked about it." Ted tousled Lucinda's hair. "I'll stay too. OK, pipsqueak?"

Lucinda nodded up at Ted.

Ceejay glanced from one to the other and raised an eyebrow. "Are you sure?" The two men nodded in tandem. "All right. Call your folks, Ted, and let them know." She turned to Noah. "We have five bedrooms. You don't have to sleep on the couch. Ted knows where the sheets and blankets are kept."

She crouched down to Lucinda's level. "I need a hug before I go to work." Lucinda rushed into her arms, almost knocking her over. She held her daughter tight. "You be good for Uncle Noah and Ted, all right?"

"I will, Mommy. You don't gotta worry about me."

"I'll walk you back to the house." Noah reached out and helped her up.

The feel of his strong, callused hand around hers settled her like nothing else could. She nodded, and he led her toward the house.

"How are you holding up?"

"I'm all right. The surgery went really well, and tomorrow she'll be moved into a regular room."

"That's good. I'll head over for a visit."

"She'd like that."

"Are you going to bring Lucinda to see her?"

"I don't think so. A hospital is no place for an active four-year-old, and Jenny will be home in a few days."

"All right." They'd reached the back door, and Noah drew her into his arms.

He kissed her. Despite all the worries she carried, her insides melted and all thought left her. God bless this man.

❦ ❦ ❦

The pathologist found cancerous cells in two lymph nodes. The oncologist's words echoed through Ceejay's head until it hurt— until the pounding accented each word individually. Ceejay gripped her purse against her chest and hurried into the hospital lobby. She jabbed at the elevator button and tried to breathe.

Why would the oncologist want to meet with her? Shouldn't he be meeting with Jenny? Her stomach lurched as the elevator started to climb. She glanced at the crumpled piece of paper in her hand, reciting the room number where she would find him.

The doors whooshed open, and she stepped out. Arrows and numbers pointed the way. Why was she rushing to hear bad news? She forced herself to slow down and headed in the direction the arrows indicated. Stopping before the partially opened door, she straightened and knocked.

"Ms. Lovejoy, come in." Dr. Johnson wiped a napkin over his mouth and gestured her into the tiny office. A boxed lunch sat on his desk, with a half-eaten ham sandwich lying on the waxed wrapping paper. "I was just grabbing something to eat. I hope you don't mind. Some days it's lucky if I find any time at all for a meal."

"No, I don't mind." The doctor had impressed her the first time they'd met. The middle-aged oncologist had seemed genuinely caring when they'd gone over the possible outcomes with her aunt. His warm, brown eyes now regarded her with an expression of concern as she took the chair beside his desk. "Why did you want to see me? Shouldn't my aunt be a part of this meeting?"

"I've already met with her." He leaned back in his chair. "She's refusing any further treatment."

Her eyebrows shot up to her hairline, and her heart knocked against her sternum.

"It's not uncommon," he continued. "She's in shock right now. I wanted to meet with you because I'm certain nothing I said got through in her present state. Cancer treatments have improved greatly over the past decade, and your aunt's prognosis is still very good. I want to order some tests to see if there are any hot spots, and—"

"Hot spots?"

He nodded. "Cancer cells reproduce much more rapidly than normal cells. This generates heat, which can be detected by—"

"I get it," she snapped, and buried her face in her hands. "I'm sorry, Dr. Johnson. I...I need a minute to absorb all of this."

"Understandable."

She drew in a breath and sat up. "The important thing here is that she's refusing further treatment, right?"

He nodded. "I'm hoping you can persuade her to change her mind."

"I'll do my best." She rose from the chair. "I'll go talk to her now."

"If I can be of any help, or if you have any questions, please call me." He stood up and handed her a business card. "We'll want to begin her first round of chemotherapy soon."

First round? Shit. That sounded way too serious. Ceejay nodded and walked out of the tiny room and down the hall toward the elevators.

"Ms. Lovejoy," he called and hurried toward her. "Your purse."

"Oh...thanks." She took her bag from him and headed for the bank of elevators. Her mind had gone blank, and shock held her firmly in its grip. She stared at the row of double metal doors without really seeing and waited for one of the elevators to open.

Walking out of the elevator and down the hall toward her aunt's room, she knew she couldn't leave Perfect. No way would she allow Jenny to face chemotherapy alone. She swiped a tear away. This wasn't supposed to happen. Not to Jenny. They'd caught it early, gotten all of the tumor during surgery. Her aunt had done everything right. Why had it all gone so wrong?

A weight had settled into her midsection the day the word *biopsy* had entered her life. Every day since, the space inside grew to accommodate the growing mass until the sheer bulk made eating and breathing impossible.

Knocking lightly on the door, Ceejay called out, "Hey, is it OK to come in?" Jenny had been moved to double-occupancy room with nothing but a curtain separating the two beds. She didn't want to interrupt someone's sponge bath or dressing change.

"No one here but me," Jenny replied. "Come on in."

Expelling the breath she'd been holding, Ceejay entered. An explosion of color filled Jenny's side of the room. Mylar balloon get well messages swayed in the air, stirred by her entrance. Red, gold, and blue ribbons dangled from the floating globes. Flowers in vases and foil-wrapped pots filled every flat surface. Cheery get well soon cards had been propped open on top of the heating and cooling unit under the window. "Wow, look at all this."

Jenny stared at the ceiling, nodding slightly. "Folks from the diner stopped by, and neighbors." She turned toward her. "Noah brought the roses."

Her heart skipped a beat at the sound of his name. "They're gorgeous. Has Sheriff Maurer been by?"

"He has, but I was sleeping." Jenny shifted in the bed and winced. "He left the box of chocolates and a card. Do you want a piece?"

"No, not now. Here, let me help you." She rushed to her side. "What do you need?"

"I'm tired of being flat on my back."

Her aunt's surly tone brought on a rush of empathy. Her nursing instincts kicked in, and she automatically checked the IV, giving it a click to send a surge of pain medication. She pressed the button to raise the back of the bed and held her aunt forward to place a pillow behind her for added support. "Is that better?"

Jenny nodded and swallowed. Moving a pile of magazines from the lone chair beside the bed, Ceejay took a seat. "I met with Dr. Johnson. He says you're refusing more treatment."

"Did he also tell you the cancer has spread? They found it in my lymph nodes. You know what that means."

"Unless you agree to have more tests done, nobody knows what that means."

"It's spreading." Jenny pressed her head back against the pillows. A single tear slipped out of the corner of her eye and trickled down her cheek.

Ceejay couldn't bear to see her cry. She moved out of the chair to stand before the window. "You have to fight this."

"Don't see the point. Chemotherapy makes you sick as a dog, and I don't know of anybody who's ever defeated the grim reaper forever. Do you?"

"Tons of people have survived cancers far worse than yours. Finding cancerous cells in your lymph system means you need follow-up treatment to prevent the spread. It's not a death sentence, Jenny. You have so much to live for, and…we need you. Lucinda and I need you." Her words filled the room and hung in the air like the Mylar balloons.

She stared out the window at the cars filling the parking lot below and murmured, "One, two, three, four—"

"Do you remember when you started counting things?"

Ceejay shook her head. "Five, six, seven..." She'd count all the red cars first, leaving the trucks for later.

"When you were little, and you got upset, I'd tell you to count to ten." Jenny sighed. "You took that advice to heart in a big way. You were such a cute little thing."

Eight, nine, ten...

"I have a will. I'm leaving the house to you, and—"

"Stop it!" Ceejay swung around to face her. "Don't talk like this. I don't want the house. What I want is for you to snap out of this doom-and-gloom outlook and fight, dammit!"

Jenny blinked rapidly, and more tears leaked out. Her lips compressed, turning down at the corners.

Shit. She'd done that. "I'm sorry. I'm sorry." Ceejay swiped at the tears flooding her own eyes. "Dr. Johnson says your reaction is normal. You're in shock. You have to change the direction your thoughts are taking you. You're young, and other than the...the..." She sucked in a huge breath. "Other than this, you're very strong and healthy. There's absolutely no reason why you can't beat this."

"Come and sit down, Little Bit." Jenny gestured to the chair. "There's something else we need to discuss."

Oh, God. Her insides tumbled. She turned back to the cars in the lot, back to numbers, innocuous and infinite. "What?"

"Your mother—"

A strangled cry broke free. "Don't want to talk about her." She circled her arms around herself.

"I know. We're going to anyway. You're a grown woman with a daughter of your own. It's time you got past this."

"*Past this?* How does one get past being abandoned by her own mother?"

"My sister did *not* abandon you. She loved you so much she was willing to put herself through hell to turn her life around. She wanted so badly to get herself straightened out." The hospital sheets rustled. "Something happened to her that first year she was away at college. Someone broke her heart and her spirit."

"My biological sperm donor, no doubt."

"Maybe. Shortly after that, she took up with the wrong crowd. Thank God she didn't start using until after you were born."

"Sure." All the anger and resentment simmering below the surface clawed at her insides. All the little-girl hurt that had never healed rose up and swallowed her whole.

"Anyway, Ann contacted me. She'd been waiting for space in this brand-new drug rehab program, and they finally had a room for her. I hadn't seen her so hopeful and determined to turn her life around for a long time." Jenny's voice broke. "She asked me to take care of you so she could kick her addiction, get herself clean, and be the mother to you she dearly longed to be."

"And then she took off," Ceejay spit out the words scalding her throat.

"No. She didn't."

She turned to face her aunt. "OK, then. She just never came back for me. Does that sound better to you? Because it doesn't sound any different to me."

"Honey, your mom died of an accidental heroin overdose the night before she was to enter rehab."

"No." Ceejay shook her head as her heart pounded against her ribs. "No."

"You don't remember her funeral, but you *were* there." Jenny gestured to the chair again. "Every time any of us brought your mom up, you'd pitch a fit. I'm sorry. Maybe we did the wrong thing. We all loved you so much, and seeing you so upset..." Her mouth turned down again. "We all agreed not to bring her up anymore."

Ceejay slid into the chair. Her mind flooded with images— fragments of memory flashed through her head. Her mother, so young and terribly thin, petite and blonde like Jenny.

"Your mother didn't leave you on purpose." Jenny stared at her. "You see?"

Somewhere during the conversation, she'd lost the ability to respond. Hell, it was all she could do to keep herself together, but her aunt needed something from her, so she nodded.

"I know how important it is for you to have your chance at a life in the big city. I want you to go ahead with your plans to move. Leaving Perfect means so much to you, and I don't want my being sick to interfere. My brothers will take care of me. I've already talked to them about this, and—"

"I'm sorry. I can't...wow, that's...this is a lot to...to take in." Ceejay shoved out of the chair and grabbed her purse from the floor. "I'll be back tomorrow." She leaned over and kissed her aunt on the cheek and hurried to the door.

"Ceejay, wait," her aunt called.

"Tomorrow, Jenny, and when I return, I want to hear you're ready to fight this. No more talk about leaving me the house, or my uncles taking *my* place as your caregiver. Got it? I'm a *nurse*." She blinked back her tears. "I'll come pick you up tomorrow. Call me once your discharge papers are all signed."

She rushed out of the room and shut the door behind her before Jenny could say any more. Leaning against the wall, she struggled to slow her heart to a normal rhythm, then pushed off to walk to the small waiting room at the end of the corridor. Once there, she sank into a seat and leaned her head back to stare at the black dots floating in front of her eyes.

Maybe putting her head down would be wiser. Leaning over, she inhaled through her nose and exhaled through her mouth until the dizziness ebbed. Ceejay straightened, pulled her cell phone out of her purse, and called Sheriff Maurer on his private cell phone.

"Harlen, this is Ceejay. We got the report from the pathologist, and...I...I need your help." Ceejay raked her free hand through her hair and brought him up to speed on everything that had happened with her aunt's diagnosis and the talk she'd had with the oncologist. Once he assured her he'd come talk to her aunt right away, she hung up and headed for the parking lot. Lord, she was glad Lucinda was spending the day with the Offermeyers. She needed time alone to process everything.

Her mother hadn't left her. She'd loved her enough to get help. All the years she believed everyone in Perfect pitied her because she'd been the poor unwanted child...had they all known the truth? She unlocked her car and sighed. Of course they knew, and like her family, they believed they were protecting her by keeping it a secret. She understood. Her mother had been a drug addict, and they had all tried to buffer her from that stigma.

People in Perfect made it their business to know, and it didn't mean they hadn't pitied her, only that the pity sprang from a different place. Still, the altered perspective kept poking at her brain. She'd lost her mom at an early age, but not because her mother hadn't wanted or loved her as she'd always believed. That changed things, and she'd have to think about it.

The drive home went by like her car had autopilot, while her mind struggled to process everything. Pulling up in front of the house, she noticed Noah's truck was gone, and her heart sank.

Missing him only added to the weight she carried around inside her. The past five days had been so hectic they'd hardly crossed paths, and besides, Jenny's cancer had reduced everything to who'd take care of what when.

Weary to the marrow in her bones, she dragged herself up the stairs and through the front door. She headed to the kitchen, dropped her things on the table, and went to the fridge for the pitcher of sweet tea they always kept full. Her hand on the pitcher, she froze. Footsteps? There weren't any extra vehicles in the driveway. "Ted?" she called. "Noah?" The sound stopped midway down the front stairs. Ceejay's heart raced, and her mouth went dry. She closed the refrigerator door and moved toward the foyer.

Moving to the end of the stairs, she frowned up into Allison Langford's startled face. "What are you doing here?"

"Noah called. He told me about Jenny, and...we came to help." She gripped a pile of linens in her hands.

"I didn't see your car."

"We flew. Noah picked us up from the airport earlier this morning."

"You shouldn't have come. I don't *need* your help. I'm a *nurse*." Didn't *anyone* think she'd step up for the woman who'd raised her? Jenny's words came back to sting her. Her aunt had already arranged to have her siblings take care of her. That's what she'd said. She'd been a mother to Ceejay her entire life, and now she wasn't going to let her to reciprocate? She'd even encouraged her to move to Indianapolis. That hurt the worst. What kind of person did Jenny think she was? "Do you think you can take better care of my aunt than I can?"

"No, of course not." Allison took another step down the stairs. "But we can help with Lucinda and the house. You're going to have your hands full."

Made perfect sense, but it didn't stop the ringing in her ears, or the throbbing pain at the base of her skull. Seeing Allison triggered memories of all the shame and rejection she'd suffered when Matt walked away, and that triggered a deeper, unhealed pain.

Something inside of her imploded, and she fell back into a frightened little girl standing on an unfamiliar veranda. Her mother held her hand, and a shabby, pink suitcase with cartoon characters on the front sat beside her. She remembered the front door opening to reveal a stranger. Her mother didn't even bother to go into the house before pushing her into the other woman's arms. Didn't even kiss and hug her good-bye before she was gone from her life forever.

"I can't..." She'd gone numb, emotionally paralyzed, and it had nothing to do with the woman standing on the stairs. Her ability to form coherent sentences, to explain, abandoned her. All she could do was stare and shake her head.

The front door opened and closed behind her. Noah? Man, when she had it back, she was going to give him a piece of her mind, but right now she couldn't even muster the energy to turn around. She continued to stare at Allison, watched the tears pool in her eyes as she covered her mouth with her hand. Nothing she could do about it. The best she could manage was to shake her head again and hope Allison understood her own reaction had nothing to do with her.

Allison turned around and fled back upstairs. Ceejay remained frozen to the spot.

"You made my wife cry again. I'm disappointed. I had hoped for a change in attitude by now."

She sucked in a breath and turned. She knew that voice. Noah had his eyes, his chin. They were the same height and had similar builds. His tyrant, tough, son-of-a-bitch father. *Great*.

Anger flared, rousing her from her stupor. What right did this man have to walk into *her* home and talk to her in that condescending tone? "Why? Because you offered to *buy* your way into our lives a few weeks ago?"

"No, because Noah is my son. He tells me you two are seeing each other."

"I didn't invite you here, and I sure don't need your help." Ceejay clenched her hands into fists. A flicker of doubt cast a shadow over her heart. Was Noah seeing her just to ensure a place for the Langfords in Lucinda's life?

"Lucinda is our granddaughter, and we Langfords don't walk away when one of our own needs help. We want to be a part of her life."

"Really. Matthew walked away easily enough."

"He wasn't a Langford."

"Whether the *Langfords* have a place in my daughter's life or not is *my* decision to make, and on my terms. And I assure you, that decision won't have anything to do with who I'm seeing."

"Humph." He thrust his hands into his pockets and jangled the contents. "I didn't want it to come to this."

"To what?" The jangling sound raked across her frayed nerves.

"If you don't allow us access to our granddaughter, I'll be forced to put my considerable resources toward seeing you have no choice."

She frowned. "What's that supposed to mean?"

"We have the right to petition the courts for visitation. Matthew Wyatt was Lucinda's father, and you've kept her from us, kept us from even knowing she existed."

"I *kept* her from you?" she cried. "Matthew didn't want her. He never acknowledged Lucinda's existence or claimed her as his. Besides, Matt didn't just walk away; he *stole* from me to do it. I still have the police report. What kind of case do you think you'd have? You have no prior history of involvement in our lives up till now."

"Doesn't matter." He jangled the keys in his pocket again. "I have the money and the lawyers to make it sound like we're the injured party. If you won't willingly let us be a part of Lucinda's life, I'll keep you in court until she's eighteen. I don't like it when my wife cries." He paused and leveled his gaze at her. "That insurance settlement won't last long if you fight me."

"Edward!"

Allison had returned and stood at the top of the second-floor landing. Ceejay's gaze swung between them. A tight band of tension crushed her rib cage. She had to get away.

Lucinda. She needed her daughter. Now.

She fled back into the kitchen, grabbed her purse and keys, and left by the back door. Why hadn't Noah asked her first before inviting his parents? Didn't he know her at all? Could this day get any worse? All the fear and stress she'd been under for the past few weeks came crashing over her. She couldn't breathe.

Pulling out of the driveway onto the two-lane highway, she gunned the engine and raced toward the Offermeyers'. She longed to talk to Noah. What were his motives for dating her? Did it have more to do with Lucinda than she wanted to admit? She swallowed the hurt, and tears blurred her vision. If she could just hold her baby girl in her arms, the world would turn right side up again.

She rounded a curve too fast and tried to compensate. Her right tires spun in the soft sand on the shoulder, and she lost control. The Honda fishtailed and jerked. Ceejay turned the wheel hard to the left and stepped on the gas. She hit something, a boulder, or a fallen log at the lip of the culvert. The car flipped.

For a second, time stopped. Ceejay hung suspended in the air, and then all hell broke loose.

Her car touched down on the incline, rolling before coming to an abrupt stop upside down. Pain radiated through her entire body, and her head swam. Even though everything had come to a standstill, the world still spun. Blackness edged in, and she slid right into it.

CHAPTER FOURTEEN

NOAH PARKED HIS TRUCK, CLIMBED out, and hurried toward
the hospital entrance. He had to get to Ceejay before she left. He
could only imagine what would go down if she arrived home to
find his parents there before he'd had a chance to talk to her.
She'd be pissed as hell, but dammit, they were a couple now. His
parents would be a permanent fixture in their lives. She had to
get used to that fact.

The automatic doors slid open, and a blast of air-conditioned
cold hit him as he followed a crowd of people to the elevators.
Knowing his stepmom as he did, he should've figured once she
heard about Jenny she'd hop on the first plane down. It wasn't
like he hadn't told her not to come. He had. His father's presence
had been the real shocker, though.

He exited the elevator and headed for Jenny's room. The
door was slightly ajar, and he glanced in to make sure she
wasn't in the middle of some procedure involving her doctor
or a nurse. The second bed was still empty, a good thing. Her
curtain had been pulled, and he heard voices, but not Ceejay's.
Sheriff Maurer?

"But…but I'll lose my hair, and—"

"Hell, Jennifer, I lost most of mine ten years ago. Are you telling me you think less of me because I'm bald on top?"

Jenny giggled like a schoolgirl. "You don't have much left, do you?"

Noah smiled. It did his heart good to hear her laugh. He stood still for a moment, unsure what to do.

"I don't care about your lack of hair, Harlen, but I...I only have one—"

"It's not your breasts I'm in love with, sweetheart." The sheriff's voice came out a husky rasp. "It's you I need, and I'm not leaving your side until you promise me you'll fight this thing."

Well, shit. Noah swiped his hand over the lower half of his face. He didn't want to interrupt, but this could go on all day. He didn't have all day. Hell, the sheriff could go all gooey after he left. Noah knocked. "Hello, can I come in?" The curtain slid back, and Sheriff Maurer glared at him. He ignored it. "Where's Ceejay? I was hoping I'd catch her before she left."

Jenny's color had improved, and her smile was genuine. "You missed her. She left about thirty minutes ago."

"Crap." Noah, blew out an exasperated breath. "My folks are at your house."

"What?"

"I didn't invite them, Jenny. I told my stepmother about your surgery. She and my dad hopped on a plane, and now they're here. Allison wants to help."

Jenny's brow furrowed. "Oh dear."

"Yeah, *oh dear*." Noah's hand automatically went to the back of his skull.

"Ceejay was upset when she left. I...I told her about how her mother died, and I told her I wasn't going through chemotherapy or any other treatment." A blush filled her cheeks, and she glanced at the sheriff, who had her hand gripped firmly in both of his. "I've changed my mind about that."

"I'm glad, Jenny." Noah smiled. "You can beat this."

"You'd better head back." Sheriff Maurer raised an eyebrow at him.

"Right." There was no way he'd get there before she did. The damage was already done. "How did she take the news about her mom?"

"Not well."

"I'd better get going, then." Noah headed for the door. "We'll see you tomorrow when you come home." He didn't wait for a reply and hurried back to his truck. Maybe he worried for nothing. Ceejay might have put her animosity toward Allison behind her, especially since he'd confronted her about taking her anger at Matt out on all of them. Maybe she'd even appreciate his family's willingness to help out. *Sure, and the pigs in Indiana are going to start smelling like roses.*

The countryside flew by as he formulated a plan for disarming Ceejay's temper. A sound argument and logic should work.

They wouldn't. Not with her. He'd have to get past her defenses. He sighed and turned into the driveway. A rush of adrenaline hit his bloodstream, turning his mouth into a desert and his insides into a jumbled mess.

The house still stood. *That's a good sign, but where's her car?* Maybe he'd gotten lucky and she'd stopped in town to run some errands before coming home. He climbed out of his truck and made for the door in double time. "Mom, Dad, you here?"

"Oh, Noah." Allison rushed at him from the living room. "I did it again. We shouldn't have come. I…I thought Ceejay would be OK with seeing me here…and…"

"Don't be too hard on yourself." *Great. Crisis not averted.* "Things have been hectic around here, and she's gotten one piece of bad news after another." He looked past her. "Where's Dad?"

"He's out walking off the ear-beating I gave him." She shook her head. "He...he threatened Ceejay. We—"

"Wait. Back up. He *threatened* her?" Noah went into battle-ready mode. "You'd better tell me what happened."

"Come sit down. Do you want coffee? I just made some."

"Sure." Noah jammed his hands into his pockets and followed her into the kitchen.

"Where's Ceejay now?"

"I don't know. She took off shortly after she found us here." Allison placed a mug of coffee on the table. "Sit."

He complied and wrapped his hands around the mug while she caught him up on everything that had gone down. *Dammit.*

"Ceejay was in bad shape, Noah. She seemed...bewildered, lost. I don't know." Allison's brow creased. "Maybe even a little hurt, like she thought nobody saw her as capable of taking care of things on her own."

"Christ." Noah leaned back and stared at the ceiling. Where had she gone? "How long ago did she leave?"

"About forty minutes ago. Maybe she went to get Lucinda."

He shook his head. "The Offermeyers only live a couple of miles from here. She would've been back by now."

"Wouldn't she have stayed to visit?"

"It's possible." Sirens broke the normal country quiet, two, maybe three. They drew closer. The sound crescendoed and passed. Another siren from the opposite direction converged. An icy finger of dread traced from the base of his skull down his spine. The area wasn't what you'd call densely populated, and the two-lane county road didn't get much traffic. "I have a bad feeling." Noah shot out of his chair and headed for the front door.

Allison ran after him. "Where are you going?"

"Those sirens…I gotta see…I have to find Ceejay." Sweat and the shakes. He had to fight the trigger, fight sinking into a flashback. His lungs labored to catch up with his pulse. Noah clenched his jaw and forced himself to concentrate on the here and now.

Allison called out, "Call me when you do."

He nodded and ran for his truck. The bad feeling had turned to shrapnel in his gut. The sirens stopped. They hadn't faded into the distance. They'd stopped. His truck bounced along the ruts in the driveway, jarring him. He gunned the engine and flew down the two-lane in the direction of the Offermeyers'.

A mile down, the road was blocked. Two patrol cars with lights flashing flanked a fire engine. An ambulance with its back open caught his eye. Two attendants unloaded a gurney and pushed it toward the edge of the culvert. Noah pulled off onto the shoulder and bolted for the ditch.

"Whoa, hold on there." An officer put his arm out to block him. "We need to keep the area clear."

Noah strained to see beyond the emergency vehicles. "I've got to—"

"You don't *got to* do anything, Noah. Let the professionals take care of her."

Hell no! His worst nightmare. All the blood rushed from his head and spots went off like fireworks in front of his eyes. He blinked and focused on the deputy. He remembered meeting him at the Fourth of July celebration. "Deputy Taylor, right?"

"That's right, and we have everything under control."

Ceejay. "Is she…" The words stuck in his throat. He couldn't force them past the lump.

"She's banged up, but her vitals are good. She's being taken to St. Mary's Warrick Hospital in Boonville."

"I need to see her."

"She's not conscious. You can see her once she's been taken care of."

"No. I need to see her *now*." He'd lay the deputy out on the asphalt if he had to. Gut-deep and visceral, his need to lay eyes on Ceejay overrode everything else. If he didn't see her chest rise and fall, if he didn't confirm for himself that she still had a pulse, someone was going to get hurt. "Move."

Deputy Taylor frowned, glanced over his shoulder at the EMTs with their loaded gurney, and nodded. "A minute. She needs to get to the emergency room. We figure the accident happened a while ago. A passerby called it in and—"

He didn't wait to hear the rest. All the air left his lungs in a rush. Noah pushed past the deputy to weave his way through the vehicles until he was near enough to see her on the gurney. The attendants collapsed the frame and started to load her into the ambulance. "Wait."

They'd strapped her to a backboard and put a neck collar on to keep her still. She had a gash on her forehead near her hairline. He didn't know where to touch her. "Ceejay."

"Sir, we need to go."

"Give me a second." Noah leaned close and put his hand on her cheek. Her skin was damp, but warm. Relief swamped him. "Honey, I'm here."

Her eyelids flickered and she moaned. "Hurts."

"I know, baby. I'm sorry. They're taking you to the hospital now."

"Lucinda," she whispered. Her eyes opened for a second, connected with his, then fluttered shut.

Her pain and helplessness slammed into him. All his fault. "I'll take care of Lucinda. Don't you worry."

The EMT stepped closer and gripped the gurney. "She may have internal injuries. Every minute we delay—"

"Yeah, I'm sorry. Go." Noah stepped back and let them do their job. The siren's shrillness shredded his heart. Seeing her injured, hurt because of him, brought him lower than he'd ever been. He should've made sure his parents understood they weren't to come to Perfect without Ceejay's OK. He turned back to his truck. She was alive. Thank God she was alive. His chest constricted, and he could hardly draw a breath.

"Noah," Deputy Taylor called. "Take this home for her." He handed Ceejay's purse to him. "That old car of hers is totaled. We'll have it towed."

He nodded and walked on shaky legs back to his truck. Sitting in the driver's seat, he glanced at her purse. Pain tore a wide path through him. He was an idiot, and he didn't deserve her.

What if Ceejay never got past her hostility toward his stepmother? How could they ever have a future with Matt in their past? He gripped the steering wheel, rested his forehead on his knuckles, and fought the urge to weep. Turning his head slightly, he glanced at his watch. The Offermeyers weren't expecting anyone to pick Lucinda up until 1400 hours. He had time. He needed to make something clear to his father before bringing Lucinda home. Someone knocking on his car door brought him up.

"You all right to drive?" Deputy Taylor rested his hands on the open window frame.

Noah sucked in a breath. "I'm a little shook up."

"I can give you a ride to the hospital if you want."

"No, thanks for the offer, though." Noah shook his head. "My folks are here. I need to let them know what happened, and then Lucinda…" His voice broke. *Shit.*

"This has surely been a tough time for the Lovejoys. You let us know if you all need anything. Me and the wife would be happy to babysit, or anything else you can think of. Jenny and Ceejay have certainly helped us out plenty of times."

"Thanks, I will."

The deputy touched the rim of his hat and walked away. Noah waited until he couldn't hear the siren anymore, turned his truck around, and headed for home. Thoughts of patricide passed through his mind.

Both Lovejoy women in the hospital, one in Evansville, and the other in Boonville, wherever the hell that was, and one little girl who would soon find herself without her mother and great-aunt. She'd be frightened and confused. He couldn't mess up when it came to Lucinda.

His jaw tightened at the sight of his father standing on the Lovejoys' front porch. Noah slammed the truck door behind him. His hands curled into fists as he strode to the steps. "What the hell did you do, Dad?"

"I made it clear to Ms. Lovejoy that *no* isn't an option when it comes to Lucinda."

"Great. Did you consider what kind of stress Ceejay's already under? Her aunt has cancer. She found out today that her mother died of an accidental drug overdose. On top of all of that you threatened her?"

"I—"

"Shut the hell up and listen. If you ever threaten her again, it's the last you'll ever hear or see of me."

"Noah, you can't mean that!" Allison cried from behind the screen door.

"I do mean it, Mom. Those sirens...Ceejay's been in a car accident, and it wouldn't have happened if she hadn't left here so upset." Tears stung his eyes. He turned away to face the orchard. "She..." He swallowed hard. "Ceejay and Lucinda mean the world to me, and I've screwed everything up enough as it is. I won't have any kind of threat hanging over her head."

"Oh, honey, we can work this out. Sit down, both of you."

Sitting was beyond him. He was keyed up and ready to spring. Noah shook his head, while his heart pounded from the adrenaline still rushing through his system.

His father made no move to take a seat either. He plunged his hands deep inside his pockets and widened his stance.

"Oh, for crying out loud." Allison sat. "You two idiots are far more similar than you realize. Both as stubborn as concrete." She sent them both a disapproving scowl. "Your father overreacted when he saw me crying. Ceejay's words didn't upset me. It's what I saw in her eyes that brought me to tears. That poor girl has been through so much. She's devastated, lost, and everything feels out of control to her."

Allison sighed. "I've been there. I had a knee-jerk reaction because it brought all those feelings back." She raked him and his father with a look he knew well from his childhood. She meant business. "Ceejay didn't tell me to leave. That's progress."

Noah glared at his father. "You're going to make this right."

"I meant what I said." His dad's stare clashed with his. "Ms. Lovejoy needs to come to terms with the fact that Lucinda is our granddaughter. If you can talk her into letting us have visitation, I'll back down. If not, I'll do what I have to."

"We can't bully our way into their lives, Ed." Allison shook her head. "Didn't we just have this conversation?"

"I think it would be best if you two head home." Noah sent a pleading look to his stepmother. "I can handle things here, and once I've had a chance to talk to Ceejay—"

"No. I'm not leaving." Allison lifted her chin. "We don't even know the extent of Ceejay's injuries yet. She might not be able to take care of herself, much less her aunt and Lucinda."

"It's my understanding she has a large extended family here in Perfect. The Lovejoys don't need us, Allie. I have to agree with Noah on this." His father shot him a determined look. "We aren't giving up, only stepping back."

"It's not about need. I'm staying because our son loves Ceejay. Noah needs our support. The Lovejoys need our support, and maybe if we try, we can get through to Ceejay."

"I doubt she'll talk to any of us after this." Noah pulled out his phone and entered the name of the hospital into a search engine for directions. "I've got to get to the hospital. I'll pick Lucinda up on the way home." He headed down the veranda steps and back to his truck for the umpteenth time that day.

Driving to St. Mary's gave him time to regain some control. How should he handle the situation with Ceejay? *Beg for forgiveness.* Noah pulled into the parking lot determined to keep it together. Two visits in one day. Two different hospitals. St. Mary's was smaller, older. Noah made his way into the lobby, stopping at the front desk for directions. He headed down a narrow corridor toward the emergency room, turned a corner, and pulled up short. "Sheriff."

Sheriff Maurer hooked his thumbs into his belt. "They just took Ceejay upstairs to surgery. She's not in the ER anymore."

"How…how is she?"

"Both her wrists are broken. Her left is in bad shape. That's why they're doing surgery." He gestured for Noah to walk with him down the hall. "She also has a fractured clavicle, a couple of cracked ribs, and a concussion."

Noah wanted to lean against the wall—maybe pound his head against the cinder blocks a few times. Instead, he kept pace with the sheriff and tried to get enough oxygen in his lungs to stay upright. Here he was, right back in the hospital's small lobby and entrance without even a glimpse of Ceejay.

"Sit." Sheriff Maurer pointed to a chrome and leather chair. "You look like you're about to drop."

Noah lowered himself into the seat. The sheriff loomed in front of him.

"You seem to have a knack for upsetting Ceejay."

"I—"

"First, you lied to her about who you are. Then you sprang Matt's mother on her without so much as a by-your-leave. Now, you've invited your folks to her home without a moment's consideration for her feelings."

"Now, wait a minute." Anger coursed through him. "I didn't invite anybody anywhere, and even if I did—"

"You gonna make upsetting her a habit, son?" Sheriff Maurer glared at him. "If that's the plan, you'd better rethink your involvement with Ceejay."

Noah shot up and went toe-to-toe with him. "What goes on between me and Ceejay is none of your business."

"Maybe it would be best for everyone if you moved on."

"Did you talk to Ceejay?" All the fight left him. "Is…is that what she said?"

"Don't need to talk to her." Sheriff Maurer's chin jutted out. "She's had two men in her life. Two. You and Matt, and you've both caused nothing but trouble."

Was it true? Had he caused nothing but trouble?

Sheriff Maurer adjusted his uniform hat. "Now I have to drive back to Evansville to tell Jenny that her girl is in the hospital. Do you know what that's going to do to her?"

Biting back the urge to tell the sheriff where to go, Noah pushed past him, strode through the lobby and out of the hospital to the parking lot. It hurt too much to poke around in the wound the sheriff's words had opened. Instead, he focused on Lucinda. He just needed to keep his mind on the task ahead. There would be plenty of time to worry over everything else later.

Noah caught sight of Gail as he drove down the Offermeyers' driveway. She stood in the front yard with her youngest perched on her hip. Lucinda and Celeste had climbed on the lowest rung of the corral fence attached to the Offermeyers' barn to get close to the mare and her two foals. Noah pulled his truck off the drive and parked in the grass.

"Hey, Noah. You're early," Gail called as she walked toward him with one hand shielding her eyes from the bright afternoon sun. "Did you happen to see what all those sirens were about a while ago?"

Noah glanced Lucinda's way. She was still enraptured by the horses and hadn't turned to acknowledge his arrival yet. He waited until Gail reached him, so he could keep his voice down. "Ceejay flipped her car into the ditch. It happened at the bend about halfway between your place and theirs."

"Oh, my God! Is she all right?"

"She has some broken bones. That's all I know. I haven't seen her yet. The ambulance took her to St. Mary's in Boonville. She was in surgery by the time I got there."

"Do you want us to keep Lucinda tonight? Brandon is at a sleepover, and I know Celeste would love having her here."

"No. I appreciate the offer, but my parents are here, and they want to see her."

"If there's anything we can do, you just let us know. Bring Lucinda over any time you need to." Gail shook her head. "I just can't believe it. First Jenny's cancer. Now this…"

Guilt poked at the open wound in his gut. "I have to get Lucinda home." He also had to call Ted and let him know what happened. Ceejay's cousin could inform the rest of her family. God, he wasn't looking forward to having them descend upon him. Maybe he'd catch a break, and they wouldn't come over until after his father left. "Lucinda," he called.

"Uncle Noah," she cried as she hopped down from the fence. "I don't wanna go yet."

He walked over to the corral with Gail beside him. "I know, but your grandma can't wait to see you."

Lucinda's eyes grew wide, and she started hopping. "Grandma's here?"

He opened his arms, and she ran to him. He scooped her up and held her close, breathing in her sunshine and fresh air scent. The sudden sting of tears took him by surprise, and he struggled to get himself under control. "She is, and she brought you something."

Lucinda leaned back and smiled at Celeste. "My grandma is going to spoil me rotten; that's what she said." She turned back to him. "Did she bring anything for my friend?"

"I don't think so, but I'll bet whatever she brought, you can share with Celeste the next time she comes over to play."

"OK." She put her tiny arms around his neck and laid her head on his shoulder.

"Don't you have something to say to Mrs. Offermeyer?"

"Thank you, Mrs. Offmeyer," Lucinda murmured, and yawned.

"You're welcome, honey. Call me if you need anything, Noah." Gail rubbed Lucinda's back. "I mean it."

"I will." They reached his truck, and he strapped Lucinda into her car seat. She was almost asleep by the time he was behind the wheel. Maybe it would be best to let her nap before breaking the news about her mother to her. He climbed in and leaned out his window. "Thanks for taking her today."

"It's no problem. She keeps Celeste busy." Her baby fussed and rubbed his eyes, and she bounced him on her hip. "We all love Ceejay and Jenny. I can't even tell you how many times they've stepped in when we needed help. I know you're new around here, and maybe you don't feel comfortable asking. Do it anyway. We owe you."

Noah nodded. It was all he could manage before turning his truck and heading home. He'd spent far too much time in his vehicle today and needed a break. His heart wrenched at the sight of Ceejay's car as they passed. Glancing in the rearview mirror, he was relieved to see Lucinda sleeping. How would he explain why her mom's car was upside down in the ditch? He inched along the Lovejoys' drive at about two miles an hour, parked, and gently disentangled her from the car seat. She sighed and snuggled against his shoulder without waking. His heart melted. He was in for life. No doubt about it.

Nope. He wasn't going to turn tail and leave just because the sheriff of Warrick County thought it *best*. He'd find a way to make things right. How, he hadn't a clue, but dammit, Ceejay and Lucinda were his, and he'd fight like hell to keep them.

His dad opened the front door for him. Noah turned so he could see Lucinda. His father's face softened as he ran a hand over her curls. "She looks like Allison," he whispered. Their eyes met, and a moment of understanding passed between them, a connection and a common purpose. If there was one thing they could agree on, it was this. Family.

"Ed, is that Noah?" Allison called from the kitchen.

Lucinda stirred, stretched in his arms, and resettled. Allison approached from the kitchen, and his dad gestured to her for quiet.

She whispered, "Let me take her upstairs and put her to bed."

He transferred the sleeping child to his stepmother, and his dad followed her upstairs. Noah walked back out to the veranda and pulled out his cell. Time to call Ted.

After everything had been settled about who would pick Jenny up from the hospital tomorrow, he joined his parents in Lucinda's room. His father studied the ABCs and 123s tapestries Ceejay had beaded for her daughter. He turned when Noah entered.

"Ceejay did those," Noah whispered. He'd been blown away when he'd first laid eyes on the pieces. How long had it taken her to create them? The alphabet had been beaded in block form with flowering vines and butterflies weaving through them, some beaded, some embroidered. The numbers were in varying colors with the same vines and butterflies so that the two framed works fit nicely together. Amazing detail. Heirloom quality.

His father's brow rose slightly in appreciation. Allison ran her fingers through Lucinda's curls as she sat next to her on the bed. Noah tilted his head toward the door and walked into the hall. His father followed.

"Would you two mind watching her for a while? I need to get back to St. Mary's."

"Go ahead. We'll be fine." His father shifted his posture. "Look, Noah, I…"

"I get it, Dad. We'd both do whatever necessary to protect our loved ones. You need to know this—Ceejay and Lucinda *are* my family. I'll do whatever it takes to keep them safe. I'll do whatever it takes to see that they have what they need." Emotion flickered through his dad's eyes. Pride?

"We'll talk later. Go." His father turned back to Lucinda's room.

When had he become the equivalent of a human Ping-Pong ball? He took the stairs as fast as his prosthetic would allow and rushed out the Lovejoys' door to his truck. Noah pulled back onto the country road and headed back to Boonville. At least Sheriff Maurer wouldn't be there this time.

He slowed down going around the bend where Ceejay's accident had happened. A tow truck, lights flashing, maneuvered around in the middle of the road, getting into position to lower the winch. Noah gave the driver a two-fingered salute as he edged his truck by, like all the locals gave in passing. It didn't matter it they knew one another or not. The small acknowledgment made him feel connected, like he belonged, and he needed that now.

Pulling into the hospital parking lot, Noah took a deep breath and let it out slowly. Surely Ceejay would be out of surgery and in a room by now. He hurried to the front desk, where a silver-haired receptionist wearing a headset sat behind a computer screen.

"I'm looking for Ceejay Lovejoy. She was in surgery earlier this afternoon."

Her fingers flew over the keyboard. "She's in room two fourteen. Are you family?"

"Yes." As far as he was concerned.

"Go on up, then. The elevators are down that hall and to your left."

"Thank you." He was already on his way as he said it. The elevator whooshed open the second he pushed the up button. It was empty. Lucky break. His gut twisted into a knot on the way down the hall. What would he say? A doctor walked out of her room just as he arrived. He glanced at the ID on her white coat. "How is she, Dr. Jordan?"

"She's going to be fine. Are you family?"

He nodded.

"She's awake, but still recovering from her surgery. Don't overtax her."

"I won't. Thanks." He pushed the door open and walked in. Ceejay had been placed in a room the size of a large closet. Her eyes were closed, and she looked so small and broken in the bed, it nearly brought him to his knees. Both her wrists were encased in casts with dark blue gauze covering them. Her left arm was in a sling-like contraption that wrapped around her torso. Multiple scratches and small cuts covered what skin he glimpsed. "Ceejay?"

He heard the intake of her breath from across the room, and his heart took a nosedive. "How are you, honey?" Noah moved to the chair beside her. She had stitches on her forehead, and the gash had swelled to an angry purple goose egg.

She turned her head to glance at him, then turned to stare at the ceiling. "I've been better."

"Dr. Jordan says you're going to be fine. Do you need anything? Can I do something to help you feel more comfortable?

She shook her head, and a single tear leaked out of the corner of her eye. Pain seared his insides as the teardrop traced down her cheek and fell to the pillow. "I'm sorry my parents surprised you like they did." He ran his hand over the back of his scalp. "I didn't invite them. You know that, right?"

"Doesn't matter."

"It does. I know how you feel about them."

Her brow furrowed. "Go home, Noah."

"Not until you tell me we're all right."

A long sigh escaped her. She closed her eyes, and her mouth tightened into a straight line. More tears leaked out. Helplessness and frustration surged through him. He couldn't even take her hand in his to offer her comfort. Her fingers were swollen, and both hands were partially encased in plaster. "Ceejay, talk to me." He waited, holding his breath, and smoothed the hair away from her injured forehead.

"Please go," she whispered. "Can't do this now."

Can't do what now? Tell me to get the hell out of your life? Had the sheriff been right after all? The woman he loved lay busted and bruised in a hospital bed, and it wouldn't have happened if it hadn't been for him.

He couldn't take any more. The tenuous hold he had on his emotions snapped as the life he'd been building for himself in Perfect collapsed all around him. He didn't want to have this breakdown in front of her. Noah shot of the chair, out the door down the hallway, down the stairs, and back to his truck.

His heart pumped a furious rhythm inside his chest, and he no longer tried to stem the tears scalding his eyes. He leaned back in the bucket seat, closed his eyes, and let the sweltering waves of the desert heat take him. This time he welcomed the parade of the dead. Their eyes couldn't condemn him any more than he condemned himself. Noah rode the flashback, no longer caring where it took him or for how long.

Sweating and weak, he came back to the present. He swiped at the wetness on his cheeks. Nothing had changed. He still sat in his truck in the middle of the parking lot. Ceejay still lay in her hospital bed in Boonville, and Jenny remained in hers in Evansville. Nothing he could do about either.

A hollowness spread inside him. He'd take hollow over the flashback. Hollow came close to calm, and calm he could handle. He turned the key in the ignition. He needed to regroup, hide out until he regained some perspective. Hell, he needed to regain his equilibrium. Lucinda didn't care about flashbacks or broken hearts. She needed him front and center.

Noah pulled his cell phone out of his back pocket and hit speed dial. Allison answered on the second ring. "How's everything on your end?"

"Good. Lucinda is still sleeping. What did you find out about Ceejay?"

"She's in room two fourteen. That's about all I know. She… she wouldn't talk to me." He swallowed the lump in his throat.

"Give her some time. She's had a lot to deal with and just had surgery. She's probably not up to talking to anybody."

"Listen, if it's all right with you, I need some time to…to…" *Get my shit together.*

"I understand, Noah. Do what you need to do."

"Thanks. I'll be in the bay area of the carriage house if you need me. Talk to you later." He snapped his phone shut and pulled out of the parking lot, heading for Perfect. Lowering the windows, Noah inhaled the fresh country air. Other than the hog stench, he loved the way southern Indiana smelled. He didn't know which scent came from which plant, but the sweetness was a balm to his raw nerves, and he never grew tired of breathing it in. By the time he parked next to Jenny's car, it was almost five p.m., and he'd spent most of the day driving from one place to another. He needed to do something physical.

The path to his apartment had a well-worn look to it, and he set his course for the carriage bays. He didn't want to think or feel. He wanted to lose himself in something completely unrelated to the day's stressors. Flipping on the newly updated overhead lights, Noah surveyed the workspace he and Ted were creating. A large piece of pegboard leaned against the wall. He'd mount it on the wall and organize his tools. Noah grabbed a tape measure, a pencil from the workbench, and threw himself into the job. It felt good to lift, drill, and fasten. None of the worry went away, but the physical activity gained him some much-needed control.

He stepped back to survey the job. Satisfied, he crossed the room for the hooks and started putting them in rows and columns.

His father walked through the door and peered around. "Nice space. What do you plan to do here?"

"Not sure yet." Not true, but he didn't feel like explaining.

"Allison sent me out here to get you. Lucinda is up and asking for her mother."

"Is she upset?"

"Not yet. The novelty of having grandparents here hasn't worn off."

Noah picked up the last remaining tools and put them in their places on the pegboard. "Let's go." Sweet Pea greeted them at the back door, and he let him outside before heading to Lucinda's room. What kind of child-friendly explanation could he offer for her mom's absence? Lucinda sat on the edge of her bed with Allison kneeling on the floor tying her shoes. She caught sight of him and slid off the bed.

"Hey, sweetheart."

She hugged his knees and peered up at him. "Where's Mommy?"

Noah picked her up. She wrapped her arms around his neck, laid her head on his shoulder, and gave his father a wary look.

"You met your grandpa?"

She nodded and her hold tightened. He moved to sit with her in the rocking chair. "It's all right, Luce. Did he tell you he's my dad?"

She leaned back to give him a dubious look, and he couldn't help smiling. "He is."

With a sigh, she settled herself against him again. It always took her a while to make the transition from nap time to fully awake. He set the rocker in motion, and his parents seated themselves on her bed. "She's not awake yet. Give her a minute."

"Grandma says she's gonna stay wif us for a while."

"That's right." He rubbed her back.

"Where's my mommy?"

Man, he wished he could turn back the clock and undo some of the mess he'd caused. "Your mom is fine, but she had an accident with her car. She's in the hospital getting fixed up, and then she'll be home."

Tears filled her eyes. "Does she got bad cells growing in her t-too?"

"No, sweetheart." Noah shifted her so that he could look her in the eye. "She broke her wrists. When she comes home, I'll bet she'll let you draw on her casts."

"What're casts?"

At least she looked more interested than upset.

Allison came over to squat at eye level with her. "Casts are a hard covering the doctors will put over your mom's wrists so they heal the way they're supposed to. Do you want to go down to the kitchen for a snack?"

Lucinda shook her head, tucked her hands in front of her, and rested against him again. She surveyed the adults in the room. "I can say my ABCs."

"Really?" His dad chuckled. "Let's hear it."

For the next few minutes, Lucinda performed all her tricks for her enraptured audience, and Noah's heart swelled with pride.

"All right, Smarty Pants, what's this letter?" His dad pointed to the T on Ceejay's alphabet tapestry.

"That's a T-tee, Grandpa."

He pointed to another letter. "How about this one?"

"H, hah," she cried and sat up straight, rising to the challenge.

"And this?" He moved to the numbers.

Lucinda held up three fingers. "Three."

Noah caught his stepmother's eye. The pride he saw there reflected his own, and he grinned at her.

"OK. You win. Do you think you might give your old grandpa a hug?"

Lucinda turned to Noah as if looking for permission. "Do you want to give him a hug?"

She nodded, setting her curls in motion.

"Go ahead, then."

He helped her off his lap, and she ran to his dad. He picked her up and made growling noises as he hugged her tight. Lucinda squealed and giggled. Noah sighed. Another hurdle passed.

"Uncle Noah said you brought me something, Grandma," Lucinda said the second her feet hit the floor.

"That's right. I did. Do you want to go see?" Allison held out her hand for Lucinda, and the two of them left the room.

Noah stayed where he was, listening to the sound of Lucinda's chatter fade down the hall.

"That one's going to break a few hearts when she grows up." His father shook his head. "Smart as a whip and well on her way to becoming a heart-stopper."

Noah nodded. "She is, isn't she?"

"What the hell was wrong with Matt?"

"Your guess is as good as mine, but I don't intend to make the same mistake."

"You're really serious about Ceejay?"

Strong emotion welled up, and all he could manage was a nod. What if she never talked to him again?

"Noah, I'm…" His father swallowed hard and studied the beaded alphabet. "Shit."

Noah's brow rose. He'd never seen his dad choke up. Had he been about to apologize?

His father swallowed a few times and turned to the door. "Is there a good pizza place in this backwater town? I'm starving, and I'll bet our little girl could go for pizza and ice cream."

"You're going to spoil her rotten."

His dad grunted. "Until her mother kicks us out, anyway."

CHAPTER FIFTEEN

Tears leaked out of the corners of Ceejay's eyes, traced down her cheeks, and fell onto the hospital pillow beneath her head in a steady drip, drip, drip. Her mother? Dead. Aunt Jenny? Cancer. Her dream job? Gone. Even if they did hold the job for her until she recovered, she couldn't leave now. Not with Jenny sick. All her dreams, all the plans she'd made sifted out of her grasp like so much ash in a stiff breeze.

And as if that wasn't enough, the conversation she'd had with her doctor right after her surgery kept bouncing around in her head.

"You were unconscious when you came in, so we didn't get a chance to ask. When was the date of your last menstruation?"

"It's been almost three weeks, and yes. There is a possibility I could be pregnant."

"Hmm. Best not to take any chances. This early, a pregnancy test would still show a negative. We'll give you a nonnarcotic painkiller."

Thinking about being pregnant added another brick of anxiety to her growing pile, and the whole mess settled in her gut. She shifted her position away from the tear-dampened spot on the pillowcase and grimaced. Moving even that little bit set off a new wave of throbbing pain. Her head ached. Hell, all of her ached—especially her breaking heart.

Her bones would heal soon enough. She could always find another job and make new plans, but Jenny's cancer? *Shit, don't go there.* She stared at the blank, white ceiling above her hospital bed. Maybe if she stared hard enough, a lifeline would drop, and she could pull herself out of the deep, dark quagmire of grief and self-pity sucking her down.

To top it all off, every time the door to her hospital room opened, her heart gave a hopeful leap, only to crash-land on the cold linoleum floor. Noah hadn't returned since she'd told him to go home, and she needed him. Desperately.

A fresh wave of misery swamped her, and a new surge of tears dampened the dry spot she'd moved to. Crap. If she kept this up, she'd dehydrate, and the nurses already looked at her like maybe it was time for a psych consult.

She heard voices in the hall and strained to hear who it might be. The door handle twisted, and her heart did its leapfrog thing. Lifting her head, she tried to wipe the tears from her cheeks. The heavy cast on her wrist smacked against the bridge of her nose, sending brand-new pain stinging through her. "Owww."

The door opened, and a strangled groan broke free. The Langfords were the last people she wanted to see. Yet here they were, staring down at her from the foot of the bed, with Ed's threats still ringing in her ears. She let her head drop back onto the soggy pillow—right back into despondency. It wasn't Noah, and the disappointment sat heavy on her chest, making small talk impossible. Not that she had any to offer.

"The nurses are worried about you." Allison grasped the strap of her purse with both hands. "They say you've been in tears since you woke up after your surgery yesterday. Is it…could it be a reaction to the anesthesia?" Her expression was the picture of caring concern.

"Could be." Let them believe whatever they wanted. Maybe they'd leave sooner. An awkward silence took up the space be-- tween them. Allison gave her husband a nudge with an elbow to the ribs.

"I owe you an apology." Mr. Langford shifted his stance as if challenging her to dispute his sincerity. "You have my word. There will be no legal action taken, but—"

"If you don't mind, I'm trying to get some rest." She went back to staring at the ceiling.

Mr. Langford stepped closer to his wife and put his arm around her waist. The protective gesture sent jealousy spiraling through Ceejay. She wanted that kind of concern, that kind of masculine protection. She wanted Noah. Could her life suck any more than it did right this minute? *Man, this self-pity pool just keeps getting deeper and deeper, with no flotation device in sight.*

"Ed, why don't you go search for some decent coffee. I think I saw a little shop across the street from the parking lot."

A look passed between them. Allison's pleading. Ed's skeptical. Their silent conversation fascinated Ceejay. She knew the moment he caved to his wife's wishes. Interesting. Clearly Allison had the tough son of a bitch wrapped up tight and tied with a ribbon. She sighed. Too bad she didn't have a clue how to do that.

"All right, Allie. I'll be back shortly." He leaned in and kissed his wife before turning to her. "Do you take anything in your coffee?"

Hell, why not let him fetch for me? "Yes, lots of cream and three packets of sugar. So much cream the color is more a light tan than brown, and don't use the fake stuff. Make that four packets of sugar. Thanks."

He let out a huffing sound and walked out of the room. Once he'd gone, Allison snatched a dry pillow from the top shelf of the narrow closet. She returned, replaced the soggy pillow with the dry one, and plumped it up before moving on to the twisted blankets.

"You don't have to do that."

"I know. I want to."

The soft, sweet scent of her perfume wafted over Ceejay as Allison tugged the blankets into some semblance of order. Ceejay relaxed into the comfort of having someone else take care of her.

"I'm sorry, Ceejay. I know what a shock it must have been to find us in your house. Noah told us about Jenny's surgery, and we came right away." Allison stepped back and sent a worried look her way. "We truly want to help. I hope you'll let us."

She was far too deep in her own misery to muster the kind of strength it took to hold on to her anger any longer. It wasn't Allison's fault her husband was a jerk, and none of what happened with Matt had anything to do with her either. "Yeah, it was a shock." She let out a shaky breath. "I was already upset, and…" More tears slid down her cheeks. "Crap." She sniffed. "I can't seem to…to s-stop."

Allison grabbed a few tissues from the box on the bedside table and wiped Ceejay's eyes and nose. "You're in quite a state."

"I know, huh." Ceejay laughed through the tears. "It's like everything I've corked up for twenty-four years is coming out in a big weepy, snotty mess."

"Do you want to talk about it?"

"I…I wouldn't know where to start." She laugh-cried again, too far gone to be embarrassed.

Allison reached over and smoothed Ceejay's hair back from her eyes. "How about we start with my son? Let's talk about Matt."

Ceejay's tensed at the mention of his name, and she turned away to hide the churning bitterness.

"You'll never know how sorry we all are for what he did. I'm still having trouble believing he could be so callous and irresponsible."

Another strangled laugh escaped. "Yeah, me too."

"You may be surprised to hear this, but I went through a similar situation with his father. He went out to buy diapers one night and never came back. Matt was only three weeks old when my husband walked out on us. I didn't have a job. I was estranged from my family. I didn't have two nickels to rub together, and only a few weeks of rent left on the apartment where we lived." She lifted an elegant eyebrow. "Which was a tiny, dilapidated dump in a very bad neighborhood, by the way."

Despite herself, Allison's revelation drew Ceejay's interest. "What did you do?"

"I thought he might come back once he cooled down. After two futile weeks of waiting, I went crawling back to my family and begged for help."

"Did they help?

Allison's expression seemed to turn inward, as if she relived those difficult times. "They gave me a job in the family business so I could help myself. My mom watched Matt until I was caught up enough financially to pay for day care, then my parents made it clear Matthew was my responsibility. Those were the toughest years of my life."

"S-seeing you the first time you came to Perfect set off all kinds of emotional s-stuff. You have no idea how awful Matt's leaving was for me. I was pregnant and unmarried. Everybody in town knew he didn't want me or our baby. Do you k-know what it's l-like to face that kind of pity every freaking day of your life?"

"I can imagine."

"I always believed my m-mom didn't want me either. Nobody even *knows* who my father is, least of all me, and then Matt d-did what he did." She didn't even have the words to express what his leaving had done to her, how it still tainted every aspect of her life.

What is it about me that makes leaving so easy?

She hiccupped. "B-being a single parent is terrifying. Everything is on my shoulders—all the responsibility, all the worries. What if I mess up?"

"I know. I had the same fears and insecurities when I was on my own with Matt. You won't mess up, Ceejay." Allison got up, sat on the edge of the bed, and put her arms around Ceejay, casts and all, to give her an awkward hug. "You're an amazing mother to Lucinda."

"Ow."

"Oh, sorry." She leaned back and patted Ceejay's leg. "I thought maybe you could use a hug."

"I could. It just hurts. Everything hurts. Thanks anyway. That was nice of you, especially considering…" In spite of the rudeness she'd shown her, Allison came back with nothing but kindness. Ceejay didn't deserve her warmth and concern, but she took it all in anyway.

The dam holding her emotions back crumbled, and words started spilling out. "My mom…she didn't abandon me. She died. My mom died, and it was an accident." She sobbed. "I…I'm so afraid for Jenny, and I feel so h-helpless. I don't know what I'll do if…"

She gulped air and squeezed her eyes shut. "I'm sure that's way more than you wanted to hear. I j-just can't seem to stop. It's all circling around inside my head, and I c-can't make it stop."

Allison patted her leg again. The gesture was so maternal, Ceejay almost lost it again.

"I think you're way overdue and entitled."

Ceejay searched the room for something to count. Folds in the curtain hanging beside her bed. One, two, three. No use. Not even numbers could fix this mess. "I've ruined everything."

Allison's brow furrowed. "What have you ruined?"

"Look at me. I can't move my left side." She lifted her right arm in its heavy cast with her swollen fingers sticking out like sausage. "I can't even wipe my own nose. How can I take care of Jenny and Lucinda when I can't even take of myself? Besides, Jenny's been a mother to me all these years, and…and she asked her brothers to look after her instead of me. It f-feels like Matt and my mom leaving me all over."

"Oh, Ceejay. Your aunt didn't mean to hurt you. She knows how important it is for you to follow your dreams. Jenny didn't want to see everything fall apart for you because of her illness. She was trying to do what she thought was best."

"I can't leave. I couldn't leave her! How could she even think I would?" She sniffed and continued to stare at the ceiling. *Plus, I've screwed everything up with Noah. I told him to go away, and he hasn't come back.* She couldn't say that to his stepmom.

"You haven't ruined anything. You'll be there for Jenny in other ways, and though you might have to delay your plans, it's not forever." Allison shifted back to the chair. "Look, I'm sorry about the shock my first visit caused, but can you imagine what having a granddaughter means to me, especially after losing my son? I came here today to get some things settled between us." Allison's voice held an edge of determination. "We're Noah's family. He lives in the carriage house on your property, and our paths are going to cross. Can you make peace with that?"

Ceejay bit her lip, and a wave of shame shook her by the shoulders. "I'm sorry I've been so—"

"Don't apologize. I would have reacted the same way. I think it's best if we let the past go and start over." Allison smoothed her slacks down with her palms. "Lucinda is our granddaughter, and—"

"I know. I know. I haven't been fair." Her tears stopped, and she felt blessedly empty inside. "It's not your fault Matt did what he did, and I'm not going to keep Lucinda from you anymore because of him."

"I'm glad." Alison's voice quavered, and her eyes grew bright. "She's an amazing little girl." The tension in Allison's posture eased. "They're letting you out in about an hour. Would it be all right if we wait for your discharge papers and take you home?"

"Is Jenny there?"

"She is. Your uncle Jim picked her up."

"How is she? Did Sheriff Maurer—"

"He's been by her side since she left the hospital."

The empty place inside her filled with relief. "How is Lucinda? She must be worried."

"We've had a few challenging moments." Allison chuckled. "That child has a mind of her own, and she wants her mommy."

"I miss her too." What about Noah? Did he miss her as much as she missed him? She kept that question to herself. Now that her tears had finally stopped, a tentative peace settled over her. She had to admit she liked Allison. The poor woman had listened to her blurt out all of her deepest, darkest insecurities and hadn't run screaming from the room.

"Coffee anyone?" Ed came through the door with a cardboard tray holding three cups with lids. A bag dangled from his hand. "I brought scones. I thought maybe after nothing but hospital food, you might appreciate the change." He looked from her to Allison as if assessing how things had gone in his absence.

Whatever he saw must have pleased him, because he relaxed, and his eyes filled with warmth. Still, she had difficulty looking at him. "Thanks. A scone would be great."

He handed the bag to his wife and took a coffee from the tray. "Lots of cream and sugar." Placing the cup on the movable tray, he smiled at her, and Ceejay's breath snagged on an exhale. His smile replicated Noah's, and seeing it sent a pang of longing through her that almost started a fresh flow of tears. Had she blown it? Had Noah had enough of her pushing him away and called it quits?

"I'm going to need a straw and some help with this." Her voice broke. She couldn't even enjoy a good cup of coffee without help. At least her legs still worked.

By the time they got all the discharge papers signed, her prescription for pain pills filled, and she'd been loaded into Noah's truck, Ceejay wanted to curl up and sleep. Exhaustion battled with excitement at the prospect of seeing her daughter, Noah, and Jenny. She was too keyed up to rest.

She strained forward on the ride up the gravel driveway. Sweet Pea's frantic barking greeted her. Noah stood on the veranda next to Lucinda. Her midsection started a flutter riot that spread to her heart. Ed helped her out of the truck, and she glanced at Noah. His eyes were riveted on her, and he took a step.

"Mommy!" Lucinda tugged free of his hand and ran for her.

Noah caught her and lifted her off her feet. "Whoa, slow down there, sweetheart. Your mom needs you to be gentle."

"It's all right. Let her go." Ceejay's eyes stung. "I've missed you so much." Would he know the words were meant for him as well? She held her right arm out, and the minute Lucinda hit her legs, she wrapped her up as much as she could.

"Grandma said you broke your bones."

"That's right." Her eyes met Noah's, and she sucked in a breath at the despair she glimpsed there. What was going through his mind?

"Are you going to let me draw on your cast?" Lucinda touched the plaster and gauze encasing her right wrist.

"Absolutely, but right now I'm really tired." She turned her attention back to her daughter. "Do you want to help me to my room?"

Lucinda nodded and put her hands under the cast on her wrist as if to lift it for her. Ceejay let her lead the way past Noah and into the house. "Maybe we could stop by Aunt Jenny's room on the way to mine."

"She's sleeping right now."

Noah's voice and nearness sent a bittersweet thrill down her spine. "How is she?"

"Good." He placed his hand on the banister close behind her and kept it there as she climbed the stairs. "She's eating well."

Her nursing instincts kicked in. "Who's been taking care of her dressings and the drainage tube?"

"I've been taking care of her," Allison said as she followed them upstairs.

Ceejay nodded, swallowed the lump in her throat, and made her way into her room with Lucinda acting as her guide. Allison closed the door, leaving Noah alone in the hallway, and helped her get into a pair of boxers and a baggy T-shirt for a nap.

"Thanks for your help." Ceejay sank into the familiar softness of her own mattress.

"That's what we're here for. I'll be up to check on you in a couple of hours."

Lucinda pulled the sheet up to her chin for her, and Ceejay smiled. "Thank you, baby. You're a good little nurse."

"Sleep, Mommy." She kissed her cheek.

Ceejay nodded and closed her eyes, already halfway there. The door closed, and she let sleep take her.

🐏 🐏 🐏

From her place on the veranda, Ceejay shielded her eyes against the early morning sun and watched Edward Langford say good-bye to his wife. The way they held each other you'd think they were newlyweds, not an older couple married for years. Even though she wasn't completely comfortable around him, for Lucinda's sake, she appreciated that he'd stayed for her first full day home.

Noah strapped Lucinda in and crossed around the hood to the climb into the driver's seat. Lucinda had insisted on going with them, and they all agreed she'd enjoy watching planes take off and land. The truck disappeared down the gravel drive, and Allison headed back to the veranda.

"Do you need anything, Ceejay?"

"No, thanks. Take advantage of the lull. Put your feet up. We've been working you to the bone."

"I might just do that." Allison smiled and sank into the chair across from her. "I'm glad we could help out. We had to wrestle with all your uncles and aunts for the opportunity, you know."

"I can imagine." Ceejay shot her an amused look. "I don't know how to thank you. You've been great, and—"

"You don't have to thank me. I love spending time with my adorable granddaughter. She's so bright and confident, and she already has a great deal of empathy for a child her age."

Her daughter was amazing, and Allison's praise sent a rush of pride through Ceejay. "Thanks."

"I know it's hard for you to be around my husband." Allison propped her elbows on the table and rested her chin on her hands. "He can be difficult, but Ed is a good man. He's generous, fiercely loyal, and protective of his family. He and I are both hoping you'll allow us to include you in that circle."

"I need some time." Could she warm up to the man who had threatened to keep her in court until Lucinda turned eighteen? What would she have done if the tables had been turned? Lucinda meant the world to Allison. Anyone could see that, and Ed would do anything for his wife. Maybe she could forgive him. Eventually.

"Take as much time as you need. As far as we're concerned, you're already family." Allison tilted her head and surveyed the grounds. "I get why Noah loves it here so much. Something about this place is calming, healing. He's doing well. I have you and Jenny to thank for that, so we're even."

"Me?" Ceejay blinked, and her brow rose. "I don't think I've had anything to do with Noah's recovery. He told me once I'm like a scab he can't stop picking."

"Exactly." Allison laughed. "Go. Rest. We got you up too early this morning."

"I could use a nap." She yawned and rose from her place. Had they helped Noah? He did look healthier, thanks to diner leftovers and working outside in the fresh air and sunshine. If only he'd talk to her. It had been two days since he'd come to see her in the hospital and she'd told him to go home. What was keeping him?

She climbed the stairs like an old lady, stiff and slow. Her ribs still hurt when she moved, and getting around taxed her reserves. She had no energy. Careful not to let her bedroom door close all the way, she made her way to the bed, sank into the mattress with a heavy sigh, and fell asleep.

Ceejay woke up and checked her clock. She'd slept for two and a half hours, and her stomach grumbled with hunger. She swung her legs over the side of her bed and pushed herself up with her good elbow. If she was lucky, Allison had tucked some easy leftovers in the fridge, and she could manage putting together a snack to see her through until lunch. She nudged her door open and started down the hall toward the back stairs to the kitchen.

Jenny's door was open a crack, and she peeked inside the room. "Hey, can I come in?"

"Of course." Jenny had a book propped open on her lap and her reading glasses on. She took them off and set them aside. "The swelling on your forehead has gone down some."

"Look at us. We got out of different hospitals on the same day. Did you ever think we'd both be in such a state?" Ceejay eased herself down on the cushy chair next to the fireplace. A snack could wait. "How are you feeling?"

"Better. More optimistic. I'm going to go through with the rest of the cancer treatments."

The air left her lungs on a surge of relief, and she leaned her head back. "That's good."

"And you?" Jenny asked.

"I think Noah is done with me." The words slipped out before she had a chance to think them through. Maybe having uncorked everything with Allison had removed any kind of filter she'd had.

"Don't be ridiculous. He's still here, isn't he?"

"Sure, probably for Lucinda." Tears stung, and she blinked them away. "He's not talking to me, and I've scarcely seen him."

"Oh, honey." Jenny raised herself against the headboard. "He thinks your accident was his fault. He believes you're the one who's through with him."

"That's crazy. He wasn't driving too fast around the bend. I did that all on my own."

"Still, it's what he thinks right now, and he's hurting. He's crazy about you."

Her heart raced at the thought. "What makes you think so?"

"He told me. I started to ask him how he felt, and he told me before I got the question out."

"He did?" The hopeful thrill expanded to a bubble of joy, then burst as the despair she'd seen in Noah's eyes flashed through her mind. "That was then, and this is now." Ceejay glanced at her aunt. "I think I might've pushed him over the edge. When he came to the hospital to see me, I told him to go away. I couldn't handle any more that day. He must've misunderstood me."

Ceejay fussed with the lace doily on the arm of the upholstered chair. "And even if we do manage to work it out, how do I know if he's the real thing or just another recipe for the same old heartburn?"

"You don't. None of us do. You have to be willing to take the chance. Happiness doesn't come easy. It's work, but well worth the effort."

"I take it Sheriff Maurer finally told you how he feels?" She was pleased to see the color flooding her aunt's cheeks.

Jenny bit her lip and nodded. "I told him I feel the same. Have for years."

"Why did it take you two so long to get around to telling each other something so important?"

"I don't know. He's been my best friend forever. I didn't want to wreck what we had in case he didn't feel the same way." Jenny lifted a shoulder and let it drop. "We see each other every day, and I tell him everything. I guess I figured that was enough."

"Well, I'm glad you got around to spilling the truth. You both deserve to be happy."

"So do you. Ceejay, you know you're the daughter of my heart, and Harlen feels the same." Jenny averted her gaze and gripped her quilt. "That's why he...Harlen did something, honey, something you need to know about."

Ceejay tensed. "What?"

"The day of your accident Harlen was upset." Jenny's expression turned grim. "He ran into Noah at the hospital and said some things he shouldn't have."

Ceejay focused her attention on the dust motes swirling in the beam of sunlight streaming through her aunt's window. Could one count particles of dust? She didn't even try. The urge to count things had diminished since she'd spilled her guts to Allison. "What did he say?"

"He told Noah he'd caused you nothing but trouble, and that it would be best for everyone if he moved on."

"No!" She shot up from her chair, wincing at the pain her abrupt movement caused. Was that why Noah hadn't talked to her these past two days?

"I'm sorry."

"Harlen needs to take it back." Her gaze flew around the room as if she'd find the solution to all her problems in one of the four corners. "What am I going to do?"

"Do you love Noah?"

"I do. I really do, and it scares the hell out of me." There. She'd admitted it out loud. No take-backs once a person said something like that out loud. She'd put up a good fight, tried to wiggle away from the fact—no more. She loved Noah, and it was the kind of love that took root and grew deeper and stronger with time. She had to fix things between them.

"Talk to him."

"How can I?" Frustration coupled with anxiety started her pacing. "He's avoiding me."

"Hmmm, you found a way that night you spent in the carriage house."

Ceejay stopped in her tracks. "You know about that?"

"Course I do." Jenny chuckled. "Not much gets by me. Find a way and talk to him."

Could she do that? She couldn't live with herself knowing Noah believed he was to blame for anything that had happened over the past week. "I will."

"Hello." Sheriff Maurer rapped on the door and came in. "Well, look at this. Both my girls up at the same time." He held two bouquets in his arms. "How are you two feeling?"

Jenny's answering smile could've lit up a moonless night, and it warmed Ceejay's heart to see it. Harlen tried to hand her one of the bouquets. The best she could manage was to press it against her chest with her cast. "Thank you. These are lovely. I'll take them down to the kitchen and put them in water."

The sheriff cleared his throat. "Ceejay, I might've—"

"I know. Jenny told me." She leveled her gaze at him. "I'm going to talk to Noah, and you should too. He didn't cause my accident, and he's done all of us nothing but good since he got here." She crossed the room and leaned down to give her aunt a peck on the cheek. "Are you coming downstairs for lunch today? You need to get out of that bed and move around."

"I will." Jenny glanced at the sheriff. "Will you stay, Harlen?"

"If you want me to, of course I will, sweetheart."

Ceejay rolled her eyes. This was going to take some getting used to. "See you later." She left the room and headed for the kitchen to see if she could fill a vase with water on her own. Flexing her fingers, she tested the dexterity. The swelling had gone down some, and her fingers didn't look like fat sausages anymore. Maybe she had to practice what she preached to Jenny and get moving.

Staring at the kitchen cabinet wasn't going to get that vase down from the shelf. Ceejay pushed a chair across the kitchen floor with her knee until it rested next to the counter.

She climbed onto the seat and reached with her right hand, barely catching the rim. She pinched it between her thumb and fingers and dragged it to the edge.

"What are you doing?"

Noah's voice sent a rush of adrenaline through her, followed by a flood of heat. His strong hands encircled her waist, holding her steady.

"You shouldn't be up on that chair."

His sudden appearance sent her heart flying around inside her rib cage. "I'm trying to get this vase so I can put these flowers in water." She brought the vase down, and it hit the counter with a thunk.

"Let me do it."

"No. I have to start doing as much as I can."

"That's ridiculous. It's only been a couple of days since your surgery."

Ceejay climbed off the chair. She pulled the vase against her chest and set it beside the sink. Her fingers weren't strong enough to hold the weight, and even though the break in her clavicle was on the left side, her movements caused a throbbing ache. Spots danced before her eyes. She hated being so weak and helpless. A fine sheen of sweat broke out on her forehead. "Maybe you're right."

Noah put his arm around her and led her to the kitchen table. "Sit down."

For days she'd longed to feel his arms around her in that protective way, and now it felt more professional than personal. "Nurses and doctors make the worst patients." She lowered herself to the chair and put her head down as much as she could. "Noah, can we talk?"

Sweet Pea started barking, and someone knocked on the front door.

"Uh...sure, but I'm in the middle of something right now. Can it wait?"

"OK. Maybe later today?"

He nodded, stepped back, and stared down at her for an intense instant, then took off out the back door without a backward glance.

She stared at the door, hoping he'd come back. What could she do if he refused to talk?

Allison walked into the kitchen, trailed by Lucinda and Gail Offermeyer. Both women had their hands full.

"Denny sent supplies," Gail announced. "Smoked bacon, smoked turkey, and a ham. I also made potato salad and coleslaw. This ought to keep you all fed for a while."

Ceejay wanted to run after Noah and make him talk to her until everything went back to the way it was before. Instead, she pasted a smile on her face and turned to greet her neighbor. "Thanks, Gail. You didn't have to do that."

"Mommy, I got to see airplanes wif Grandpa and Uncle Noah. Can we go on one?" Lucinda came to lean against her legs.

"Someday." She'd already quit her new job and canceled their trip to Disney World and the appointments to look at houses to rent in Indianapolis. How had her life backslid into limbo so quickly?

Gail started toward the refrigerator. "Consider the food payment for all the late-night, panicky phone calls we've made over the years about screaming or sick babies."

"Put that stuff on the counter, Gail. I'll take care of it." Allison set her own load down. "I was about to make lunch anyway. Do you want to help, Lucinda?"

Lucinda moved to climb onto the chair Ceejay had moved to the counter. "Yes, Grandma. We have to have a vegetable or a fruit too."

"That's right, sweetheart." Allison cupped Lucinda's face in her hands for a second, and then turned to Ceejay. "You two head out to the porch, and I'll bring you some iced tea."

"I'll get the tea, Mrs. Langford." Gail opened a cabinet, took two glasses down, and set them on the counter before heading for the fridge.

"Thanks, and call me Allison." She smiled.

Feeling useless, Ceejay rose from her chair and waited for Gail to join her on the way to the veranda. "Thanks for stopping by."

"Believe me, the pleasure's all mine. Denny's mom came over to watch the kids." Gail sighed audibly as she placed the glasses of tea on the table and sank into a chair. "I hardly ever get time away from the house without my entourage of short people."

Ceejay laughed and took a seat. "I don't know how you do it with three. One is hard enough."

"Do you want more children?"

"I haven't really thought about it." She wasn't about to admit out loud how much she longed for a family of her own, with a husband, and siblings for Lucinda. She frowned as her conversation with Dr. Jordan echoed through her head. *Yes, there's a chance...* She dismissed the thought. What were the odds? Wouldn't she be eligible for some kind of world record book if she got pregnant *twice* because of a torn condom? Not to mention both fathers being from the same family. No. Way. Couldn't happen. Except... wasn't that the way things always went for her? No. Not this time. "I guess I would if the circumstances were right."

"I'm so glad you and Noah are seeing each other. Denny and I have been desperate for another couple to do things with. Maybe we can go out for a beer one night soon."

Ceejay's calendar count stopped. "Noah doesn't drink."

"Not even beer?" Gail's expression turned to surprise.

"Nope, not even a beer. He says too many veterans with post-traumatic stress disorder self-medicate with drugs and alcohol, and it only leads to more problems. He doesn't want to take the chance."

"He's a good guy, Ceejay."

"I know." She had to fight the urge to run off the porch to the carriage house to make Noah listen to reason.

Gail sipped her tea. "He's really good with Lucinda too. He'll be a great dad someday."

Ceejay couldn't help smiling at the memories triggered by Gail's words. Noah sitting in the wet grass by the sandbox, their trip to the zoo with Lucinda's constant barrage of questions and chatter, Noah holding her daughter's hand or holding her on his lap. "He is good with her. She adores him." *So do I.*

"Are things serious between you two?"

I wish. If his abrupt departure from the kitchen was any indication, not so much. "We've only been out once. It's way too soon to say."

"Sure, but he lives here, and you see him all the time."

Lucinda pushed the screen door open and came over to them. Sweet Pea ambled out behind her. "I'm done helping, and Grandma said to sit wif you and Mrs. Offmeyer."

"What do you have there?" Gail asked.

She held up the two Barbie dolls Allison had given her. "My grandma brought them for me. Where's Celeste?"

"She's home with her grandma. Would you like to come over and play with her sometime this week?"

Lucinda nodded, climbed into a chair, and started playing with her Barbies.

"You know what would be fun, Ceejay? Your aunt, Sheriff Maurer, my folks, and your uncles and aunts all get together to play bridge once a month. What if we started something like that, only we could play poker or something? There's you and Noah, me and Denny, and we could get a few other couples involved. We could start our own tradition."

"Maybe." She would be leaving Perfect soon, wouldn't she? Her gaze strayed to the orchard spanning several generations. The notion didn't carry the same urgency. Everything in her life had changed, and she hadn't had a chance to catch up, that was all.

"I desperately need a social life. I'll arrange everything." Gail leaned back in her chair with a grin. "You haven't touched your tea."

"I can't lift it." Embarrassed, Ceejay held her right cast in the air. "I need a straw."

"Oh, my God. I'm sorry." Gail jumped up and headed for the door. "I'll get you one."

"Thanks." A social life. Even though she'd known everyone in Perfect forever, she'd never tried to form close friendships with her neighbors. Dreams of leaving had kept her from reaching out to the people she'd known all her life. Now Gail had reached out to her, and the whole idea pleased her far more than she thought possible. If she were honest, she'd even have to admit she'd always been a little envious of the close ties her aunt had in their community.

Her own notions about the pity-tinted glasses everyone looked through when they saw her had been more isolating than she'd realized.

The sound of Ted's Mustang on the gravel drew her out of her thoughts. He wore jeans and work boots, and his tool belt hung from one hand. "Hey, Ted. What're you up to?"

"Hey, Ceejay. We're moving the scaffolding around to the back of the house today. Gotta get started on the back side." He came up the steps. "How're you feeling?"

"Banged up, but on the mend."

"What you got there, little Luce?"

"Barbies. Grandma gave them to me."

"Cool." He tousled her hair. "I'm going to go find Noah."

Even the sound of his name caused a physical reaction. Tonight. She'd talk to him tonight.

Gail came through the door and placed a straw in Ceejay's iced tea. "Hi, Ted."

"Hey, Gail."

"I have to get going. I'm meeting Denny in town for a child-free lunch at Jenny's diner." She slung her purse strap over her shoulder and fished for her keys. "I'll get back to you about the card night, Ceejay."

"It's going to be a little while before I can do anything involving holding things in my hands."

"Oh." Gail frowned. "Right. Let's see a movie and go out for a bite, then."

"Sounds good. Let me know when you want Lucinda for a playdate."

"Can I bring my Barbies?" Lucinda looked up. "Celeste and me can share."

"Celeste and I can share," Ceejay corrected.

Ted raised his eyebrows. "You still play with Barbies, Ceejay?"

Gail laughed and headed down the steps with a wave. "Bring Lucinda tomorrow. She can stay for lunch."

Allison came to the door as Gail drove off. "Lunch is ready. Ted, would you go get Noah?"

"Sure."

Ceejay's heart stomped on her broken ribs. She had to make it right with him.

CHAPTER SIXTEEN

SEEING CEEJAY STAND ON THAT chair had nearly stopped his heart. Hearing her say she wanted to talk stopped it cold. Noah wasn't proud of the way he'd boot-scooted out the back door, but he couldn't bear hearing her say she didn't want to see him anymore. Right now, he didn't want to think about what she might say. He didn't want to think about anything but wood and tools.

He started a fresh pot of coffee brewing and studied the pattern he'd designed for the cradle while he waited. *Focus on the task.* He grabbed his iPod, stuffed it into his back pocket, poured himself a mug of the fresh brew, and tucked the pattern under his arm before heading to his shop.

He stepped through the door and surveyed the newly updated shop space with satisfaction. Inhaling deeply, Noah took in the dry, woody scent of the old timber structure, and a fraction of his tension eased. The plans for the cradle lay flat on the workbench. He put his iPod on the dock and cranked some tunes. Running his hand over the pieces of walnut he'd chosen for the head- and footboards, he savored the feel of the wood against his palm. Memories of his uncle Gabe's shop, of the hours spent learning the craft, sprang into his mind, and fondness for his stepmother's brother warmed the corners of his battered heart. Maybe he'd give him a call tonight.

He'd gotten several stools and placed them strategically around his workshop so he wouldn't have to stand on his prosthetic too long in any one spot. He pulled one close to the workbench and grabbed a pencil. Laying the pattern out on the wood, he started tracing. Once he was finished transferring the pattern, he put on the safety goggles and moved to the table saw. When the pieces were reduced to a more manageable size, he moved to the jigsaw for the tricky part—cutting the dovetails.

He leaned close and maneuvered the wood around the blade with painstaking precision. Tapping his foot to the beat of the music, he dove deep into the task, letting go of everything he'd screwed up, the dead who haunted him, and his lack of any discernible career path. Getting each notch perfect became the focal point of his universe.

Noah finished the first side and scrutinized his work for flaws. Excitement thrummed through his veins. He smiled, pleased with his efforts, and turned the headboard around to dovetail the other side. His fingers itched to carve the old English rose in the center. He'd chosen the pattern because the petals resembled hearts. Any child of his would know without a doubt he or she was loved.

He sat up and frowned. After what Ceejay had been through in the accident, what were the odds she'd still be pregnant? If she had been to begin with, that is. He didn't know, but his heart broke a little thinking they might have lost something so precious. Giving himself a shake, he turned back to his work.

Wood, tools, and working with his hands. Focus.

What kind of finish did he want to use? Black walnut had a rich, mellow color and a distinctive grain. Maybe clear acrylic for protection would suffice. He laid the dovetailed headboard on the table and began chiseling around the edge of the English rose traced on the surface. Ted walked into his shop. Noah spared him a glance and a nod.

"Is that country music you're listening to?"

"When in Rome…"

Ted laughed and moved to peer at his project. "What're you working on?"

"Just tinkering." No way did he want to explain his need to make a cradle. "Trying out a new pattern."

"Cool. I took woodshop in high school, and I really enjoyed it. You'll have to teach me how to do this." Ted reached out and traced the emerging relief for the rose. "I've been sent to fetch you. Lunch is ready."

Noah wasn't ready for another confrontation. "Is Sheriff Maurer there?"

"Yep. He's turned into some kind of permanent fixture at the old homestead since Jenny's surgery."

Lunch also meant seeing Ceejay again, and his heart couldn't take another hit today. "I'll pass. I have food here."

Ted studied him. "You can't hide out in here forever. Maybe—"

"It's just lunch." Noah sorted through his tools, picking out a smaller chisel. "You can see I'm in the middle of something."

"It's not just lunch." Ted took a step closer, keeping his eyes fixed on the project under way. "You've been avoiding Ceejay since her accident. You should—"

"I should get back to work. Don't need lunch."

Ted stepped back and stuffed his hands into the back pockets of his jeans. "We still gonna move that scaffold this afternoon?"

"Sure. Come get me around one thirty."

Ted continued to stare at him like he wanted to say more. Noah bent back to work and hoped he'd take the hint. He didn't want to talk—didn't want to reveal even a smidgen of the hurt robbing him of sleep. Lunch? Hell, he couldn't eat.

"OK. Catch you later."

Once Ted left, Noah let out the breath that seized every time he thought about Ceejay. He forced his attention back to the project he had laid out on the workbench. He couldn't make a mistake, or he'd have to start all over. This piece had to be perfect. He soon settled into the tapping rhythm of the chisel and mallet against the wood.

A throat clearing near the door almost sent his chisel skidding across the walnut. Noah glared at the source of the interruption.

Sheriff Maurer stood in the doorway, out of uniform, with a plate of food in his hand. "The women sent me out here. I guess they're worried you'll waste away to nothing if you skip a meal."

"Put it over there on one of the shelves." Noah pointed with the chisel in his hand. "Thanks."

The sheriff placed the plate where he'd indicated and crossed the room to stand next to him. *Damn.* "You need something, Sheriff?"

"I do."

If this was to be a repeat of their last conversation, Noah would be facing assault charges. He kept working. *Tap, tap, tap.* "What now?"

"I owe you an apology. I know you didn't cause Ceejay's accident any more than you caused Jenny's cancer. They've both made it clear I'd better make it right between us." He crossed his arms in front of him. "I was upset."

Not the *why are you still here* he expected. Noah's brow rose, and he ducked his head to his work. "Apology accepted."

"I care about Ceejay."

"So do I."

"I don't want to see her hurt again."

Noah squared his shoulders, widened his stance, and fixed the sheriff with his best commander stare. "And you're certain I'm out to hurt her?" Hell, he was the hurting party here. Did no one get that?

"No. I may have been a little hard on you. I'm overprotective is all."

"I get it, Sheriff. Now it's time to back off. Like I said before, what goes on between me and Ceejay is none of your business. She's a grown woman."

"Right. I'm off the case."

Noah nodded. "Good."

"You might want to talk to her."

Noah went back to navigating the difficult curves of the rose petals with the tools gripped in his hands. So much easier than navigating the mysteries of the human heart. "Didn't you just say you're off the case?"

Sheriff Maurer chuckled and started for the door. "Don't let things go for as long as I did, son."

❦   ❦   ❦

Physical exhaustion was a good thing. Noah couldn't hold on to a thought long enough to get worked up about anything. He leaned back in his recliner, glad to be on his ass, and channel-surfed for something mindless to watch on TV. He and Ted had wrestled the scaffolding around to the back of the Lovejoys' house. Tomorrow afternoon they'd start on the gutters. That gave him the morning to work on the cradle.

"Noah?" A knock accompanied Ceejay's muffled voice through the door.

His tired body rushed headlong into turmoil. His lungs froze while his heart made up for the lack of movement. Leaping out of the chair, he reached the door at the speed of sound. God, he hoped she didn't expect him to talk, because the inside of his mouth had turned to suede, and he didn't think he could get his tongue to move.

Noah opened the door. The past week had left him feeling like a dry sponge, and Ceejay was fresh springwater. He soaked up the sight of her. She wore a ridiculous, ratty pair of pink cut-off sweatpants and an overlarge T-shirt with her one good arm through the sleeve. Her feet were bare. Beautiful.

"We need to talk."

"OK." His spirits hit the dirt. No good ever came from a conversation beginning with *we need to talk*. Especially not with a woman you were dating. *Shit.* He grabbed the remote control from the arm of his recliner and clicked the off button.

Ceejay lifted her chin and faced him down. "You didn't cause my accident, Noah. I did. I was driving too fast when I took that bend in the road. You weren't at the wheel. I was."

"I know, but you wouldn't have been driving so fast if my father hadn't upset you." His hand went to the back of his skull. "Which makes it my fault."

"Don't do that." Ceejay moved close and tugged the front of his shirt with her thumb and forefinger.

He stared at her in confusion. "Don't do what?"

"You always rub the back of your head when you're upset."

"I do?"

She nodded. "You're going to give yourself a bald spot." She looked up at him and her eyes grew bright with tears. "You never came back to the hospital for me. Why didn't you come back?"

"You told me to go away."

"I didn't mean forever." She sniffed. "I've missed you so much, and…and…"

"You have?" His insides took a slider, melting into a warm pool of relief. "I've missed you too. I thought you were pissed at me because my parents were here. I didn't invite them. Allison is impulsive that way. She always has been. I should've known she'd hop the first flight down here once I told her about Jenny."

His hand automatically headed for the predicted bald spot at the back of his skull. He forced it down and shoved it into his front pocket. "How could I have known my dad would come with her? I'm sorry he threatened you, honey. I won't let it happen again. I—"

"Noah?"

"Yeah?"

"Stop blaming yourself. I was upset before I got home. Jenny's cancer, learning about my mom, and yes, seeing your parents when I wasn't expecting them was a shock, but they aren't responsible for my accident either. They came to help, and I appreciate it."

"Yeah, but you wouldn't have been driving so fast if—"

"Why didn't you come back to the hospital?" Her chin quivered. "When I told you to leave, I was drugged up and in pain. I couldn't carry on a conversation."

"I thought you were telling me you didn't want me in your life. Sheriff Maurer said—"

She bit her lip and shook her head. "I know what he said. He was way out of line, and wrong besides."

"I can't take any more of your pushing me away, Ceejay." He took her face between his palms and lost himself in her baby blues. "We need to come to some kind of understanding."

"I know." She moved closer. "I wasn't pushing you away. I'd just reached my limit for the day. Sometimes that happens. Can we come up with some kind of code word or something? Like, I need a little alone time, and it's not about pushing you away; it's about me trying to process things?"

"Sure." He swallowed hard and let his eyes roam all over her face, memorizing each freckle, the tiny scar above her left eyebrow, the fullness of her lips. "We can do that." His heart soared. She wanted to work things out, and he could hardly take it in.

"Are you going to kiss me soon?" Tears got caught up on her eyelashes as she blinked.

"Yeah." He drew her close, casts, bindings, and all, and dove deep into the welcome she offered. All the fear, hurt, and tension he'd suffered since the day of her accident dissipated. A rush of longing set his blood on fire—and certainty. They belonged together and always would. He loved her.

The axis in his life tilted, righting itself. His heart and lungs settled into a normal rhythm for the first time in days. Normal for his aroused state, anyway. This kind of normal he could live with. He broke the kiss and threaded his fingers through her silken curls. "I know you can't be *with* me until you're healed up a little better, but could I just hold you for a while?"

"I'd like that." She studied him back. Her gaze traveled over his face, and her pupils had dilated.

The force of wanting her nearly brought him to his knees. Noah ushered her into his bedroom. "You might be more comfortable if I helped you out of those clothes."

She made that deep-in-the-throat chuckle that set his blood on fire. "Only if you take yours off too."

"I can do that." Noah slipped out of his jeans, boxers, and T-shirt almost before the words left his mouth. "Come here."

He tugged her shorts and panties off, then eased her arm through the one sleeve of the shirt she wore. Lifting it over her head, he groaned. No bra. Sweet. He reached out to cup one lovely breast, gratified to hear the quick intake of her breath. He pulled the blankets back and helped her lie down. Scooting in beside her, Noah drew her scent deep into his lungs.

Need pulsed through him at the feel of her soft skin against his. He wanted her, but for tonight, having her beside him was enough. "This is good. Spend the night with me."

"All right, but wake me early. I don't want Lucinda to get up in the morning and find me gone. She's been more upset by everything than she lets on."

"I will." He snuggled closer, sliding one arm under her head and the other around her waist, at ease for the first time in a solid week.

"Noah," Ceejay whispered.

"Hmmm?"

"I think if we're real careful, we could…"

His eyes flew open, and he smiled against the bare skin of her neck. "Could what?" he asked, nuzzling the tender spot behind her ear.

"You know."

"Say it."

"I want you to make love to me."

"I want that too." Noah propped himself up on one elbow. "I'll do all the work. All you have to do is relax and enjoy. Tonight is for you." He kissed her, careful not to put pressure anywhere near her injuries. She moved restlessly beside him. He ran his thumb over one sensitive nipple and felt a shiver run through her body.

Leaning in, he took the other into his mouth, and his blood rushed to his groin at the sound of the throaty groan she made.

He knew exactly what he wanted to do to her, something he'd fantasized about since the day he had seen her sweet backside bobbing away in the garden. He'd never wanted to taste a woman the way he wanted to taste Ceejay—never wanted that level of intimacy with anyone but her.

"Don't ever do that again," she said on a sigh.

She didn't like having her breasts fondled and sucked? He lifted himself to peer down at her, lust clouding his brain. "Never do what again?"

"Don't shut me out the way you did. You're not the only one with issues. Don't you get what that did to me?"

Her eyes were filled with the same hurt and insecurity he'd suffered. His chest tightened with regret. "I won't. If something is bothering me, I promise to let you know. The same goes for you. If something is bothering you, tell me. If you're feeling insecure, all you have to do is let me know, and I'll do my best to—"

"Good enough." She put her arm around his neck and drew him to her. "No more talking."

She kissed him, her sweet tongue delving into his mouth in search of his, and he surrendered to the joy only Ceejay could bring to his life. Noah kissed and caressed his way down her delectable curves, edging closer toward learning her taste. He wanted to watch her in the throes of an orgasm. Anticipation sent his heart racing. Spreading her wide beneath his hungry gaze, he was filled with awe. His woman. He traced the shape of her with a finger and watched her reaction.

Lowering himself between her thighs, Noah indulged in his fantasy, reveling in the sounds of passion he elicited from her, almost coming himself when she shuddered against him with her release. He raised himself and reached for a condom in the bedside table. Slipping it on, he stared down at her, overwhelmed by her beauty.

"Noah." His name came out a breathy sigh. "That was... mmm...that was amazing." She stretched, enticing him with her body and her look.

He sank back down, careful to support his own weight. "We're not done yet, sweetheart."

"I was hoping you'd say that." She moaned and drew him to her for another mind-blowing kiss.

Mindless with desire, he entered her. Her name echoed through the room as he lost himself in the feel of her slick heat surrounding him. Ecstasy. Peace and an irrevocable bond wound around his heart as he collapsed beside her in a satisfied heap. She sighed beside him and scooted close to his side.

He wrapped her in his arms as gently as he could. "I hope that's a sigh of satisfaction."

"It is," she purred. "Most definitely satisfied here."

"Go to sleep, honey. Everything is going to be all right."

"Is it?"

Nodding, he let contentment wash over him and closed his eyes. He hadn't slept well for days, and having Ceejay in his arms changed everything. He drifted off with images of cradles filled with redheaded babies floating around inside his mind. So much better than the hollow-eyed accusations of the dead.

Noah hurried up the veranda steps. It had been hard to let Ceejay leave his bed so early in the morning, and he wanted to be with her again. Opening the door, he gravitated toward the sound of feminine voices in the kitchen. Allison, Jenny, and Ceejay were all seated at the kitchen table, with a black-and-white hatbox sitting on the table in front of Ceejay. Warmth spread through his chest at the sight of his stepmother and the woman he loved sitting peacefully together. "Where's Lucinda?"

"Harlen took her to the Offermeyers' for a playdate. Do you want coffee?" Allison started to rise.

"I'll get it, Mom." Noah helped himself to coffee and brought the pot back to refill her cup and Ceejay's. "Do you want more iced tea, Jenny?"

"No, I'm fine, thanks."

"You're looking good, by the way. How are you feeling?"

"Better every day." The corners of her eyes creased with familiar warmth. "I'm starting chemo in a few weeks, and I'm already looking forward to putting all of this behind me."

"That's good. What do you have there?" He gestured toward the box as he leaned down and gave Ceejay a peck on the cheek. He straightened and returned the coffee to the warmer.

"This box holds all that remains of my mom's possessions." Ceejay sighed. "Jenny told me my mom didn't abandon me. She died of an accidental drug overdose."

Noah slid into the seat next to hers and put his arm around her shoulders. "I'm sorry."

"Thanks." Ceejay swallowed hard. "I was wrong about her, and maybe I'm wrong about my dad, too. He might not know I exist, like all of you never knew about Lucinda." She waved toward the box with a forlorn gesture. "I was looking for clues about who he might be. I couldn't find anything." Ceejay pressed herself against the back of her chair and stared at the cardboard container, disappointment plain on her face.

"Do you mind if I take a look?"

"Be my guest."

Noah removed the lid and pulled out an envelope, opened the flap, and took out the stack of photos tucked inside. Pictures of Ceejay as a newborn, and then as a chubby-cheeked baby with bright red hair. He went through them one at a time, stopping when he came across the photos including her mother.

"Let me see those photos," Allison said, reaching out her hand.

Noah handed them to her, and she placed them in a row in front of her. "You were an adorable little girl, Ceejay."

"Were?" Noah raised his eyebrows. "She's still adorable." Color rose to Ceejay's cheeks. Man, he loved making her blush. He gave her shoulder a squeeze. "And little."

Ceejay made a disgruntled noise, and Noah couldn't resist kissing her on the forehead.

"Of course she is." Allison laughed and turned back to the pictures. "I can see the resemblance between you, your mother, and Lucinda, although Luce's coloring is different. She has the Wyatt dimples and chin."

"She has your eyes." Ceejay's expression was open and friendly as she glanced at Allison.

Noah had to swallow back the surge of emotion welling up. He turned the empty envelope over and studied the faded scrawl on the front while the women continued to fuss over the photos. The penciled writing was barely legible. "J. C. Flynn, care of the University of Evansville?"

"My mom went to school there." Ceejay glanced his way.

"I wonder…"

"What do you wonder?" Ceejay asked, as Allison and Jenny turned to listen.

"An envelope addressed to him with pictures of you inside." Noah handed Ceejay the worn, yellowed envelope. "Reverse his initials."

She gasped. "C.J." She swiveled in her chair to stare wide-eyed at him.

"Wait," Jenny broke in. "Like I told Ceejay earlier, I found the envelope with the rest of what's in this box when I went to pick up Ann's things. I put the pictures inside because it was convenient. I can't even be sure that's my sister's handwriting on the front."

"Still, it's a lead." Noah shrugged. "And it gives us a place to start. Maybe he was a friend of hers. If he's still around, he might be able to tell us who your sister was seeing at the time."

"I agree." Ceejay's eyes lit up. "Will you help me do a directory search, Noah?" She held up her encased wrists.

"Of course. Let's go to my apartment. We can use my laptop." He got up and took his mug and Ceejay's to the sink. "Unless either of you needs me for anything right now." He turned to his stepmom and Jenny.

"We'll be fine," Allison answered. "I'll call your cell when lunch is ready."

"Thanks." He followed Ceejay out the back door. "Don't get your hopes up, Ceejay. This may end up being a wild goose chase."

"I know." She frowned at him. "Even if it's not a wild goose chase and we do find my father, there's no guarantee he'll want to have anything to do with me."

"I can't imagine that." He placed his hand at the small of her back.

"Yeah?" She chuffed out a sound of amusement. "Don't you think you might be a tad biased?"

"Nope." He swung around her to get the gate, and then his door. "Have a seat on the couch, and I'll get the laptop."

For the next hour, they searched out all the Flynns in the Evansville area. Three were women and six were men. Noah compiled a list with their names, addresses, and phone numbers.

"Let's check the University of Evansville. Maybe J. C. Flynn was one of my mother's professors."

"All right." He entered the university into the search engine and clicked on the website. Next he clicked on the faculty directory and entered the name. "Look at this, Ceejay. Dr. Jeffrey C. Flynn. He's a history professor."

She sucked in an audible breath. "I can't believe it. What if he's my father? What do I do now?"

"Says here he has regular office hours between two and four, Mondays through Thursdays. Make an appointment and go see him."

"I can't do that. What would I say?" She shot up from the couch and paced around the room. "You do it."

"Do what? Ask him if he's your dad?"

"No." She huffed in exasperation. "*You* make an appointment to see him. Tell him you're interested in an advanced degree in history or something like that, and—"

"Why not start with a phone call and introduce yourself? Let's not make things more complicated than they need to be."

"Please, Noah? I want to see him face-to-face."

He could practically feel the tension pulsing from her, and her eyes held a pleading expression he couldn't refuse. "All right." He fished his cell phone out of his back pocket. He entered the phone number listed on Flynn's page, and a secretary answered. "Hello, my name is Noah Langford, and I'd like to make an appointment to talk to Dr. Flynn about obtaining a master's in history." He waited while the woman on the other end checked the professor's calendar and came back with some choices. "This Thursday at two would be great. Thanks."

"If I could clap my hands, I would." Ceejay sank down beside him on the couch and rested her head on his shoulder. "Thank you."

"You're welcome." He put his arm around her. "I don't want to see you set yourself up for hurt or disappointment. Things might not turn out the way we hope."

"I know." She patted his leg before getting up. "I'm going to head up to the house and figure out what I'm going to wear to this meeting on Thursday. I'm really sick of elastic waistbands." She leaned over and kissed him on the lips. "See you at lunch."

After she left, he decided to work on the cradle for a while, and he headed for the workshop. The frame had posed a challenge. He wanted something hip high, so Ceejay wouldn't have to bend over too low every time she needed to pick up the baby. He also wanted the cradle to swing in a smooth, soothing motion. The frame he'd devised ended up being like the old-fashioned, double porch or swing-set type of mechanism. Definitely safer with siblings around to set it in motion with too much enthusiasm.

All that was left was the final sanding and applying the finish, and the piece would be done. He opened the bay doors, turned on the floor fan, and set to work with the finest-gauge sandpaper he had. Working with his hands to create the piece satisfied and calmed him in a way he hadn't experienced since the hours he'd spent in his uncle's shop. Remembering the phone conversation he'd had with his uncle brought a smile to Noah's face. Maybe he could talk him into a visit once the construction season slowed down.

Noah reached for a cotton shop cloth and wiped away the sawdust from the cradle. Taking a few steps back, he admired his work. The insides of the headboard and the footboard had the English rose carving. He'd cut small open hearts, three on each of the sides. Not big enough for little hands to get caught, but large enough to allow for airflow.

"Whoa. This is what you've been working on all this time?" Ted let out a low whistle from just inside the open bay doors. "It's really something. I had no idea you could do shit like this." Ted reached out and set the cradle into a smooth, silent glide. "Can you make other stuff?"

"Yep." Noah's chest swelled. "I can design and build anything."

Ted stopped the cradle midswing and moved closer to examine the carvings. "Will you teach me?" He regarded Noah with serious determination. "This is what you should do, man. Forget about sanding peeling paint and gutters."

"I can teach you, sure, but I don't know about—"

"This is it, Noah. I'm telling you. We can sell furniture over the Internet. You'll never have to deal with people face-to-face."

A buzz started in Noah's head. He forgot about PTSD when wood and tools were in his hands. The satisfaction woodworking gave him, the thrum of excitement—could this be his passion, or did all these feelings happen because the cradle was for Ceejay?

"Why a cradle?"

Noah's attention came back with a start. Ted's gaze fixed him with an intensity he'd never seen from the younger man. He scrambled for something plausible to say. "I haven't worked with wood for years." He picked his tools up, crossing to the pegboard to put them away. Reaching for a can of acrylic finish from the shelves, he answered, "I wanted to start with something small to get back into it before trying something bigger."

"Humph."

The incredulous sound forced Noah to look his way. The intensity of Ted's gaze hadn't lessened, and Noah's palms started to sweat. "It's not what you think."

"Oh, yeah?" Ted's face hardened. "What do I think?"

Noah stared back. Currents of adrenaline-laced energy traced through his limbs. His heart hammered, and his mouth felt full of the sawdust he'd recently swept away. "I'm not like my stepbrother."

"I know you're not. Matt never would've bothered making a cradle before he took off."

"Does it look like I'm leaving to you?"

"We gonna get to work on those back gutters, or what?" Ted turned his back on Noah and headed for the door.

"I'll be right there." This new tension bothered him. He'd come to like and respect Ceejay's cousin. The way Ted looked up to him and sought his company meant a lot to Noah. He grabbed his tool belt and bucket of supplies and followed. Climbing the scaffold to take his place beside his silent coworker, Noah struggled to come up with something to say that would alleviate Ted's concern.

"I'm in love with her," he rasped out. *Great.* Not exactly what he'd intended to say.

"No shit." Ted kept on sanding his patch of dilapidated gutter. "Any fool can see you're in love."

"What's the problem, then?"

"Is she pregnant?"

"I don't know. She hasn't said." He shook his head. "I think it's too early to tell."

Ted's arms dropped, and he turned around to lean against the limestone. "Ceejay deserves so much more than having to get married because she's knocked up. Don't you get it?" He shook his head. "Even if you do stick around, even if you marry her, it's always going to be in her mind that you did it only because she's carrying your baby. After everything else she's had to deal with in her life, can you imagine what that would do to her?"

"Oh." He recalled how she'd reacted when he'd told her he'd marry her if she was pregnant. He rubbed his chest over his aching heart. "I've gotta do something to prove otherwise."

"Yeah, you do." Ted pushed off the wall and turned back to sanding the gutters. "Don't wait too long."

"I won't." His mind raced, searching for some grand gesture that would convince Ceejay he wanted her with or without an unplanned pregnancy between them. What if she didn't want to marry him?

"I'm serious about the furniture, Noah."

"Huh?"

"I want to do this. I want to make things with my hands and be proud of the product. You know I've been trying to figure out what to do with myself, and the one thing I'm certain of is that I want to be my own boss. When I look at that piece of workmanship, I get a buzz of excitement I've never felt for anything else. You can be damn sure I've never gotten this excited about hog farming." He lifted an eyebrow.

Noah laughed. "I get it."

"What if I commit to taking some business and marketing classes? Would you consider striking up a partnership with me then? You teach me how to make furniture, and I'll handle the business stuff. You handle the creative and production end." Ted blew out a breath. "I've never seen a cradle like that. It's like a fine antique, only new."

Noah stood still. Something inside him shifted, snapped, and clicked into place. "Langford Newtiques, Heirloom-Quality Handcrafted Custom Furniture."

"Shit." Ted spun around. "I want in on this. Full partners, and I'll put my heart and soul into making it pay. I swear."

Noah's grin spread wide. "Langford and Lovejoy Newtiques. It has a good, solid ring." *Speaking of rings...*

Ted grabbed Noah's hand and shook it. "You won't regret this."

"I know I won't. I want to see you enrolled in classes. In exchange, you've got a deal." He pulled his cell phone from his pocket and hit speed dial.

"Who're you calling?"

"My sister. We need some help setting this up, and she's working on her MBA at Harvard." He turned his attention to the call. "Hey, Paige, how's my favorite little sister?" His grin grew wider still. He had a career path, and the way before him lay clear. "Listen, Mom is here, and I was wondering if you have any free time to join us for a while. You want to meet your niece, don't you?" He surveyed the sloping lawn and the Ohio River. He loved this place and the people in it. He envisioned Langfords and Lovejoys living here for generations to come.

"I need your help." He waited for her response. "I want you to help me pick out an engagement ring—" He held the phone away from his ear and winced at the squeal loud enough for Ted to hear. "You'll meet her once you're here. Yeah, yeah. Lucinda too. I know waiting has been hard on you." He smiled at Ted while his sister rattled on. "OK. Listen, I also need some help setting up an Internet business. You know how to create websites, right?"

He gave her the details and only half listened while she ticked off things he'd have to do and paperwork that needed to be filled out. "We can take care of all of that when you're here. I'll see you in a couple of weeks, and thanks, Paige. You're going to love Ceejay, Lucinda, and Jenny. They're going to love you too." He ended the call and faced his new business partner. "Done." Now, all he had to worry about was whether or not Ceejay would say yes.

CHAPTER SEVENTEEN

"THIS IS NINETEEN HUNDRED LINCOLN AVE." Noah nodded toward the brick building before them. "We're here. Dr. Flynn's office is on the second floor."

Ceejay's palms started to sweat, and the sound of the blood rushing through her veins rang in her ears. She could hardly breathe. Noah's strong arms encircled her. She must've gone pale, because he guided her to the bench next to the Metro Bus sign on the sidewalk and pushed her down to sit. He sat beside her and rubbed her back.

She forced air into her lungs. "I don't think I can do this."

"You can." He kept rubbing.

Closing her eyes, she let the soothing motion of his hand work its magic. Her breathing slowed, and her heart rate soon followed. "Maybe we should come back another day—once I've adjusted to the idea."

"We're here now."

"I know." She sighed. "My whole life I've wondered who my father is and why he left me." The gentle pressure of Noah's hand gave her strength. "I've always believed he didn't want me, just like I believed my mother left me on my aunt's doorstep for the same reason." She blew out her breath. "The same way Matt didn't want me and Lucinda."

"I want you. If you'll let me, I'll stick around, and that's a promise."

"Really?" Tears filled her eyes as she met his steady gaze. She blinked them away and laid her head on his shoulder. "That's the sweetest thing anybody has ever said to me."

He stroked her hair and kissed her. "Don't you know I'm nuts about you?"

"Then you really are nuts." She smiled at him through her tears. "Because I'm a mess." Shoot. Just when she'd gotten her heart rate under control, Noah sent it leapfrogging inside her chest again. "Let's go meet this man. I was wrong about my mom. Maybe I'm wrong about my dad too."

He helped her up, and they climbed the concrete stairs to the wide, glass doors. "Noah," she whispered as they entered.

"Hmm?" He leaned close.

Heat flooded her cheeks. "I'm crazy about you too."

"Then you really are crazy, because, honey? Between the two of us, I really am a mess, and I have the papers to prove it."

Ceejay reached for his hand. "Not as far as I'm concerned."

Turning his palm around, he laced their fingers together around her cast. She surveyed the inside of the building. The turn-of-the-century campus hall boasted a marble floor with an inlaid geometric design. The dimly lit hallway was large and cool, even without air-conditioning. Staircases with wooden banisters stained almost black and covered in about ten coats of varnish stood at either end.

The stainless-steel double doors of the modern elevator in the center looked out of place. "Can we take the elevator? I don't feel up to taking the stairs."

"Sure. The elevator is easier for me, anyway." Noah hit the button. "He believes I'm here to talk about a master's in history. I'll do the talking. When you're ready, let me know by putting your hand on my arm."

She nodded, and the elevator doors opened. They rode to the second floor in silence, stepping out into a much less ostentatious hallway. The narrow corridor had a linoleum tile floor typical of the fifties. Doors with black numbers painted above them lined both sides. Was she supposed to feel like this? Like she was walking through wet cement toward her own execution?

They stopped in front of a door with a small, brass bracket holding a name card. Dr. Jeffrey C. Flynn. Noah rapped his knuckles against the wood.

The door opened. Ceejay's insides tumbled into a messy heap as she stared at the short, wiry man before her. They had the same freckles, the same blue eyes and wild, curly reddish hair, although his was thinning and streaked with gray. Ceejay couldn't have uttered a word if her life depended on it. She reached out and grasped Noah's arm for support.

"Now?" Noah asked, frowning down at her.

"What?" She turned her gaze to him, her brain frozen in shock. He looked pointedly at the hand on his arm. The signal. "Oh. No." She snatched it back.

The professor looked from her to Noah and back to her again. "Can I help you?"

Noah stepped forward. "I'm Noah Langford. We have an appointment."

Dr. Flynn's expression cleared. "Right. Come in." He stepped back and held the door while they filed through. The small office had a single, narrow window with an air conditioner whirring away. Shelves lined one wall, sagging from the weight of leather-bound reference books and stacks of file folders.

"This is my girlfriend, Ceejay."

Hearing Noah call her his girlfriend shot a pulse of pleasure straight through her heart. How sweet was that? The thrill temporarily distracted her from the emotional chaos ricocheting around her healing rib cage. Was Dr. Flynn her father? The resemblance was uncanny. He must be. Would he want to know her?

The professor moved another pile of stuff from a chair in the corner and carried it over to the spot next to the seat already positioned by his desk. He gestured for them to sit. "What happened to you?" He surveyed her cast, the sling, and the fading bruise on her forehead.

"Car accident," she muttered as she took a seat. Noah sat beside her.

"Sorry to hear it." Flynn sank into his chair and fiddled with the keyboard on his computer. "You're interested in a graduate program in history, you said. What is the specific region and period you're interested in? Do you plan to get a master's first, or would you prefer to get into the PhD program right away?"

"Did you know Ann Lovejoy?" Ceejay blurted. "She attended the University of Evansville twenty-six years ago."

The professor's hands dropped to his lap, and his chin dropped. His eyebrows came together as he stared at her. "What's going on here?"

"Ceejay," Noah took her hand, "I thought you were going to let me do the talking."

"I was, but look at him." She gestured toward the professor. "Don't you see what I'm seeing?"

"What's this about Ann Lovejoy?" Dr. Flynn's upper lip beaded with sweat, and he wouldn't meet her eyes.

Ceejay leaned forward in her chair. "Did you know her?"

"I'd just started teaching back then. She was in one of my classes. Why do you ask?"

"How well did you know her?"

The professor studied her for a few seconds, and then scrubbed at his face with both hands. "Well enough."

"My name is Ceejay Lovejoy." She turned to Noah. "Show him the pictures and the envelope."

Noah pulled the envelope out of his back pocket and handed it to the professor. Ceejay searched for any sign that Dr. Flynn might be happy to discover he had her for a daughter. She watched as he took the photos out and went through them. Slowly, he studied the penciled words on the outside.

"Could you be my father?" Ceejay held her breath and waited. His eyes were glued to the envelope. Silence filled the tiny office while the window air conditioner hummed a tuneless song.

"That was a difficult time in my life. I was married. My wife and I were having some problems. I'm not proud of my actions back then, and—"

"I don't care about any of that. Is there a chance you're my father?"

"It's...possible." A pained expression clouded his face. "Yes, but if Ann was pregnant, I never heard about it." He squirmed in his seat. "Things ended abruptly between us once she discovered I was married."

"Why would she have told you about me? I mean, with you being married and screwing around with her at the same time and all." Ceejay couldn't keep the bitterness out of her voice.

"Look, I'm remarried now, and I don't want this ancient history blowing up in my wife's face." Dr. Flynn raked his fingers through his thinning hair. "Did Ann say I'm your father? Is that why you're here? I'm sure I'm not the only guy she slept with during her college years."

"Hey," Noah ground out. "Watch it."

Ceejay seethed. What a weasel, trying to make it sound like her mother was loose, after already admitting he was married while they were seeing each other. "She never said. My mom died when I was three."

"Look, I'm sorry to hear your mother died. I really am." Flynn eyed her with a wary expression. "What do you want from me?"

"I...I just wanted to know who my father is." He didn't want her, didn't even want to know she existed. Everything in Ceejay's world stuttered to an abrupt and painful halt. His rejection squeezed her insides into a frozen lump. She stared at Noah, hoping he'd pick up on her silent plea to get her out of there. She didn't want to breathe the same air as this man. Noah slid his arm around her shoulders and drew her close. *Ow.* It hurt, but she wasn't about to complain.

"We don't want anything from you." Noah's voice carried a sharp edge. "You couldn't possibly have anything we need. Ceejay grew up without knowing who her father is. Now that we've met you, I'm certain she's relieved." He stood, bringing her up with him. "We have a lovely little girl, and as far as I'm concerned, she'll never know you exist."

Noah had used *we.* He'd claimed Lucinda. His protectiveness kick-started her frozen heart, leaving a rush of love for him in its wake. If she hadn't been certain about him before, she was now. Her knees went weak. Crap. Her legs were about the only functional appendages she had.

"Come on, honey. Let's go." Noah guided her through the door.

"Wait." Dr. Flynn shot out of his chair. "This is the last thing I expected to hear today. I need time to adjust." He followed them out of the office. "Where do you live? How can I reach you?"

"You don't need to reach me." Ceejay lifted her chin and squared her shoulders. "I've managed without a father my entire life, and I'm fine. We're fine."

The professor's shoulders slumped. "I'm sorry."

She turned away and let Noah lead her to the elevator. Once inside, he drew her into his arms. "Are you all right?"

She snuggled against his chest, inhaled his scent, and let the tears flow. "He didn't know about me."

"Are you certain he's—"

"Did you *not* get a good look at him?" She gestured to her own face. "I have his eyes, his bone structure, his coloring and freckles. I think they're even in the same pattern."

"Yeah, I noticed."

"I…I feel so bad for my mom." She sniffed and swiped at the tears on her cheeks. "That man broke her heart."

"I'm sorry, Ceejay. What can I do?"

"You're doing it now, Noah. You're here with me."

"I've got your back, babe. Always."

The elevator door opened. Noah put his arm around her shoulders and headed them in the direction of his truck. Always. He'd said always. Warmth spread through her, chasing away the pain of rejection she'd just received from Dr. Flynn. Ceejay turned her thoughts away from the excruciating encounter and focused on something more pleasant. "Allison said your sister is coming to Perfect with your dad next weekend."

"Yep. She's planning to stay for a few days. Do you mind? She only has a week off before she starts school."

"No. I don't mind." The Langfords would outnumber the Lovejoys at the old homestead. Her head ached, and she worried about how all the activity and company would affect Jenny. Most of all, everything in her life kept shifting, and she couldn't find firm footing. "Once I'm out of these stupid casts, I'm going on a vacation."

Noah gave her shoulders a squeeze. "You haven't been working for three weeks now. What do you need a vacation from?"

"The Langford invasion." She nudged him with her shoulder, reveling in the sound of his laughter.

❦ ❦ ❦

Ceejay smiled as Noah's sister got out of Ed's SUV. How different everything seemed since her accident a month ago. She could honestly say she didn't mind Ed's presence in her life anymore. Paige had her father's coloring, but she definitely got her good looks from Allison. Carefully styled shoulder-length tawny hair brushed her shoulders. Her jeans still held a crease where they'd been pressed, and the sleeveless silk button-down blouse screamed casual elegance.

Ed went to the back of his car and unloaded their suitcases. Paige headed straight for her.

"Oh, my God, I'm so glad to finally meet you," she gushed. "I already know we're going to be good friends." She surveyed Ceejay's casts and sling. "I'd give you a hug, but it looks like that might be painful."

"Thanks." Ceejay felt a little overwhelmed and took a step back. She placed her hand on Lucinda's curls. Her daughter stared wide-eyed at the newest Langford. "This is—"

"Wow, are you the cutest little niece ever, or what?" Paige went to her knees on the veranda. "Hey, Lucinda, you and I are going to have to spend to some serious girl time together. I'm your Aunt Paige."

The two fingers that had been firmly planted flew out of Lucinda's mouth, and a look of awe replaced her natural trepidation. "Are you my uncle Noah's sister?"

"I sure am." Paige stood and held out her hand, and Lucinda took it. "Your grandma is my mommy."

Lucinda turned her face up toward Paige like a flower to the sun. "She is?"

"Do you like to play dress up?"

Lucinda nodded.

"Good, because I brought some of my old favorites with me. How'd you like to be a princess for the day?"

Lucinda glanced at Ceejay over her shoulder. "Mommy, can my aunt Paige make me a princess?"

"Sure she can." Ceejay sent Paige a look of gratitude. She'd already decided she liked Noah's outgoing sister. "Go on in. Allison and Jenny are in the kitchen preparing a feast for dinner."

"Where's Noah?" Mr. Langford set the luggage on the porch.

"He's in his shop with my cousin." Ceejay reached for the screen door and hooked her fingers into the handle to open it. "I'll show you where to put Paige's things."

"Are we OK, Ceejay?"

"Umm…" Whoa. Ed was nothing if not direct. A surge of adrenaline charged up her insides. Were they OK? She did a mental inventory, pleased to find no lingering angst. "Sure."

"That's good. Noah told us about your meeting with Dr. Flynn." He put a hand on her shoulder for a second. "You want me to have a little talk with the man? Give him a black eye or two?"

She was about to laugh until she met his eyes, and her breath caught. He meant it. Allison's words came back to her. This was his way of letting her know she had allies. She shook her head. "I appreciate the offer, but I'm really OK about how it turned out. It's not like he's ever been a part of my life."

"You ever need anything, all you have to do is ask." He followed her up the stairs.

"Thank you, Mr. Langford."

"Call me Ed. I'll just put these bags where they belong, and then head out to the carriage house with the men."

"I can let him know you're here. He'll come to the house."

"Don't bother. I'll tell him myself."

She led the way down the hall to the bedroom they'd prepared for Paige. "You and Allison are in the same room you were in before. We plan to eat in about an hour. Would you let my cousin know he's welcome to stay?"

"I'll do that." Ed placed his daughter's suitcase on the freshly made bed and headed to the room he shared with his wife.

Ceejay took the back stairs to the kitchen, drawn by the sound of women's voices and the delicious smell of peach cobbler wafting through the house. Counting Harlen and Ted, they'd have nine people staying for supper. Nothing like the Thanksgiving and Christmas crowd, with all the Lovejoys gathering at the ancestral home, but enough that they'd eat in the dining room. "Lucinda," she called as she walked into kitchen, "I need you to help me set the table."

"I can help." Paige lifted Lucinda off her lap and rose from her chair.

"Thanks." Ceejay lifted her right cast. "I can't wait to have these off."

"I can imagine. Tell me where everything is, and we'll get it done in no time."

Paige followed her through the double doors to the dining room, and Ceejay pointed to the sideboard. "Everything is in there."

The hour passed quickly, and soon the men's voices added to the congenial atmosphere as they trooped in through the back door to wash their hands at the kitchen sink. Frustrated with her own helplessness, Ceejay moved out of the way while Allison and Paige brought the food-laden platters and bowls to the dining room. "When did you get here, Harlen?"

"About forty minutes ago," he said. "Been admiring all of Noah's new toys out back."

At the mention of his name, Noah came to stand beside her. "I'm starving. We've been smelling that turkey smoking on the grill all afternoon." He leaned in and gave her a kiss.

An electric shock shot down her spine. "Jenny made a cobbler with peaches from our orchard. It's a recipe handed down through the family all the way back to—"

"The Civil War." Ted sauntered past, coming to an abrupt halt when he caught sight of Paige. "*Hello. She's* your sister?" He shot Noah a questioning glance.

"Yep, and she's out of your league, buddy."

"Tell me what league you're talking about, and I'll sign up today." Ted's eyes widened. "You gotta put in a good word for me, bro."

Noah laughed. "Good luck. She's older than you, and a Harvard graduate."

"Doesn't matter." Ted stared at Paige from his place in the kitchen. "Ceejay, if Noah won't put in a good word for me, you will, right?"

She nudged him toward the dining room. "You're on your own."

"Uncle Noah"—Lucinda grabbed his hand—"can I sit wif you?"

"Of course you can." Noah scooped her up in his arms. "I want you on one side of me and your mom on the other. That way I can take care of both of you."

"Thanks." Ceejay took the seat he held out for her, and then he settled Lucinda into her booster and sat between them. Ceejay glanced around the table at the happy faces. Something settled inside her, and she savored the happiness. The old house was made for gatherings like this, for children and family. She'd miss it once she found a new job in the city. At least she knew it would always be here to come home to. "Everything looks great."

"Light meat or dark?" Noah took the platter being passed around the table.

"Dark, and Lucinda likes white."

Noah maneuvered a little of everything onto their plates, then he started cutting their food into manageable pieces.

"You're going to make a great daddy someday, Noah." Paige nodded at him from across the table. "You're a natural."

Ceejay's heart raced. Had Noah mentioned the possibility to his sister? No, he wouldn't. She could no longer deny she was late, but trauma could also cause a woman's cycle to get out of whack. And stress. Stress could definitely be the cause. It would just be too weird, too much of a freakish coincidence to find herself in the very same predicament twice in her life. She felt the color rising to her face. Stealing a sideways glance Noah's way, she found him staring at her with an intensity that stole the air right out of her lungs.

"I hope so." He turned to Paige. "You want to drive into Evansville with me tomorrow?"

"I'd love to get out of this house and take a trip into town." Ceejay put her fork down. "I've been feeling restless."

Noah gave her good shoulder a squeeze. "I don't think you want to come this time. I have some business to take care of, and Paige has offered to help. Plus, I haven't spent any time alone with my sister since—"

"Oh, right." Stung, she turned back to her plate. "Another time."

"Tomorrow I'm spending with my big brother, and then I think we should plan a girls' night out." Paige looked around the table. "What do you say, Mom? You, me, Jenny, and Ceejay. Dinner out and a chick flick?"

"Can I come?" Lucinda practically bounced out of her booster.

"If you go, who will take care of me and your uncle Noah?" Ed gave Lucinda a mock scowl. "How about we have our own little party right here? Pizza and Disney."

"And ice cream?"

"That sounds great." Noah tousled her hair. "And ice cream."

"Count me in." Harlen nodded. "I'll bring the ice cream."

Ted had taken the chair next to Paige. His total absorption with Noah's sister had to be obvious to everyone. He turned to face her. "Do you want children someday, Paige?"

She took a sip of her sweet tea without looking at him. "I haven't given it much thought. I'm not finished with my MBA yet, and I want to get started on my career first. I'm not even dating right now."

"I want kids. At least two, maybe more."

"Good for you," Paige mumbled and caught Ceejay's eye. "Where do you want to go for our girls' night out?"

"You know what? I've never had a pedicure." Ceejay's excitement about the venture grew. "Can we do a spa thing before dinner and the movie?"

"Absolutely." Allison rubbed her hands together. "I suppose we'll have to head into Evansville for that. Leave it to me. I'll find the spa and make the appointments. My treat."

Ceejay frowned. "I can't let you do that. You've already done so much."

"Just try to stop her." Ed sent Allison a love-filled look. "She has a stubborn streak a mile wide."

"Listen to who's talking." Allison fussed with her napkin. "He's right, though. I want to do this." Her glance connected with Ceejay's, shifted to Noah, touched on Lucinda, and came back to her. "You may as well accept it now, because I'm not taking no for an answer."

❦   ❦   ❦

Ceejay sat on the veranda and admired her freshly manicured feet for the umpteenth time. Maybe she'd buy a toe ring to go with the glossy red polish on her toes. Once she was back to work, she'd make pedicures a regular thing.

Yesterday's girls' days out had been so much fun she was already thinking about setting up another one, and this time she'd invite Gail. Her friend had been such a huge help since the accident and Jenny's surgery, and nobody deserved a day of pampering more. Thinking about their growing friendship brought a smile to Ceejay's face. Anticipation for the double date they'd planned for the Monday after the Langfords left filled her thoughts.

The screen door opened behind her, and she turned to grin at her aunt.

"I thought you might like some coffee while you're out here." Jenny set a mug with a straw in it on the table before settling herself into a chair. "I'm glad I caught you. I have something I want to talk to you about."

"I'm all ears." Ceejay relaxed back into the cushions.

"My chemotherapy starts next week and continues for six weeks. After the first round is finished, Harlen and I are getting married."

"That's so exciting, Jenny!" Ceejay squealed and sat up straight. "I'm happy for you both."

"And...I'm going to sell this old place."

"What?" Ceejay blinked at her. "You can't sell this house! Tobias and Mary Lovejoy must be trying to claw their way out of their graves right now." Her heart pounded, and her mouth went dry.

"You said you didn't want the house, Ceejay. I've talked with my brothers and cousins, and they all have homes and property of their own. Nobody wants to take it on. It's too much for me and Harlen. I'm going to move into his place."

"So rent it to someone once I'm gone. You can't sell. Our entire family history is here, and...and the orchard. What about the orchard?" The world spun around her, and spots danced in front of her eyes. "Why not sell the diner?"

"I can't sell the diner. It's my income. Harlen has decided not to run for sheriff again. He's going to take early retirement so we can travel. That's another reason why I don't want to hold on to this place anymore. Harlen and I have got a lot of time to make up. We have things we want to do, and places we want to go. Besides"—Jenny stared at the table—"my health insurance isn't going to cover all the bills for my surgery and the chemotherapy. I need the money."

"Take the money I got from Matt. Just don't sell the house."

"No. You're going to need that insurance settlement to fund your own plans, and don't forget you don't have a car right now. All you've ever wanted was to get as far from Perfect as you possibly could. Don't let this old place hold you back."

"But—"

"Once you're out of those casts, you're going to want to follow your own dreams." Jenny lifted her chin. "My mind is made up."

Ceejay stared out over the front yard and struggled to draw a breath. The world closed in around her. She didn't say another word to her aunt, walked down the steps and straight into the middle of the fruit trees where she collapsed onto her back on the prickly, dry grass. She stared up into the canopy of the recently harvested peach trees while her entire world fell apart.

Tears blurred her vision, softening the early autumn tans and greens spinning around her. Everything she wanted, everything she'd believed about herself and her place in the world had gone topsy-turvy.

She couldn't lose this place. The land and the house held her family's history spanning all the way back to the Civil War. All the way back to Tobias and Mary, her great-great-great-grandparents. Her heritage. Lucinda's heritage.

In a flash that came too late, she realized she didn't want to leave. Not now. Not ever. Even if she did use the insurance settlement as a down payment, no way could she get approved for a mortgage big enough for a riverfront property like theirs. And besides, no job meant no mortgage.

Digging her hands into the grass by her sides, she made a desperate effort to hold on to one simple thing while everything else in her life spiraled out of control. Panic stole her breath and threatened to take her down for the count. She shifted her gaze, glomming onto the ripening apples, and started to count for all she was worth. *One, two, three...*

CHAPTER EIGHTEEN

NOAH PEERED OVER PAIGE'S SHOULDER while she adjusted the pictures of the cradle on their Langford & Lovejoy Heritage Furniture website. They'd been in his shop since the early hours. She, Allison, and the Lovejoy women had all gone to town yesterday for their spa day. He and Paige had spent the day before that picking out a ring, filing all the appropriate incorporation papers, and setting up their business accounts. Today he planned to scoop up any of the gold nuggets of business and marketing advice Paige gave him.

"I owe you big-time."

"Yeah, you do, and don't think I won't call in the favor one day." She shot him a wry look. "How did Dad take the news?"

"What news?" Their father strolled through the opened bay doors.

Shit. Noah hadn't wanted to have this conversation until his year was up—until he had something to show for his efforts besides a single cradle he never intended to sell. No avoiding it now, though. *Soldier up.* "I'm starting my own business. I'm going to design and build custom furniture and sell it on the Internet."

His dad put his hands deep into his pockets, jangled the contents, and stared at the site Paige was working on. "Sounds more like a hobby than a feasible way to earn a living."

Noah tamped down the frustration flaring up and braced himself for the rest of the argument. This was nothing new. "I'm not going to work for Langford Plumbing Supplies, Dad. I had no interest before I went to war, and I have even less now."

"It's your responsibility. A Langford has always stood at the helm. You're next in line." *Jangle, jangle.*

Noah caught movement out of the corner of his eye as Ted came around the corner of the carriage house, ready for work. He turned back to his father. "Not this Langford. Paige is the genius when it comes to business management. Put her to work."

"It's always been the Langford *men* who have led LPS." Ed shook his head.

Noah glimpsed the hurt in his sister's eyes before she averted her gaze.

She stared hard at the computer screen. "That's right. Heaven help us if a *girl* should be in charge. The world as the Langfords know it would turn upside down."

"Oh boy. I'm interrupting something. Sorry." Ted started backing away. "I'll just come back later."

"Wait, Ted. I need to make a run into town to drop your proposal for the carriage house off at city hall." Paige rose from her stool and snatched up the manila envelope sitting on the workbench. "Could you give me a ride?"

"Absolutely." Ted lit up like a flare.

Noah quirked an eyebrow. "Did you drive the Mustang or that beat-up old piece of shit you call a truck?"

"Oh, crap," Ted muttered. "I drove the truck. Give me your keys, bro."

"They're on the dinette in my apartment. You mess up *my* truck and the Mustang is mine."

"Over my dead body." Ted turned and followed Paige out of the bay. "If I mess up your truck, I'll fix it."

Noah waited until the two were out of earshot before turning back to his dad. "Why do you do that to her?"

"Do what?"

"Paige is brilliant. She graduated from Harvard with honors, and you put her down every chance you get."

"I'm not putting her down." Ed frowned. "I know she's bright. She's my daughter."

"Then why won't you put her to work for the family business?"

"She's not emotionally equipped for the job."

"How can you say that?" Noah shook his head. "Why put her through Harvard if that's the way you feel?"

"Plumbing and construction are still predominantly male. Paige is brilliant, but she's also naive and mostly fluff. She's led a sheltered, pampered life." Ed picked up one the chisels and turned it in his hand. "You know as well as I do she wears her own designer brand of rose-tinted glasses." He set the tool down and leaned back against the edge of the table. "I'm trying to protect her, Noah. If I hired her, she'd be resented. She'd be eaten alive at LPS, more so because she *is* my daughter."

"Have you told her why you won't hire her, the part about the resentment she'd face?"

He grunted and crossed his arms in front of him. "Course not. It's not open for debate, and I don't want to start an argument with her she can't win. Look, I have no doubt Paige will find her own way, and whatever she settles into, I'm certain she'll be very successful." He shrugged. "It just isn't going to be at LPS."

"I'm not joining the family business either." Noah blew out a breath. "The reality is, I have PTSD, and it's not going away. I don't handle conflict or stress very well. I don't like being around people." He reached out to touch the tracking ball on his laptop, bringing their website back up on the screen. "Working with my hands makes me happy. It brings me peace. I'm going to turn what I love to do into a successful business."

"So, fine. Build furniture in your spare time. Maybe the best way to conquer this PTSD thing is to get back into the fray, learn to deal with the stress and the conflict again. You used to be so competitive. Put that to work for you now."

"PTSD is not something you conquer, Dad. It's something you learn how to cope with. I need you to accept that." Noah recognized the concern and the love in his father's eyes. Even if his father didn't understand, Noah had no doubt he meant well. "I have."

Ed sighed and pushed himself off the workbench. "You plan to stay here in Perfect?"

"I'd like to. We'll see. Ceejay would rather live in a large city, and I plan to be wherever she is." If only he could convince her to stay here. He loved the old place with its long history and Lovejoy roots. He wanted to continue restoring the house, maybe add some updates.

The river meandering by, the country roads with no traffic, the peaceful sounds of birdsong in the early mornings, and the sweet scent of green growing things in the summer soothed his fractured mind. Hell, he'd even grown accustomed to the occasional whiff of hog stench.

Noah could easily see himself spending his life here, building his business and raising a family in the same house that had been home to Ceejay's ancestors. He even looked forward to getting together with the Offermeyers. Now, that was progress.

"You really are serious about her?"

"Yep." The ring Paige had helped him pick out lay nestled in its leather case, tucked into his dresser drawer. He'd have to plan a romantic night out so he could pop the question. Soon.

"Allie and I just want you to be happy, son. I hope you know that." His father rested a hand on his shoulder and gave it a squeeze. "If you change your mind, LPS will still be there waiting for you."

"You're nowhere near retiring, Dad. Maybe there will be a grandchild or two who will take over the family business."

"Maybe. Speaking of family, I think I'll go see what my granddaughter is up to this morning." He chuffed out a laugh. "She's quite the pistol."

Noah nodded, relieved. "That she is. I have a few more things to do here, then I'll be up to the house for lunch."

"Good." Ed gave Noah's shoulder another squeeze. "I'm taking my wife and daughter back with me when I leave on Sunday. Paige starts school on Wednesday, and we want to give her time to get settled in."

"I know. I can handle things from here on in. Jenny is recovering from her surgery, and Harlen's around most of the time." He met his father's gaze. "I appreciate everything you and Mom have done to help out. Ceejay and I are grateful to you both."

His dad nodded, stuck his hands back in his pockets, and left. Noah watched him go. Their conversation had gone much better than expected, and a weight lifted from his shoulders. Affection for his dad warmed his heart.

Noah pulled his cell phone out of his pocket and sat down in front of his laptop to do a search for lumber suppliers. He needed to order a supply of oak, ash, and maple so potential customers had a range of choices. Once the lumber was delivered, he'd stain small samples with the various tints. He'd better have Paige teach him how to upload photos to their website. Everything had to be in place before she left.

"Noah?"

Noah's brow rose. "Jenny, what brings you out here?"

"Ted told me about his partnership with you. I wanted to see what you've done out here." Her gaze roamed around the bay. "Wow, it's really something. I want to thank you. I don't think any of us have ever seen Ted so excited about anything other than that old Mustang."

"Turning my hobby into a business was his idea. I couldn't do it without him." Noah gestured to his laptop and rose from the stool. "Do you want to see our website?"

"I do." She took a seat and navigated around their site. "Did you know Ted has already registered for a couple of night classes? He told me he's getting his prerequisites at a junior college, and then he's going to transfer to the University of Southern Indiana. They have a business college there."

"Yep. I know." He'd had a positive influence, been a contributor to something good, and the pride swelling his chest sent a lump to this throat. He was the one who'd gained the most through their partnership.

"Can I see the original?"

"Huh?"

"The cradle pictured here. Can I see it?"

"Oh, sure." Noah moved to the corner of the room where he'd covered the cradle with canvas. "I'm working on designing a matching crib and armoire. We should start production next week." He pulled the canvas off and ran his hand over the walnut. "Here it is."

"It's beautiful." Jenny set the cradle in motion. "You're very talented."

This feeling pride again would take some getting used to. "Thanks."

She sighed and stopped the cradle's swinging motion. "I came out here to give you a heads-up. I'm afraid I upset Ceejay this morning."

"How?"

"Harlen and I plan to get married."

"That's great news." He frowned. "Why would that upset her?"

"I also told her I plan to sell the house."

"Oh." Shock turned his insides into a scrambled mess. "This is the original Lovejoy homestead site, right?"

"Yes, but it's too much for me and Harlen. He's going to retire once his term is up, and we want to do some traveling. He has a nice little place in town. It's much more manageable for the two of us."

Noah's mind spun. "Have you had a market analysis done? When is it going up for sale?"

"I've spoken with a Realtor in Perfect. The appraisal is going to be done sometime in the next month." She blinked several times and stared at the cradle. "Ceejay said she didn't want the place, Noah. I had planned to leave it to her, but she's always wanted to move away from here. I…it seems like the more I try to do what's best for her, the more upset she gets." She bit her lip. "I don't know what to do anymore."

"Don't worry about it." Noah drew her in for a bear hug. "Do me a favor?"

"Anything."

"Don't put the house on the market just yet. I might have a buyer for you, and you can save a lot of money if you sell it on your own."

She looked up at him, and her brow rose. "Who?"

"I don't want to say anything in case it all falls through. Where is Ceejay now?"

"I think she's in the orchard. That's where she headed after we talked."

"I'd better go find her." He'd wanted a romantic night out with just the two of them, not the middle of the morning with Langfords and Lovejoys hanging around. Fate had a mind of its own, though, and he wasn't going to argue about the timing. Noah passed through his apartment, grabbed the ring from his drawer, and stuffed it into his pocket before heading for the orchard.

Sweet Pea greeted him at the gate. "Hey, big fella. I suppose you come with the house." He scratched behind the mutt's ears and was rewarded with a deep groan of doggy joy and tail-wagging. The minute he let himself through and aimed for the orchard, his heart started a wild rhythm. His mouth turned into a desert, and his hands shook.

This took more guts than facing an unseen enemy in Iraq. What would he do if she said no? He couldn't predict the outcome. He and Ceejay hadn't been a couple long enough to talk about the future, but dammit, time wasn't going to change his mind. "Ceejay?" he called.

"Here."

She sounded so forlorn. The urge to protect her and to fix everything in her world propelled him through his fear of rejection. He found her lying on her back, staring into the branches of the fruit trees, tear tracks still fresh on her cheeks.

They'd been here before, only now everything had changed. He loved her, Lucinda, and Perfect. Noah lowered himself beside her. She scooted closer, and he eased his arm under her shoulders and held her close. "You want to talk about what brought you out here?"

She nodded. "I've been all wrong, and now that I realize my mistakes, it's too late." She sniffed.

"What have you been wrong about?" He held his breath.

"My whole life I've wanted to get as far from Perfect as I possibly could. I hated it here, and...and..." She swallowed hard a few times.

"That's changed?" She nodded against him again, and he had to bite his lip to keep from grinning like a fool.

"Jenny is going to sell my house." She sobbed and buried her face against him. "I don't want to move. I don't want to leave the orchard, or the river...or...or the Offermeyers."

He did have to chuckle at that last part. "The Offermeyers?" He smoothed the curls from her forehead and peered down into her stricken face.

"You know what I mean." She blinked up at him. "I've never let myself get close to anyone around here because I always thought they pitied me. I don't think that anymore."

"You've had quite the summer, haven't you?" He brushed a kiss against her lips.

"Ya think?" She sighed. "At least in this economy it will probably take a year or more to sell." She sniffed. "It's gotta be worth close to a million—half a million at the very least. Not something I can afford on a nurse's wages."

"Come with me. I have something to show you." He boosted her to her feet before getting up himself.

"What does showing me something right this minute have to do with any of this?" She pouted.

He took her hand and tugged her along behind him. "You'll see."

She didn't utter another word all the way to the carriage house. Noah placed his hands on her shoulders and guided her into the carriage house bay.

"I've seen your shop already." She stepped away from him and did a once-over of the space. "It's great, but—"

Pressing a few keys, he brought their website up on his laptop and moved back. "Look." She glanced at the images and the banner and then straightened, giving him a confused look. "What's this about?"

"I know what I want to do, honey." His hand went to the back of his skull. "Ted and I have started a business together. We aren't even live yet, but we have plans." His breathing did a shallow, trippy thing, and his heart stuttered away in his chest. What did she think? Would it be enough? "You said I had to have a life before I had a life to share. Do you remember?"

"Of course I remember." She bent back to the computer screen. "Langford and Lovejoy Heritage Furniture," she read aloud. "Are you excited about this?"

"Yeah, I am." The hopeful expression he saw when she looked his way gave him courage. "Look, I know it's not much yet. We're starting out small, but I intend to put everything I have into growing this business into something I can be proud of. Something *we* can be proud of." Her face lit up, sending his head spinning.

"I'm already proud of you, Noah. You're an incredible man. I've always known you were something special."

"That's good. That's really good. Come and see the proto-type." He rushed over to the covered cradle and whipped the canvas off with a flourish.

"Oh," she gasped as she ran her hands over the first piece of furniture he'd made in years.

"You inspired me, Ceejay."

"It's beautiful. I can see the care you took with this. The craftsmanship is outstanding."

Excitement sent a buzz of energy through him. "You were right. I forget about everything when I'm working with wood. I get a deep satisfaction I'd forgotten existed. I have all kinds of ideas for things I want to design, and I—"

She laughed and cupped his face with her good hand. "I'm happy for you."

He covered her hand with his. "I have you to thank. You and Ted, that is. He's my business partner."

"Really?" She shot him an incredulous look and went back to the cradle. "It's such a shame you're going to sell this. Is the black walnut from the pile here?"

"Yep. Walnut from this land. Lovejoy land. We aren't selling it, Ceejay. This cradle is ours."

"Ours?" Her brow rose almost to her hairline, and an audible whoosh of air left her lungs. *It's now or never, soldier. Man up.* He swallowed hard, turned her to face him, and kissed her first. For courage. "I love you, Ceejay, and it's the kind of love that grows and lasts. I want a life with you. I want to have a family together. I want to grow my business, and play cards with Gail and Denny once a month, and I'll even help butcher hogs this fall. What do you think?"

Tears slipped out of the corners of her eyes. "I think that sounds like heaven, but…"

"Listen to me." He cupped her face and stared intently into her eyes. "Making furniture is my passion, and you know I love Lucinda. But you're my life. You own my heart and always will."

She sniffed and swiped at her eyes. "You haven't asked about—"

"I know I haven't. I'm not going to. This is about you and me and everything coming together for us the way it has—the way it was meant to. If you're pregnant, we'll fill the cradle sooner rather than later. If you aren't, we'll decide together when we want another child. OK?"

She nodded and sniffed. He took that as a good sign. Noah dropped to his good knee and pulled the ring out of his back pocket. "Ceejay Lovejoy, will you marry me?" He opened the box, took the ring out, and held it up to her with his heart in his throat. "Things will be tight at first. The mortgage for this place is going to take a good chunk of income, plus I'm investing heavily in our new business venture."

"You want to live here? We can buy my house?" She laughed and cried.

"I can't imagine living anywhere else, and I can't imagine a life without you and Lucinda."

"OK." She beamed and blinked. "Let's do this. You're going to have to put that ring on my finger, because I can't. I'm shaking too much."

He came back up from the floor, and the world blurred into a kaleidoscope of dizzying bliss. She was his, now and forever. Slipping the ring on her finger sent a rush of pride and possessiveness through him. "You haven't said what I need to hear yet."

"Noah Langford, I love you more than I can even say, and I have for some time now."

"Would you marry me even if I didn't want to stay in Perfect and buy the house? Even if you aren't pregnant? You're really OK with how messed up I am, the scars and the—"

"Stop it. Don't you get it? You're the hero of my heart." She gazed up at him, her eyes lit with love and bright with the sheen of tears. "Never doubt that I love you for you. I'm the one with the scars. Somehow you've managed to get past all the crazy. I'm the lucky one here."

He didn't see it that way, but he sure wasn't going to argue her out of saying yes. "Come on, sweetheart. Let's go tell everyone."

"Don't you want to know? You aren't going to ask?"

"Do you want to tell me?"

"I'm not certain. I haven't taken a test, or anything, but I...I have this weird déjà vu vibe going on. It...brings back memories." She glanced up at him, and the haunted look nearly broke his heart.

"Don't go there, sweetheart. This is completely different." He drew her close, kissed her, and headed them toward the door. "I want you, and I want children with you—whenever they come to us."

Noah clasped her hand and led her toward the big house and their family. The smile he couldn't suppress made his cheeks ache. He took in a huge breath and reflected upon the unexpected direction his life had taken.

His mind conjured the images of the men and women he'd served with in Iraq, and a twinge of pain erased the smile. He had so much to be thankful for. His family had everything to do with his recovery. Many soldiers weren't so lucky. Noah swallowed the lump closing his throat. If he had the chance, he'd find a way to help.

"What's wrong?"

"I was thinking about how lucky I am. I know there are veterans out there who are struggling with the same kinds of issues I am, only they don't have the support I do." Noah took a deep breath. "I wouldn't be where I am today if it weren't for you, Lucinda, Jenny, and my folks."

"Maybe once the dust has settled around here you can find a way to reach out to some of those veterans."

"Good idea."

"Before we go inside, can we discuss a few things?"

"Sure." A cocoon of well-being surrounded him, and he kissed her again just because he could.

"I want to keep working. I called Deaconess, and once my casts are off, I'm going to start picking up floater shifts until something opens up on a more permanent basis."

"I wouldn't ask you to stop working if that's what you want to do. I know how hard you struggled to get your nursing degree."

"Good. One more thing. I want to use the money I got from Matt's insurance policy as a down payment on the house."

"Hmmm. Can we negotiate that one?"

"Noah..."

"I think we should put that money away for Lucinda's education. I'd like to believe it's what Matt had in mind when he took out the policy." He gave her shoulders a squeeze. "I have to believe it's what he intended."

"All right." She sighed. "If it weren't for Matt, we never would have found each other." She rested her head on his shoulder.

They'd reached the veranda. "Ready?"

She nodded. "Let's go. And Noah?"

"Yeah, babe."

"I think we should discuss what kind of tree we need to order to plant in the orchard come spring."

"You think?" A thrill shot through him. He was going to be a daddy.

"I do."

EPILOGUE

CEEJAY GLANCED AROUND AT EVERYONE gathered in their orchard. *Their* orchard. Hers and her husband's. She never got tired of saying it. *My husband.* She touched her wedding rings with her thumb, giving them a turn around her finger, and went back to the faces filling every space between the peach, apple, and pear trees. Neighbors and relatives looked on as her father-in-law and Harlen lowered the brand-new plum tree into its freshly dug hole.

They'd decided to start a new kind of fruit tree to celebrate the christening and their new beginnings. The homestead had passed on to the next generation of Lovejoys, thanks to the generous help of her in-laws, who had given them the down payment as a wedding present.

She smirked at Ted, who'd spent the morning hovering around Paige like a bee after pollen. Poor guy didn't stand a chance.

He sauntered over to her. "Hey, did Noah tell you we have another order for one of your beaded state bird and flower combos?"

"He did, and I've already started on it." She'd taken up beading again, since she was still on maternity leave from her nursing job at Deaconess. Making a little extra money from her beading helped her to feel like she was contributing to their household income and to the growing family business. Her attention turned at the sound of her daughter's voice.

"Daddy, I want to hold baby Toby." Lucinda reached up and tugged at Noah's sleeve.

Ceejay's heart swelled at the sound of her daughter calling Noah "Daddy." Would she ever get used to it?

He nodded toward Allison, who held their sleeping son in her arms. "How about we let Grandma and Aunt Jenny share him today. You can hold him all you want once they've gone home." Lucinda's expression turned into a pout of disappointment.

"Come here, sweetheart. You aren't too big to let me hold you, are you?"

"No, but I will be when I start kindergarten this fall."

She and Noah shared an amused glance over their daughter's head as he lifted her.

Lucinda wrapped her arms around his neck and laid her head on his shoulder. "I wanna hold my baby brother."

"I know. We don't always get to have things our way, though, do we?"

Lucinda shook her head.

"It's how you handle the disappointment that counts, right?"

"I guess." Lucinda sighed and leaned back to look him in eye. "Daddy?"

"Hmmm?"

"Can I have a pony?"

Those close enough to hear the conversation chuckled. Ceejay's heart nearly burst. She had everything she'd ever wanted. Friends and relatives, a man she adored, a family of her own, the homestead that had sheltered the Lovejoys stretching all the way back to the Civil War, and all of it was right here.

Noah grinned her way. "You'll have to ask your mother."

"We'll talk about it when you're ten." She smoothed the curls out of her daughter's eyes.

"Ceejay." Jenny approached, her short curls bouncing around her head with each step. She'd just had another cancer-free checkup, and Ceejay almost needed sunglasses to look at her. Maybe it was being so happy in love that made her so bright and vibrant.

"The Flynns just called. They missed the turnoff and said to tell you they'll be here soon."

"Thanks." Her mind went back to the phone call she'd received a week after she and Noah had gone to meet the professor. He'd told his wife everything, and it was she who encouraged him to reach out. Ceejay had agreed to at least give him a chance, and a fragile bond had begun to form between them. She wasn't ready yet to tell Lucinda she had another grandfather, but they were getting closer to that day.

"I'm starving." Noah put Lucinda down and watched her run to his dad. Noah slipped his arm around Ceejay's waist. "You ready to head up to the house for the feast yet?"

"Sure. Why don't you let everybody know lunch is ready."

"I will, but first I want a kiss." He drew her into his arms and planted one on her lips right in front of everyone. He chuckled. "I never get tired of that."

"Of what?" She fussed with his collar and scowled up at him.

"Of making you blush."

"I'll never get tired of that either," she whispered. "I love you, Noah."

"I know you do, honey. I love you too." He turned, keeping her in his arms. "It's time to eat," he shouted. "Everybody head up to the house."

Everything she needed and wanted was right here. She followed the crowd toward the house, and a deep-seated contentment filled her. Her whole life she'd believed leaving her hometown would help her build a new life, and now she knew the truth. Her life was perfect.

**Read on for a sneak peek of Barbara Longley's
next novel set in Perfect, Indiana**

THE DIFFERENCE A DAY MAKES

Available April 2013 on Amazon.com

"MISS LANGFORD, MR. WEIL WANTS to see you right away," the receptionist said. "I'm to send you right up."

"OK. I'm on my way." Paige smiled at the young woman. Her boss probably wanted to congratulate her on the way she'd handled Meyer Construction's latest deal. She'd been pleased to be assigned one of Ramsey & Weil's largest accounts, especially considering she'd only been with the company a little over two months.

Better drop her things off in her office before heading to the boss's suite. Sliding her coat off as she went, Paige walked down the hall to her tiny office. Tiny, yes, but she had a window. Straightening her burgundy gabardine skirt and brushing off a few specs of lint from the jacket, she headed back out for her meeting with Mr. Weil.

His secretary glanced at her over the rims of her glasses. "Miss Langford. Mr. Weil is waiting for you."

"Thank you." Mrs. Hadley's expression was as dour as ever. Apparently she'd worked for Ramsey & Weil from the beginning. She had to be close to seventy. Throwing her shoulders back, Paige knocked on Mr. Weil's door.

"Come in," he barked.

Smoothing her face into a professional mien, she opened the door and strode in. One look at his expression and she faltered. He looked serious. Seriously unhappy.

"Have a seat, Langford." He moved a pile of folders aside.

She took one of the chairs in front of his desk. "You wanted to see me?"

He scowled. "Meyer Construction needed our bid five days ago. They never got it. They've gone with another supplier."

Adrenaline hit her system, and her heart leaped to her throat. She gripped the arms of the chair. "That's impossible! I sent that bid with a same-day courier two days before it was due."

"Like I said—they never got it." He leaned back in his leather chair and fixed her with another scowl. "I've also had two of your other accounts complain that our bids were late. If it weren't for Anthony Rutger, we would've lost those accounts as well."

"Anthony?" Her mind spun with the implications. *Anthony?* No, he wouldn't purposefully sabotage her. They were a couple.

Her mind raced to the day the courier had come for the Meyer bid. She'd been in the middle of a call, and Anthony had offered to take the envelope to the lobby. At the time, she'd thought it was sweet. Come to think of it, he'd also offered to put other bids into the office's outgoing mail bin for her.

Heat filled her face. "I'm sorry. It won't happen again."

"Damn straight it won't. You're fired."

"Oh, no. There's been a mistake. I'll get the Meyer account back somehow." She sucked in a breath. "From now on, I will personally put things in the out bin myself, and—"

"Miss Langford, you're done here."

The expression in his eyes was pitying, and she got it. Mr. Weil knew what had happened, but ultimately, she was responsible. She'd been so naïve, so trusting...*Oh, my God! I've been sleeping with the enemy.* No wonder Anthony insisted they keep their relationship a secret. Paige couldn't get enough air into her lungs.

"Paige," Mr. Weil's tone softened, "learn from this, and you'll know better next time."

She tried to swallow, but her mouth felt like the wool that her designer coat had been cut from. "Give me another chance. I can't be *fired,*" she croaked out. Harvard graduates didn't get *fired.*

"It's already done. Security is here to escort you out." Mr. Weil stood up and moved to the door. He swung it open, and George, the security guard, waited for her in the hall. He wouldn't meet her eyes.

Humiliation. Shame. Mortification. A maelstrom of ugly emotions threatened to overtake her, and white-hot anger followed. *Anthony.* He'd done this to her. Why? She blinked away the sudden sting of tears. No time to deal with that now. She rose on shaky legs, lifted her chin, and walked out of the office without looking at Mr. Weil or George. Aware of the security guard's presence behind her, she made her way to her office with as much dignity as possible. Was that a smug look on Mrs. Hadley's face? Paige lifted her chin a bit higher.

"I'm sorry about this, Miss Langford," George murmured once they were in the elevator. "You'll come out of this all right."

Harvard grad fired from her first real job.

She choked back the sob rising in her throat. How could she face her parents?

"Bye, George. Thanks for being decent about this."

"You take care, Miss Langford. Something better is going to come along. Give it some time, and you'll see."

"Sure." *Not effing likely.*

The worst part? Anthony's betrayal and the way he'd used her. It was all so calculated, so deceitful. Shame stole her breath. A short half hour ago she'd been thinking he was *the one.* Nausea roiled through her, and a cold sheen of perspiration dampened her forehead. She covered her mouth and hurried to her car. Once inside, she gripped the steering wheel and rested her head against her hands. Sucking air in through her nose, she let it out through her mouth until the nausea receded. She had to get out of here. She started her car and sat up.

That's when she saw him. Anthony watched her from the front entrance with a smirk on his face. He lifted a hand, saluted her, and turned to walk inside. She gave him the finger, not that it did any good. He didn't even see it. Paige pulled out of her parking spot and headed for her condo.

Once she was behind closed doors, the tears came. What was she going to do? Word would get back to her dad, and she didn't want that to happen until she turned things around.

Noah. "Yes!" She could visit her brother. Her mind raced. She'd have a place to hide until she could figure out the rest of her life, and nobody would have to know what had happened until she got back on her feet.

She swiped the tears off her cheeks. She stared out the balcony doors at the Philadelphia skyline. Could she manage to sneak away before news of her demise hit the grapevine? Anthony might crow about his deed to his buddies. Her face grew hot, and anger stiffened her spine. She grabbed her cell phone and hit speed dial. Noah answered on the third ring.

"Hey, big brother. How're things in Perfect?"

Paige glanced at the clock as she turned in to Ceejay and Noah's driveway. Almost midnight, and she didn't want to wake them. They'd given her a key to the carriage house when she'd come down for Toby's baptism, and she still had it. Noah wouldn't mind if she crashed there tonight. It would be far better than waking up the entire household at this hour.

She parked next to an old Chevy pickup—perhaps Ceejay's cousin's?—grabbed her stuff, and headed toward the carriage house. Praying their dog Sweet Pea wouldn't sense her presence and start barking, she tiptoed along the path from the gate to the door. All she had to go by was the scant light of the new moon.

So far, so good. Sweet Pea remained blissfully quiet. She dropped her bag on the concrete and rifled through the pockets of her purse for the key. "Aha. Got you." She fumbled a few times in the darkness, trying to insert it into the lock. Finally she got the key in, turned it, reached for the knob, and pushed, just as a light turned on inside. The door was yanked from her grasp so suddenly she fell inside, right into a naked man—a naked man holding a gun.

"Aaah!" She scrambled back to regain her footing and stared at the wild man before her. Shaggy blond hair hung down to his shoulders, and a tangled mess of a beard hid most of his face. Panic-filled brilliant blue eyes were riveted on her with a haunted look that stole her breath.

"What the hell?" He dropped the hand holding the gun to his side. He snatched something from the inside wall and covered his interesting bits.

A cowboy hat? She blinked. He stood five or six inches taller than her five-foot-five frame, and there was nothing to him but wiry muscle and bone. He had a nasty scar that extended from his right hip all the way down the front of his leg almost to his knee. Plus, he was bare-assed-like-the-day-he-was-born naked. Her brother wouldn't allow anyone dangerous near his family, but still… "Put that thing away."

"If you insist." He tossed the cowboy hat to the recliner.

"The GUN!" She slapped a hand over her eyes. "I meant the gun."

"Well, that's not where you were looking."

ACKNOWLEDGMENTS

I WANT TO THANK ALL of the everyday heroes in our armed forces who put their lives on the line in the name of duty. Bless you. Kevin Hanrahan deserves a shout-out for graciously answering all the questions I threw his way. To my wonderful agent, Nalini Akolekar, thank you for your belief in my work, and a big thank-you to Lindsay Guzzardo and all the folks at Montlake who have helped me polish this novel until it shines.

ABOUT THE AUTHOR

As a child, Barbara Longley moved frequently, learning early on how to entertain herself with stories. Adulthood didn't tame her peripatetic ways: she has lived on an Appalachian commune, taught on an Indian reservation, and traveled the country from coast to coast. After having children of her own, she decided to try staying put, choosing Minnesota as her home. By day, she puts her master's degree in special education to use teaching elementary school. By night, she explores all things mythical, paranormal, and newsworthy, channeling what she learns into her writing.